Praise for *All Tha*

"This subdued tale of learning to forgive is Bartels's best yet."

Publishers Weekly

"*All That We Carried* is a deeply personal, thoughtful exploration of dealing with pain and grief. . . . Erin Bartels makes it shine."

Life Is Story

"Bartels proves herself a master wordsmith and storyteller."

Library Journal, starred review

"Erin Bartels has a gift for creating unforgettable characters who are their own worst enemy, and yet there's always a glimmer of hope that makes you believe in them. The estranged sisters in *All That We Carried* are two of her best yet—young women battling their own demons and each other as they try to navigate beyond a shared painful past and find their way to a more hopeful future."

Valerie Fraser Luesse, Christy Award–winning novelist

"*All That We Carried* is so much more than just a beautiful novel—it's a literary adventure of both body and spirit, a meaningful parable, a journey of faith. Erin Bartels creates amazingly realistic characters in two sisters wrestling with their past and with one another. Not only did this story make me want to pull on my hiking boots for my own adventure, it propelled me to search out a deeper faith. Simply stunning. A novel not to be missed!"

Heidi Chiavaroli, award-winning author of
Freedom's Ring and *The Tea Chest*

Praise for *The Words between Us*

"*The Words between Us* is a story of love found in the written word and love found because of the written word. It is also a novel of the consequences of those words that are left unsaid. Bartels's compelling sophomore novel will satisfy fans and new readers alike."

Booklist

"*The Words between Us* is a story to savor and share: a lyrical novel about the power of language and the search for salvation. I loved every sentence, every word."

Barbara Claypole White, bestselling author
of *The Perfect Son* and *The Promise between Us*

"If you are the kind of person who finds meaning and life in the written word, then you'll find yourself hidden among these pages."

Shawn Smucker, author of *Light from Distant Stars*

"Vividly drawn and told in expertly woven dual timelines, *The Words between Us* is a story about a woman who has spent years trying to escape her family's scandals and the resilience she develops along the way. Erin Bartels's characters are a treat: complex, dynamic, and so lifelike I half expected them to climb straight out of the pages."

Kathleen Barber, author of *Truth Be Told*

THE
GIRL
WHO
COULD
BREATHE
UNDER
WATER

Books by Erin Bartels

THE GIRL WHO COULD BREATHE UNDER WATER

a novel

ERIN BARTELS

Revell

a division of Baker Publishing Group
Grand Rapids, Michigan

Published by Revell
a division of Baker Publishing Group
PO Box 6287, Grand Rapids, MI 49516-6287
www.revellbooks.com

Printed in the United States of America

Library of Congress Cataloging-in-Publication Data
Names: Bartels, Erin, 1980– author.
Title: The girl who could breathe under water : a novel / Erin Bartels.
Description: Grand Rapids, MI : Revell, a division of Baker Publishing Group,
    [2022]
Identifiers: LCCN 2021023644 | ISBN 9780800738372 (paperback) | ISBN
    9780800741105 (casebound) | ISBN 9781493434206 (ebook)
Subjects: GSAFD: Suspense fiction. | LCGFT: Thrillers (Fiction)
Classification: LCC PS3602.A83854 G57 2022 | DDC 813/.6—dc23
LC record available at https://lccn.loc.gov/2021023644

22   23   24   25   26   27   28   7   6   5   4   3   2   1

for those I've failed
and those I've forgiven

All good writing is swimming under water and holding your breath.

F. Scott Fitzgerald

1

The summer you chopped off all your hair, I asked your dad what the point of being a novelist was. He said it was to tell the truth.

Ridiculous.

"Nothing you write is real," I said. "You tell stories about made-up people with made-up problems. You're a professional liar."

"Oh, Kendra," he said. "You know better than that." Then he started typing again, as if that had settled things. As if telling me I already had the answer was any kind of answer at all.

I don't know why he assumed I knew anything. I've been wrong about so much—especially you. But there is one thing about which I am now certain: I was lying to myself about why I decided to finally return to Hidden Lake. Which makes perfect sense in hindsight. After all, novelists are liars.

"It will be a quiet place to work without distraction," I told my agent. "No internet, no cell service. Just me and the lake and a landline for emergencies."

"What about emailing with me and Paula?" Lois said, practicality being one of the reasons I had signed with her three years prior. "I know you need to get down to it if you're going to meet your deadline. But you need to be reachable."

"I can go into town every week and use the Wi-Fi at the coffee shop," I said, sure that this concession would satisfy her.

"And what about the German edition? The translator needs swift responses from you to stay on schedule."

We emailed back and forth a bit, until Lois could see that I was not to be dissuaded, that if I was going to meet my deadline, I needed to see a lake out my window instead of the rusting roof of my apartment building's carport.

Of course, that wasn't the real reason. I see that now.

The email came from your mother in early May, about the time the narcissus were wilting. For her to initiate any kind of communication with me was so bizarre I was sure that something must be wrong even before I read the message.

Kendra,

I'm sorry we didn't get to your grandfather's funeral. We've been out of state. Anyway, please let me know if you have seen or heard from Cami lately or if she has a new number.

Thanks,
Beth Rainier

It was apparent she didn't know that you and I hadn't talked in eight years. That you had never told your mother about the fight we'd had, the things we'd said to each other, the ambiguous state in which we'd left our friendship. And now a woman who only talked to me when necessary was reaching out, wondering if I knew how to get in touch with you. That was the day I started planning my return to the intoxicating place where I had spent every half-naked summer of my youth—

because I was sure that in order to recover you, I needed to recover us.

The drive north was like slipping back through time. I skirted fields of early corn, half mesmerized by the knit-and-purl pattern that sped past my windows. Smells of diesel fuel and manure mingled with the dense green fragrance of life rushing to reproduce before another long winter. The miles receded beneath my tires, and the markers of my progress became the familiar billboards for sporting goods stores and ferry lines to Mackinac Island. The farm with the black cows. The one with the quilt block painted on the side of the barn, faded now. The one with the old bus out back of the house. Every structure, each more ramshackle than the last, piled up in my chest until I felt a physical ache that was not entirely unpleasant.

In all our enchanted summers together on the lake, there had been more good than bad. Sweet silent mornings. Long languid days. Crisp starry nights. Your brother had thrown it all out of whack, like an invasive species unleashed upon what had been a perfectly balanced ecosystem. But he hadn't destroyed it. The good was still there, in sheltered pockets of memory I could access if I concentrated.

The first step out of the car when I arrived at the cabin was like Grandpa opening the oven door to check on a pan of brownies—a wave of radiant heat carrying an aroma that promised imminent pleasures. The scent of eighteen summers. A past life, yes, but surely not an irretrievable one.

On the outside, the cabin showed evidence of its recent abandonment—shutters latched tight, roof blanketed by dead pine needles, logs studded with the ghostly cocoons of gypsy moths. Inside, time had stopped suddenly and completely, and the grit of empty years had settled on every surface. The same boxy green plaid sofa and mismatched chairs sat on the same defeated braided rug around the same coffee table rubbed raw by decades of sandy feet. That creepy stuffed screech owl still stared down from the shelf with unblinking yellow eyes. On tables, windowsills, and mantelpiece sat all of the rocks, shells, feathers, and driftwood I'd gathered with my young hands, now gathering dust. Grandpa had left them there just as I had arranged them, and the weight of memory kept them firmly in place.

Each dust mote, each dead fly beneath the windows, each cobweb whispered the same pointed accusation: *You should have been here.*

For the next hour I manically erased all evidence of my neglect. Sand blown through invisible cracks, spiderwebs and cicada carapaces, the dried remains of a dead redstart in the fireplace. I gathered it from every forgotten corner in the cabin and dumped it all into the hungry mouth of a black trash bag, leaving the bones of the place bare and beautiful in their simplicity.

Satisfied, I turned on the faucet for a glass of cold water, but nothing happened. Of course. I should have turned on the water main first. I'd never opened the cabin. That was something an adult did before I showed up. And when I went out to the shed to read the instructions Grandpa had written on the bare pine wall decades ago, I found it padlocked.

Desperate to cool down, I pulled on my turquoise bikini and walked barefoot down the hot, sandy trail to the lake. Past Grandpa's old rowboat. Past the stacked sections of the dock I had only ever seen in the water—yet another thing adults did that I never paid any attention to because I could not conceive of being one someday.

At the edge of the woods, I hesitated. Beyond the trees I was exposed, and for all I knew your brother was there across the lake, waiting, watching.

I hurried across the sandy beach and through the shallows into deep water, dipped beneath the surface, and held my breath as long as I could, which seemed like much less than when we were kids. As I came back up and released the stale air from my lungs, I imagined the stress of the past year leaving my body in that long sigh. All of the nervous waiting before interviews, all of the dread I felt before reading reviews, all of the moments spent worrying whether anyone would show up to a bookstore event. What I couldn't quite get rid of was my anxiety about the letter.

Out of all the reviews and emails and social media posts that poured in and around me after I'd published my first novel, one stupid letter had worked its way into my psyche like a splinter under my fingernail. I had been obsessing about it for months, poring over every critical word, justifying myself with logical arguments that couldn't take the sting out of what it said.

Kendra,

Your book, while perhaps thought "brave" in some circles, is anything but. It is the work of a selfish opportunist who was all too ready to monetize the suffering of others. Did you ever consider that antagonists have stories of their own? Or that in someone else's story you're the antagonist?

Your problem is that you paid more attention to the people who had done you wrong than the ones who'd done you right. That, and you are obviously obsessed with yourself.

I hope you're happy with the success you've found with this book, because the admiration

```
of strangers is all you're likely to get from
here on out. It certainly won't win you any
new friends. And I'm willing to bet the old
ones will steer pretty clear of you from here
on out. In fact, some of them you'll never
see again.

Sincerely,
A Very Disappointed Reader
```

Maybe it was because the writer hadn't had the courage to sign his name—it had to be a him. Maybe it was because it had been mailed directly to me rather than forwarded on from my publisher, which could only mean that the writer either knew me personally or had done a bit of stalking in order to retrieve my address. It hurt to think of any of my friends calling me a "selfish opportunist." But the thought of a total stranger taking the trouble to track me down in order to upbraid me gave me the absolute creeps.

But really, if I'm honest with myself, it was because deep down I knew it had to be someone from Hidden Lake. Who else could have guessed at the relationship between my book and my real life?

Whoever this Very Disappointed Reader was, he had completely undermined my attempts to write my second book. I knew it was silly to let a bad review have power over me. But this wasn't someone who just didn't like my writing. This was someone who thought I was the bad guy. He had read my novel and taken the antagonist's side—your brother's side.

Now I closed my eyes, lay back, and tried to let the cool, clear water of Hidden Lake wash it all away. But the peaceful moment didn't last. The humming of an outboard motor signaled the approach of a small fishing boat from the opposite shore. Hope straightened my spine and sent shards of some old energy through my limbs and into my fingers and toes. And even though I knew in my heart that it wouldn't be you, I still deflated a bit when I saw your father, though in almost any other context I would have been thrilled.

He cut the motor and slowed to a stop a few yards away. "Kendra, it's good to finally see you again," he said. "I was sorry to hear about your grandpa. We wanted to make it to the funeral, but Beth and I were out of state."

"Yes, she told me."

He looked surprised at that, then seemed to remember something. Perhaps he knew about the strange email.

I swam to the boat—not the one I remembered—and held on to the side with one hand, using the other to shade my eyes as I looked up into his still-handsome face. I didn't ask him where you were that day, and he didn't offer any explanation. More likely than not, he didn't know.

"Beth's in Florida now," he continued. "It's just been me since Memorial Day. I was hoping to catch your mother up here before she put the place up for sale."

"It's not going up for sale."

"No? Figured she would sell it."

"It's mine. Grandpa left it to me."

"That so?" He glanced at my beach. "I can help you put the dock in tonight, around five? I'd help now, but I'm off to talk to Ike."

"Ike's still alive?"

"Far as I know."

I smiled. "That would be great, thanks. Hey, I don't suppose you've heard from Cami? No chance she'll be coming up this summer?"

He looked away. "Nothing yet. But I've seen Scott Masters once or twice this month. And Tyler will be up Friday."

He waved and headed out across the lake to Ike's. I tried to separate the thudding of my heart from the loud chugging of the outboard motor that receded into the distance.

Of course Tyler would be there. Every paradise needed a serpent.

2

My buoyant mood sinking at the prospect of having to face Tyler in a matter of days, I toweled off and finished unloading the car in my swimsuit. I lugged in five boxes of books, each volume carefully selected from my personal library to inspire me to write something that would show that my first book's success had not been a fluke. That I had more to offer the world than just the story of my own pain. That the letter writer was wrong. I'd wanted to bring my entire library, but it would have required a U-Haul. Anyway, I wasn't planning on staying forever, just for the summer.

I installed my literary muses onto the shelves Grandpa had made with two-by-sixes in the unfinished interior wall of the living room and then shoved my full suitcases one by one up into the loft. The last met with unexpected resistance, tumbled down, and nearly yanked me off the ladder with it. I poked my head up over the threshold. The space that had been my room, my treehouse, my pirate ship, my enchanted castle tower, was filled with patio furniture, beach umbrellas, and plastic folding beach chairs.

I thought of Grandpa's emaciated body in the casket a few months earlier, of how he'd moldered in a nursing home for two years before his death. How had he gotten all of this up here? He'd always been wiry, small but muscular, his body sculpted by a lifetime of working with his hands. "Never pay someone to do something you can do," he'd told me one stifling August afternoon when I'd asked why we couldn't just buy firewood and have it delivered. He went back to splitting logs, and I went back to stacking the pieces that tumbled away from his keen axe.

He must have declined quickly at the end. And I hadn't been here to help.

I pulled the suitcases back down, lined them up on the living room floor, and took an overdue bathroom break, which reminded me that I still hadn't managed to get the water turned on. I couldn't flush, couldn't wash my hands, couldn't rinse the lake off when it was finally time to go to bed, which I also couldn't get to because of all the junk up in the loft.

Maybe things at Hidden Lake looked the same on the surface, but in some deeper place they were askew. What was this place without old Fred Brennan? What was my life without my grandfather? Fresh grief welled up inside of me, and I wanted to sit on the toilet and cry. But that wouldn't get the water turned on.

I searched every kitchen drawer for the key to the shed. Then I remembered the desk in Grandpa's bedroom. On its richly lacquered surface sat the old gray typewriter my grandparents had purchased secondhand for my mother when she had to take a summer correspondence course in order to graduate high school. I wrote my first story on that typewriter. You hated it.

In the drawer, everything was just as it had always been: Bible, pens, typing paper so thin the sun shone through—and a small dull gold key. A few minutes later the shed was open, the water was turned on, and the toilet was flushed.

Back at the desk, I dug an envelope out of my purse and pulled out the sheet of folded paper inside, slicing my finger on the crisp white edge. I sucked at the blood that bubbled out and read the words I already knew by heart. Bizarrely, it had been typed on a typewriter, the *a* sagging slightly below the rest of the letters. I slipped a piece of typing paper out of the drawer and rolled it into place. My fingers hovered over the keys for a breath, then began chopping out the words.

Dear Disappointed Reader,

I looked at that line a moment, then pulled the paper from the typewriter and crumpled it up. What use was there trying to respond? There had been no return address on the envelope. No one would ever read any sort of response I could muster up. Though if I could answer the letter's claims in writing, maybe I could see in black and white that they were baseless and get to the writing I actually needed to be doing.

I slipped another piece of paper from the drawer and rolled it into place.

Dear Disappointed Reader,

Three words on a blank page. It was more than I had written in a week. I sat back in the stiff wooden chair and folded my hands across my pale stomach. It had been at least five years since I could remember seeing definite tan lines in the mirror, and the constant idleness before my laptop had produced a roll of fat that hadn't been there before. I straightened and pulled in my abdominal muscles. Still there.

Gravel crunched outside. A moment later there was a light knock at the screen door, and I abandoned the letter on the desk.

"Come on in."

Your dad stood in the doorway in boat shoes and cargo shorts and an open white button-down shirt. Against his tanned face, his clear blue eyes, so unlike your unfathomable dark brown ones, positively glowed. He'd obviously spent the last few weeks doing little but lying outside, probably with a sweating beer in hand. Why didn't he have a belly?

"You look like you're ready to get back in the water," he said.

"Why bother getting dressed at the lake?"

"Exactly." He scanned the shelves I had stuffed full of books and picked a hardcover from a low shelf. "This is a good one."

I laughed. "You know the author signed that one."

He opened the cover. "Ah, yes. 'To Kendra. Someday you'll be signing one of these for me. Love, Robert.'"

I tried to keep the pride from showing on my face as he placed the book back on the shelf, but I knew I was failing. It felt good to fulfill the promise of that inscription, written so long ago to the girl I once was. The girl who wanted so desperately to make a mark on the world.

"You know, I'm still waiting," he said.

My stomach clenched. Hadn't he read my book? It had been out for a whole year. After the letter, I almost hoped he hadn't, hoped he wouldn't, hoped he'd simply put it on his shelf and forget about it.

"I have a few in the car."

"Let's get that dock in the water. Then you can get one for me."

A mixture of relief and disappointment swirled in my gut. Maybe I didn't really want him to read it anymore, but I wanted him to want it, to not be able to wait until he got his hands on it. Didn't he remember what it was like the first time? Or was publishing so old hat to him now that books had ceased to be magical?

We walked out into the still-hot evening and, section by section, reassembled the dock until we were in water up to our thighs. But at that point, the water should have been up to my waist.

"How long has the lake been this low?" I asked when the last section was secure.

"It's been dropping the past few years, though it's not usually this bad until August. Not enough snow the past couple winters. Not enough rain this spring. Ike says it hasn't rained more than twice since March, and it was already in the eighties in May."

"Well, if Ike says so."

He laughed at that, but I didn't get much satisfaction out of it. It was an easy joke to make.

"How about that boat?" he said.

"The boat can wait. I'd rather you help me get the beach stuff out. Grandpa apparently stores it all in the loft over the winter."

We walked back up to the cabin beside one another in perfect step until we got to the door, where your dad hung back to let me go first. With me above and him below, my childhood sanctuary was restored in less than twenty minutes and the beach stuff was piled in the weeds just outside the cabin door. Piece by piece, everything would be set right. I was sure of it. Or at least I was trying to be.

"Thank you, Mr. Rainier."

"You're what, twenty-five?"

"Twenty-six."

"Either way, you can probably just call me Robert at this point."

I wrinkled my nose. "Feels weird to start calling people by their first names once you hit some magic age, but I'll see if I can get used to that."

He didn't need to know that you and I had always referred to our parents by their first names when they were out of earshot, which was rather often since Jackie never came up to the lake and Robert and Beth were nearly always busy. I wonder if things might have turned out differently if we'd just had a bit more supervision.

Robert regarded me a moment and then clapped his hands together. "How about some refreshment? I've got a cooler in the boat."

He took off for the beach, and I followed close behind. "That's a new boat."

"Fairly. I've had it a few years."

"What did you do with the old wooden one?" I hoped it had been sold. Or sunk.

"It's just sitting back behind the garage." He reached the boat and pulled out a red and white cooler, the same cooler I knew often held bait.

"Why don't you get rid of it?"

He twisted the top off a bottle and handed it to me. "You want it?"

"No," I said with perhaps a bit more force than I meant to. I put my lips to the bottle and got a whiff of dead minnow. I'd never been a beer drinker, and the pungent ghost of fish guts did nothing to increase my appetite. "But no reason to junk up the yard with it."

"I could give it to Ike. He could add it to his compound."

He turned to look across the lake, and I took this opportunity to pour out half the bottle at the base of a poplar sapling. "It would fit right in."

"There's still a bit of light left if you want to tackle that boat."

I shook my head. "Nah. Mosquitoes will be out soon. Anyway, I don't think I'll be up early tomorrow morning to go fishing. I'm exhausted."

"I'll leave you my extra gas can. Fred's is stale by now if there's anything left in it. And don't worry about mosquitoes. That's one nice side effect of the dry spring. Haven't seen even one since I came up."

I looked for another opportunity to inflict the beer upon the sapling, but Robert was looking through the trees to the cabin behind me. I forced down a swig.

"I'm glad you're not selling this place," he said. "Lot of memories wrapped up in it."

I nodded, though I was fairly sure that his memories of growing up on Hidden Lake bore little resemblance to mine.

"I'd hate to see someone come in and tear it down," he continued. "Build a McMansion there. Once you get one of those on a lake, it's only a matter of time before that's all you've got. They're like that garlic mustard in the woods or what's that other stuff—purple loosestrife. No matter how you fight it, it just keeps spreading."

He headed back to the boat, and I quickly dumped the rest of the beer out and kicked some sand over it before he returned with a small red plastic gas can.

"So where's that book?" he said.

I stowed the gas can in the shed, popped the trunk on my car, and lifted a copy of *That Summer* out of a box. It gave me a thrill, even so many months after I signed for the first shipment that arrived at my apartment, to see it, to hold it. My story. Finally out of my head and resting safely in a block of wood pulp, where it couldn't torment me. Though the elation was tempered now as I thought again of the letter.

`Your book, while perhaps thought "brave" in`
`some circles, is anything but.`

I slammed the trunk.

Inside, your dad was flipping idly through *If on a Winter's Night a Traveler* by Italo Calvino, which makes a story out of several first chapters of books that were doomed never to be finished. I'd packed it because of the lyrical style and amusing wit.

Now the abandoned storylines, each so fascinating the reader wished they would go on, just reminded me of all my aborted attempts at writing my second novel. Only mine weren't even remotely fascinating.

I held out my book and tried not to look giddy and maniacal about it.

"Did you sign it?"

"No." I snagged a pen out of the desk, sat down on the couch, and opened the book to the title page as Robert replaced Calvino on the shelf and picked up another luminary to whom I would never hold a candle.

Robert,

I stopped. What could I say? How could I begin to thank him for the encouragement, for believing in me, for acting like a father to me when I had none, for opening his home to me, for the water skiing and the meals and the endless cans of Coke? This wasn't like signing a book for a fan in line at a bookstore or an aspiring writer at a conference. My standard quips about telling your truths or pushing toward your goals made no sense.

Robert Rainier had made it long ago. He was a household name. His books had been made into movies and miniseries. Rabid fans with no sense of boundaries occasionally knocked on his door. Remember that summer Beth called the police on that freak with Robert's author photo tattooed on the back of his neck when he showed up, apropos of nothing, and wouldn't leave?

"You don't have to do it now," he said. "Think about it and give it to me whenever you're ready."

I closed the book. "It's not that I can't think of anything to say. It's just that there's so much to say."

A look of pride settled on his face. "I'm really happy for you."

Now in the failing evening light he actually did look much older than the last time I had seen him. Lines of shadow edged his mouth, and dark circles hung like two hammocks beneath his eyes. I wondered if you were the reason for them.

"I'll get it to you tomorrow," I said.

"Don't set deadlines for yourself. You've got enough of those in your life now."

A half laugh, half groan erupted from deep within my chest.

"Dare I ask how the next book is coming?" he said.

"It isn't. That's the problem."

He nodded. "Been there."

"How did you get past it? My next manuscript is due in September, and I've got nothing—nothing—down on paper. It took me four years to write *That Summer*. I only have three months left." I didn't like the panic I heard in my voice, the dread that came welling up again from my stomach. "I'll never get it done."

"Sure you will. I wrote *The Soldier* in a three-week marathon fueled by nothing more than coffee, cigarettes, and NoDoz, and it's my bestselling book. Time doesn't matter. It's passion that gets books written."

I flopped back on the couch, resenting the confidence that oozed from him, that always oozed from him. Robert Rainier had nothing to worry about in this world. His publisher probably salivated at the thought of doing his bidding, and if they didn't fall into line, there were probably half a dozen others waiting to scoop him up. What was a deadline to him? When had he last opened a notice from a collection agency?

He sat down next to me. "It'll come."

I fiddled with the edges of the patch that covered a cigarette burn from Jackie's wayward teen years. Grandpa had never spoken willingly of those times. When asked, he gave answers that seemed to me like the beginning of a great story, then he'd get busy doing something else. I'd have to conjure up the rest of it, what might have happened before, what could have happened after. It was during those moments I became a storyteller.

It was easy in those days. Just the imaginings of a girl with more questions than answers. But now, with the stakes raised and the specter of failure brooding over me like a thunderhead, I had never felt less up to the task.

"Did you ever worry that what you were writing wouldn't be good enough?" I said. "That it wouldn't live up to what you'd written before?"

He sat back and crossed one leg over the other, which is exactly the pose he is in whenever I bring him to mind. "Maybe early on. But at some point you realize it's not about that. Every story has its own story. You can't compare them."

My dissatisfaction with his breezy answer must have shown, because he leaned forward, stared at his hands, and tried again.

"It's like comparing your kids. They each have their own life, their own trajectory. I can't compare Tyler and Cami. One has been very successful against the odds. And one has sorely tested my faith and my patience. But just because one kid is thriving and one is floundering doesn't mean I love one more or the other less. I was disappointed with the initial reception of *Blessed Fool*, but I still think it's the best book I've ever written." He patted my knee. "You'll get there. Just sit down and write whatever comes."

I thanked him again and walked him out to his boat. We had missed the sunset. Grandpa and I had always watched it my first night on the lake each year. And the next morning, after we'd been out fishing, he would drop me at your dock and summer would officially begin.

Now as your dad's new boat disappeared into shadow, I wondered where you were . . . and if I would ever see you again.

3

I have always taken every scrap of advice that has ever come my way, especially if it came from your father. You always did the opposite. I'm sure you thought I was too easily swayed by the opinions of others, just like I thought you were too stubborn to see what was in your best interest. Truthfully, at this point I'm not sure one approach is better than the other.

After Robert's pep talk, I spent three mornings on the couch, staring at my laptop and trying not to look at the letter I had started in the typewriter on Grandpa's desk, which I could plainly see through the bedroom doorway over the top of my screen. Three mornings, butt in chair, following the illustrious Robert Rainier's directive to write whatever comes, and I was no closer to overcoming my paralysis.

I knew why. I couldn't stop thinking about the fact that on Friday Tyler would be there, across the lake, in the flesh. He had been haunting me for so long I had ceased thinking of him as a real person. He was a ghost, a phantom, an oppressive presence lurking ever in the shadowy background of my mind. And now he was slinking into the foreground like a cat that had gotten a bead on a mouse.

I was convinced that my writer's block would not exist were it not for the letter from the Very Disappointed Reader. The letter would not exist were it not for my first book. My first book would not exist were it not for Tyler. It stood to reason, then, that the way to deal with my inability to write was to start by dealing with Tyler, which was something I had successfully avoided doing for nearly a decade.

Disgusted by my lack of focus when I'd been so sure being at the cabin would fix everything, I slammed my laptop shut, dumped it on the coffee table, and climbed into the loft to get into a suit. My favorite red halter top bikini was uncomfortably snug. My sedentary ways ended now. Nothing cleared the mind and tightened the muscles like good, hard swimming. A trip to Mermaid Island was in order.

Whether the place had a real name before we christened it and planted our pink bandana flag on its frog-rich shores, I still don't know. No matter. Significant places are often renamed when they are conquered by new civilizations. Only the old maps attest to the existence of Gaul and Persia and Yugoslavia. Mermaid Island was our announcement to the world that you had come and conquered a small inland lake community in northern Michigan.

When you came home with the Rainiers from Korea, Robert explained to me that you didn't speak any English. That you'd grown up in an orphanage. That your biological parents had given you up because of a birth defect called clubfoot.

But I could see no defects in you. You were beautiful in all of the ways I was not. Your hair was shiny and stick straight and obedient while mine was too wavy to be straight, too straight to be wavy, and invariably a frizzed-out bird's nest on humid days, which was most of the summer. I was prone to heat rashes and blushed easily. Your skin was smooth as a wave-tumbled stone. And while you may have limped on land, you were an elegant swimmer. You never lost a race or a contest to see who could stay under water the longest. That first summer we may not have been able to talk much, but we didn't need to. We did whatever would make you smile, because making you happy made me happy.

"Boat," I said as I clumsily rowed us across the water to the island. "Row."

"Boat. Row," you repeated.

I sang "Row, Row, Row Your Boat" over and over until you joined in through your giggles. Everything I did, every word I said seemed to make you laugh. You laughed when I jumped out of the boat and dragged it to shore. You laughed when I showed you how you could eat the wild mint that stretched its rhizomes out in all directions just beneath the sand. You laughed when I skipped a flat stone across the glassy surface of the lake. I thought you must be the happiest person alive, and I wished I were you.

"Stick," I said, showing you the driftwood branch I was fashioning into a pole. "Dig," I said as we dug down into the sand with our fingers until water welled up in the hole.

I held the stick straight as you pushed the sand back in around the base. Then I untied the bandana that held my tangled hair away from my face. I tied two corners to the stick and waited for the wind to make it flutter grandly, but it was a windless day. I held the bandana out with my hand and made it ripple by my own power.

"I declare this land Mermaid Island," I shouted. "And we are its queens." You laughed hardest at that.

You helped me gather oxeye daisies, and together we made crowns for each other, bowing as we placed them on each other's heads, me solemn, you smiling. When we left our domain for supper that night, I wished we had a younger kid we could make into a servant who would row the boat for us—it was so tacky for a queen to row her own. But at least on the way home we each took an oar, sitting close on the bench seat, me on the right, you on the left, making our way home, together.

I knew from the start, that's how we fit. Side by side. Just the two of us.

Which is why when the next summer rolled around, I was shocked at your sudden ease with your adopted language and violently jealous of the girls at your school who must have been teaching you. It was hard to imagine that your life went on somewhere else, that you weren't in some sort of stasis Up North while I rushed through the school year to rejoin you the next June. It never occurred to me that things might be happening to you at the same time they were happening to me.

That was a big year for me. I'd grown nearly four inches, which you could see, and started wearing a training bra, which I think you suspected. What I'm sure you didn't know is that, just days before leaving home for the summer, I had my first period. My mom explained the mechanics of sex and sent me off to Hidden Lake with a stern warning to watch out for boys, so I left home disgusted with biology in general and boys in particular.

Next to you, I now felt more hulking and clumsy than ever. Even though we were both ten, I privately imagined myself in the role of big sister and felt a little better. I would watch out for boys for both of us, from sunrise to Magic Time, when the sun dipped behind the forested hills and the fireflies and moths and bats danced in a crushed-velvet sky.

That was the last perfect summer on Hidden Lake. The next year, you had an older brother.

"He's not my real brother," you were quick to explain. "People think since he's Korean he's my real brother, but he's not. He's just some big kid no one wanted. Beth and Robert said I needed a sibling. I told them I wanted a little sister, but they said Chin-Hae needed a home more than another cute little girl. Well, Tyler now."

The moment I laid eyes on Tyler Rainier, I was glad you had gotten a big brother. I was also sure that he was just the type of boy my mother had warned me about. At fifteen, he was already four years older than we were, yet he seemed older still, almost like an adult. His mouth was set in a permanent frown, just like my mom's. His eyes were two black camera lenses that recorded everything, and behind them was a mind that was constantly processing, considering, coming to conclusions he did not share with his new little sister and her friend.

"I think something's wrong with him," you said in a conspiratorial whisper. "He was adopted before—more than once—but he ended up back at the orphanage."

"Does he speak English?"

"Not much."

I kept a neutral expression on my face, but inside I was tingling to think that I might be the one to teach him. Maybe I could teach him enough that he'd know English before he went back downstate and some other people got to him.

For several days, you and I did our regular stuff—floating around in inner tubes, looking for cool rocks, catching crayfish and minnows and toads—and Tyler drifted by like an extra in a play who had no lines, just there to give the audience a sense that the main action was playing out in the midst of a real world that contained other people. But once Scott Masters realized that there was another teenage boy on the lake, Tyler morphed into a secondary character whose own storyline occasionally crossed paths with ours.

What Scott and Tyler did with their time wasn't always clear to me. They could be seen heading around corners and emerging from the woods, and though I still couldn't read emotion on Tyler's face, I could tell Scott was up to something. Maybe they were drinking and smoking in secret. Maybe they were torturing small animals. Maybe they were building a tree fort. Or a bomb.

In early July, our storylines merged. We were forced to defend Mermaid Island from Tyler and Scott as they lobbed a shower of tiny bait fish at us from the old green wooden rowboat. We answered with rocks found along the shore. I tossed them underhand, getting close to the boat but not close enough to do any real damage. You threw them overhand as hard as you could. You were remarkably accurate, hitting your new brother half a dozen times in the arms and chest until he sat down hard, started the outboard motor, and left amid a string of syllables that were unintelligible to me but that you must have understood.

At the time, I was annoyed. Tyler was cute in his long, brightly colored swim trunks. I liked how he only put a shirt on at night, when the temperature dropped and the mosquitoes came out. I liked how his sleek black hair flopped over one eye and how the other eye held brazenly steady when I caught him looking at me. I was always the first to look away.

As my hands and feet cut through the water now, propelling me toward our old haunt, I couldn't quite decide if I wished Tyler had never come to live on Hidden Lake at all. Yes, he'd ruined everything. But didn't I also owe him the barest sliver of gratitude?

My knee struck the bottom of the lake, and a sharp stone dug into the space between my kneecap and tibia. Eyes watering, I rubbed the spot vigorously and stood in water up to my calves. Mermaid Island was smaller than I remembered, though the low lake level should have made it bigger. Networks of dried roots stretched along the shore like veins in the white of an eye. A woodpecker tapped among the stand of trees that I would not enter. I knew nothing was there now. But the pain of the past is not so easily erased as the pain from a stone in the flesh.

There was another time on this beach, the memory of which holds no anxiety for me. You and I were building an elaborate series of obstacles in the sand—holes, tunnels, berms, walls—in order to conduct the First Annual Frog Olympics, which turned out to be the Only Annual Frog Olympics. We captured a couple unwilling amphibian athletes and set them down at the starting line, fully expecting them to race through the obstacle course toward a future filled with accolades and honors from their fellow frogs. Instead, either they didn't move or they hopped off in the wrong direction, forcing us to retrieve them and set them back on the right course again and again, trying to coax them by poking their pointy green butts with one hand and holding the other along the edge of the course to keep them going the right way, until we couldn't breathe for how hard we were laughing. Easily one of the top five best days of my life. So strange how one place, one person, can elicit equal parts joy and confusion.

A moment later, with nothing else to do, without having even stepped onto dry land, I turned my back on our grand old kingdom to head back to the cabin.

It had been years since I'd swum that far that fast. My younger self would have had a thing or two to say to me about wasting every summer in front of a computer screen instead of spending them in the water where I belonged. My lungs and muscles pulsed with pain. I started home, slower, switching up my strokes every few minutes. I half hoped your dad would come out in his boat to offer me a ride. I'd have even accepted a ride from crazy old Ike Fenton at this point. But, as usual, no one came to my rescue.

By the time I hauled myself out of the lake, I was limp and waterlogged, like a tangle of kelp washed up on shore. I snatched my towel from the chaise lounge and rubbed the water from my hair as I walked up the sandy path to the cabin. For the first time in a long time, I felt tired in body rather than tired in spirit. I liked the feeling.

I wiped the wet sand from my feet, spread the towel over the porch railing to dry, and swept through the door, ready to get back to work, which really only meant I was ready to get back to sitting and staring like an idiot.

At the slam of the screen door, a man jumped up from the couch where he'd been sitting, dropping a book on the floor in the process. A cold blade of panic punctured my lungs, and for a moment I was mute, immobilized. Was this the anonymous letter writer? A whacko stalker?

I know what you would have done. You would have sauntered over, never missing a beat, and asked him what kind of pomade he used or where he'd gotten his shoes. Whatever you were feeling inside—terror, rage, lust—it would not have shown on the outside.

But I'm nothing like you. My darting eyes found the phone on the kitchen wall, scanned the room for a blunt object. I tried to force my lungs into an obedient rhythm, but they were in charge now, not me.

"Wh-who are you?"

"I am Andreas," the man said in some sort of accent. Russian? "I am the translator."

German.

Breathe.

Breathe.

He picked up the book he had dropped. "Lois said you were expecting me." He looked me up and down. "Obviously you were not."

I reached back out the door, grabbed the towel, and covered the evidence of my unpreparedness. "No, I wasn't. Lois said the translator would be making arrangements to *talk*. Not that he'd be involved in a breaking and entering at my cabin. And I was expecting a woman. Andrea."

"Andreas," he said, emphasizing the *s* and holding out his hand. "Andreas Voelker. And I didn't break in. The door was open."

I clutched the towel around my chest, heart still thumping against the inside of my ribs. "I guess I thought the *s* was a typo. But that doesn't explain why you're here or how you even knew where *here* was."

He took back his unshaken hand and rubbed his stubbled beard. "Lois told me she was having some trouble communicating with you. She gave me the address and said she told you I was coming."

"Yeah, well, she didn't."

"I'm so sorry. I didn't mean to scare you. If you like, I will go outside until you are . . . dressed."

You know what happened then. My stupid face broadcast my stupid embarrassment. Like this ridiculous situation was all my fault. I could feel the blood boil up behind my skin, red and full of betrayal. Never so self-possessed as you. You who never blushed for anyone.

"Yes. I could use a few minutes," I said.

"Of course."

He put the book down on the table. My book, the one I had started to sign for Robert. The screen door whapped shut, and I watched him walk down to the water. He was shaking his head and raking his fingers through his wavy brown hair. I took some comfort in the idea that the surprise encounter had been as embarrassing to him as it had been to me. I hoped his cheeks were burning as hot as mine.

As soon as he was beyond the trees, I pounced on my phone. No voicemail, no texts. Of course. Despite the ugly towers that seem to pop up on every once-beautiful hill in northern Michigan, we still didn't have reliable service at Hidden Lake. It was a feature that seemed to commend itself to the writing process—no cell phone, no internet, no distractions—but now the lack of modern technology was exasperating.

What had Lois been thinking? I'd given her the landline number, told her I wouldn't be reachable by conventional means. Why hadn't she called? What was this guy *doing* here?

I threw shorts and a T-shirt over my suit and tousled my damp hair. I didn't dare look in a mirror. I snatched the phone from the cradle and dialed Lois's number. It took more thought than it normally would have. The muscle memory of punching numbers with my thumb interfered with the kind of memory I needed to access to make a call on the ancient rotary phone, which had never been replaced, because why would you replace something that still worked? I waited through three rings, then the call went to voicemail.

"Lois, it's Kendra. I had a bit of a surprise today when the German translator showed up. At my house. I was not expecting him. And I was not expecting a *him*. Please call me on the landline number I gave you. If I don't pick up because I'm out on the lake, please try calling back."

I hung up and looked out the window over the kitchen sink, expecting to see a Volkswagen or a BMW in the drive. The sight of a dusty Ford pickup might have made me laugh out loud if not for the jumble of memories it conjured up.

I found the translator standing at the end of the dock, looking out over the water. Dressed in dark blue jeans, a close-fitting chocolate-brown button-down shirt, and what looked to be expensive shoes, the man with the unkempt hair and scruffy beard was decidedly out of place on the dock. He looked more like an ad for cologne than a book translator.

"Mr. Voelker, we got off to a rough start." I stuck out my hand. "I'm Kendra."

He shook it firmly. "Nice to meet you."

"Welcome to Hidden Lake."

A wry almost-smirk bloomed on his face, as though I had said or done something humorous. Did he find the handshake overly formal? My mistake about his gender certainly deserved a laugh in hindsight. But something in me didn't think he was exactly amused at our situation so much as he was amused at what I had just said.

It made me think of you. Always churning little jokes out of some snark factory in your brain, never quite letting me in on what was so funny. Or maybe you tried and I just didn't get it.

"Why don't you come inside and we can have a drink and something to eat and get this wrinkle ironed out," I said. "I assume you've been on the road for a while." I led the way into the kitchen and took two glasses down from the cupboard. "All I have to drink is Coke, iced tea, and milk, and the water's good."

"Water is fine, thanks."

I cracked some ice cubes into the glasses and turned on the faucet, which sputtered a moment before the stream ran steadily. "I'm sorry I don't have anything much better than ham sandwiches or PB and J at the moment, but I wasn't expecting guests." I spun around, glasses in hand, water running colder in the sink behind me. "This isn't something that could have been done over email?"

"It is, but Lois said you didn't have email access up here."

I filled the glasses. "Right, but it couldn't be done over the phone? This whole situation seems highly unusual."

"It's not a short conversation," he said as I placed a glass in front of him. "There are questions throughout the entire book. German is a very precise language. English is more . . . up for interpretation. There are ambiguities in the imagery—metaphors, comparisons, wordplay—things that sound beautiful in English but can sometimes sound rather crude in German. In some cases, I may have to change what is said entirely and write a new passage that conveys the same feeling. And I want to get it right. I want to do right by your story."

I pulled out two plates and four pieces of bread. "I appreciate that. Really. I'm just . . . I guess I'm surprised they'd actually send someone from Germany over here to do this. I'm nobody. And it must be crazy expensive."

He laughed lightly. "I live in Chicago."

"Oh. Still." Feeling more than a little stupid, I busied myself with a jar of strawberry jam. This made absolutely no sense. "Did you come all the way up this morning?"

"Yes. I left the rental place at six."

"You rented that truck? Seems like an odd choice for such a long highway drive."

"I had requested something smaller, like a Jetta—better gas mileage. When I told him I was going to a cabin in the woods in northern Michigan, he handed me the keys for the truck."

I finished spreading the peanut butter and pressed the two sides of the sandwiches together. They must have seen him coming a mile away. Surely renting a heavy-duty truck cost a lot more than a compact car. "And have you found it particularly useful now that you're here?"

"No. Not yet."

I put one of the plates down in front of him, sat, and took a bite of my sandwich.

"I'm allergic to peanut butter," he said.

"What?" I snatched the plate away from him and started to stand up. "Why didn't you say so?"

He put a hand on my wrist to stop me. "I'm kidding. Only kidding. To lighten the mood."

I hesitated but settled back down in the chair at the light pressure he continued to exert on my wrist. I was about to twist my arm out of his grasp when he let go, picked up the sandwich, and took an enormous bite.

"That's not funny," I said. I took a drink of water. "Food allergies are dangerous."

He was struggling to stop smiling even as he chewed. "I'm sorry," he said, his cheek filled with PB and J. "I shouldn't have done that. You're a very serious person."

I'd heard that one before. I set down my drink a little harder than I meant to. "Some things are serious."

His smile faded. "Of course."

I lightened my tone. "So where are you staying while you're up here?"

He shifted in his seat. "Yes, I need to talk to you about that. I hadn't realized how busy it would be here when I decided to come. It seems like every hotel, motel, and Airbnb is booked solid."

"Well, yeah, it's tourist season. When it's warm in Michigan, everyone goes Up North, everyone goes to the lakes."

"I see that now."

He said nothing more, and I knew he was waiting for me to supply a solution to his problem. But what was I going to say?

"I thought," he ventured, "that since it was your suggestion to have me come up, you might know of a room somewhere."

"My suggestion? This was my suggestion?"

"Well, yes. Wasn't it?"

Was it? I had no memory of this.

"I'm not picky," he said. "I'd take a tent and a sleeping bag as long as I can charge my laptop somewhere."

"No tents," I said forcefully.

He looked to me for more.

I sighed. "Just . . . I'm not going to make you stay in a tent. There's an extra room here."

"Are you sure?" he said too quickly. "I don't want to put you out."

I wasn't.

"I'm sure."

4

So now I had a roommate. And the spot above the fireplace where Grandpa's shotgun used to hang was empty. I wondered who had gotten the gun when they settled the estate. Surely not my mother.

Andreas tucked his suitcase beneath Grandpa's bed and asked me why I didn't sleep in what was clearly the only real bedroom in the place. I searched for the reason among the haphazard folds of my thoughts.

"I don't know. I never even considered it. It's my grandpa's room. I've always slept in the loft."

"You aren't going to need this?" He tapped the desk a few inches from the letter I'd left there.

I picked up the letter, folded it, and slipped it into my pocket. "I have a desk upstairs."

"Do you want the typewriter?"

"I don't write on it." I pulled the incriminating paper from the rolls and looked for a deflection. "Is that all you brought? One suitcase? You must not anticipate staying long," I hinted.

One corner of his mouth quirked up. Maybe it was just the

way he smiled. Maybe he was just a little crooked, like the horizon line of your shoulders, the left one always sinking slightly lower than the right, drawn down by your bad leg.

"Surely you know that Germans are very efficient," he said. "My deadline to finish the initial translation is the first of July, so I should be out of your hair very soon." He tugged lightly on the curtain in the doorway. "What is this?"

I remember you asking about that a long time ago. I remember asking Grandpa. I remember him saying that the curtain was there because there wasn't a door, and when I asked him why there was no door, he told me that most of the time doors weren't as necessary as people made them out to be.

"I have no idea," I said to Andreas. "There's never been a door there, just the curtain. There was never really a need for much privacy."

Until now.

"We'll stay out of each other's way," he said, perhaps sensing my discomfort.

The phone rang. Probably Lois calling to apologize. I was happy for a task that took me out of that bedroom. It was only now fully hitting me that I was going to be sharing my cozy cabin with a strange man I'd never met before, and the only interior door in the entire cabin was for the bathroom.

Grandpa had been wrong.

But it wasn't Lois on the phone. It was Robert, with an invitation.

A moment later I swung my head back around the bedroom doorjamb to find Andreas leaning over the desk, looking out the window toward the lake. "How would you like to have dinner tonight with a friend of mine, another author?"

He straightened and turned. "*Wunderbar.*"

"He's just across the lake," I said. "Robert Rainier. Have you heard of him?" His expression of dopey disbelief pleased me deeply. "I'll take that as a yes."

I went back to the kitchen phone to confirm with Robert. When I hung up, Andreas was standing in the living room with his hands on his narrow hips, looking like he expected to find he'd been pranked.

"Robert Rainier?"

"He lives across the lake. Well, summers there. I've known him for forever. His daughter's my best friend." Could I still call you that? "Let's get the boat ready. Give me a hand outside?"

"I don't know much about boats."

"I don't need your brain, just your brawn." I looked at his shoes. "Do you have flip-flops or sandals?"

Andreas yawned. "No."

"Just go barefoot then. Don't want to ruin those shoes."

He sank into a chair and removed his shoes and socks. His feet were even paler than mine had been a few days earlier.

"You burn easily?"

He yawned again. "I'm not sure."

"Not sure?"

"I don't get out in the sun much. I generally work at night. Fewer distractions in a busy city—easier to immerse myself in the work."

"Would you rather stay here and take a nap?"

"And miss dinner with Robert Rainier?" He stood up. "Where is this boat?"

I led him down the sandy path through the trees, stopping at the silver fishing boat. We flipped it easily and marched it down to the water's edge, me at the bow, him at the stern.

"The motor's kind of heavy," I said when we got to the shed, but he had already hoisted it up and was heading back down to the lake. I grabbed the plastic gas can Robert had left me and a nylon rope and hurried after him.

Minutes later, the boat was in the shallows, rope fastened securely to the front, engine resting on the back. I filled the tank with gas, pulled the choke, and gave the cord a solid yank.

Nothing.

I tried again with the same result. The scent of gas mingled with the odor of an unfortunate fish that had washed up on shore some yards away and was now being picked at by noisy gulls.

Andreas stood on the dock, pant legs rolled up to his calves. "Want me to try?"

I had grown up in this boat. I was not about to let some smirky German nightwalker who didn't know anything about boats start an outboard motor for me. "Choke needs cleaning," I said with feigned authority. I'd heard Grandpa say that before.

A quick perusal of the shed revealed no cans of choke cleaner, nor any other likely tool for engine maintenance—or at least, none I knew how to use. I felt a presence behind me and spun around.

Andreas pointed to two wooden oars hanging on the wall near the door. "What about those?"

"I guess that will do for now. We better get moving if we don't want to be late."

Back at the lake, I dragged the boat into water nearly up to the hem of my shorts, tossed the line to Andreas on the dock, and hoisted myself up beside him.

"Where are the life jackets?" he said.

"This isn't Lake Michigan. We don't need life jackets. No one's ever drowned in Hidden Lake."

Andreas made no move to get into the boat.

"You know how to swim, right?" I said.

"No, I don't."

I don't think I have to tell you that I had never met an adult who couldn't swim. Everyone in Michigan can swim. Water is our birthright, our natural habitat.

"You don't know how to swim?"

He shook his head. He didn't even look embarrassed. No red in those cheeks.

"Would you rather drive over?"

He held up his hand. "It's fine. What can happen, right?"

"Trust me. It's a straight shot across the lake. The only scary part will be getting in and getting out, but if you can ride a bike, you can get into a boat."

"How does riding a bicycle prepare you for boating?"

"Balance. Inner ear. All that stuff."

He gave a resolute nod and committed himself to my care. I secured the boat in place with the line, slipped back into the water, and pushed the side of the boat right up against the dock so that Andreas could see no strip of water between them.

"Sit down on your butt and hang your legs over the side of the boat," I said. "Now slide onto that middle seat, facing me, just like you were sliding into a booth at a restaurant."

Andreas took a breath and accomplished the maneuver. My tight hold kept the boat from rocking in the water.

"See? Easy."

"But how do you get in?"

I tossed the line into the bow behind him. "Scoot all the way to your right, and when the boat tilts, just lean the opposite way."

"Wait, why is the boat going to—"

I hoisted myself up over the side and into the boat in one fluid motion. Andreas jerked to counter my weight, then looked at me, wild-eyed and gripping his seat.

"See? Easy," I said. "Now grab the oars."

I wouldn't normally be so pushy with someone I'd just met, but I didn't know of any other way to master my fear of being alone in a boat with a strange man who had picked up a fifty-pound motor and walked practically a hundred yards with it while emitting nary a grunt. There were only two men I trusted enough to be in this position with—one was dead and the other was waiting on us to arrive for dinner. I took some comfort in knowing I could jump out at any time without worrying that Andreas might follow—it wouldn't be the first time I'd done something like that. He may have gotten the upper hand by surprising me when I walked into the house in a dripping-wet bathing suit, but out here I had the clear advantage. And I intended to keep it.

It took Andreas a few minutes to find an efficient rowing rhythm, but soon the boat was skating across the water like a merganser. The sun threw down a constant thrum of heat on my face and arms and thighs. The chirruping of a bald eagle skipped like a stone over the glassy surface of the lake. A school of sunnies sculled in the deeps, their secret realm revealed by shafts of sunlight piercing the water.

If I didn't look at my companion, I could imagine it was you in the boat, taking us to your house for fresh-squeezed lemonade. For just a moment, my soul opened up like a water lily. I was eleven again, and nothing had happened to me that I hadn't made happen. I presided over my days, my nights, my mind, my body, the unchallenged sovereign of a small but pleasant life.

"You set the book here, didn't you?" Andreas said. "Hidden Lake is Clouded Lake, isn't it?"

My petals closed. "What makes you say that?"

He stopped rowing. "The white birch trees there, the six hills,

46

the birds, the dock, even the dead fish on the beach. They are all in your book."

I feigned indifference to the line of questioning that always caused my heart rate to tick up and let my standard answer spill from my suddenly dry lips. "I drew from this place, of course. Everyone draws from real places. But it's not Hidden Lake."

Only it was, and I was sure by his expression that Andreas knew that. He wasn't smirking anymore, but the thoughtful set of his mouth was almost worse. That was the look a person got when he was putting two and two together, and I had made it my mission for the past year to make sure that equation never came out right.

Andreas resumed rowing. I fixed my eyes on an arbitrary spruce tree to the northwest. Nothing more was said until we reached your dock, where I jumped out without warning, setting the boat to rocking and hopefully throwing him as much off balance as he had thrown me. I wound the line around the cleat and extended a hand. Andreas's face was pale as the inside of a catfish.

"If you were in swim trunks you could just get out into the water—it's shallow here—but I'm afraid wet jeans are not going to be terribly comfortable for dinner."

He scooted to the edge of his seat. The boat tilted, and he leaned away from my hand to counter it.

"The trick is to go fast," I said. "Like ripping off a Band-Aid."

He gave me a doubtful look.

"Kendra!" Robert shouted from the deck above.

As soon as your father spoke, Andreas clasped my hand and jumped out of the boat. The move was so sudden he almost pulled me into the water. He straightened his shirt, unrolled his pant legs, and ran a hand through his hair, looking very much like a man meeting his future father-in-law for the first time.

Robert trotted down the stairs to the dock and pumped Andreas's hand. "You must be ze German. My great-grandfather shot twelve planes out of the sky over France."

I threw him a horrified glare, which he met with an easy smile.

"Relax, Kendra. It was for the Kaiser." He poked an elbow into Andreas's arm. "My grandpa made up for it in the next war, though. Come on up. Steaks are ready for the grill."

I tried to send Andreas a telepathic apology, but he wasn't looking at me. He was fixated on the yellow cottage up the stairs that Robert was taking two at a time. I tried to see what he was seeing, to look anew at a place that was so much a part of the fabric of my being that I almost ceased to take note of it. Then I realized that he was probably trying to match up this house to the one in my book.

"Sorry about that," I said as I started up the stairs. "He must be spending too much time with Ike."

Andreas followed a step behind. "You'd be surprised how often people tell me war stories when they realize I'm German. And I'd expect it from him anyway. Who is Ike?"

"This crazy old veteran who lives on the northeast shore. Supposedly he was the only one from his battalion to survive D-Day, though I have my doubts about that. He'd probably shoot you on sight if he knew you were German."

The crooked smile was back. "I'll try to avoid him, then."

Before I could open the back door, Robert swung it open himself, a platter of raw steaks in one hand, spatula in the other, open bottle of beer shoved in his back pocket. "Beer's in the fridge," he said. "Liquor's in the icebox. Help yourselves."

Andreas followed me into the cool shadows inside the house. "An icebox is a fridge, right?"

"In this case, no. It's an icebox. Like, an actual icebox, from before electricity. But no ice in it. Just a cupboard now. It's in the living room."

"Ah," he said. "Would it be too stereotypical for me to choose beer?"

I had to smile. "Very much so. But have what you want."

I grabbed a beer out of the fridge for him and filled a glass with ice and lemonade—store-bought in your mom's absence—for myself. On the way back out, I peeked into the living room and stopped short.

The icebox was still there, but other than that it was like an entirely different house. The rug was new. The couch was new. The lamps were new. The ancient tube TV had been replaced with an obscenely large plasma screen hung on a wall and banked by skinny high-end speakers. A glance through the door into your parents' bedroom revealed a new bedspread, new pillows, new paint color. Grandpa's cabin may have been frozen in time, but life on this side of the lake had gone on at full speed without me.

Andreas was waiting for me in the kitchen doorway. I clinked my glass against his bottle in an attempt to be casual. "Cheers."

"*Prost.*"

Out on the deck, your dad reclined in a white Adirondack chair as the steaks sizzled on the gas grill. I took the chair next to him. Andreas sat across from me on the long edge of the chaise lounge, his face open and bright. No smirk for Robert Rainier.

"Andreas, right? Kendra tells me you're translating her book."

"Yes, that's right. Have any of your books been translated into German?"

"A couple. I've never had a translator work with me in person, though." He narrowed his eyes. "Seems highly unusual."

"Yes, I would normally do such work over email," Andreas

said. "But Ms. Brennan has no access here and we have a tight deadline. The German edition is scheduled to release in time for Christmas."

Robert frowned. "And you're just starting now?"

"No, no. Most of the work is done. I am only here to clarify parts that are not simple one-for-one translations." Andreas put his beer on the deck, leaned forward, and began to talk with his hands. "For instance, you might use a metaphor that is very meaningful to English speakers—and Ms. Brennan's writing is full of such beautiful metaphors—but a wooden translation of the words into German may mean something very different or nothing at all."

Robert nodded and looked pointedly at me. "You're lucky they're putting such care into this. Sometimes I don't even hear about a foreign edition until the complimentary copy shows up at my door."

Somehow I doubted that was true. Or perhaps his books were so utterly in demand that he just couldn't keep track of his own success anymore.

"I have read many of your books, Mr. Rainier," Andreas said. "But not in German. I would be interested in taking a look at one."

"My first book came out in German, but there wasn't much interest from Germany for the war books. They're all on the shelf in my study. You can borrow anything you like while you're here. And call me Robert." He stood up. "How do you like your steak, Andreas?"

"Medium rare."

He slapped Andreas on the back. "*Gut Mann.*"

"*Guter Mann,*" Andreas corrected with a smile.

"Ah!" Robert scowled down at me. "You still going to force

me to insult the cow that sacrificed its flesh by insisting I cook this thing dry?"

I rolled my eyes. "I'll take it medium. No less, though."

Robert winked. "That's progress anyway."

Across from me, Andreas smiled. A real, full smile. He had a friendly face, boyish despite the beard, with twinkling eyes. With his sleeves rolled up, elbows on his knees, and the bottle held loosely in his fingers, he looked perfectly at ease. I liked seeing him across the deck. Tyler had always sat too close.

"Your arms are already looking medium rare," I said. "Let's eat inside."

Besides the steaks, Robert produced a container of store-bought potato salad and a bag of chips.

"Does your wife know you're eating like this?" I asked.

He tucked a piece of steak into his cheek. "What do you think?"

"Beth's a health nut," I explained to Andreas. "Especially when it comes to greasy stuff like potato chips. Big no-no for a dermatologist."

"She'll never catch me," Robert said. "She probably won't even be up until after the Fourth." A flicker of a shadow passed across his face.

"She's going to miss the fireworks?" I said.

"I don't think she'll *miss* them."

Andreas pointed. "Ah, you see? Right there. *Miss*. One word, two meanings. One is to be absent—*fehlen*—while the other is to feel the loss of something or someone—*vermissen*. And there are many other meanings besides those two. That witty bit of conversation couldn't happen in German. It would have to be altered or the double meaning would be lost."

"Your English is excellent, though," I said.

"But I am not a native speaker. I learned in school, and not even American English so much as British English. So I am never confident it is perfect."

"It doesn't have to be *perfect*," Robert said. "Nothing is."

I choked a little on my steak, recalling the reams of marked-up pages I used to get back from him when I started writing.

"In most cases I would agree," Andreas said. "If I were writing a story myself in English, I would not worry if it was perfect. But I am not writing my story; I am writing Ms. Brennan's story. I want German readers to have the same full experience of her book that American readers do."

Robert pointed his fork at me. "I'll say it again: you're lucky to have him, Kendra."

Heat crept up my neck as I locked eyes with a beaming Andreas across the table. The men prattled on, bouncing from books to boats to Chicago haunts they had in common. I kept silent, hoping to be forgotten, missed. *Fehlen?* Or *vermissen?*

I cleared the dishes in Beth's stead—I have never seen Robert clean up after a meal—washing great pink puddles of blood and fat from the white plates as the men drifted off to the deck for cigars and another beer. I refilled my glass with lemonade and joined them as the sun began its slow tumble from the sky.

"Want one?" Robert asked, indicating his cigar.

"Why not?"

No, I haven't taken up smoking cigars, but I couldn't help wanting to be just one of the guys. The less you stick out, the less likely you are to take on the shape of a target. That had been my mistake with Tyler. I'd been too girly. I never should have shrieked when he grabbed my legs under water. Never should have blushed at his stares. Never should have gone along to get along.

I would never make that mistake again.

5

Andreas waved over my shoulder to Robert, then took up the oars and started to row. Getting into the boat had been smoother this time, and I was sure the presence of another man had induced this swift improvement in technique. Once Andreas was seated, he offered me his hand. Though dizzy from the cigar—which I'd smoked far too fast in my eagerness to seem like I knew anything about smoking cigars—I would not accept the help. I might have welcomed the assistance were it not for your father's parting words as he handed Andreas the German edition of *Blessed Fool*.

"Kendra's on a deadline of her own. Probably do her good to have someone else there, keeping her accountable. I don't think I'd ever make a deadline if it weren't for Beth's nagging. Keep on her, Andy."

Andreas had wisely said nothing, but that couldn't take the patronizing sting out of what Robert said. No one had been keeping tabs on me when I wrote my first book. Books get written when they get written. You can't rush the process. I know. I've tried. When I'd gotten the two-book deal I'd been ecstatic; my next book was guaranteed to be published. Now I couldn't stop myself from resenting my success, and even resenting Robert's a little. There's nothing like a successful man to make you feel small.

A crescent moon had risen in the eastern sky before the sun had quite given up for the day. The little silver fishing boat floated between these two heavenly bodies, skimming waters that mirrored the russet and rosé tones of the thin clouds that had moved in during dinner. Magic Time. I kept my eyes locked on the faint line of my dock. I'd forgotten to turn on the porch light—Grandpa always did that—and the trees had swallowed up the cabin entirely. I didn't need the light to get from the dock to the cabin door, but it would have helped in setting the right course across the lake.

"You were signing a book for him," Andreas said into the almost-silence. "I was flipping through it before you came in."

"I started to." I debated on whether to say more, to explain my inability to write even a short note to my mentor.

"He must have been a great influence on you. I mean, you write on very different subjects, but to be so familiar with such a famous author must have influenced you to become a writer yourself."

"I'm sure it did. He was always writing when I hung out with his daughter, Cami. Except when he was avoiding it. He definitely had his own bouts of writer's block. I don't know why he was making such a big deal about mine."

"How far are you on your next book? What is it about?"

I briefly considered lying to him. But that would mean his opinion mattered to me. And why should it? I just met the guy. "It's not about anything yet because it doesn't exist."

"You haven't started?"

I let a wisp of fatigue waft out in a small sigh. "Starting isn't the problem. I've started ten stories. Twenty. It's getting beyond about five thousand words that's proving difficult."

For a moment the only sound was the swoosh and trickle of the oars dipping in and out of the water, that lovely liquid melody of all my best and worst memories.

"Will you let me know if there is anything I can do to help?" he said. His voice was too kind, and I felt those months of private frustration closing in on my heart. "Or if I am making it difficult for you to concentrate? I don't want to be a distraction."

"I'm sure you will be." I wasn't sure he could see my smile in the darkening twilight. "But that's okay. You have a job to do. And it's nice to have some company."

It really was, though I was surprised my words were more than mere politeness. I had been living alone for some time. My schooling and all of the socialization that went with it was over. My work was solitary. And even the social interaction that came with being an author was superficial because I made sure it was. Maybe I'd missed being with people without knowing it.

Andreas surprised me by jumping out onto the dock before I even got the boat tied. He took the line and tied it himself, then held his hand out to me. This time I took it.

"Better grab that book," I said. "If you leave it out all night it will be ruined by dew. I have the English version on my shelf if you want to compare them."

He followed me up the dark path to the cabin, stumbling a little on the unfamiliar terrain. Inside I flicked on the light, and he drifted over to the bookshelves in the wall. He stared at the spines for a moment.

"Are these organized in any particular way? They're not alphabetical, by author or by title."

"You're right, but they are organized, very deliberately." I let him stare a little longer. "You'll never get it."

He snagged Robert's debut novel off the lowest shelf. "Chronological? But then why would Chinua Achebe be over here?"

I grinned. "That's a good question. Why *would* Chinua Achebe be over there?"

His fingers drifted lazily along a row of spines. "It's a map," he said finally, definitively.

"Wow. Very good."

"Clever way to arrange them. Chronological by continent." His eyes drifted north. "There is more to Europe than England and Ireland."

"This is only a fraction of my library. And if you look carefully, I have France, Spain, Italy, Poland, Russia, and Greece represented on the next shelf down—all in English, of course."

"Germany?"

I pointed. "Kafka."

"He wasn't German. He wrote in German, but he was born in Bohemia."

I wasn't sure I saw the distinction, but I wasn't about to argue.

"And there," he continued, "is a fine example of the problems translating. Gregor Samsa did not necessarily awake one morning to find himself transformed into an enormous insect. The word simply means 'vermin,' an unclean animal. Kafka was Jewish, so to be turned into an unclean animal, an animal not fit for sacrifice, is the point. This meaning is lost."

"Okay, Kafka doesn't count. So make me a list of who I should be reading."

He released an enormous yawn and gave both sides of his face a couple light slaps.

"Now you better get to bed," I said. "I need to wash the lake off, but I can wait until you've brushed your teeth."

"Oh, I won't be sleeping tonight. My schedule will get all 'out of whack,' as you might say."

"You're really going to stay up all night? How do you intend to ask me all these translation questions when I'm sleeping?"

"No, you see, this will work out best. You sleep at night. And when do you write?"

"From about seven to noon—when I *do* write."

"Fine then. I work until, say, three or four o'clock in the morning, then I go to sleep. You write in the morning without anyone in your way. Then I get up, we eat lunch, and in the afternoon we work through the passages together, which prepares me for the next night's work."

"So I won't see you until noon? That could work." A part of me was relieved. The less time we spent together, the less I would feel the need to play hostess and the more time I could devote to busting through my writer's block. And if he wasn't awake until noon, he'd never see me braless in my pajamas.

"So, now I will go into my room and leave you alone." He gave me a little wave. "Good night, Ms. Brennan."

"*Gute Nacht*, Mr. Voelker. But really, you can just call me Kendra."

He put a hand to his chest. "Andrea*s*."

Then he was gone into Grandpa's room, and the curtain slid across the doorway. I stood there a moment more, listening to the chair being pulled out from the desk, the drawer being opened, a piece of paper being rolled into place in the typewriter. The keys began to click, slowly at first, then with more purpose. When I was there so long it felt like spying, I snuck away and went up into the loft. I gathered up a pair of light cotton PJ shorts, a tank top, and a fresh pair of underwear, tucked it all under my arm, and headed for the bathroom.

While Grandpa had installed a door in the bathroom, there was no lock. I had never felt the lack of one until this moment. I showered and dressed as quickly as possible, brushed my teeth, then scanned the room for any embarrassingly female items. I gathered up my dirty clothes from the past few days, which

I'd carelessly left hanging on hooks and in little piles on the bathroom floor, and brought them to the closet in the kitchen that held the washing machine.

Or used to hold the washing machine. Now it held only a scattering of mouse droppings and a huge dead moth. Clearly I'd missed this during my cleaning spree earlier in the week. At a loss but too tired to deal with it right at that moment, I dragged the clothes up to the loft and dumped them on the floor at the foot of my bed. I crawled under the old quilt, handmade by the grandmother I'd never known, and closed my eyes.

Two hours later, I was still awake, staring at the crescent moon that had found its way to my window. It wasn't the moon's fault. And it wasn't the letter this time, though it had kept me up on other nights. It was the man directly below me. The noise of the typewriter had already ceased by the time I was out of the shower, but his mere presence—awake, alert— unnerved me.

What had Lois been thinking, giving this guy my address? I tried to imagine the man in the room below was actually just my grandfather, as it always had been. If I had heard the reassuring sound of snores, I might be able to get some sleep. As it was, all I heard were the normal cabin sounds—whispers of pine needles dropping onto the roof, wispy footsteps of mice on the floor, the whine of a trapped and dying fly at the window screen.

Finally I gave up and quietly slipped outside. I walked down the long, bouncing dock and lay on my back. The Milky Way split the night sky the same as it always had in June, its twin mirrored in the still lake. Each star maintained its place among all the trillions of others, knew its prescribed path. The earth spun at the same speed it always had, hurtling through space yet lulling its creatures into a false sense of stability. My lake, my stars. My fixed points.

I remember the night we lay on the dock making up new constellations. We jettisoned the Greek gods and Native American legends for myths of our own making, crowning the Crayfish King and locating his Jellyfish Jester a few stars over to the left. We built him a castle in the sky using parts of Ursa Minor and Draco, gave him a scepter he could hold in his claw, and designated a cluster of stars as his subjects.

Lying there now I could still see all of them, could identify them far more easily than the constellations of old, the ones that had directed mariners for centuries. Where might you and I have ended up if we'd followed the old maps? If we'd taken Polaris for our guiding light rather than the slowly shifting tentacles of the Jellyfish Jester? It's lucky for us Hidden Lake is disconnected from the great waterways of the world, that there is no way out, or we might have both been lost forever.

I closed my eyes. The *gloop* of bullfrogs in the water tickled the still-conscious part of my brain even as every other sensation fell away. There was no hard dock beneath me. Only a forgiving cushion of air that lifted me into the arms of sleep, into a supreme softness blanketed with clouds and feathers and a single light throwing silhouettes upon the wall. Then there was nothing but the scratching of a pen. Then even that was swallowed up in darkness. The light morphed to a muted glow that filtered through my shut eyelids. And then I was awake.

It took only a moment to realize that the ceiling above me was too far away and too flat to be the eaves above my bed. I was in Grandpa's room, Grandpa's double bed. And it was morning.

I felt my way, dry-eyed and squinting, out of the room to find Andreas on his side on the couch, a ratty afghan covering him from shoulders to ankles. Confused, I tiptoed into the kitchen and started the coffee maker, hoping it would not wake him but not caring enough to forgo the morning ritual. If ever I needed coffee, it was now.

With a steaming mug in hand, I stepped out into the mid-morning haze and walked along the narrow lakeshore path that had been formed and maintained by countless silent generations of deer. As I brushed through the tall grass and wildflowers, a flood of familiar smells—wet sand and crushed mint and something sweet I have never been able to identify—washed over me in gentle lapping waves of memory.

I followed the shoreline west to our favorite rock-picking spot on the far side of the big dead tree, still not quite decomposed even after all this time. I thought of all the stones left unpicked during my eight-year absence, of the ones that had returned to the sediment in the bottom of the lake when I did not pluck them from obscurity and add them to my carefully curated collection. I should have made time for this place. For Grandpa. For you.

I remember the summer we were obsessed with skipping stones. It was all we did all day every day for at least a month. Seeking out the flattest, smoothest, roundest stones we could find. Standing on my beach in the morning before any wind whipped up the water. Sending them flying across the surface like hoverboards, which we were sure existed somewhere and were being kept from us by a vast parental conspiracy. My record was eight skips. Yours was twenty-three. I never would have believed you if I hadn't seen it with my own eyes. Though I still maintain that it was only twenty-two.

"Do you think magic is real?" you had asked as you held the stone in your hand, testing its weight.

"No."

You looked at me like I'd just blasphemed the name of the Almighty. "You don't? Seriously?"

I shrugged. "I mean, I used to. I used to think unicorns were real too. You just grow out of those things."

You rubbed the stone with sand, like someone chalking a pool cue. "I don't."

You whispered something to the stone, kissed it, and sent it sailing. Twenty-three skips. Well, twenty-two. Either way, impossible. You met my slack-jawed gaping with a self-satisfied smile.

"Magic," you said.

And for a little while longer, you made me a believer.

The sun warming my back, I squatted here and there in our favorite spot to scan the shallows, sorting through a rainbow of stones and fossilized coral, resolved to choose only the very best. I found nothing suitable for skipping. But I did fill my pockets with little treasures. Then I drained my coffee and filled the mug with more. As the weight of the stones slowly grew, my heart felt lighter than it had in months.

Back at the cabin, I let the screen door slam, and Andreas shot upright on the couch.

"Oh! I'm so sorry!" I said in an intense, pointless whisper. "I forgot you were here."

He shielded his eyes from the light. "What time is it?"

I scooted, red-faced, into the kitchen and looked at the clock. "Eleven thirty," I said in disbelief.

I emptied my pockets and the mug onto the countertop. I'd wash the stones later. For now, I rinsed my cup, refilled it with coffee, and filled a clean mug for Andreas. When I came back into the living room he was lying on his back, his chest and stomach bare, with one arm slung over his eyes. I quietly placed the mug on the table near his head.

"*Danke.*"

"Do you need milk or sugar?"

"Nah."

I sat down on one of the wingback chairs. "I'm so sorry I woke you. I completely forgot you were here."

"No, it's fine."

He sat up and ran his fingers through his hair, a motion that I could now see must be a standard tic when he felt ill at ease, a way to smooth out the wrinkles, wipe the canvas clean. I made a mental note of the mannerism. Perhaps I could use it.

He took a long drink of the dark brew and gave me that confounding half smile. "Rough night?"

I suddenly remembered waking up in Grandpa's bed and crossed my arms over my chest.

"I heard you leave," he said. "When you didn't come back after a while, I thought I should go out to look for you. I found you asleep on the dock. I thought maybe if I left you there, you might roll off into the water and drown."

I couldn't ask him how he'd gotten me back to the cabin. I hoped I had walked, even if it was with assistance. If he'd dumped me headfirst into a wheelbarrow, it would have been better than being carried, unconscious, and laid down on someone else's bed. I felt the old clutch of panic rising in my chest and took a few deep breaths to push it back down.

"I'm sorry I took your bed," I said. "You could have gone up to the loft. The couch is terrible."

He rubbed one bare shoulder. "I've slept on worse. But you— you've missed your writing time, haven't you?"

I took a sip of coffee. "Ugh, this is cold. Why didn't you say so?"

I snatched the mug out of his hand before he could take another sip, dumped it in the sink, and started a new pot. When I turned around, my half-dressed houseguest was leaning in the doorway, a square of white folded paper in his hand.

"Before I forget, I found this on the floor outside the bath-room last night. It must have fallen out of your pocket."

I unfolded it. Andreas was looking at a spot on the floor.

"Did you read this?" I asked.

"Only enough to figure out what it was. I'm sorry."

I folded it up. "It doesn't matter."

"If it didn't matter, you wouldn't be saving it."

I tossed it on the counter with practiced indifference and opened the fridge. "Eggs and toast?"

"Sure."

"You're not allergic to eggs? Or wheat?"

He smiled. "No."

"And after that we'll go to town. Your truck will come in handy after all. I need a washing machine, you wanted a life jacket, and I imagine we both need to check emails."

I busied myself with breakfast preparations and ignored the shirtless man in the doorway. A moment later he left, and I shoved the letter back into my pocket. When Andreas reap-peared he was dressed in a pair of jeans, an embroidered bur-gundy shirt, and those same expensive-looking brown leather shoes.

"We're also getting you some flip-flops."

I struggled to stay alert as the rental truck rolled down the packed dirt road that curves away from Hidden Lake toward the county highway, but the sun was streaming through the window and the gravel sent soothing vibrations up through the tires and into the gray upholstered seat. Only my driver's occasional requests for directions at intersections and comments about the surrounding landscape kept me from drifting off entirely.

It was far more comfortable traveling down this road in the

cab of a pickup rather than the bed like we used to, bouncing all around the rusty metal rectangle of your dad's beater truck, pretending we'd been abducted, whispering our escape plan into each other's ears. We'd hide under the old woolen blanket, you with the biggest wrench from the toolbox, me with a tire iron, and when our kidnapper opened the tailgate to drag us into the woods and murder us, we'd bash him over the head from both sides, steal the truck, and leave him for dead. Robert was such a sport to play along with us.

"What happened to all these trees?"

I focused in on Andreas. "What trees?"

"The dead ones."

I scanned the rolling hills. "Those are ash trees. Emerald ash borers got them."

"What's that?"

"An invasive insect. It bores between the trunk and the bark and cuts off nutrients to the canopy. They've been working their way north for a decade. That's why there's a ban on moving firewood. They're trying to stop the spread to the Upper Peninsula. It's good of them to try, but it won't work."

"Why not?"

"Campaigns like that never do. People are selfish. They think the rules don't apply to them, or that just this one time it won't hurt. They do whatever they want, whatever suits them, and never think about the fact that others might suffer because of their actions."

He looked away from the road and caught my eye. "You're a pessimist, then?"

I shrugged. "I'm a realist."

"All pessimists think they're realists." He motioned out the window at the fuzzy white puffs dancing their way through the sky. "And what is all this?"

"Cottonwood seeds."

"Are those native?"

I thought for a moment. "You know, I have no idea."

Ten minutes later, Andreas eased off the highway and onto the main drag in Gaylord, which was choked with the typical summer traffic—cars topped with kayaks, RVs with bikes strapped on the back, trucks pulling boats or trailers laden with four-wheelers and jet skis. Everyone in a churning frenzy to experience summer before it slipped away.

I chose the cheapest washing machine I could find at Menards and brought the slip with the barcode on it up toward the checkout lines, where Andreas was waiting for me. He had picked out a life jacket but no footwear.

"Shoe store next?" he asked.

"What for?" I motioned to an enormous cardboard bin full of flip-flops marked $3.95.

"Those? I thought I'd get some nice leather sandals."

"You buy leather ones and they'll get ruined by the water or end up at the bottom of the lake. Just get the cheapo foam ones. They work, they float, and you're not out any money when they get ruined."

I grabbed a pair from the bin, then snagged the life jacket out of his hand. "I'm buying this too. It's not like you're going to take it back to Chicago with you. We'll just leave it at the lake in case someone else needs it."

I really didn't want to spend money on any of this stuff, but more than that I hated the thought of appearing hard up for cash.

"Then at least let me buy you coffee wherever we're going for Wi-Fi," Andreas said.

After loading the washing machine into the truck bed, we fought our way back into the sluggish river of traffic and then into the parking lot of Biggby Coffee. Once we were seated, I lost no time tracking down every email I had exchanged with my agent for the past six months.

It quickly became clear that I really did have only myself to blame for Andreas. I'd misread the name, my overwrought brain registering *Andrea* every time. And just as Andreas had said, I'd even been the one to blithely suggest "Andrea" stay at the cabin to placate Lois's fears of the German edition getting behind schedule after my impulsive decision to head up to a Wi-Fi dead zone.

I had also gotten an email from my editor, who was eager to hear a status report on the new manuscript. I moved it to a folder marked URGENT and put it out of mind. When I finally got to the end of my inbox, a new message from an unfamiliar address popped up.

Wie lange möchtest du noch bleiben?

"I don't speak German, you know," I said across the table.

Andreas lifted his eyes from his laptop and twisted the corner of his mouth. "*Nicht mal ein kleines bisschen?*"

I sighed. "It's not polite to do that."

It was a full smile now. "You said good night in German."

"Everyone knows *some* German. Schnell, Fahrvergnügen, lederhosen, 99 Luftballons."

Andreas leaned back and laughed. "It's nice to know my culture translates so readily. Eighties songs and car commercials. And where did you learn *schnell?*"

"It's what all the guards are yelling in *Schindler's List*. And everyone in Michigan knows what lederhosen are. Big German population back in the day."

He held my gaze, eyes twinkling, mouth fighting another smile. "*Ich kann mich glücklich schätzen, mit so einer schönen Frau Kaffee trinken zu dürfen.*"

"Ah, there's another one. *Frau*. Like *Fräulein*. Fräulein Maria. *The Sound of Music*. And I think I heard coffee in there."

"*Das ist gut*. Very good. Are you ready to leave, Fräulein Brennan?"

I shook myself out of his steady gaze and focused on my laptop. "Yes, I think so. You?"

"*Ja*."

We packed up our things and headed for the door. Andreas got there first and held it for me. I kept my face turned toward the window during the drive back to the lake in order to hide the dumb smile I could not seem to force from my lips. How had this intruder so quickly infiltrated my defenses?

Then I remembered the last guy who had so easily charmed me, and what had followed, and the smile drifted off with the cottonwood seeds.

6

The cottonwoods were in seed the first time I was ever alone with Tyler. It was the day you got yourself grounded for stealing Ike Fenton's best fishing pole, which would have been any other man's worst. I'd been too chicken to join your ill-fated escapade. My cowardice kept me from punishment, but it couldn't save you. The string of lies you told to cover your tracks was impressive, but you should have known Beth would see through them. She always did.

When you were sent to your room for the rest of the night, I made an awkward exit and headed down to the dock. A moment later Tyler followed.

"My mother tell me take you home."

The prospect of riding across the lake alone with Tyler had me secretly pleased with your confinement. He manned the outboard motor, and I sat across from him in the middle seat, our knees nearly touching. I made a point of not looking at him as we cut through the water, focusing instead on the reddening clouds to the west.

After a minute, I felt his fingers brush the crease below my bent knee. It was just the barest touch. Perhaps he hadn't noticed what he was doing. I moved my knee slightly, just out of reach, to see if his fingers would follow. They didn't. And then I couldn't move my knee back to where it was without him noticing, without him knowing that I didn't mind his touch.

Suddenly the engine sputtered and ceased, and the boat slowed to a stop.

"What happened?" I asked.

Tyler shrugged. I didn't know if the shrug meant that he didn't know why the engine had stopped or if he hadn't understood what I said. We were still a hundred yards from the south shore. I could swim the rest of the way, but that would leave Tyler stuck in the middle of the lake. I wondered if there had been any swimming lessons at the orphanage. Your first summer on the lake, you didn't go out in water deeper than your chest.

I joined Tyler in the back of the boat and looked at the engine.

"Gas?" he asked.

I opened the gas cap, but in the dim light it was impossible to tell. I looked to the south, to the light that winked on the little brown cabin beneath the trees. "Can you swim?"

He shook his head.

"Swim?" I said again, making a swimming motion with my arms.

He shook his head again.

I expelled a breath. What now? I looked to Tyler for an idea. He only shrugged again and smiled. Then his pinky finger was brushing my thigh. I didn't move this time. Didn't look at him. Didn't look at anything at all. We sat there next to each other in the little wooden boat, paralyzed. I don't know how much time passed as the clouds in the western sky shifted and purpled, but I did know that we couldn't sit out there forever. People would begin to wonder where we were.

"I can swim to shore and ask my grandpa to bring some gas out in his boat."

Tyler looked intently from my eyes to my mouth and back again. I had never kissed a boy, though at your insistence we had tested our technique out on each other through the modest barrier of your pillowcase. Jackie had said nothing about that, so I figured it was okay. But as Tyler edged closer, I started to think of all that my mother *had* said. That kisses led to touches, which led to babies, by way of the act that sounded awkward and painful and just plain weird.

I was in the water before I knew I had jumped out of the boat. I kicked off my favorite sandals and started for shore at a fast crawl, not looking back until I could stand in the shallows. I would send Grandpa out with the gas can. When my feet hit the shore, I heard the motor spurt to life again. Tyler turned the boat around and headed back to where we had come from. I never found my sandals. At the end of the summer I lied to my mother, telling her I'd grown out of them and given them to you.

The next day I did not go to your house. Nor the next. On the third day, you knocked on the cabin door and Grandpa made me open it.

"Where have you been? Tyler and Scott have taken over Mermaid Island. We have to take it back."

You grabbed my wrist, but I made no move to go.

"What's wrong with you?" you demanded.

"Nothing."

"Then let's go get them."

"Why?"

"Don't you listen? They've got all their junk on Mermaid Island. But I've got a plan. We're going to steal their boat. Hold it for ransom. Tyler can't swim."

"So?"

"So he can't come after us."

"Just leave it alone."

I left you standing there on the doorstep with no explanation for my rejection and climbed back up into the loft. I watched from my window as you stomped back to the lake. For just a moment my body tried to go after you, but my brain threw up a roadblock.

You can't tell her. That's her brother. And he's a bad kid. Wanting to be touched by a bad kid was something only another bad kid would want. And if you found out I was a bad kid, Beth would find out—because she always found out—and then she wouldn't let me play with you anymore. She barely tolerated me as it was.

"Kendra?"

I peeked over the edge of the loft to find Grandpa standing below, newspaper in hand.

"Whatever happened between you and Cami, make it right. No sense in being at odds with your friend."

I didn't tell him it wasn't you I didn't want to see. And I certainly would never tell him what had almost happened in the boat. I couldn't avoid seeing Tyler forever. But I could put it off just one more day.

Friday morning dawned clear and bright. Tyler would arrive at Hidden Lake sometime this afternoon. I had to face him, to confront him. I would make him explain himself. I would know that it had all been real, that it had been wrong, and that I had gotten it right. Then I would burn that letter and move on. I would write my next book, secure in the knowledge that I had told the truth, as all good novelists should.

I spent the quiet morning at my little desk in the loft, making notes and outlines. I'd had an idea on our excursion to town, and I needed to follow it a ways, to see if it was any good. But I kept finding myself looking out the window across the sliver of lake I could see through the trees. Looking for movement. When I reached the end of my patience with the mounting heat, I shut my laptop, slipped into a suit, and crept outside, careful to guide the screen door closed with a steady hand. I tiptoed through masses of accumulated cottonwood seeds as more floated down around me in a summery snow globe.

The lake started warm and shallow and easy, but with each step the temperature dropped a little more and the water pressed more firmly against my body. I walked as far as I could, until the sandbar disappeared and my muscles contracted at the sudden cold rising up from beneath me. I drifted slowly, head just above the water, until the feathery tips of seaweed ceased grasping at my swirling toes.

I filled my lungs, sank beneath the surface, and opened my eyes. The sun shivered in patterns of light and color across a school of minnows that scattered at my intrusion into their realm. Dull green fronds waved lazily. I scanned the dim reaches of the lake bottom for the opalescent shimmer of mussel shells. Because even at its deepest—Ike claims it is one hundred fifty-eight feet, two inches, exactly—Hidden Lake is too clear to hide much of anything for long.

I surfaced, swam a few yards, and dipped down again. The world drifted beneath in waves of deep blue and green and brown. I came up for air, dropped back into the abyss, again and again. Then a glint. Something shining within a twist of exposed roots. The watery atmosphere bent and shifted, but the object itself did not move. I plunged down, cutting through the cold in my ungainly way—never as graceful a swimmer as you. I grabbed at the silvery object, planted my feet on the cold, soft, sandy bottom, and propelled myself in the direction of the light.

At the surface, I wiped the water from my eyes to examine my find. Seven silver bangles held together by a silver ring. A bracelet. Your bracelet. The one you never took off your wrist. Why would it be in the lake?

"What are you doing way out here?"

The voice came from behind me.

The dark silhouette of a man in a boat loomed against the sun-drenched sky. He'd always been bigger than me—tall, muscular, heavier than he looked—and in the remembering, his stature had grown even more. I had hoped that when I saw him again, I would see that he was more manageable than memory had made him out to be. But with his head haloed by the sun and mine bobbing beneath his feet, Tyler Rainier was as big of a problem as he had always been.

"Looks like you're searching for treasure."

I dropped my hand into the water, but there was little point. His eyes never missed anything.

"I was just . . . I found this at the bottom of the lake."

I held the object out for Tyler to see. Suddenly it was in his hands and my fingers were left grasping at air.

"Those are Cami's," he said, though he didn't need to.

"Give them back, Tyler."

The boat drifted, and I turned in the water to maintain eye contact. That was what my self-defense instructor had harped on in college. Maintain eye contact. Let them know that you can identify them. Show them you're not afraid, even if you are.

"Give them back," I repeated.

He tossed the bangles in my general direction, just out of reach. I immediately dove down to get them, but even as I did

I wished I hadn't. It was just one more opportunity for Tyler Rainier to demonstrate that in our brief and confusing association, he was the one in control.

I came up out of the water with your bangles safely on my wrist and smoothed back my wet hair. "Is she here?" I asked.

Tyler looked off to the shore in the direction of my grandfather's cabin—my cabin, though it was still hard to think of it that way. "You on your own over there now?"

I was sure he didn't need to ask about my living situation. He'd have figured it out within an hour of getting back up to the lake, even if Robert hadn't told him, which of course he would have.

"Was she up earlier this season?" I asked.

The boat kept drifting. A cottonwood seed caught itself in Tyler's black hair, tragically unaware that this was not fertile soil. It would likely drop off into the lake and drown when the boat started moving again. It would never be a tree.

"Don't know." He looked directly at me. "We haven't talked since May of last year."

The month my book had come out.

"I came out here to tell you my dad invited you over for lunch," he said. "I can take you over now if you want to hop in."

I held his calculating stare. Tyler knew about Andreas. Robert certainly would have included him in the invitation. "He only invited me?"

"Oh, your German can come along. I'll follow you over there now and take you both back across the lake with me."

"I have a boat."

"With a busted motor."

How did he know that?

"I could have a look if you like."

"No thanks," I said. "As I recall, you're not very good with engines. Yours always seems to crap out on you. Andreas and I will be along soon."

The boat's motor chugged to life. I turned my back on him to swim to the Brennan side of the lake. And even though reason told me he'd be facing away as he returned to the Rainier side, I couldn't shake the feeling of Tyler's eyes on me the entire time.

7

Andreas strode down the dock in jeans and his cheap new flip-flops.

"Don't you own a pair of shorts?" I shouted from the boat.

"Of course."

"Then why wear jeans on these hot days? You really ought to be in swim trunks. I don't suppose you have any, though, if you can't swim."

"I do have one pair with me. I got them for the hot tub in my building."

"Go put them on in case you want to cool off in the lake. I have my suit on under this."

Andreas did an about-face and disappeared into the trees. I futzed with the outboard motor. If I could get online, I probably could have the thing running again, but the motor hadn't been on my mind during the trip to town. Anyway, Robert would know what to do. I gave up and settled into place at the oars as Andreas reappeared wearing the shortest green swimming trunks I'd seen outside of a yellowed photo from Jackie's 1980s childhood.

I covered my mouth and faked a cough. "How long have you lived in the US?"

"Seven years. Why?"

I shook my head. "Untie the line and hop in."

Evidently a fast learner, Andreas easily entered the small craft and took the seat in the stern. "I'll row," he offered.

"You did last time."

"I don't mind."

"Neither do I."

Andreas had come in handy installing the washing machine since I didn't have a furniture dolly, but I was strong enough to row my own boat. And anyway, in those short trunks, he had no business sitting with his knees that far apart.

Several minutes later we were up on the Rainier deck, and Tyler was gripping Andreas's hand like he expected them to be best friends. Seeing their palms touching made mine itch.

"Dad will be out in a bit. Let me get you a beer."

The shadow hanging in the back door swallowed Tyler up, and Andreas said, "He's Robert's son?"

"Adopted. Beth couldn't carry a child to term."

I searched for movement in the kitchen window, but all I could see was a reflection of trees and sky. I felt sure Tyler was watching us from behind that counterfeit summer. Inside my pocket, the corner of the folded-up letter poked into the crease between my leg and my pelvis. I'd wait until after dinner, let Andreas and Robert get involved in some writerly conversation, maybe let Tyler follow me down to the fire pit, where we'd have some privacy but still remain within view of the house. He'd read the letter and tell me who was right. Me? Or Disappointed Reader?

I invited Andreas to sit, deliberately touching his shoulder so that Tyler could see through the kitchen window, then situated myself across from him, perching on the long side of the chaise lounge.

Tyler finally appeared with three beers and began to distribute them.

"No thanks," I said.

"It's already open," he said.

"You should have asked me what I wanted instead of assuming I'd want what you want."

He sat beside me on the lounger and rested his free hand on the seat behind me. Not touching, but close enough to show he could if he wanted to.

I stood up. "I'll put it in the fridge, and one of you can have it after you've finished those. I'll make myself something else."

Tyler stood.

"Stay there," I said. "I know my way around."

I deposited the open beer in the fridge and looked out the window over the sink so I could see what Tyler might have seen from that vantage point. The men were talking—strange to think of Tyler as a man. I could see Andreas's face. He wasn't smiling. All I could see of Tyler was his back. He had put a shirt on for his guests, though he hadn't bothered to button it. His skin was already the color of sand at sunset, a tone he was probably able to maintain year-round since he'd moved to California. Next to him, Andreas looked like he'd just popped over on his way to the morgue. Had he put sunscreen on before we left?

Your silver bangles jingled on my wrist as I grabbed a tumbler, filled it with ice, and brought it over to the antique icebox. I squatted down and shifted the bottles inside. Vodka, rum, brandy, cognac, whiskey, peach schnapps. No gin. I straightened up to go look again in the kitchen—maybe Robert had left it out—and when I turned around I was face-to-face with Tyler. Or I would have been if I'd been a few inches taller.

"Need some help?"

I felt the oak icebox at my back, immovable, and stepped to the side to extricate myself from the tight spot. "Where's the gin?"

"Should be in there."

"It's not."

"Strange. Dad never runs out of basics." He made his own cursory appraisal of the stash. "How about whiskey?"

I knew I could keep my wits about me with gin. But one cocktail with whiskey and my head would be fuzzy. Tyler was sharp. I had to stay sharp around him.

"I'll just make it with vodka."

"Make what?"

"A martini."

"In a tumbler? With ice?"

"It's hot out, and the glass hardly matters."

"The wrong glass ruins the whole experience."

"This is just lunch with friends on the lake."

"So we are friends?"

My throat caught. I wasn't ready for this conversation yet. Not in here.

"Sure." I said it so quietly I couldn't be certain if I'd actually gotten past the *sh* sound.

Tyler smiled, that same smile that always formed on his face before he pressed his advantage. It was his tell.

"Good. I was hoping we were still friends." He picked a cottonwood seed out of my hair and took the glass from my hand, letting his fingers linger on mine for a moment, though he could easily have avoided touching me. Had it been someone else, it might have elicited the sweet shock of electricity you get when you realize someone wants you to know he's interested in you—that lightning that starts in your gut and screams through your extremities, looking for the ground. But Tyler's touch only turned my stomach.

"I'll get you your martini," he said. "You better run on out to that German of yours. He's probably lonely out there."

Andreas. Out there alone, getting baked.

"Do your parents still keep sunblock in the basket on the screened porch?"

"I'm sure they do," Tyler said over his shoulder as he headed for the kitchen. "Nothing ever changes up here."

He couldn't have been more right, despite the updated decor. I rushed out of the room, snagging the sunscreen on my way back out to the deck. Andreas's face lit up when he saw me.

"You need to put on some sunscreen." I held out the bottle to him.

Andreas put down his half-empty beer. "Where's your drink?"

"Tyler's getting it."

Andreas was slathering sunscreen on his legs when Tyler came out with a martini glass filled to the brim with milky gray-green liquid and garnished with fat green olives on a bamboo skewer.

"You like it dirty, right?"

I felt heat rush up my neck and into my cheeks. I took the glass from him, trying not to touch his fingers. But the maneuver failed, and a few drops escaped the glass and trickled over both of our hands. I got the glass safely onto the table next to Andreas, wiped my hand on my shorts, and sat in a chair that Tyler could not share with me. Tyler licked his own fingers clean, then settled casually into the chaise lounge I had abandoned.

"Where's Robert?" I asked.

"He should be here soon. Had to run to town."

He wasn't in the house. And Tyler had invited only me at first.

"So you and Kendra grew up coming to this lake?" Andreas said.

"I grew up coming to the lake," I jumped in. "Every summer of my life until I went to college. Tyler didn't start coming here until I was eleven."

"And how old were you?" Andreas asked him.

"Fifteen." He took a sip of his beer. "I was adopted very late in life. Probably too late."

Andreas tipped his beer to his lips and narrowed his eyes.

"Do you need sunglasses?" I asked. "I'm sure Robert has a couple extra pairs inside."

Andreas stuck out his bottom lip and shook his head a little. "I'm fine. Tyler, you said you're an agent?"

"Talent scout."

"Sports?"

"Screen. Commercials, TV, movies. You ever get to California?"

"No. This is the first time I've left Chicago in a couple years, actually. It is a nice break. It's so quiet and peaceful here."

"It's been a few years for me too. I haven't been up since Mom and Dad kicked Cami out after that winter she lived here. You ever hear about that, Kendra?"

"I heard enough."

Truthfully, I hadn't heard much. A letter from Grandpa had mentioned that you were staying at the cottage over the winter of my senior year at college. I found it hard to picture you huddled up by the fireplace while Ike was ice fishing out on the lake with a little kerosene heater to keep from freezing to death. Robert wrote me the next spring, telling me about your many false starts in various cities, speculating about unsavory friends and drug use. He asked me to see what I could do to show you that people cared about you. I swallowed my pride and tried calling a few times. You never answered the phone, never returned my messages.

Tyler took a swig of beer. "This place was absolutely trashed when she got done with it. Mom said it looked like Ike's place. That's why there's a new couch and TV and stuff. You should have seen what she did to my room."

I tipped my head toward Andreas. "I'm not sure Cami would appreciate you airing her dirty laundry to someone you just met."

At that, Tyler sat up straight. "Are you kidding me? You—"

"I'm back!" came Robert's voice from inside the cottage. Then his body followed it outside. "Sorry that took so long. Hey! Andreas! Kendra! Give me a minute and I'll get the burgers on."

I didn't wait for Tyler to finish saying what I knew he was going to say. "I'll give him a hand," I said and headed into the house. But I didn't go into the kitchen to help Robert. I went straight to the bathroom and poured the martini out into the sink. If Tyler had made it, I sure wasn't going to drink it.

8

don't know how long I had been staring blankly into the mirror over the bathroom sink when I heard a knock on the door.

"Kendra, are you in there?" Andreas asked.

I tried to answer, but nothing came out.

"Are you okay?"

I opened the door and found him leaning with one hand on the wall, a concerned twist to his brow.

"Is everything all right?"

"Yes, I'm fine."

"The burgers are ready."

I made a move to go, expecting to be blocked as I so often had been in this very spot, but Andreas stepped back to let me pass.

Outside, your dad was seated at his usual place, as was Tyler. Andreas pulled out a chair for me directly across from Tyler—your chair—then he sat himself in what he didn't realize was actually my spot, nearest to Robert. I tucked my feet beneath the chair, out of reach, and made an effort to eat, but the burger tasted like ash. Each bite lodged itself in my throat and had to be chased with a mouthful of water to get it down past my chest and into my stomach, where it fell like a stone.

"I was reading *Blessed Fool* in German a bit last night," Andreas was saying to Robert, "and I wondered if I might ask—is the story based on something that really happened?"

Robert squirted a blob of mustard onto his burger. "Truth has a way of working itself into any story, whether the writer means it to or not." He glanced my way, then looked back to Andreas. It was so quick I wasn't sure if it had really happened. Had he read my book after all? Did he know?

I leaned back until Andreas blocked Robert's sight line. From this new vantage point I saw the back of Andreas's neck. "Didn't you put sunscreen on your neck?"

He felt the tender red skin. "I guess not."

"Why don't we move this inside? Andreas is getting burned to a crisp."

"He can just switch spots with me," Tyler said. "I'm in the shade over here." He stood and took up his plate.

Andreas hesitated a moment, then followed suit. In my mind, a silent protest mounted, but there was nothing for it. Tyler settled himself next to me. I leaned away to compensate.

The meal and the conversation continued without me. And, I came to notice, without Tyler. Robert was in his element with an adoring fan to talk to, and it was soon clear that Tyler and I could have put on a puppet show or committed seppuku without them noticing. While Andreas peppered Robert with questions about his writing process and Americans' views on the war, I drifted to a different meal at a different time at this table.

It was a few weeks after the incident with the boat and the almost kiss. Everyone was where they were supposed to be— Robert and Beth at the head and foot, you and me on the lake side looking at the house, and Tyler on the other side looking at the lake. Or rather, at me. Even when he spoke to others, which he did as little as possible, he still held me in his gaze.

You said something to him in Korean. I could tell it was cutting by the way your eyes narrowed to sharp obsidian. He said something back, smiling at me.

"English at the table, please," Beth said.

"He won't stop staring at Kendra," you said.

"He's not staring."

"Yes he is. Isn't he staring at you?" you asked me.

You knew I hated confrontation. I'd told you how hard I worked all fall, winter, and spring to keep on Jackie's good side, to avoid giving her any reason to yell at me or even talk to me if possible. All I wanted out of my summers was the kind of relaxed happiness I saw in my friends downstate during the school year, whose expected and even longed-for births hadn't ruined their mothers' lives as my unexpected and unwanted one had.

I didn't answer you. And Tyler continued to stare. Which was okay with me, really. I liked the attention. Seeing Tyler again after I jumped out of a boat to avoid kissing him hadn't been as hard as I'd thought it would be. In fact, it was like it had never happened. We didn't talk about it and no one else knew, and everything fell into its old rhythm.

So when Tyler stretched out his foot and touched my bare toes with his beneath the table, unseen and yet right in front of everyone, I didn't pull mine back. As he ran the ball of his foot up my shin, I went on eating, pretending nothing was happening. I was glad I'd started shaving my legs, and that I'd remembered to do so that morning.

Later that night when the four of us were swimming, you and Scott drifted into deeper water while I lounged in the shallows not far from your brother. It was nearing Magic Time, and pretty soon your mom would yell from the kitchen window that it was time for us to get out of the lake and get ready for bed. Scott and I would get in our boats and slip off to our own docks while you and Tyler climbed the steep wooden stairs to the cottage. But for another ten minutes or so, the night was ours.

Tyler was lounging on his back in eight inches of gently lapping water. I lay close by on my stomach, propped on my elbows, watching the last wisps of sunset. Neither of us had spoken for a long time when Tyler said into the quiet, "You don't like me."

I twisted a bit to look at him. "Of course I like you."

"You don't."

"Why do you say that?"

"You don't want to kiss me."

I released a nervous laugh, killing time as my brain searched for the right response. "Just because someone doesn't kiss you doesn't mean they don't like you." I turned back to the sunset, disappointed to find there was no more pink. Just a dull gray-purple glow. The stars would be out soon.

Then something slid beneath me, and I jerked away from the bottom of the lake. In one swift motion, Tyler swept me onto his stomach, holding himself up with one elbow, the other arm snaked tightly around my bare waist.

"What are you—"

"Kiss me."

I didn't. He rolled me over so my back was against the sand and his body blotted out the sky. I struggled to get my arms under me, but Tyler pressed against me until only my face was above water.

"Let me go, Tyler."

"Kiss me."

"No, Tyler. Let me go."

His smiling face was inches away from mine. "Come on."

"Cami! Tyler! Time to come in!" came your mom's sing-songy voice from the kitchen window right as the water came up over my ears.

Tyler sat back, still pinning my legs to the sandy lake bottom. Then he stood and held out his hand. When I didn't take it right away, he reached down, gripped my wrist, and pulled me up anyway. You and Scott came splashing in from the deeper water and hurried past us to where your towels lay near the fire pit on the little spot of beach. You didn't ask what was going on. You hadn't seen a thing.

"Kendra?"

I crashed back to the present. Someone at the table had asked me something. I flipped through the last couple minutes in my mind, searching for the words, but all I could access was Tyler's aggressive smile.

"I'm sorry, what?"

"Where were you just now?" Robert said. "You looked like you were a million miles away."

"No, I was right here." I glanced at Tyler out of the corner of my eye. "Almost exactly here."

"I was telling Robert I thought you had started writing," Andreas said.

"How did you know?"

He shrugged. "There was something different. After we came back from town."

"But I've hardly seen you since then." I turned to the others. "We keep different schedules."

"But you are writing?" Robert said.

"Almost. Just notes and outlines so far."

"Who will you be crucifying this time?" Tyler said.

"Tyler—" Robert started.

Andreas stood up. "I hate to be a—what do you call it?—wet blanket, but Kendra and I have some translation work to do, and I think I better get out of the sun. Thank you for lunch."

I stood and pushed in my chair, your silver bangles tinkling against the metal frame. "Yes, thank you. Tyler, how long did you say you would be here?"

"I'm staying at least until after Mom arrives, if she ever does."

"She'll be here," Robert said with an edge of irritation in his voice. "Door's open as long as you're up here, Andy. Drop by any time and we'll get the war all sorted out between us."

Andreas tipped his head at his host and followed me down the stairs to the dock.

"Oh," Robert called after us, "the engine."

"We can talk about it later," I said.

Robert started down the steps. "Just leave it with me. I'll give you a call when I've figured it out."

He detached the motor and took it to the garage. Andreas offered his hand to me at the boat. I didn't want him to feel the shake I knew was manifesting itself in the tips of my fingers. But that was also what made me yearn for a sure grip. I allowed him to steady me, just for a moment, then let go.

"I'll row," he said.

I did not argue.

Andreas pulled us across the lake with long, powerful strokes. When we were about a hundred yards out, he paused his rowing. "So that's him."

There was no use pretending I didn't know what he meant. "Yeah, that's him."

9

When we got back to the cabin, I handed Andreas a bottle of aloe vera gel. "Here, put this on your neck. And next time you're going to be out in the sun, don't forget the parts of you that you can't see."

"Ich mache mir mehr Sorgen über den Teil von dir, den ich nicht sehen kann."

He said it so quietly under his breath I couldn't even be sure it wasn't English. I ignored him all the same.

"Let's get down to business. What questions do you have for me? About the translation."

Andreas wiped the excess aloe on his bare legs and stood. "Let me get my notes."

"While you're in there, why don't you change? I can't take you seriously in those short shorts."

He turned back at the bedroom doorway. "They're too short?"

I smiled. "They would have been fine before the Wall came down."

"Why didn't you tell me before?"

"I like to be prompt. If I'd known it was just Tyler waiting for us, I wouldn't have hurried."

Andreas closed the curtain but kept talking. "He's obviously read the book. What does he have to say for himself?"

I forced my eyes away from the small gap in the curtain through which I could see movement—a flash of green, of flesh, of denim. "That's the first I've seen of him since I was eighteen." The bangles on my wrist caught my eye. "Well, the second. He showed up unexpectedly earlier today. He has a tendency to do that."

Andreas came out of Grandpa's bedroom wearing the jeans I'd told him to change out of earlier. He settled on the couch next to me and placed a laptop on the coffee table. "How can you sit at the same table with him?"

Since I didn't have an answer to that beyond the fact that my primary impulse in life has always been to avoid ruffling feathers, I deliberately changed the subject. "I expected to see something typed on paper."

"Why?"

"I heard the typewriter the other night."

"Oh." He jumped up and retrieved a piece of paper from the bedroom. "That was my list of German writers for you. You should be able to find at least something in English by them. But it may have to ship from the UK."

I scanned the list. Andreas had added the umlaut above some of the vowels by hand in blue pen, as well as every letter *u*.

"What's with the *u* key?"

"Stuck. I tried to fix it, but my typewriter repair skills are worse than my understanding of post–Cold War American swim fashions."

I laughed. "You seriously would have been fine if you were here when Robert was a kid."

"He grew up on this lake too, didn't he?"

"Yes. And his wife, Beth, and my mom, Jackie. And my friend Scott's dad, Paul. They were kind of a foursome, like Cami,

Scott, Tyler, and me. Is that what you were talking about with him?"

He gave me a puzzled look. "Not exactly. You really were in your own world there at lunch."

I shook my head. "Sorry."

"I've started reading his first book. There are similarities to yours in the setting. Hints here and there that make it seem autobiographical in some ways. Like yours." Andreas scratched his chin. "How based in reality is that character? Where does fact end and fiction begin? He obviously didn't drown like he did in the book."

"Unfortunately, no." I cringed at my own words. "Sorry. I . . . I find this hard to talk about."

Andreas opened his laptop. "Let's drop it. We have work to do."

The screen came to life, revealing two open documents. One was my manuscript in English, laced with notes and queries in red. The other was in German.

"This looks exhausting," I said.

"It will be easy. All you have to do is answer some questions about what you've already written. No one knows the story better than you."

I knew that should be true. But with the accusations in the letter still unanswered and the memories twisted by time, I wasn't so sure. What was fiction? What was fact? What had I gotten wrong? Thankfully, Andreas's questions were focused on just the first few chapters, and the answers to his queries were fairly straightforward, merely a matter of saying yes or no—*ja* or *nein*—to two or more translation possibilities.

Yet I could see that before too long, things were going to get uncomfortable. During the interviews I'd had up to that point, the host would agree ahead of time not to ask personal questions about what may or may not have happened in my own life that led me to write such a story. We spoke in general terms, and I always shared the phone number of a help line that listeners could call. But I'd never had to get into the gritty details with the often male interviewers.

At book signings, the crowd was mostly women, and I always chose passages that were easy for me to read aloud without getting emotional. Nothing that might throw me too far back into the memories. Inevitably at least one reader—often more—would approach me afterward to tell her own story, so my already heavy load of melancholy grew ever more burdensome as I collected a bit of hers to add to the pile.

A counselor in college told me I probably had post-traumatic stress disorder, but I felt ridiculous claiming such a diagnosis. PTSD was for people who'd been bombed, who'd seen their friends blown to pieces, who'd lost limbs or had third-degree burns over most of their bodies. It wasn't something you could claim when you still weren't sure how much you had only yourself to blame for your troubles.

Andreas was right; Tyler had read the book. But it took only a moment of thought to know that he couldn't be Disappointed Reader. He knew it had happened—that *something* at least had happened. So if not him, then who? There were only a dozen or so families on the lake, and I didn't really have much to do with most of them anymore. How many of them even knew I'd written a book?

When I'd answered Andreas's questions, he moved back into Grandpa's room to work and I looked for motivation to get back to my own laptop. But amid all the jumbled thoughts in my brain, it was hard to come by. Instead of heading back up to the loft to write, I crept to the bedroom doorway. Andreas was sitting on the bed, propped up by pillows, computer on his lap.

"How much of that letter did you really read?"

Andreas looked up from his screen. "What letter?"

"The one you found on the floor."

"Oh, that. Not much. As I said, just enough to know what I should do with it."

"I don't suppose as a translator you ever get a letter from a disappointed reader who thought you should have used *vermissen* instead of whatever that other word was."

"*Fehlen.*"

"That one."

"No, but I've gotten a pretty nasty letter about an article I wrote."

"You write too?"

"Sure. All the best translators are writers first."

I smiled wistfully at his confidence. I missed feeling that. That glow of self-assurance that rose up from within and had powered the writing of my first book. Would I ever feel it again?

"What did you do? When you received that letter?"

Andreas tilted his head as if to get the memory to roll into place. "I got in a fight. At a bar."

"I don't know if I can picture you in a bar fight."

He grinned. "You could if you heard me yelling in German. This was in Chicago. I don't think anyone knew why I was upset. They probably thought I was some sort of raving neo-Nazi."

"German can sound awfully angry. But still. You seem so even-keeled."

He set the laptop to the side and leaned forward. "I am, generally. But you know what it's like when someone attacks your writing. Criticize me about anything else—what I look like, what I drive, what my ancestors did to your ancestors—who cares? But my writing, your writing . . . that's the real you, isn't it? That's what is inside you. To have it thrown back in your face is just the worst feeling in the world."

I knew that feeling. I'd known it long before receiving the letter that had so easily thrown me off course.

"Was it from someone you knew?" I said.

"No. The letter came from just some reader. I didn't know the guy at the bar either, and of course he had nothing to do with it. He was just in the wrong place at the wrong time. Believe me, I wasn't proud of my behavior."

I pulled the letter from my pocket and held it out to him. It was creased and warm and getting worn from handling. "Read it," I said.

"It's none of my business."

"Read it. How do you say 'please' in German?"

"*Bitte.*"

"*Bitte*, then."

I stood at the foot of the bed, watching his eyes travel down the page. It was just one page. I'd probably written thousands of pages over the years. And one page held me prisoner.

"That's one reason I'm here," I said when he finally looked up. "To try to remove a roadblock. I can't write because I'm second-guessing everything. Hemingway said when you weren't sure where to start, you should just write one true sentence, the truest sentence you know, but now I worry that everything I try to write is nothing but lies."

"But it is fiction."

"You know what I mean. It's got to be true, even if it's made up."

"And this letter is stopping you because it makes you question what is real in your book? Or in your experience?"

"My experience, I guess. The book obviously rings true, otherwise it wouldn't have gotten the response it has."

"Then what is the problem? The book works. Your writing works. You can put in as much or as little reality as you like. And whoever wrote this letter did not have the experience you had. You did. You know what is real, you know what happened. So you can ignore this reader who was not even man enough to sign his name."

"You think it's a man?"

Andreas glanced over the letter again. "Don't you?"

"I did at first. Now I'm not so sure. No matter who wrote it, the point is I need to figure out what really happened."

"But you know what happened."

"I thought I did." I sat on the edge of the desk. "There are some things you think you'll never forget. They're carved into your mind like words on stone. Then the more you run your fingers over them, the more you rub off the hard edges, until you can tell *something* was there but you can't tell exactly what. And still you can't let go of it. So you start writing about it in your journal, and that doesn't help, so you fictionalize it, thinking that now you can end it any way you want, that you can end it at all. And it works. For a while. Until someone comes along and tells you you're wrong, and you look again and all you have is this collage of real and almost real and fabrication, and there's no telling for sure anymore what actually happened and what you just imagined happening. So what can you do but ask the only other eyewitness?"

I paused, though I didn't expect Andreas to answer.

"I need to talk to Tyler. To ask him how he sees the events that night. I was going to do it today, but then . . . I don't know. It didn't seem like the right time."

Andreas swung his legs over the side of the bed to face me and held out the letter. I folded it and put it back in my pocket.

"If he's the one who wrote that letter, you already know what he thinks."

"He didn't write it," I said. "It's not his style. To address the matter at all . . . he never did that. Anytime I got myself into a situation with him, he just pretended it hadn't happened, and everything went on as it always had. He wouldn't bother writing a letter. And he sure wouldn't hide behind an anonymous moniker. He'd just blatantly put it out there. He was about to today before you cut him off."

Andreas nodded. "Then who do you think wrote it? Just some random reader?"

I shifted my weight on the hard edge of the desk. "It has to be someone I know. And, honestly, I think it has to be someone from the lake."

"Why do you say that?"

"It just seems like this person . . . knows something."

Andreas yawned and glanced at his watch.

"I'll get out of your hair," I said.

"It's fine."

"No, you finish what you were working on and I'll get together some dinner."

"Maybe something light? I don't normally have half-pound burgers for the first meal of the day."

"You got it."

I was slicing a cucumber for a salad when Andreas walked into the kitchen ten minutes later. "It's not even close to ready," I said. "I'm a very slow chopper."

"When are you planning to speak to Tyler?"

I laid the knife on its side. "Soon. I have to get past this so I can stop thinking about it and start writing."

Andreas picked up the knife, edged me out of the way, and

started slicing where I'd left off, more than doubling my speed. "You don't plan on going alone," he said.

"How do you do that so fast?"

He stopped slicing two inches from the end. "You keep the end of the knife on the board, anchored, see? And then you just bring the end closest to you up and down, like a paper cutter." He demonstrated, and in a breath the job was done.

"Well, I hope you like cucumber," I said, "because I was going to stop and put the rest back in the fridge before you usurped my position."

"*Ach herrje! Tut mir leid.* Sorry."

"No big deal. Here, you can chop this carrot for me."

"Kendra?"

"What?"

"You don't plan on going alone to talk to Tyler."

I let out a little sigh. "It's not something someone would talk about in front of another person. I thought we'd talk out on the dock."

"Your dock?"

"Or his." I put a bottle of Italian dressing on the kitchen table.

"I can see the end of this dock from the window," he said.

I smiled. "I appreciate your concern. But I'm a big girl now. It won't be like it was then."

I'd make sure of it.

10

The summer we were twelve, not three days went by without a thunderstorm that rattled the old cabin windows. Moisture swelled every plant cell. Bloated mushrooms bloomed on fallen logs, and the forest floor was spongy underfoot. The low places were constant pools quivering with mosquito larvae. Each step outside the cabin brought their bloodthirsty mothers swarming, and every time the door opened a few would get inside to terrorize me and Grandpa as we tried to read or play cards or sleep.

In the mornings we wore long pants and long sleeves and masked ourselves in a cloud of bug spray to go fishing. Still, they found us, and even with showers, the smell of EPA-approved poison lingered on our skin like mist off the lake. Puzzles that had not been attempted in years were hauled out of cupboards and spread out across the coffee table. I became well-versed in solitaire, gin rummy, and Crazy Eights. Some days you came over to play Monopoly or set up long rows of dominoes to tip. Other days I braved the mosquito gauntlet to your air-conditioned palace to watch fuzzy network TV and draw pictures of the unicorns I no longer believed in.

Every sticky night I tried to ignore my discomfort enough to fall asleep, and every night I failed. So I escaped into books. Though I never knew her, it was obvious from the books she left behind that Grandma Leila had been a fairly practical woman. Cookbooks, a book of crochet stitches, a beat-up book on parenting a difficult child. Grandpa mostly read the newspaper, but he did have a number of nature guides—books on identifying edible plants, wildflowers, fungi, and insects. I was surprised at how many different varieties of mosquitoes there were and took pains to kill them gently when I found them in the house so they would not be unidentifiable smears. Already by the third week of June I'd killed many specimens of *Anopheles quadrimaculatus*, *Coquillettidia perturbans*, *Culiseta inornata*, and *Aedes albopictus*.

But it wasn't long before I grew tired of such practical reading. Your house was filled with books—mostly novels and histories and biographies, and mostly on the floor-to-ceiling shelves that lined every wall of your dad's off-limits study.

One particularly wretched night in early July, the dermatologist part of your mother allowed me to spend the night at your house to see if the persistent and itchy heat rash across my stomach would go away. Grandpa took me and my overnight bag across the lake after a miserable dinner of wilted salad and tuna sandwiches that stuck like mortar in my throat.

"It's almost enough for me to consider getting an air-conditioning unit," Grandpa said, "but I've lived this long without it."

You ran down at the last second to meet us at the dock and hustled me out of the boat. "Mom says to invite you in, Mr. Brennan," you said over your shoulder when you were already halfway back to the stairs.

"Tell her thanks, but I'll be getting back. Heat's worse once you've felt cool and comfortable for a while."

Inside your house it was seasonless. Every trace of the primordial dampness had been filtered out of the heavy air, and the hum of the AC was like the steady, life-giving buzz of those machines in hospitals that keep people from meeting their natural end. I dumped my overnight bag on the floor and flopped blissfully onto your cold, dry sheets.

"Can't I just live here this summer?" I moaned.

"That would be so cool! This summer's the worst. I'm bored out of my mind. If I see another jigsaw puzzle, I think I might kill myself."

"If your mom would just chill out about us swimming in the rain, it wouldn't be so bad."

"Yeah, like we'd die or something."

We sat there a minute more without saying anything, me soaking up the cold until I shivered and pulled your blanket up.

"What, are you going to sleep?"

"No. It's freezing in here."

"Hey." You glanced at your closed bedroom door. "I do have one thing we can do that we haven't yet." You crawled halfway under the bed and emerged a moment later with a shoebox full of contraband. You snatched a pack of cigarettes out of it and slid the lid back into place before I could get a proper inventory of the box's remaining contents.

"Where'd you get those?"

"Tyler got them from Scott, who got them from Ike Fenton. He said he thinks Ike thought Scott was his dad."

"Ike thought a teenager was his dad? That guy's nuts."

"No. Scott's dad. Paul. Ike thought he was Paul."

"Oh. How'd you get them from Tyler?"

"I took them when he was busy drawing. You know that's his new thing? Beth's teaching him art. Like, for real. Not the fooling around we've done with her old supplies. She's got him taking lessons from her every morning now until we go back home and he can go back to his real teacher."

I frowned. Why hadn't Beth ever asked me if I wanted art lessons?

"Why don't you learn too?" I said. "Maybe we all could."

"No thanks. She's too fussy. You can't just draw something. You have to draw it her way. Like she knows everything there is to know about art. She's a dermatologist, not an artist."

"I don't know. Her stuff is pretty cool."

You snorted. "That abstract nonsense? Like that's the thing—how can she say I'm doing it wrong when her stuff doesn't even resemble anything in real life?"

"I thought they were all like close-ups of skin cells and follicles and stuff."

"Yeah, and skin diseases. *Diseases.* I'm surrounded by diseases."

I laughed. "Anyway, taking art lessons would be better than sitting around doing nothing."

You shook two cigarettes onto the bed and looked at me with a catlike grin. "We're not doing nothing."

A light rain had begun to patter against the windowpane, a prelude to another storm that would keep me awake even though I was finally cool and comfortable.

"We can't smoke in here." Actually, I didn't want to smoke—anywhere.

"We'll open the window."

"The rain will get in, and you know we'll get caught anyway."

"No we won't."

I rolled my eyes. "Beth will know. She always knows."

"She doesn't know everything. And you worry too much."

"You didn't think you'd get caught when you brought the raccoon in the house. You didn't think you'd get caught when you TP'd Scott's place. You didn't think you'd get caught when you started messing around in your dad's office."

"Ugh. I still can't believe he wrote that stuff."

"Point is, you always get caught. And I'm not sure I want to get dragged down with you."

"Oh, please, you love getting dragged down with me." You gave me a playful wink. "What else is there to do? What is she going to do, ground me? I'm already stuck in the house doing nothing."

I could see the logic in that. And it was a deliciously bad thing to do. It was strange—whenever I was with Jackie or Grandpa, I always wanted to do everything right. I didn't want to let them down—Jackie because she was never pleased with me and Grandpa because he was always pleased with me. But you were always coming up with mischief. Nothing truly destructive, just playfully subversive schemes I would never come up with on my own.

"Shouldn't we lock the door?"

"No way. Locked doors make Beth furious."

I slid open the window. "And cigarettes don't?"

You cracked the bedroom door and yelled, "We're going to bed now!"

"Don't yell in the house, please!" came Beth's shouted reply.

You shut the door and skipped over to the window. The sill was already splattered with rainwater, and the carpet beneath was speckled with little shining droplets like morning dew on grass.

"There are matches in the medicine cabinet," you said. "Go get them."

"Why me?"

"Because you haven't brushed your teeth yet. Beth would expect to find you coming out of the bathroom. But I got ready for bed before you came. Just go and bring the matches back when you're done."

I rummaged through my bag to find my toothbrush and scooted down the hall to the bathroom across from Tyler's room. I shut the door, quickly dispensed with the necessary bathroom rituals, and scanned the medicine cabinet for matches, but there were none to be found. Ashamed not to be able to complete your simple directive, I picked up my toothbrush, opened the door, and nearly screamed. Tyler was on the other side of it, leaning against the doorframe. I waited with my hand on my chest for him to move aside so I could go through the door, but he remained where he was.

"Ex*cuse* me," I said.

"What are you girls up to tonight?"

"If I can get out of this bathroom, I'll probably be sleeping in a few minutes."

Tyler kept his eyes locked on mine and smiled.

"So excuse me," I said again.

He didn't move. "What were you looking for?"

"Nothing."

"Yeah you were. I heard the medicine cabinet."

"Don't you think it's a little weird to listen to someone else in the bathroom?" I searched for an explanation that didn't involve matches or diarrhea. "I was looking for something for this mosquito bite."

Tyler pushed his way into the small space and opened the medicine cabinet. The hydrocortisone cream couldn't have been more obvious if it had been in my own hand. He plucked it off the middle shelf and held it out to me. I reached for it to bolster the ruse, but he snatched it back. "That's not what you were looking for."

I gave an affected sigh and turned to go, but Tyler reached over my shoulder and shut the door.

"Knock it off, Tyler."

"What?" he said with an incredulous smile. "What were you looking for? I just want to help you find it."

"Matches," I mumbled.

"What for?"

"Nothing. None of your business."

He pulled a red lighter from his shorts pocket and held it out to me. "Don't light the house on fire, little girl."

His grip tightened on the lighter for a moment before he released it to me. I slipped it into my pocket and tried the knob again. This time he let me go, and I scuttled down the hall. One last glance revealed Tyler hanging in the bathroom doorway like a spider.

"What took you so long?" you whined after I closed your door.

"No matches. But I have a lighter."

"Where'd you get that?"

"From the bathroom."

You gave me a weird look, then shook your head. "Whatever. Come on, let's do this before my whole room is flooded."

"I guess I should have brought a towel too." I stuck a cigarette between my lips and you held a flame to the end of it, your other hand cupped and touching my cheek.

"You have to breathe in," you said.

I sucked in a huge breath and coughed so violently the cigarette flew out of my mouth and landed on the floor. I gasped and scrambled to pick it up.

"Shhh!" you hissed.

"I'm—*cough*—tr—*cough*—trying!"

You pinched me hard. "Shut up!"

I clamped down on my cough and put the now damp cigarette firmly between my teeth, hacking quietly around it as you lit yours without incident. "H—how'd you do that?"

"I don't know. I didn't inhale it."

"You said to . . . breathe in."

You shrugged. "Sorry. That's how people do it in movies."

I wiped the tears from my eyes and leaned toward the open window to blow a cloud of smoke out of the room. The rain-soaked carpet had kept the errant cigarette from leaving a burn mark, but now ash was building up at the end.

"You need to take this screen out," I said.

You popped the screen out and set it on the ground just outside the window. "That's how the raccoon got in, you know."

"Pfft. Like you didn't have a plate full of crackers and peanut butter in here to lure it."

You laughed and leaned against the windowsill, your bare arms glowing in the lamplight. "That was a fun night."

I had to smile at your always selective memory. "Was it fun cleaning up raccoon poop?"

"That was better than dealing with Beth." You blew a stream of gray smoke out into the night.

"Blech. This is gross," I said, giving the cigarette a disappointed look. "Your mom's not so bad. I mean, she's not so great either. But at least she cares about you."

You rolled your eyes dramatically. "Yeah, right."

I tried to flick my ash out the window with an air of nonchalance, but it wasn't as easy as it looked. Not for me, anyway. A couple more puffs and the lit part met the wet part and started smoldering. I leaned out into the rain to put it out and dropped it on the ground outside.

"That's littering," you said.

"What else am I supposed to do with it? Just get it tomorrow morning."

You took a long puff, held it in your mouth, then blew it out in little bursts.

"If you're trying to make smoke rings, you're failing," I said.

"How do people do that?"

"I don't know. Maybe—"

The door opened. You threw your cigarette out the window and shut it before you realized it was just Tyler. "What do you think you're doing in here?"

"Oh, nothing," he said. "I just thought you might want to know that Beth is coming."

He rolled casually along the doorjamb back toward the hall. I shoved the lighter and the pack of cigarettes under my shirt, and we scrambled beneath the covers as though we'd been there all along. Beth's face appeared where Tyler's had just been.

"All right, girls. Lights out—" Beth stopped and tilted her nose. "Camilla Ho-Sook Rainier, were you smoking in here?"

"What? No."

"Then why do I smell smoke?"

"I don't know. Maybe Ike Fenton is prowling around outside." You turned to me. "Didn't I tell you I thought I heard someone outside the window? Do you think maybe he's spying on us? Eww!"

Beth walked over to the window. "Cami! This floor is soaked! You know the air's on. Why did you have this window open in the rain?"

"We didn't!" Your voice held so much indignation I wondered if you believed your own lies.

Beth leaned over the bed and took a good whiff. "Do you think I'm an idiot? You've obviously been smoking in here. What's the matter with you? Where did you get cigarettes?"

You put on your most penitent face. "They're Tyler's! He gave them to me!"

"Use your head. Smoking's terrible for your skin, it's terrible for your health, it's illegal for someone your age, it's against the rules of this house, and it's a disgusting habit that will drain your bank account and slowly kill you from the inside. I thought you were smarter than that. Kendra, were you smoking too?"

Before I could say anything, you broke in. "No, she didn't want to. It was just me."

I could always count on you to take the brunt of the punishment. Always.

"We'll talk about this in the morning, but for now I don't think you deserve to have a friend stay the night."

You sat up. "You can't send Kendra home! She didn't do anything!"

"I'm not sending her home. She'll sleep on the couch."

"But—"

"I don't want another word out of you. Kendra, please get into your PJs and then come out to the living room. I'll make you a bed."

I pulled the cigarettes and lighter from my shirt and handed them to your mother. She sighed heavily.

"You better punish Tyler," you said. "He's the one who got them."

"Don't you tell me what to do, young lady."

You rolled your eyes but said nothing else. Beth walked out and shut the door. I started slipping out of my clothes. I remember I didn't want you to see the ugly heat rash on my stomach. I needn't have worried. Your eyes were boring holes into the closed door.

"Tyler will get off scot-free. Just watch. He gets away with everything."

I pulled my nightshirt over my head. "That's not fair."

"No kidding."

"Well . . . I guess I'll see you in the morning."

You flopped over onto your side. "Good night."

"Hey, thanks for covering for me."

You turned back to me and managed a weak smile. "Of course."

It took your mother no time at all to toss a couple blankets and a pillow on the couch. I settled in quickly and quietly as she fiddled around in the kitchen a few minutes. Then she was at my side.

"Kendra, I'm sorry that Cami exposed you to cigarettes. That shouldn't have happened. I understand if you need to tell your grandfather, and please let him know he can call me to discuss it if need be."

"My mom smokes," was my practical reply.

Beth pressed her lips together. "I know she did when we were teenagers. I kind of hoped she might have stopped by now." She raised her eyebrows in a knowing way. "But there, you see? It's a hard habit to break, so you don't want to let yourself get into it."

She flicked off the remaining lights and disappeared down a hallway on the opposite side of the house. I closed my eyes and tried to focus on falling asleep. That's when the storm really got going.

Three hours later I was still awake. I crept into your father's office, shut the door, and turned on the small lamp on the big gray metal desk. His typewriter was flanked by two stacks of paper. On the left were blank sheets. On the right, the growing draft of his latest manuscript. I asked him once why he still used a typewriter to write his books when a computer was so much easier.

He looked at me with a thoughtful scowl. "I guess it's fear."

"Why would you be afraid of computers?"

"No, it's not that I'm afraid of new technology or anything. It's just that I've always written on a typewriter—on *this* typewriter—and I'm afraid I might not be able to write on something else. The sound of the keys and the hammers and the ding at the end of a line . . . it's all part of the process. I guess I don't want to change things up and jinx the whole thing."

I picked up the last typewritten page on the stack, read a paragraph, and put it down, then scanned the packed shelves for something interesting. When I came to the section that held Robert's own titles, I stopped and picked one off the shelf. I'd seen it before. It was the one you sneaked into your room earlier that summer. You pulled it out when I was over that evening and showed me all the sections you had found where characters were making advances or making out or downright making babies.

I'd been more than a little embarrassed by the fact that someone I knew—someone who cooked me burgers and handed me cans of Coke when his wife wasn't looking—had thought up some of the stuff those characters were doing.

I was especially intrigued by one character, Misty. When Jackie had taught me about sex, she'd made it sound like boys were the ones who did it all, and that girls had to come up with all sorts of ways to keep them from doing what they wanted until you got married. I figured she had just not been very good at that, which was why I didn't have a father. But in that book, Misty was the one who was starting all the funny business. It had never occurred to me until then it might go the other way around.

I sat down on the floor, leaned back against the wall of books, and flipped through the pages to find the passages you'd read to me a couple weeks earlier. But I couldn't find what I was looking for, so I opened up to the first page. Maybe it would all make sense if I knew what the whole story was. I was only a few pages in when the door creaked open.

"Kendra? What are you doing in here?"

11

slammed the book shut and scrambled to my feet. "I'm sorry, Mr. Rainier. I couldn't sleep with the storm."

He tipped his head to get a better look. "So you went right for my stuff, eh? Knew that would be boring enough to send you off to dreamland?"

He was smiling, but I felt heat rush into my cheeks. "No, not at all. Your writing is very interesting."

He held out his hand, and I placed the book in it. He looked from the cover to me, then sat down at the desk, retrieved a pen from the top drawer, and opened to the title page. "So, what do you want to do with your life?"

What? What kind of a question was that?

"I don't know." I thought about the mosquitoes and the insect guidebook. "Maybe be an entomologist?"

"Really?"

I shrugged. "I don't know."

"Well, that's a fine thing to be, I just didn't realize you had such an interest in insects."

"I don't. Not really. I mean, I like knowing what I'm looking at. But I'm not sure just what an entomologist does after

identifying them. I wouldn't want to dissect them or anything."
I thought a moment. "I like rocks."
He put the pen down. "A geologist then?"
I screwed up my face. "I like to collect rocks and figure out what minerals they're made of. I like sorting them into groups. It drives me crazy that Cami just throws them into a jar without even washing them." I glanced over your mother's painting of magnified cancer cells on the wall. "Maybe I'll be an artist, like Mrs. Rainier. Or maybe a writer, like you."

He smiled. "I bet you'd be a great writer. You know how I know that?"

I shook my head.

"Because you notice things. You're a lot like me. You sit quietly and take it all in."

"How does that make you a good writer?"

He motioned to the leather chair across the desk, and I sat down. "Because in order to write something true to life, you have to observe life. You have to know—really know—what you're looking at, just like you said about rocks and insects."

"But isn't the stuff you write about stuff you've never seen before—like battleships and tanks?"

"Actually, I have seen a lot of those on research trips, but you're right that I've never been in a war. Wars you can research by reading about them and interviewing people who were there—people like Ike Fenton. But the real story even in a war story is the characters you create, and if you start by being a good observer of human nature, you can write in any setting at any time and make it believable, because human nature never changes."

"You don't think people are better than they used to be?"

He snorted. "No, I don't."

I thought for a moment. "Women can vote. There's no more slavery."

He tipped his head in some measure of concession. "Human societies may change here and there. But human nature? Nah. People are always people. And people are broken." He suddenly looked very sad. He picked up the pen and began scribbling in the book. When he finished, he blew across the ink, shut the cover, and held it out to me. "This is for you."

"Thank you, but . . ." I looked at the shelf. "You don't really want to give me your copy, do you?"

He laughed. "I wouldn't worry about that. *Blessed Fool* was my debut, and it didn't sell all that great at first. They released a new edition after the Iron Cross series sold so well, but I still have a whole box of these first editions. You hang on to that. It could be worth something to you someday."

I nodded.

"Sounds like the storm's passed," he said. "Maybe you should try to get a few hours of sleep before everyone else is up."

"What about you?"

"I'm going to get to work. This is the best time for me. I have at least four solid hours before Beth gets up, five before Tyler, and six before Cami. Hopefully the typewriter won't keep you up."

I turned to go, then hesitated. "How do you do it?"

"Do what? Write?"

"Yeah. Like how do you come up with a story and characters and stuff?"

"I guess different people do it different ways. My advice to you is to start a journal. Write in it every day, whatever comes into your head. You spend enough time recording your thoughts and observations and one day you'll see a story there. It will rise out of the pages like fireworks, and you'll be amazed it came from your own mind when you weren't looking." He smiled indulgently. "Now go to sleep. Oh, and don't let your mother know you have that book. Or your grandfather."

For just a second, he looked like he regretted giving it to me, like he was going to take it back. Then he shook his head and inserted a clean sheet of white paper into the typewriter. I shut the door behind me and snuggled under the covers on the couch, placing the book under my pillow and listening to the interplay between the now-soft rain on the roof and the mechanical singing of the typewriter.

That was an important night for me. For you, it was just another bit of shenanigans, another bit of wood in the cross you moaned about bearing—a mother who was concerned about you and a father who was actually there, things I would have given almost anything to have. But for me . . . that was when I was commissioned. When one of the most successful writers of his generation touched his burning torch to mine and sent me down the road I am still trying to walk today.

You smoked half a cigarette. I became the bearer of a sacred flame.

Sunday afternoon I slathered myself in sunscreen, slipped into a swimsuit, and parked myself on the sun-drenched sand with *Tess of D'Urbervilles* and a glass of iced tea. I read two chapters and then couldn't continue. I saw too much of myself in the ineffectual, pliant Tess. I tossed the book on the sand, turned over on my stomach, and drifted in and out of sleep in the intense heat until a buzzing, grumbling sensation pricked the blackness of my subconscious. A motor. Someone shouted my name.

Squinting into the spotlight of the sun, I could barely make out the figure of a man.

"Kendra! Come give me a hand with this."

Your dad was kneeling and fiddling with something on the

floor of his boat. I quickly checked my top half to make sure I hadn't undone the back of my suit to avoid tan lines, then jumped up to help.

"Turns out it was an easy fix," he said, lifting Grandpa's old motor out. "Tune-up, more or less."

We walked the outboard through the shallow water to where my boat was tied and positioned it on the back of the stern.

"Hop in and give it a whirl," he said.

I pulled myself over the side of the boat, and Robert launched himself onto the dock, water dripping from his shorts. I primed the engine and pulled the starter cord. It roared to life on the first try.

"Woo!" I shouted over the noise. "Thank you!" I stopped the motor. "That will make things much easier. I might even go fishing one of these mornings."

"You haven't been fishing?"

"Not yet. Actually, I've barely thought about it. It was always Grandpa who got everything ready and woke me up and dragged me out to the boat. I mean, I enjoyed it once I was out there, but if it weren't for him I wouldn't have gotten out of bed, that's for sure."

"You should go."

"You want to come with me some morning?"

"Sure, we could do that."

I couldn't help noticing the slightest hesitation before he agreed.

"Of course, you're probably writing at that time, aren't you?" I said to let him off the hook.

"Usually, but I imagine you are as well."

I smiled. "I should be."

"I thought you'd started."

"Almost. I'm almost ready."

He pulled me up onto the dock. "How about that signed copy? Manage to write that at least?"

"Shoot! No. I can do it right now for you."

He held up a hand. "No pressure. I don't need it right now. Wait till it comes to you, what you really want to say."

We sat in the low-slung beach chairs, the nylon seats nearly touching the sand, and looked out across the dazzling lake.

"Let me go get you something," I said. "Tea? Lemonade?"

"Tea's fine."

I trotted up to the cabin and into the kitchen, half expecting to see Andreas getting his "morning" coffee, but my houseguest must have been sleeping late. On the way back, I tried to catch a glimpse of him through the curtain in the doorway, but the crack only revealed the typewriter sitting primly on the desk.

Two days after my non-sleepover with you when I'd chatted with Robert in his office in the wee hours, I'd sat down at that very typewriter and started a story. Though I destroyed it a week later, I still remember the first sentence.

```
Once there was a girl who could breathe under
water.
```

It was a story about a girl discovering her secret ability and using it to search for sunken treasure and make friends with the fish and the frogs and the turtles. She spent so much time under water that the people on land began to forget her, and she discovered it became harder and harder to breathe air and walk across the hot sand. Eventually she couldn't come out of the water at all and had to live there. But her new underwater friends could never accept her as one of their own, so the lonely girl cried the rest of her days, and her tears flooded the surrounding land until all the people had to move far away, leaving her all alone.

At twelve years old, I thought it was quite profound and well written. I'd hoped your dad would read it with a kind of breathless urgency, introduce me to his publisher, and send me hurtling down the road to fame as a literary prodigy. But first I showed it to you. You thought I was making fun of you—the way you walked with a limp and how you were adopted and must have always stuck out as different from everyone around you.

"It's not you," I protested.

But you still wouldn't speak to me for two days, not until I told you I'd burned the story in the fireplace. I didn't actually burn it—it was far too hot and wet for fires that year. But I knew you'd like it if I had, and I just wanted to make you happy, because I'd begun to notice that so often you were not. That the ever-present smile and easy laugh you'd had during your first summer on Hidden Lake were more and more infrequent.

In reality, I ripped the story into pieces so small that no more than two or three typed letters were linked together. I surreptitiously sprinkled the fragments out on the lake one dark, rainy, miserable morning in the fishing boat with Grandpa. Some were eaten by fish, some sank into the depths, and some washed up on shore in a goopy mass later that day. Your dad never saw it.

Once I was back outside in the blazing sun, Robert and I sipped our iced tea in thoughtful silence.

"How are you, anyway?" he finally said. "Other than the writing. Got any new hobbies? New friends? Lovers?"

I had to laugh. "I don't have time for any of that. I've spent most of the past year speaking, doing interviews, writing articles . . . you know what it's like."

He nodded. "Those were tough years for us. Beth wanted

kids, I was gone all the time, then she couldn't get pregnant, then she couldn't stay pregnant. We nearly didn't make it. I think adopting Cami was the only thing that kept us together. We put the love into her we couldn't quite put into each other anymore. And things did get better."

"What is Cami doing now, anyway?" I ventured. "I don't think I've talked to her in years."

"Neither have I."

I wasn't exactly surprised to hear this. In a time when everyone in the world was getting more connected by the day, you were conspicuously absent. I'd looked you up on more than a dozen occasions over the years, hoping to make up for lost time online, or at least to check up on you, make sure you were okay. But you were nowhere. No social media profiles, no pictures, no job descriptions. Whatever you were doing, it was no one's business but your own. It was like you didn't even exist.

In the empty space left in the conversation, I heard a killdeer cry out, trying to draw some predator away from its rocky nest down the shore.

"She hasn't been taking calls from us," Robert continued. "For a while we thought it would be best to just give her some space, but then . . . well, that's what Beth's doing right now, trying to track her down. She's following up on a lead in Florida from an old friend of Cami's."

I balanced my glass on my bare knee, letting the cold seep into my skin. "Have you gotten the police involved?"

"Not yet. I mean, she's disappeared before. Just not for this long."

"Why didn't you say something? Why didn't anybody call me?"

He glanced my way and looked back out onto the lake. "I didn't think the two of you were on good terms anymore. It's none of my business, but I think when you stopped coming up

117

to the lake she took it personally. She never had an easy time holding on to her friends at home. They drifted in and out of her orbit pretty quickly."

I could easily guess why, if your brother treated your other friends the way he'd treated me.

"I didn't stop coming up because of her," I said. I hesitated a moment before adding, "I stopped because of Tyler."

Robert squinted into the sun and said nothing, and I was left to wonder again whether he'd read *That Summer*, and if he had, if he'd made any of the connections Andreas had so easily made despite no knowledge of my history at Hidden Lake.

"I had once thought you two might . . ."

"Oh, no. No, no, no, no."

Robert nodded slightly. "How about this Andreas fellow? He seems like a nice guy."

"He is, but why would you assume—"

"I'm not assuming. I'm just asking."

"Why?"

"I just . . . everyone should find someone who treats them right. And maybe it's a little harder for writers, you know? It's hard to find someone who understands."

"That's really very nice of you. My grandfather would appreciate that. He had such a wonderful marriage, and I know it always made him sad that Mom didn't have that." I twisted in my seat to face him. "You knew my mom back then. Why do you think she never got married?"

Robert took a long drink of iced tea. "I think that's a question for her."

I sat back in my chair. "Maybe. But she's never been all that forthcoming."

"That sounds like Jackie." He took another sip. "You ever actually read that book I signed for you way back when?"

"I read it right when you gave it to me."

"You did?" He grimaced and sucked some air through his teeth. "I probably shouldn't have given it to you when you were that young. It's not really PG."

"You don't need to tell me that." I laughed. "I remember."

"Well, I guess it can't be helped now. You remember the character named Misty?"

"Sure."

"Jackie inspired that character."

I didn't have to try hard to recall Misty's antics in *Blessed Fool*. The character was wild and reckless—and loose. I'd always known my mother must have some skeletons in her closet, but not that many. I mentally tallied up Misty's conquests, then stopped myself. Misty may have been based on Jackie, but that didn't mean Jackie had actually done anything Misty had.

Inspiration was a tricky little imp, and characters inspired by real people often ended up very different from their progenitors. Yes, Tyler had inspired Blake in *That Summer*, but they were nothing alike. Tyler was Korean, with dark hair and eyes and flawless skin. Blake was a ginger with green eyes and pale, freckled arms. Tyler was quiet and calculating. Blake was bombastic and impulsive. Their mannerisms were different, their crimes were different, and their fates were different. Tyler was the inspiration, but Blake was a character with a life and backstory of his own, totally independent of Tyler's.

"I'm sure I was too young to really get it back then," I said. "I'll have to read it again. Maybe I'll find some other people I know in there."

He gave me a little smile. "Maybe."

"Andreas has been reading the German edition. I'd say he's already halfway through."

"Probably trying to get through it before he heads back to Chicago."

I frowned. "Yeah, I guess."

"Ah! There it is," he said, pointing.

"What?"

"You like him."

I know I blushed. "It's just a little crush, that's all. It's the accent. I'm a fool for accents. And he's not too shabby a dresser."

Robert leaned back and looked at the perfect blue sky. "He's obviously pretty crazy about you as well."

"Why would you ever think that?"

He looked like he was about to speak, then he stopped himself. Finally he said, "The fact that he's here at all. Like this couldn't all have been done over the phone? And the way he looks at you. The whole time I was talking to him at lunch, he kept looking over at you."

"Oh, he did not." But even as I protested, a small part of me hoped it was true. "Anyway, he's leaving in a week. We're already halfway through the book. I'm not sure he'll need me much longer."

"I hope he'll stay for the Fourth."

"I'll ask him. I'll tell him Robert Rainier can't bear to see him go. He might stay on your account."

Robert stood up. "I better get on home. Tyler and I are going to play a round of golf before dinner. You think Andreas might want to come?"

"I can ask him for you. But you don't think Tyler might rather have it just a father-son thing? I don't imagine you two have seen a lot of each other lately with Tyler in California."

"Maybe, but I like Andy."

"Maybe you're the one with the crush." I poked him in the arm as we walked to his boat.

"Send him over in the next half hour if he's going to go with us."

"Will do." I hesitated. Then I forced myself to say, "Would you let Tyler know I'd like to talk to him about something?"

"Come over for dinner tonight."

"No, I've got work to do here. Would you send him over after dinner?"

"I'll let him know."

He started the motor, made a wide arc, and headed for the birches across the lake. I picked up his abandoned iced tea, and your silver bangles clinked hollowly against the glass.

Why was your bracelet here if you weren't? Had you lost it the last time you were at the lake? Had Ike talked you into ice fishing only for you to drop it down the hole? Did you have a falling-out with Scott and throw it away in anger? Robert had said Scott was up on the lake. Maybe I should ask him.

Inside the cabin, Andreas was up drinking coffee and reading Robert's novel in German. He looked up a moment when the screen door slammed, then focused rather deliberately back in on his book, which reminded me of my skimpy attire. Why is it that a bikini on the beach is totally normal, but the minute you walk inside it feels like you're wearing just your underwear? His good manners were touching, though I thought I caught a sidelong glance as I passed by to put the glasses in the kitchen.

"How's the book?" I asked.

"*Wunderbar.* He is such an excellent writer in English, but the translator of *Blessed Fool* did a fine job capturing his voice in German. This is so different from his war books. It's like a completely different author."

"How so?"

"Haven't you read it?"

I busied myself washing the glasses. "A long time ago."

Andreas raised his voice to be heard over the faucet. "This is very literary, heavy on style, and there is a pervasive sadness. The other books are very active, very plot driven, more triumphant. It's probably why they were more popular."

I turned off the faucet and poked my head around the doorway. "I don't remember it being sad. But I was pretty young when I read it."

Andreas furrowed his brow. "You should read it again."

"I will. Someday. So many books to read."

"You should make time for this one."

"He'd like to know if you want to play golf this afternoon before dinner," I said.

"Really?"

"Do you golf?"

"No, but I would go. I'd go just to carry his clubs and discuss his books some more."

"Full disclosure, Tyler will be there."

The light on his face dimmed. "I see. Will you let him know I'll have to pass, regretfully?"

"You'd still be able to talk to him."

"No, I'm sure they would value the time together. And we have some things we must go over for the translation anyway. My deadline is looming."

I put the glasses away. The part I'd been dreading was upon me, and there was no escaping it. Today I'd have to face it on two fronts—in fiction, when I answered Andreas's questions about the book, and in fact, when Tyler came over after dinner.

"We can get started once you're dressed," came Andreas's voice from the living room.

"You're sure you don't want to go golfing?"

"I'm sure. The last thing I want to do is spend more time with Tyler. I am spending more than enough time with him in your book."

"Well, Blake isn't exactly Tyler."

"Maybe not. But I don't like either one of them."

12

My troubles with Tyler started when I was twelve. My troubles with you started when we were thirteen. That was the year you turned into a different person and everything we had loved doing together was suddenly "so stupid."

No more games or make-believe, no more rock collecting, no more chasing grasshoppers and butterflies. No more sandcastle building or stone-skipping contests. No more Frog Olympics. All you ever wanted to do was flip through *Seventeen* magazine, paint your toenails, and braid hair—yours, mine, it didn't matter whose, but it had to be braided. Sometimes you'd wrap a section of hair in the colorful embroidery thread we used to make friendship bracelets. It took forever. In the meantime, there were worlds going unexplored, beetles going unidentified, birds' nests going unexamined, imaginary kidnappers going unthrottled.

That was the summer you began to prefer tanning to swimming. I suspected that your sudden need to lay out on the beach to tan had more to do with drawing attention from Scott Masters than developing the perfect shade of skin you saw in your magazines, which almost never featured girls who looked like you.

That was also the summer Scott's little cousin Sarah was up to visit, and once you had painted her toenails and braided her hair, she was ready for games.

"Hide-and-seek is a kid's game," you said. "It's so stupid. I need to work on my tan."

"Hide somewhere sunny then," Scott said.

"I'll play," Tyler said. "And I'm seventeen."

"So?" you said. "I don't care if you eat paste and do finger painting. I'm getting a tan."

"Oh, can we do finger painting?" Sarah asked hopefully.

Tyler laughed. "No. Our mom's paints aren't really for finger painting."

Sarah shrugged. "Anyway, I want to play hide-and-seek now."

"We don't need Cami to play," I said. "Four is enough."

"Fine, I'll play," you said, because you hated to be left out. "But only two rounds and only if I don't have to be it."

"I want to be it!" Sarah said.

"You're it, then," Scott said. "Rules are you have to hide outside—no going in the house. Safe is the fire pit. Count to one hundred and no peeking!"

"Ready? Go!" Sarah shouted, then she squeezed her eyes shut, covered her face with her hands for good measure, and started to count.

Scott ran into the trees and you followed behind, slower and with the loping gait you had just begun to try to hide from people you'd known for years. I waited to see which way Tyler was headed, then tiptoed in another direction. I snuck behind the garage and searched for a spot between the yew bushes.

"In here," came Tyler's voice from the garage side door.

He must have gone around the front. I shushed him and stepped between two overgrown yews.

"In here!"

"You can't hide inside," I whispered loudly.

"Scott said not in the house."

"He said you have to hide outside."

Tyler slipped out and grabbed me by the wrist. "I've got the perfect spot. Come on."

I allowed myself to get dragged into the dark garage. Tyler opened the tailgate of Robert's truck and pushed me ahead of him into the bed. Then he shut the tailgate as quietly as possible.

"Get in the middle, away from the sides," he said. He sat down behind me, his legs on either side of mine, and pulled the old wool blanket up to my waist.

"Dude, back up. There's plenty of room."

He wrapped his arms around my stomach and pulled me into his chest. "I don't want her to see me."

I wriggled in his grasp, and he gripped me tighter. The air in the garage was hot, stale, already stifling. Tyler's arms restricting my diaphragm made me feel like I was going to pass out. I was about to elbow him in the ribs when he loosened his hold on my stomach to cover my mouth with one hand.

"Shhh! I hear someone," came his hot breath in my ear. He leaned back so that he was lying on his back, taking me with him, pulling me up until we were stacked lengthwise like lumber beneath the blanket.

I could only hear my own heart thumping loudly. I wondered if Tyler could hear it too. I couldn't hear his. I tried to twist free. Then I did hear something. Footsteps running along the side of the garage. I went still. I could taste the sweat from Tyler's hand. My own sweat dripped down the backs of my knees and under my arms and beaded up on my forehead beneath the scratchy wool. I could almost feel a heat rash blooming on my stomach. I had to scratch. Had to breathe. Had to get out from under this blanket.

The side door of the garage creaked open, and I could see a shaft of sunlight through the wool. With each shallow breath Tyler took, I felt myself rise just a little. One hand was still over my mouth. The other now worked its way under the damp hem of my T-shirt and onto my clammy stomach. A moment later the fingers reached my ribs. And someone was creeping around the outside of the truck, scraping small flip-flops across the sandy concrete floor.

"Is anyone in here?" came Sarah's voice.

Tyler's grip on my mouth tightened.

"Hello?"

The other hand was now resting on my rib cage, one finger probing under my bikini top.

"You can't hide in here," Sarah admonished.

I squirmed. Tyler squeezed my face harder.

Footsteps running away. The garage door slammed shut and the darkness returned. I dug my nails into Tyler's hand and ripped it away from my face.

"Hey!" he whisper-shouted. He pulled his other hand out of my shirt. "What do you think you're doing?"

I sat up and threw the blanket off. "Me?" I crawled to the tailgate, pushed it open, and jumped down to the concrete. I walked out the side door into the glaring sunlight and down to where you and Scott were talking, safe at the fire pit.

"What were you doing?" Scott said, eyebrows raised.

I frantically glanced down at my shirt for any sign I'd just been groped. "What do you mean?"

"Your face is all red."

"I'm just hot. It's too hot for hide-and-seek."

"See?" you said. "Let's just lay out. Take off your shirt."

"No!"

You took a step back. "Calm down, crazy. What's the matter with you?"

I didn't know. But obviously something was. Why was this happening to me? And why did I know at the most elemental level that I couldn't tell anyone about it? Not even you. Especially not you.

Sarah marched up, grinning widely and dragging Tyler by the wrist. "I caught him!"

"Where'd you find him?" Scott asked.

"Behind the garage. He must be really good at hiding because I didn't see him the first time I was there. But I got him! Now Tyler's it."

"I'm done playing," you said.

Sarah stomped a foot. "But you said two games!"

Tyler patted her head. "We can play with four people."

"No thanks," I said. "I'm out."

"Why?" Sarah whined.

"I just don't want to play anymore."

"She's going to get a tan," you said.

"No, I'm not. I'm going home." I walked down the dock and got into Grandpa's boat.

You yelled at me in Korean.

"I'll see you tomorrow," I said. "Just you."

I untied the boat, started the engine, and did not look back.

Sitting on one of the tattered old chairs in the living room, I braced myself for an hour or so of awkward translation work with Andreas. But he skipped the scene that I had refused to reread since I'd sent in the last edits to my publisher. He had a question or two near the beginning of that chapter—What was a brazen star? How could someone's gaze make you itch?—that

I had trouble explaining. But when it came time for Jess and Blake to get into that green wooden rowboat, he moved on to the next chapter. I moved on with him, not asking why because I thought maybe I knew. And whatever good feelings I'd already developed for this stranger in my house increased tenfold.

We covered a lot of ground—too much—and ended the day's work with the lead-in to the story's climax, where Jess finds her courage and puts her plans for Blake into motion. It might only be a few more days before Andreas had all his questions answered, packed up his efficient German suitcase, and left for Chicago.

He closed his laptop. "What are your plans for tonight?"

"I asked Robert to send Tyler over after dinner."

He frowned a little. "We will be having dinner together, though? Just us?"

"Sure. I thought maybe I'd make brinner."

"Brinner?"

"Breakfast for dinner. Brinner. Like pancakes or something."

"People joke about Germans combining words, but Americans do it too."

I laughed. "But ours aren't twelve syllables long. They're snappy."

He shrugged. "I was thinking we could go out for dinner tonight. That is, if there's anywhere to go."

I schooled my features so as not to give away how pleased I was about this invitation. "Northern Michigan is no Chicago," I said. "But of course, that's why people come here. Hemingway's family vacationed up here, did you know that? Not on this lake, but not far from here. And they lived in the Chicago area. Oak Park."

"Did the Hemingways have any favorite restaurants?"

"Not anything that would be less than an hour's drive away

if it still exists. I know the perfect place, though. It's not too far. Maybe thirty minutes. I think you'd feel right at home there."

"Then let's go there. I can drive. You just tell me where to go."

I gleefully watched Andreas's face as we pulled up to a low, sprawling structure that appeared to be going for an air of Bavarian charm but only pulled off looking vaguely Germanic with a healthy helping of hick. Like everything else up here.

"*Willkommen* to Der Lindenhof," I said in my best German accent. "Or, as my grandfather always called it, The Restaurant."

"The Lime Farm?"

"Is that what that means?"

"*Linde* is lime, and *Hof* in this case is short for *Bauernhof*, which is farm."

"That's funny. No one's growing limes up here." I got out of the car and started across the parking lot. "Maybe it's the key lime pie, which at this moment doesn't strike me as particularly German. Anyway, the food's fairly decent, or it was when I was a kid and I had no discernable taste. Grandpa took me and Cami here every summer the day before he had to drive me back to meet my mom in Mt. Pleasant."

Well, every summer except for the last one.

"Your mom didn't come up to the lake?" Andreas said as he opened the door.

"She's never wanted anything to do with the place since she was eighteen."

We seated ourselves in a booth and pulled the menus out from behind the salt and pepper shakers.

"Why?" he asked.

"I don't know. I always figured it had something to do with her mom dying. She died the same year I was born. I thought maybe she didn't want to be reminded of it." I examined the menu. "That and the fact that summer was the only time she could get rid of me and not have the responsibility of a kid. Huh. This menu's different."

The waitress came by and took our drink order. I thought she was just a tad too flirty with Andreas.

"What about you?" Andreas said once she'd left. "Why did you stay away so long?"

I looked intently at the new menu and avoided answering the question. How could he not know?

The waitress came back to take our order. When she scooted away again, Andreas said, "It wasn't because of Tyler."

I adjusted your bangles on my wrist. "Of course it was."

"It couldn't have been. Otherwise you wouldn't have come back after . . . But you came up after that."

"I don't know. I guess I just got too busy. College, trying to write something worth publishing."

"Did you take classes in the summer?"

"No."

"And you couldn't write up here?"

"No, I couldn't."

"Why not?"

I thought of your dad's typewriter, of his fear that he couldn't write on anything else. Once I was in college, I wrote everything on laptops that slowly increased in functionality even as they decreased in bulk. I could have brought them up to the lake. I could have written as Grandpa quietly read the newspaper and smoked his pipe. I would have been happy to do so. If not for one thing.

"It wasn't Tyler," I admitted.

But you already knew that, didn't you?

13

'd rather not talk about this," I said as the waitress set a bottle of red wine and two glasses on the table.

"Of course. I'm sorry."

"It's fine. I'm just . . . frankly, I'm sick of talking about myself." This was not true. I loved talking about myself. But on my own terms. "I feel like I've been talking about myself for a year with all the publicity stuff for the book. I'd much rather talk about you—why you came here, why you chose Chicago, where your family is. All that stuff."

The waitress zipped by again and deposited a basket of warm rolls.

"My family is in Germany. I came to work for an investment firm that had dealings with companies in Germany and Switzerland, etcetera, and that job put me in Chicago."

I couldn't hide my surprise. "You're in finance?"

"Not full-time anymore. I still invest, but I am more of a private contractor since I got my green card." He buttered a roll. "Most people in America don't speak a second or third language. Once people discover you do, translation jobs begin to pop up."

"How many languages do you speak?"

"Five. German and English, of course, and French, Dutch, and Italian. I can also read some Spanish and Portuguese."

I spoke the only language I knew around the bite of bread I'd just taken. "Wow."

"Anyway, I enjoyed those little jobs—reading old family correspondence for a woman doing genealogical research, translating some poetry. I've even done subtitles on a couple international films. These projects were always rewarding in a way that numbers were not. They weren't about wealthy people making more money. They were about regular people understanding other regular people. So I started looking for them."

Andreas spent the next several minutes relaying fascinating and heartwarming anecdotes about the people he had met through his freelance translation work. Each one could have been a novel. I basked in his enthusiasm for their stories and in the delights inherent in being human, in having relationships, in facing adversity, in achieving personal triumph with the help of a kind stranger. Such a beautiful jumble of setting and character and plot. Would my life be similarly changed by his short involvement in it?

"How did you end up translating my book?" I finally asked.

Andreas smiled sheepishly and took a sip of wine. "I heard an interview on the radio the day *That Summer* came out. I bought the book that moment and started reading it on my phone. And I didn't stop until I finished it the next night. I couldn't. I had to read by the outlet because of how fast my battery was draining."

Our conversation paused as the waitress came by with our food. Andreas refilled both of our glasses and held out his hand across the table. "May I?"

I put my hand into his, not knowing why until he bowed his

head and said what must have been a quick blessing in German. Then he released my hand, leaving it empty on the table.

"I apologize for the German. I've never gotten comfortable praying in English."

"That's fine. I'm sure God speaks German too."

His mouth quirked in a smile, and he took a bite of pecan-crusted whitefish.

"You never prayed before any meals at the cabin or at Robert's," I observed wryly. "Nothing on the table to be thankful for then?"

Andreas laughed. "Not that. I was just following the custom of the house. But you are here at this quasi-German restaurant as my guest, so here I am the host."

"Ah, I see." I speared a maple-roasted carrot. "So how did you end up doing the translation?"

He looked embarrassed. "This may sound crazy."

"Crazy how?"

"After I finished reading, I contacted your publisher and your agent to see if the German rights had been sold. They hadn't. So I contacted an old school chum of mine back in Frankfurt who works at a publisher there and encouraged him to buy the rights and let me do the translation."

"Wow, I'm flattered."

He paused for a moment to take another bite of fish. "After negotiations started, it was clear that his very small publishing house could not offer enough money—you have a very good agent, you know."

"I'll let her know you said so."

"When my friend told me this, I was . . . devastated. I had become obsessed by the idea that I would translate *That Summer*, and in fact, I had already started working on it. So I gave him the funds."

"What do you mean?"

"I gave him the funds," he said slower. "So his company could purchase the rights."

"You paid for the right to translate my book?"

"*Ja.*"

"But who's paying you for the work?"

He shrugged. "No one."

"So your trip up here, the car rental, that's all out of your pocket?"

"*Ja.*"

He was smiling, but my stomach twisted. I thought of the weirdo with the tattoo who had sought out your father on the lake. Somehow, even with the letter mailed directly to my house, I had never really thought that someone might seek me out as well.

"I told you it would sound a little crazy," he said. "But don't worry. I'm not a crazy person. I'm just someone who loved your book. I really did not know that translating it would mean meeting you in person, or staying at your house." His eyes twinkled in the soft light. "Though, I'm not unhappy with how things have turned out."

I tried to take another bite of my food, but my stomach was having none of it. I was flattered and humbled and cautious and thrilled all at once, and I couldn't see a way out of this uncomfortable feeling. It was like the time Tyler had asked me to look at his drawings in his room and I'd found that several of them looked vaguely like me.

"Will you pose for me sometime?" he'd said. "It would be easier to make a portrait if I could look at someone."

It had been a month since the truck incident with no further trouble. He hadn't apologized—had never even acknowledged that it happened—but he also hadn't so much as brushed by me in the hallway at your house. I thought maybe he'd realized he'd pushed things too far and I wasn't interested. Or at least, I wasn't interested in the same things he was interested in.

"Sure. I could do that sometime."

Tyler smiled. I read it as him simply being happy that our friendship had survived hide-and-seek. Because that was what I wanted it to be.

Andreas was smiling at me now. His smile seemed to apologize for what he knew must seem like stalking. But could that smile be trusted? Could I trust my own judgment of others at all? Had your dad been wrong when he told me I would be a good writer because I was a good observer?

"This may sound like I'm fishing for compliments or something," I said, "but what was it about my book that would make you go to such lengths to translate it? I mean, I think it's good, but it's not world-changing or anything. It's not going to win a Pulitzer or a Nobel Prize. And men in their—what, thirties?—aren't exactly the core demographic."

Andreas stopped eating and seemed to be considering the best way to answer that question. "There was a sadness there that I think connects with the modern German sensibility. A sense that innocence is gone and there's nothing you can do to change the past. But then your Jess does not remain in this sadness. She knows she cannot change the past, but it doesn't become this weight around her neck. She does something about it. She acts. She is not simply acted upon. Does this make sense?"

"Of course."

And it did make sense. Jess was strong. Brave. Resolute. I wanted to be just like her. Why shouldn't a German investment banker?

Dinner continued, and our conversation swung around to other things—Michigan weather and wildlife, the state of the

European Union, favorite films, trips on bucket lists. It was pleasant and should have been wholly engaging, but as the evening wore on I began surreptitiously checking the time on my phone beneath the table. I needed to talk to Tyler. I couldn't wait another night. I needed to be Jess, not Kendra.

Eventually Andreas caught on, and his expression turned serious. "We should go."

I tried to pay for dinner after the evening's financial revelations, but Andreas wouldn't hear of it.

"I asked you out to dinner," he said.

"But you're losing money on me."

He put his hand up as if to say "not to worry," and it struck me that as an investment banker for the very wealthy, as someone who had enough money to blithely buy translation rights to my book, Andreas might actually be a fairly wealthy person himself.

"Well, *danke* for dinner," I said.

"*Bitte. Es war mir ein Vergnügen.*"

"*Bitte* is 'please,' right?"

"It can also mean 'you're welcome.'"

"And what was the rest of that?"

"'It was my pleasure.'"

14

An orange sun hung in the western sky when we pulled up to the cabin. A few gaunt clouds drifted impotently in front of Earth's untiring star. The browning grass around the cabin was crisp and brittle. A scattering of parched leaves dropped by distressed trees went stumbling across the gravel drive at a sudden gust of dry wind. We needed rain—something beyond our power to obtain. The worst thing to need.

That was how I'd felt for months as I struggled to write, struggled to cope with Disappointed Reader's accusations. The struggle would end tonight.

Tyler was sitting on the couch, open book in hand, when Andreas and I walked through the door. I needed to start locking that door.

"There you are," he said, letting the book rest on his lap. "I was beginning to think you were just messing with me."

"Sorry," I said. "Dinner ran a bit late."

Andreas walked through to the kitchen with the leftovers.

"It's not a problem," Tyler said. "I was keeping myself busy."

He indicated the book he'd been reading. "If you want to finish the inscription, I can bring it back with me."

I took the book from him and slid it onto the shelf beside *Blessed Fool*. "No thanks. I'd rather give it to him myself."

Andreas parked himself in the kitchen doorway.

"So where did you two go for dinner?" Tyler said.

"Lindenhof," I said. "I hadn't been there in a while. It's nicer than I remembered it. Probably should have dressed up more."

"New ownership," he said. "A few years back Scott and his dad went in and bought it."

"The Masters? Really? A restaurant?"

"I guess it's something Paul had always wanted to do, and since he retired he thought it was the time to do it. Scott's a contractor now, so he did a lot of repairs. They hired a new chef. The whole nine yards."

"I didn't know you two still kept in touch."

He stretched. "Everyone on the lake has kept in touch, Kendra. You're the one who dropped off the face of the earth."

"Well, me and Cami, apparently."

"You first."

"Kendra," Andreas broke in, "I'll be at my desk if you need me." He gave me one last meaningful look and then slipped behind the curtain.

"Dad said you had something you wanted to talk about," Tyler said.

"Let's talk outside. Do you want something to drink?" I headed into the kitchen.

Tyler stood up. "That depends. What do you have?"

I opened the fridge. "Tea. Coke."

He came up behind me. "No beer?"

"I hate beer."

"Your German doesn't like beer?"

139

I pulled the tea out. "He's not my German. And I guess he doesn't feel the need to drink with every meal."

"You don't have any liquor here?"

"There's never been liquor here."

"Oh, that's right. I forgot your grandpa was a teetotaler."

"Tea then?" I took two glasses down from the cupboard.

"I guess so."

I filled the glasses with ice and tea and handed them to Tyler. "I'll be out in a moment. There's just something I have to get."

With Tyler out the door, I climbed up into the loft to retrieve the letter. I expected it to be waiting for me on my desk, but the surface was bare except for my laptop. I sifted through the books beside my bed, flipped through a notebook, swept my finger through pants pockets. It was nowhere to be found. Never mind. I didn't really need it. I knew what it said, knew what I needed to ask him.

I climbed back down the ladder and stood for a moment, looking through the screen door. I took a deep breath.

"Kendra?" came Andreas's voice from behind the curtain a few feet away.

I walked over and pulled it aside.

"I'm right here," he said.

I offered him a reassuring nod and walked out into the evening glow, letting the screen door slam behind me. The trees were dark sentinels draped in dusty sunbeams. The sand was still warm, each step revealing a cooler layer just beneath the surface. Tyler was at the end of the dock facing west, bare feet dangling in the water, bare chest soaking up the last of the ultraviolet rays. The low sun glinted off his black hair and the two sweating glasses of iced tea beside him.

What might have happened if things had gone differently that summer? Robert had thought Tyler and I were an item.

Perhaps we had been in Tyler's eyes. Perhaps I'd led him on somehow. Could it really be just a terrible misunderstanding?

With every step, I had less time to decide how to start this conversation, whether to be angry and confrontational or hurt and confused. Whether to be blunt like Jess would have been or try to get him to bring it up himself, which was my natural inclination. Then suddenly there were no more steps to take.

I sat on the dock, leaving a buffer of space between us, and dipped my toes in the water, which, if it were possible, was even lower than it had been when I'd arrived a week ago. I took a sip of tea.

"Whoa," I croaked.

"Tequila," Tyler said. "I had it in the boat."

"Why would you have that on you?"

He shrugged. "You never know when you might need a drink. When your father tells you that the woman who wants you dead needs to talk to you, you figure maybe this conversation would be easier with a little anesthetic."

He took a long drink of his doctored tea. I set mine on the dock.

"I don't want you dead," I said.

"No? You've got a funny way of showing it."

I let out a long sigh. "You're not Blake. And I'm not Jess. And anyway, Blake didn't even die in the first draft."

"Just in the version that the whole world would read."

"Some early readers didn't like that he never suffered for what he did, so I changed it. It's not as true to life that way, but that's what people wanted."

"So you just gave the people what they wanted. A revenge story."

I threw up my hands in surrender. "People like bad guys who

are bad, good guys who are good. They'll tolerate some gray, but they won't tolerate a weak heroine. They're 'unlikable.'"

I took another sip of tea, forgetting Tyler's addition to it, then immediately poured it out into the lake. He rolled his eyes and cursed under his breath.

"Seriously? Can you blame me?" I said.

He said nothing.

The sun painted a few wisps of cloud in the purest orange and pink, colors I'd always loved to see splashed across the fading blue-green sky. Unpredictable and fleeting. Muted to mauve and rust before you could quite imprint them permanently in memory. Grandpa had once said that God did that on purpose, to keep us looking for new signs of him every day.

"I was afraid to write it how it really happened," I finally admitted. "I was afraid of what people might say about me."

"You mean you were afraid of not selling as many copies."

I wanted to protest. But what could I say? Of course I wanted it to be a success. Anyway, it was fiction, not memoir. It didn't have to be true, as long as it was *true.*

"I don't blame you," he said. "I don't. I've done some things I'm not proud of."

"I'm glad to hear you say that. But I never said I wasn't proud of it."

We stared at the sky, feet swirling in the darkening water, almost touching, drifting away.

"Tyler, how do you see what happened that night?"

He expelled a little burst of air between his lips. "How I see things doesn't really matter."

"It does. It matters to me."

He turned toward me a little. "Then why didn't you ask me that before? Before you turned me into a monster?"

I looked down at my hands. "I didn't turn you into anything. Blake's not you."

He gave a derisive snort.

"Look," I said, "I should have asked you about this before. I'm sorry. But I'm asking now. And I need to know if . . . I just need to know if you see things the way I do."

Tyler was quiet for a long time as he stared at the tree line behind which the sun had finally sunk. The edge of the black forest blinked with the tentative green lights of fireflies searching for love.

He stood up and held his hand out to me. "Come on. Let's go to Mermaid Island."

I looked back to the cabin where I knew Andreas was watching. He could not watch over me if I left in a boat with Tyler. I would not get into a boat with Tyler. Never again.

"I'm not in the mood for a boat ride."

His hand fell to his side. "Fine. No boat. Let's swim it." He shrugged out of his open button-down shirt and hiked up the shorts he was wearing. "Go get a suit on."

"I have a suit on." Why did I say that?

He lifted his palms a little as if to say, "Well?"

"It's late."

"You wanted to talk. You want to talk to me, I'll be on Mermaid Island." He performed a shallow dive off the end of the dock into the glassy water, came up, and smoothed back his wet hair. "You coming?"

I glanced back at the cabin again. Jess wouldn't hesitate. You wouldn't hesitate. And hesitation had gotten me nowhere. Maybe I needed to stop tiptoeing around the edges of this problem. I pulled my shirt off over my head, shimmied out of my shorts, and dove in headfirst.

I started in the direction of the island at a steady crawl. I could hear Tyler following a few yards behind and to the left, cutting swiftly through the water. Very quickly he was in the lead as my energy began to wane. Though I pushed myself harder and harder, I fell farther and farther behind as the last traces of day melted away. I paused to tread water and get my bearings. The moon was nothing but a sharp sliver, and I could not see the island but I could make out the Crayfish King, whose scepter pointed more or less in the right direction in midsummer. And I could hear Tyler swimming. I followed the stars and the splashes through the inky blackness. Then the splashes ceased. Tyler had reached the shore.

"Kendra?"

I stopped swimming and caught my breath. "I'm here."

"You okay?"

"Yeah." I switched to a breast stroke. "Keep talking. I can't see a thing."

"You've let yourself get a little out of shape sitting in front of your computer all the time, eh?"

I didn't answer, just followed his voice.

"You don't look it," he said. "I didn't mean that. You look great. But you used to give me a run for my money in the water."

My knee hit the sand. "You always caught me eventually."

"I could never catch Cami."

"No one could."

I tried to stand, but my legs were limp as kelp. Tyler jogged into the shallow water, slung my arm around his shoulders, and pulled me to my feet. I twisted away from his touch and sat on the sand, catching my breath. My stomach hurt, but whether it was because of the hard swim or simply the fact that I was back here, with him, I couldn't say. I tried to channel Jess, to channel you, to be the person I always wished I was—confident, self-assured—but I was all too aware that I was just me, and maybe I'd never be anybody but me.

"How could you even see where you were going?" I asked between breaths.

"I don't know. I can just feel it. Surprised you can't."

"I used to. I think."

Tyler draped his arms over his knees and pointed. "You can see Ike's place from here."

A dim string of red and green Christmas tree lights twinkled across the water.

"I can't believe that man is still alive," I said. "He was a thousand when we were kids."

Tyler let out a little laugh. "I haven't seen him yet this summer, have you?"

"Not since the memorial."

"Then he might be dead after all, slumped over in his chair with all the deer heads and stuffed raccoons and squirrels. Just another little mummy. You ever been in his place?"

"Certainly not."

"It's a trip. I was over there with Scott last year, and Ike was going on and on about catching an eight-foot sturgeon in the lake."

"There's no sturgeon in this lake. They don't live in isolated lakes like this."

"Yeah, well, I asked him where it was and why he didn't have it hanging on his wall with the other fish and game, and he told me he'd let it go."

I snickered. "You believe him?"

"I never have before, so I guess I don't know why I'd start now. Didn't have a photo to prove it or anything, but he was adamant. Real angry when he could tell we didn't believe him."

"Yeah. It hurts when people don't believe you." I let that

statement hang in the air a moment before continuing. "What is it about Ike that everyone always assumes he's making stuff up, anyway? I've always said it because everyone else always said it, but maybe that's not fair to him."

"Oh, come on, Kendra. Have you heard some of his war stories? Dad's always said that if he told them in one of his books the way Ike tells them, no one would take him seriously as an author. They're just impossible, that's all."

Were they? Or was it just that people's minds were already made up? Why couldn't he have caught an eight-foot sturgeon in Hidden Lake? Why couldn't you just take a man at his word? Just because something was unsubstantiated didn't make it untrue.

I leaned back, supporting myself with two hands planted in the sand behind me. We were both quiet, taking in the Milky Way above and its twin reflected in the now-still water, evidence of our passage nothing but a memory.

"That night was a lot like this one," I ventured.

Tyler remained silent.

"No moon," I continued. "Lots of stars. Still water."

"Only Scott and Cami were here."

"They were at the fire pit."

"No. They were with Scott's boat."

"No, they were at the fire pit," I said. "When we left, they were still there roasting marshmallows."

"That was my parents. Remember, you guys told them you were taking a night trip to Mermaid Island."

I fought hard to remember.

"Only you weren't going to Mermaid Island," Tyler said. "Scott and Cami wanted to go skinny-dipping."

"But I didn't want to." I remembered clearly now the thought of getting caught, the thought of Jackie finding out. "Then you showed up."

15

You and I had seen the tent in the woods on Mermaid Island that morning. It was stuffed with sleeping bags, a flashlight, a half-eaten box of stale graham crackers, and, deep in one of the pillowcases, the *Sports Illustrated* swimsuit issue. That was where you'd gotten the idea for skinny-dipping—a picture of some model, probably not much older than we were, slick with oil, lying on her belly in the ocean's foamy surf, her bare breasts just grazing the sand, her butt like two stones rounded by the constant action of the waves. No swimsuit in sight.

"I wish I looked like her," you said, looking down at your flat chest. "Or at least like you. I've got nothing up here."

"You will, I bet. And anyway, you know those models are all airbrushed."

"So? They have to start out looking pretty good to be models."

I scooted over to the flap of the tent. "Come on. Let's get some frogs and fill the tent with them."

"Oh, who cares about frogs?"

I slumped where I was. "Okay, then what do you want to do? And don't say French braid."

Your eyes got that mischievous glint in them. "Let's go skinny-dipping."

"Here? In broad daylight?"

"Why not?"

"Uh, duh, because people will see us?"

"So what?" You indicated the magazine. "She's not worried about being seen, and a lot more people are looking at her than would see us."

"She's degrading herself." It was a word I'd learned in school the last year. "I'm not skinny-dipping."

You flipped through a few more pages. "Do you think this is Scott's or Tyler's?"

"Ew. I don't want to think about that."

"I bet it's Tyler's. He's messed up, you know. I heard Mom telling someone on the phone that in one of the places he was before he came to live with us, some people abused him—like touched him and stuff. Just like this one teacher at my school went to jail for touching some boys in the Scout troop he ran."

"That doesn't make any sense. Why would a guy touch another guy?"

You shrugged.

"And even if he did," I said, "wouldn't that make him *not* want to be like that?"

"Like what?"

"Like *that*. Like touching people who didn't want you to touch them."

The narrowing of your eyes sent a jolt of fear through me that I had overplayed my hand, that I was in imminent danger of blurting it all out.

"What are you talking about?" you said.

For the barest moment, I almost considered telling you about what had happened in the truck. Then I didn't. It would be too hard to explain. And what if you got mad at me? What if you told Tyler I'd been spreading rumors about him, and your family found out and I was never allowed to see you again?

"I was just saying that it's weird," I finally said.

You gave me a last suspicious glance but dropped it. "Well, whosever it is, I bet Scott would go skinny-dipping with me if you're too chicken."

Scott didn't take any convincing. As Magic Time descended, the three of us set off in one boat, leaving Tyler, who was taking a shower, behind. When we reached the lonely cove where Ike Fenton occasionally fished in the early mornings, you wasted no time stripping down to nothing and diving into the water, leaving me queasy and rocking in the boat with Scott. I could just see the curve of your shoulders and the sheen of your wet hair in the starlight. I couldn't see anything else. All I had to do was strip as fast as possible and jump in. No one would see anything.

But I couldn't. This was exactly the type of thing my mother would not approve of. If she had ever met you, she would have told me to steer clear of you.

"Come on," you urged.

I waited to see if Scott would go. But he seemed to be waiting for me. When I didn't move, he shrugged and started pulling off his clothes. I looked the other way. The boat rocked again. A splash. I was alone in the boat.

"Come on!" you insisted.

We all heard it at the same time. The sound of another boat approaching. You shrieked, and you and Scott started swimming away. I tried to hide your clothes beneath a tarp in the boat. My mind rapidly concocted an excuse for being out on the lake alone after dark.

But the person in the other boat wasn't my grandfather or any other adult on the lake. It was Tyler.

"What gives?" he said. "Were you trying to ditch me?"

"No," Scott said at the same time you said, "Yes." I said nothing.

"What's going on?"

You and Scott started laughing.

"They're skinny-dipping," I said.

"And you're not invited," you said.

"Oh, wow, my feelings are so hurt. I don't get to swim around naked with my sister and some other guy. Gross."

"You could swim around with Kendra," Scott said. "If she ever gets up the nerve."

"Shut up, Scott," you and I said in unison.

"She doesn't want to skinny-dip," you said.

"She doesn't have to," Tyler said. "Kendra and I can do something else. We'll take a trip to Mermaid Island. Leave you two to your own dirty devices."

"Oh, please!" you said.

"Okay," I said. This sounded eminently better than baring it all in front of two guys and risking getting caught.

Tyler brought his boat around and helped me climb in.

"Don't do anything I wouldn't do," he said to Scott, then he started the engine and turned us toward the island.

Until Tyler beached the boat on the shore of Mermaid Island, I hadn't remembered the tent. But as he led the way through the trees, the tent and all of its contents came rushing back.

Tyler unzipped the flap and held it open. "Quick, before the mosquitoes get in."

In the space of a breath we were both inside. Tyler zipped the flap closed and turned toward me in the darkness. The stagnant plastic air reminded me too much of the close air in the garage during the game of hide-and-seek.

He wasted no time pulling me toward him, pressing his

mouth onto mine, aggressive, almost hostile. I pushed hard on his chest, but with every push he countered with a tighter embrace. Then his tongue was in my mouth, and I felt like I might gag. I somehow got a foot up against his stomach and heaved him away to the other side of the tent.

"What's wrong?" he said, anger tingeing his tone.

"I don't want that, Tyler."

"Every girl wants to be kissed."

"Not like that! You idiot."

Ruined. My first kiss was ruined.

The singing of skin against nylon sounded as Tyler slid closer.

"Cami kissed Scott."

You hadn't told me that. Why wouldn't you have told your best friend about your first kiss?

"Well, that's her business," I said. "It doesn't mean I'm going to kiss you."

"What are you talking about? The other day when you were posing for me, you were practically begging for it."

"I was not!"

"Yeah, you were! You were sitting there in your bikini—"

"I was already in the bikini. I didn't put it on for you. You were the one who asked me to pose so you could work on your drawing, and you said you were just drawing my face. I said yes because I'm a nice person. It doesn't mean I want to kiss you or do anything else with you. And I don't see why you need a real live person anyway when you could just look at all the girls in your gross magazine and draw them."

He slid even closer, pushing me into the corner of the tent so I had to hunch over. "You were going through my stuff!"

Static electricity pulled my hair up against the vinyl tent. "Your sister was going through your stuff. I wanted to leave. Just like I do right now."

I pushed my way to the flap of the tent, unzipped it, and stumbled out of his reach into the black night. Tripping over roots and rocks I couldn't see, I made my way quickly to the shore and ran into the water to swim home.

"Kendra, wait!"

I kept going.

"Wait!" Tyler caught up to me in water up to our knees. "Wait," he said, quieter now. "I'm sorry. I shouldn't have done that. I just . . . you know I like you. I thought you liked me too."

I sighed and fought back tears. "I *do* like you. That's why this sucks so much!"

"Shhh." He put his arms around me and pulled me into a hug. "I'm sorry. I'm sorry."

Ready for flight just seconds ago, my stiff muscles softened. Arms that had hung by my sides lightly encircled Tyler's bare waist. I gave a shuddering sigh and wiped one eye on his shoulder. He stepped back and held me at arm's length. I could just see his face in the starlight, his eyes black pools like the deep lake in which we stood.

"I'm sorry," he said, this time in barely a whisper.

I looked into his eyes for a moment too long, tipped my head a few degrees to the right. Then I kissed him.

Yes. *I* kissed *him.*

And it didn't end there.

Tyler lightly grasped my hand and led me to the boat. He pushed it out into deeper water and got in. I thought he was going to take me home, but he didn't start the motor. We drifted farther out into the lake. He unfolded an old blanket. That blanket wasn't anything that would get me home. It was something to make me more comfortable where I was.

Tyler tugged gently at my hand, and I sank off the seat to the bottom of the boat. I focused on the castle of the Crayfish

King as he removed the swimsuit I hadn't wanted to remove to go skinny-dipping. I focused on the frog chorus as he lowered himself onto me. I focused on the sharp pain of my neck against the plank seat when I felt the sharp pain between my legs.

I wanted it to stop. Wanted it to stop. Wanted him to stop. To stop hurting me. I should push him off, push him out of the boat. But I thought it would be over soon. It would be over soon. And everything would just go back to normal again. I felt the rough wool in my hands, the seeping of the bilge water through the blanket. A mosquito buzzed in my ear, but I couldn't swat it away, couldn't swat him away, couldn't crush him like I had so many mosquitoes, couldn't identify him in a book, label him, and then throw him away.

Why was he doing this to me? Why did I kiss him? I'd wanted to kiss him, a real kiss, but I didn't want this. The pain in my neck was unbearable. He was breaking my neck. He would crush me. When would it stop?

And then it did. He kissed me again. How could he kiss me? Why didn't I feel like one of those women in the magazine? Why did I feel like the bloody Band-Aid I'd seen on the ground at the gas station when Grandpa and I had filled up the gas can a few days earlier?

I groped in the dark for my suit and got back onto the seat, though it was uncomfortable to sit with the hot pain radiating from between my legs. Tyler started up the motor and brought me to my dock. I got out of the boat. Without another word or glance, he turned the boat around and melted into the night.

When I took off my swimsuit to take a shower that night, there was blood and something else. It wasn't my period. He'd done something to me. Something terrible. Maybe something that would never be repaired.

16

grappled for a moment with the memory that I had kissed Tyler that night of my own free will. I looked for a line that might have been crossed. How the decision to kiss him had morphed into what had happened on the boat. The moment that something I had done became something done to me. Was it when he took my hand? When I got in the boat? When he laid out the blanket?

When was the moment I should have said *stop*? Would he have listened if I had? I'd never know.

"Tyler, I got a letter. From a reader who assumed I had taken the story from my life, but that I had gotten it wrong, had misread the situation entirely. And that letter has kept me from being able to write this next book, because it has me doubting my own memory."

He snorted. "I thought you said I wasn't Blake, you weren't Jess."

"Of course, and that's true, but I did start with the truth. Obviously. It's in there. The plot may be different, but the feelings I put in it, the emotions, the revelations I had while writing it—those weren't fake. I was telling the truth."

He crossed one ankle over the other and rested his hands on his knees. "Kendra, I didn't write that letter."

"I know you didn't," I said, "but someone I know did. Someone who knew my home address."

"It's the easiest thing in the world to track someone down. Have you done a search on your name lately? You're all over the internet. People know what city you live in. You even describe what your apartment building looks like in the bio on your website. All someone needs is a few bucks and Wi-Fi and they can pinpoint you."

I stood up. "You're not listening."

"Where are you going?"

"Home. You're not listening. This is important."

Tyler got to his feet. "You want to know what I think happened that night? I pushed too far too fast in the tent and got rejected. Then you kissed me and I thought all was forgiven."

"So you thought that meant I wanted to have sex with you?"

"If you didn't want to, why didn't you just say no? You could have said no. You had that option."

"I was fourteen. I shouldn't have had to say no. I should be asked to say yes. I never said yes."

He spun away from me and then back again, kicking a little shower of sand over my toes in the process. "What about the next summer? And the summer after that? And the next one?"

I clamped my mouth shut. This was what I could not bring myself to put in my book. My regular capitulation to him. My shame at my feeble excuses. My fear that if I didn't keep him happy, if I didn't keep everyone happy, I would lose everything. I could see now how ridiculous that was, how illogical. But at the time, it had felt so much bigger, so nearly out of my control. And my self-respect had seemed a small price to pay to keep everything at Hidden Lake the same.

I forced the words I had to say past my clenched jaw. "But will you admit that . . . that the first time was—" I couldn't even say the word.

He threw up his hands and paced a little circle in the sand. "Sure, you happy? It was all my fault. Can you write your precious book now?"

"Why are you so angry with me?" I shouted. "I'm the one who should be angry with you!"

"And you're not? You killed me off in your book!"

"It's not you!"

"Yes it is, Kendra, and everyone who knows us who reads it knows it's me. Cami knew. She was just getting her life together— she was clean, she had a job lined up, had an apartment—and then she read your stupid book and disappeared, and no one's seen her since."

"I seen her." The voice came from the direction of the lake, creaking like the rusted spring on a screen door. "I seen Cami was up here in March right before I drove down to Fred's funeral. Talked to her even."

I searched the void for the source of the voice. Ike Fenton's bent form in a fishing boat slowly materialized out of the black. How long had he been listening?

"You talked to her?" Tyler said.

"Oh, yeah. Couple times."

"What did she say?" I asked.

"Not much. Told me she was up at the cottage working on something. Then she wasn't there anymore when I came back up. I was kinda surprised she didn't go to the memorial. I woulda brought her with me, but—"

"She didn't say where she was going?" I said.

"Nope. Don't think so."

"Thanks, Ike," Tyler said. "I'll let Mom and Dad know."

"Glad to help. Now quit shrieking. You're scaring all the fish away."

He floated off and merged with the night.

My anger spent, I walked into the lake, ready to go home and get a decent night's sleep. I was right. Disappointed Reader was wrong. That was all that mattered. Tomorrow I could start writing my next book. With luck—a lot of luck—I might possibly be able to meet my deadline and keep my apartment.

"I know it's probably not easy to admit that kind of mistake," I said, quietly so as not to disturb Ike's fish. "And I'm sorry for the way Cami took it. I really thought I had changed enough in the book."

Tyler said nothing, and we began the trip back to my little stretch of shore. It seemed to take longer than the swim to the island, but home was easy to find. Andreas must have turned on every light in the cabin to guide me. Tyler beat me to shore and readied his boat. I was about to walk past him and back into my sanctuary when his hand on my arm stopped my forward motion.

"Look, Kendra, I'm sorry about what happened that summer. And all the summers. I really am."

I nodded. "I just—I just don't understand why you did the stuff you did to me. Why didn't you just do things a normal teenage boy would do when he liked someone? Like Scott did with Cami." I held up my arm. "Why didn't you just give me a bracelet? You never even gave me a chance to just like you the way normal teenagers like each other."

Silence stretched out between us like a thick black snake.

"I don't know," he finally said. "I don't know why I did those things."

I sighed heavily. It wasn't enough. But I was done talking

about it. "Okay," I said, because I couldn't bring myself to say, "I forgive you."

Tyler's fingers grasped tentatively at my hand. "I really did care for you, you know."

I looked into the dark pools of his eyes, searching for sincerity, for some indication that this wasn't another manipulation. I held his gaze a moment too long, and he kissed me.

For the space of a breath I forgot to resist. I forgot to channel Jess, to channel you, to be anyone but me, the one who always goes along to get along. Then I stepped back.

"Don't, Tyler."

And before he could say anything to draw me back in, I turned and walked away.

17

I did not need coffee the next morning. I woke twenty minutes before my alarm, mind swirling with the first words of my new book, fingers trembling to get them down before they disappeared. I dared not wait for my laptop to wake up but instead snatched the closest piece of paper and a pen from my little desk under the window. Your inexplicable bangles tinkling on my arm, I scrawled the line out by hand.

Leila Marie was never late, never early, never on time. She was never any of these things because she was never invited, not even to her own funeral.

My grandmother's beautiful name, perfect for my protagonist. To see it in print brought a sting to my throat. How much had I missed by having no family but Jackie and Grandpa? I pushed through the prick of melancholy, unwilling to slow my racing thoughts. I'd wasted too much time already, and I felt sure that this time the story would work.

The morning fled in a flurry of words, the click of keys a constant drone, like an August cicada. Line by line, I filled the white space of the open Word document, which continuously unfurled before me, a never-ending riverbed to receive the creative overflow of my mind. I tried to tamp down my elation. This had happened before. Thousands of words into a draft and the flow would slow to a trickle, then dry up completely. It could not happen this time, though. I'd been right. The letter was settled.

Only . . . it wasn't. When I finally stood up to make coffee, I realized that it was still there, lodged firmly in the folds of my cerebral cortex. And when I went to throw away the piece of paper on which I'd jotted that first line, I saw through the thin white sheet something typed on the other side. I turned it over.

`Dear Disappointed Reader,`

I stared at the response I had started but never finished. The letter writer was wrong. I knew it. But they didn't know it. That person was still out there, angry and disapproving, thinking they were the only one who knew the truth. But I knew the truth. I had told my story honestly. It didn't matter that someone out there didn't understand. People were free not to like my work, not to like me. I crumpled up the paper and threw it in the little wastebasket under my desk.

Listening to the coffee gurgle in the kitchen, I pushed the letter out of mind. It was pointless to keep obsessing over it. I was right, they were wrong, and I wouldn't let whoever it was sabotage my career. I poured my coffee and climbed delicately up to the loft, careful not to spill, then hunkered back down in front of my laptop. I reread the last paragraph I'd written, then added a page break, centered the cursor, and typed "Chapter Two" at the top of the page.

Then I sat.

I took a sip of coffee.

I went back and read that last paragraph again.

More coffee.

Crap.

No, it was fine. I just needed to stretch my legs.

I took the coffee back down the ladder and walked out to the beach. Things were stirring. The lake, which had been smooth as glass last night, rippled and shimmered in the intense morning sunlight. A strong breeze trembled the cattails and shook some of summer's dust from the trees. It rose like mist in the folds of the gentle hills rolling off to the north and west. The silvery undersides of poplar leaves flashed like a school of fish. A seagull cried. A few promising clouds hurried across the sky. Maybe the weather was changing. Maybe soon we'd finally get some rain.

A spot of white caught my eye, and I set my empty mug in the sand. Halfway to the end of the dock I recognized the clothes I'd left there the night before. My shirt had caught the breeze and separated itself from my shorts. Not far away, two glasses stood at attention. I laid the clothes over my arm and took the glasses by the rims in the other hand, dumping Tyler's out at the roots of the same little tree that had absorbed my beer the night Robert and I put the dock in. It already seemed like so long ago.

Time was running, ever running, slipping through my fingers. I had to get back to work.

I suddenly remembered the urgent email from my editor that I had filed away unread when Andreas and I went into town. I couldn't just leave that hanging. I didn't have enough clout to ignore my responsibilities. Who did I think I was, anyway? Yes, I'd managed to produce a winner for my publishing house, but I knew that meant little when it came to the next one. Second books often flopped—miserably.

A few minutes later I was in the car, heading for civilization. I'd clear my inbox, touch base with my agent and my publisher, be a responsible adult. Then I'd be able to buckle down again, reenter the creative flow that had carried me along in the morning.

Great drifts of yellow coreopsis were blooming in the vacant lots and meadows along the county road. All the old markers passed away behind me, things I didn't even see anymore, they were so commonplace—the olive-green alpine-style house, the RV with the roof built over it in the middle of a field, the enormous stacks of pine logs at the lumberyard, the tiny gas station with the old pumps that still counted out the gallons with analog numbers ticking by in an unending circle. I turned onto the state highway, headed for the interstate.

A moment later I sat up straight in my seat. Something was missing. Had I somehow turned the wrong way? I pulled over and craned my head out the window. No, this was the right direction. I slowly backed the car up to where I knew the old burned-out house with its blackened bones and stone chimney stack should be. There was nothing there but a dirt lot peppered with weeds.

How strange. Not that someone would finally tear the thing down, but that I would notice it because of its absence. If it had been there where it had always been before, I wouldn't have thought twice about it.

At Biggby Coffee I tucked myself into an overstuffed purple velvet armchair, read the email from my editor (as well as a painfully polite follow-up email she'd sent a few days later), and tapped out my tardy response.

Hi Paula!

Sorry it's taken me so long to get back to you. No Wi-Fi and all that. I've been making great progress of late. Clear plan, words are flowing. I'm sure I'll have no trouble making the deadline.

Not sure how much you want to know about the story itself, but I'd prefer not to just lay it all out there when it's in process. It's a little different than the proposal that was approved by pub board, but it's better, so . . . all is well!

Talk soon,
Kendra

The note wasn't strictly true, but it wasn't entirely false either. I had made progress lately—a lot compared to earlier efforts. I hadn't exactly outlined the book and, in fact, didn't have a clue how it would end or how I would get there, so perhaps it was a stretch to say I had a clear plan. Whether it would be better than what I had originally proposed certainly remained to be seen.

A half hour later I had culled the spam, answered some mail from readers, and even managed to post a little something on social media to remind everyone I was still alive and writing. I was about to shut the laptop when a response from my editor showed up.

Kendra,

So good to see your name pop up in my inbox today. Glad to hear that the writing is going well. I understand not wanting to go into details yet about the story, but we need to know *something* about it as we head into marketing and positioning work for that season. And I've had a few industry pubs asking for just a teaser. Any chance you have a logline floating around I could throw their way? Any advance buzz helps. Hope to hear from you again soon.

Best,
Paula

A logline? A teaser? That's practically all I had. I copied and pasted my first lines into a response and hit send. Now I was committed, despite my murky plans.

Another email popped up.

Oh, Kendra, how intriguing! So much promise in those lines. I can't wait to read the full manuscript.

—Paula

I shut the laptop to avoid seeing any more incoming messages. There was definitely something to be said for living with no Wi-Fi. It kept the outside world where it should be—outside.

I dawdled a bit in town and picked up some groceries. In the parking lot I watched the English house sparrows come and go from their messy nests tucked in the *A*'s and *R* of the Walmart sign. When I could think of no more legitimate errands, I headed back to my own nest.

When I pulled up to the cabin, Andreas was shutting the pickup truck's passenger door.

"Were you about to come looking for me?" I said as I stepped out onto the gravel drive.

"No, I was just packing up."

"Packing what up?"

"My things." He glanced into my car. "I can help you with those bags."

Bags? What bags? He was packing?

"You're leaving?" I almost didn't recognize my own voice. "When?"

Andreas opened the back door of my car and retrieved two grocery bags. "This evening. After I run through just a few more items with you." He disappeared into the cabin.

I caught up with him in the kitchen. "You really need to leave tonight? I thought you were staying until the end of the month."

He shook his head and put a carton of orange juice into the fridge. "After we go over a few things in the last chapter, I'll have all I need. I can get out of your hair."

He lost himself in the brown paper bags, pulling out peanut butter and apples and bread and placing them on the counter near the pile of rocks I still hadn't washed and organized. When the grocery bags were empty, he folded them up neatly and said, "I'll get the others." A moment later the screen door was slapping the doorjamb.

I stood dumbly at the counter strewn with food I had bought for us both. What could I say? I knew he only intended to stay a short time, that he had a job to do, that I had a job to do, that I needed to buckle down. Still, I thought I'd have a few more days at least.

He was back with the last bag and a gallon of milk. Who would drink all of that milk?

"I had hoped you'd get to stay for the Fourth of July," I said lamely.

"I'm sorry I'll miss it."

"I guess Chicago will have better fireworks anyway. All we get up here are Ike's, which I suspect may be homemade."

Andreas chuckled at that and pulled a six-pack from the bottom of the last bag.

"You can take that with you," I said. "I don't drink beer."

He finally stopped moving and looked me in the eye. He seemed about to say something, then raked his fingers through his hair and left the room.

Mechanically, I put all of the groceries away, hearing Grandpa's voice in my mind. *"No sense feeling sorry for yourself."* He'd said it a couple days after what happened in the boat. I hadn't told him anything about that shameful night, but he knew when I was down because I stopped talking and started answering him only in nods and shrugs and grunts.

"No one ever did himself any good that way," he'd said. "Self-pity just shackles you to something you can't change. Best thing to do is take your mind off it."

The writing. I would immerse myself completely in my draft and not come up for air until it was done.

The afternoon flew by too quickly. The morning breeze strengthened and whisked through the cabin's open windows, rustling papers and occasionally sending errant strands of hair across my face. I gathered and tugged at it absentmindedly as I explained the last few remaining problem passages to Andreas. When he closed his laptop, it was not unlike the closing of Grandpa's casket back in March. Another chapter of life ended, this one before it had had time to truly begin.

His suitcase already packed and stowed, Andreas zipped up his laptop case and gave the bedroom a quick once-over. "I know a guy who could probably fix that *u* key," he said. "Want me to take the typewriter to him?"

"Oh, sure." A spark of hope lit in my heart. If he took the typewriter with him now, he would have to return it later.

"Not sure when he'll have time to take a look at it, but I'll let you know when it's ready."

I nodded.

He scooped up the typewriter in one arm and his laptop case in the other. I walked him to the truck, trying to come up with something intelligent and generous to say.

"I'll leave the door unlocked," was all I could come up with.

Andreas smiled and deposited the two machines in the truck. Then he jogged back toward the cabin, saying, "I nearly forgot." He came out again with two books. "This belongs to Robert."

He handed me the German edition of *Blessed Fool.* "Please give him my regards. And this . . ." He held out my own copy of the English edition. "You should read this."

"I'll try to get to it after some of your German writers."

"Forget the Germans. Read this. Start tonight."

I took the books from him. "Andreas." I paused, unsure of how to continue. "I— Thank you. For how much you care about my book."

He ran his fingers through his hair once more. "It's been my great pleasure." He smiled weakly. *"Aber du bedeutest mir mehr als dieses Buch, und ich kann nicht einfach hierbleiben und zusehen, wie du den Mann küsst, der dir deine Unschuld geraubt hat."*

"I don't speak German," I reminded him with a sad smile.

"I know." He opened the driver's side door.

"You have this number?"

"Yes." He pulled out his wallet and handed me a card. "And here is mine. Happy writing, Ms. Brennan."

"Danke."

Andreas smiled and waved as he turned the truck around, but the gesture seemed artificial. This man whose manner had been so relaxed and genuine. For the last couple hours he had been stiff and awkward and . . . sad? I watched the dust kicked up by the tires dissipate in the wind and walked into the house to the sound of the phone ringing. I lifted the receiver, hoping to hear his voice confessing something he wished he'd said face-to-face, something I wished I'd had the courage to say to him. But he wasn't yet far enough from Hidden Lake to get a cell signal.

It was Tyler's voice I heard on the other line. "Mom's back."

My breath stuck in my throat. "Did she find her?"

"No."

I let the breath go in a defeated sigh. "I'm coming over."

18

Time is capricious. Clocks would have us believe that it is dependable, constant, tick tick tick. But it isn't. Whenever things are lovely, it runs out on you. Whenever things are unendurable, it sticks like burdock seeds. Time with Tyler was interminable. Time with you was breathless. We raced from one moment to the next, trying to beat the sun across the sky, trying to outrun bath time and bedtime and fireflies.

It was my fifteenth summer at Hidden Lake when I recognized that what we had was not going to last forever. In a few years, we would both finish high school. There would be jobs and college classes—you off to Berkeley, me to Ann Arbor. There would be other friends, more for you than for me, I was sure. There would be boyfriends. Already it was happening. You and Scott were always together, and when you made time for just me, he was all you talked about.

"Where'd you get that bracelet?" I asked you one morning.

You shook the silver bangles on your delicate wrist. "Scott gave it to me."

"Let me see it."

You held out your arm.

"No, I mean let me see it."

"Uh, no. I'm never taking this off."

I rolled my eyes and changed the subject, but inside I burned with jealousy. Why did you get to be loved by a boy who gave you things when the only boy who paid me any attention was one who took things away?

While my lazy summers with you were running out, I took solace in the fact that I would only have to deal with Tyler for a couple weeks in July when he was able to get off work. But with you and Scott attached like two halves of the same clam, I felt like one of those little black leeches that latched onto your ankles if you stood too long in the shallows.

I found myself spending more time with your dad than you, which had its own rewards, of course. But it wasn't the same as floating around in inner tubes with your best friend and swapping dreams about the future. Robert gave me writing prompts and assignments. He read and critiqued my short stories. He had me read my revisions out loud to him while he sat behind his desk, eyes closed, experiencing the words. Sometimes he read his own stuff out loud to me so I could hear the cadence, get how the sweep of the story could be expressed in miniature within a single paragraph. He loaned me books and debated their merits with me.

One muggy afternoon we sat in his air-conditioned office mulling over the meaning of various characterizations in Faulkner's *As I Lay Dying*, and I blurted out, "I feel like I'm still in school."

"Why shouldn't you be?" Robert returned. "The only reason school lets out for summer is because people used to need their children to work on the family farm. You're not a farmer, are you? Or a farmer's daughter. So why not keep learning?"

"I might be a farmer's daughter," I said. "I never met my father. I could be anyone's daughter."

Robert studied me a moment and then said, "You're not a farmer's daughter."

"How do you know?"

"I can just tell. There isn't a farming bone in your body. Have you ever grown anything?"

"We had to grow African violets in sixth grade science class."

"And how did yours grow?"

I frowned. "I forgot it in my locker and it got all moldy and died. I felt really bad about it."

"There you go."

I did enjoy those times talking Faulkner or Steinbeck or Hemingway with your dad. I was the only one he ever invited into his office, and I took some measure of pride in that. But it was summer, and my swimsuit rarely needed to be hung on the line to dry overnight.

I was so lonely I was almost glad when Tyler finally did show up on the afternoon of July 4th. That night as Ike shot fireworks off his dock, Tyler kept refilling my lemonade for me. Your parents laughed and told stories with a few other adults out at the fire pit. You and Scott snuck off somewhere to make out. And when I began to feel sleepy and a bit dizzy, Tyler led me by the hand into his room.

He gave my shoulder a light tap, and I tipped over like a tree being felled, landing on his bed, glad that for a moment the room had stopped spinning. He got out his big drawing pad and his charcoals and sat down across the room, but a moment later he was up again, pulling my shirt over my head.

"What are you doing?" My words sounded like someone else across the room had said them.

"I want to draw you."

I felt my shorts glide down my legs.

"That's enough," the voice across the room said.

"Relax. Go to sleep."

I felt him move my leg there, my arm here. Felt him lift my head and arrange my hair. Then the movement ceased and the sound of a pencil scratching seemed to be saying, "Relax, relax, relax. Sleep, sleep, sleep."

I woke in a blackness thicker than any I had ever seen. My foot found the floor, and I slid down to it. A headache descended like a grand piano in a cartoon, immediate, intense. I was crawling over the floor, hands searching for something, something, something. My clothes. I was searching for my clothes. A light flickered on, sending spasms of pain down my optic nerves.

"What are you doing down there?"

It was your voice. Your room. The too-short nightie I wore was yours.

"Get back in bed, psycho," you said gently.

I crawled back under the covers of your double bed and curled into the fetal position, facing the outside of the bed in case I threw up, which felt imminent. Our feet touched and neither of us pulled away. For that moment, at least, I was the other half of the clamshell, the other part of you. Like I used to be.

The light went out. A tear slid across my cheek, making a wet spot on the pillow. The bed jerked a little as I stifled a sob.

You didn't ask what was wrong. At the time I thought it was because you were mad at me for something. But now I wonder if you didn't ask because you already knew. Had you walked in and seen me on your brother's bed? Did you know what he had done last summer? Did you know how much I needed you then?

How much I have always needed you?

The wind that had been strengthening all day was full of empty promises. What I had hoped were signs of a new weather pattern to break the incessant heat turned out to be little more than the hot breath of some malevolent spirit. Rather than rain, it delivered only Beth Rainier to the lake, along with the knowledge that no one who knew you knew where you were.

Your last roommate hadn't seen you since the last week of January. You'd stopped answering calls, texts, and emails right before Christmas. You'd fallen out of the habit of going to your support groups in late October, stopped showing up to work last July. You'd blocked Tyler's cell number a year ago, not long after my book came out.

It was Beth who put this all together after weeks of tracking your movements. It was Tyler who relayed it all to me as I stood on the back deck at your cottage.

"I'm not sure you should come in," he said.

"Why not? Maybe I can help. Maybe I can think of something new. Somewhere to look." Even as I said it I knew it was absurd.

Tyler shook his head. "Mom's not real happy with you right now."

"With me? Why would she be mad at me? What did I do?"

Tyler rolled his eyes. "Why do you think?"

"What, the book? Please. Beth's been stone-cold to me as long as I can remember, and Cami's been making bad decisions just as long. I had nothing to do with any of this. I'm just trying to help."

"So the whole falling-out between the two of you had nothing to do with you either? You're just some poor, innocent bystander in your own life?" He slumped his shoulders and put on a pathetic expression, eyes wide, mouth in an exaggerated frown. "Everything happens to me. Poor me."

I wanted to slap that look off his face. "There was never any real falling-out. Unless you count her completely dropping me when she became obsessed with Scott. Maybe you should ask him what happened between them."

Tyler steered me away from the back door. I yanked my arm out of his grip. Your bangles clanged in a minor key.

"Go home," Tyler said. "Come back on the Fourth. The police are looking into it now. Maybe by then we'll know something more and Mom will be ready to talk to you."

I turned to go, then hesitated. "Robert doesn't think this has anything to do with me, does he?"

"Believe it or not, you are not at the top of our discussion list right now."

He went into the house, leaving me at the precipice of the stairs. I don't remember descending the steps, starting the boat, or crossing the lake. When I got to my dock, my eyes were so clouded with tears it took a moment to register that it was not actually my dock. I'd followed the wrong light. I put out into the water again and tried to get my bearings. Where was the birch grove? Where was Ike's string of Christmas lights? Did the sun still set in the west? I followed the shore until I saw some familiar beach chairs.

I tied the boat and stumbled into the cabin, only to be met with the memory that Andreas was gone. I was alone.

Blessed Fool was on the coffee table.

"Read this. Start tonight."

I threw the book as hard as I could against the wall, and the stuffed screech owl plummeted to the floor. I sank onto my knees and fought to contain the tears that threatened to pour forth. I picked up the owl and looked into his vacant glass eyes. Unseeing, unhearing, unknowing. Unable to do anything but stand dumbly by while life went on around him.

I took a deep breath, stood up, and put him in his place on the highest shelf. Then I picked up the book Robert had signed for me so long ago. Its sudden flight and crash landing against the wall had torn the dust jacket and broken the spine. Several pages were folded and creased. Whatever it might have someday been worth, it was now worth less.

I smoothed it all out, sat down on the couch, and opened to the inscription.

To Kendra. Someday you'll be signing one of these for me. Love, Robert

I turned past the title page and read the dedication.

For my inspiration and my best mistake

When I'd read *Blessed Fool* at age twelve, I'd mostly been interested in the educational aspect of the naughty parts. I skimmed through a lot of it, and as a result I didn't always understand what was going on. Now I wondered. Had Robert written this book for Beth? Was she his inspiration? How could someone be an inspiration and a mistake? Or was this two different people? Who was Robert's mistake?

"Don't let your mother know you have that book."

19

I avoided your house for a solid week, but I couldn't avoid thinking of you.

We used to make plans to run away together. To pack a couple bags, steal some food and some money, and head off on foot toward the train tracks that carried stacks of logs downstate and, ostensibly, out of Michigan at some point.

"We'll just slip into a boxcar and take the train to, I don't know, Tennessee or something," you said, "then switch to one going west."

"How far west are we going?"

"I dunno. Montana? It looked nice in that *River Runs Through It* movie."

I nodded. "Then we can live in a cabin in the mountains."

"Yeah, and we can open an animal sanctuary and have horses and goats and pets nobody wants anymore."

Where we would find this cabin and how we would pay for the upkeep of all these animals were not things we concerned ourselves with. We only wanted escape. Or maybe not even escape as much as the prospect of it. I didn't really understand why you wanted to run away, but I knew why I did.

Had you finally done it? Simply jumped onto a train and disappeared? Did you just need some space and time to work something out? Or had something terrible happened to you? I followed trains of thought until I'd built up terrifying scenarios in my mind, trying to convince myself that if I thought of them, they couldn't be happening in real life. If I could create some dreadful fiction for you, the facts would turn out to be tame and commonplace. You'd turn up at the lake one day soon, fresh from backpacking across Europe, and have a good laugh at all the fuss that we'd made of you.

In the meantime, I doggedly tapped away at my laptop, determined not to waste my exile. What was a stupid critical letter in the face of all that was happening? The pages were racking up, and slowly my confidence was returning. Characters appeared, spoke, filled in their own particular backstories at opportune times. I conjured none of them. Each existed already on some other plane, and I was left to simply draw away the veil that had obscured them. Scene led inexorably to scene. This event caused that, that conversation revealed this, and I trembled a little to think that at any moment I might lose my grip on this mystical curtain and it would fly back into place.

If the mornings were magical acts of staying out of my own way, the nights were spent in anguished and exacting deliberation as I meticulously combed through my memories of those last few summers on Hidden Lake, searching for evidence to exonerate myself in your mother's critical eyes.

Yes, there had been increasing distance between you and me—there always is between people who have been friends from a young age as each grows into her own self, which might be a self that neither anticipated on those warm summer nights when they had pledged their undying friendship to one another, staring up at millions of stars, each representing a possible future. I searched those same ancient heavenly bodies now, wondering what choice could have led you to one future rather than another, what could have driven you off course and into the black hole your life had become. You'd always had a rebellious streak, but it couldn't be that alone. You were clever, beautiful, charismatic . . . you could have made something of yourself. So why hadn't you?

Between morning and night, in the hot afternoon hours, I read *Blessed Fool*. I searched its pages, as I searched my memories, for what I may have missed, for the reason Robert had advised me to hide the book from Jackie and Grandpa, the reason Andreas had insisted that I read it.

On the surface it appeared to be a typical coming-of-age story, with its attendant angst, disillusionment, and eventual acceptance of a new, adult reality. I recognized the lake, your cottage, my cabin, and even a slightly younger version of Ike Fenton. Mermaid Island appeared as the rather more prosaic Frog Island. The nearby town of Evergreen was called Bakersfield. The four young characters could have been Tyler, Scott, you, and me. I knew at least one was modeled on Jackie. But, I constantly reminded myself, as I had recently reminded Tyler, just because a real person might be a jumping-off point didn't mean the resulting character shared much in common with them.

Characters paired up, fell in love, and committed acts of betrayal or were betrayed. Revenge was taken, feelings were hurt, and consequences of decisions were met with either stoic acceptance or reckless denial. No one ended up with who I wanted them to. Characters I wanted to see punished failed to even comprehend their wrongs. Characters who deserved a happy ending were miserable.

When I read the last sentence on the morning of Independence Day, I felt a deep sense of dissatisfaction. What was the point of it all? Why had Robert, who claimed so long ago to be in the business of telling the truth, written this story? Nothing was resolved and everyone was unhappy. No wonder it hadn't sold well.

A distant rumble of thunder drew me to the window. Clouds had been gathering and passing by all week. The wind had been whipping the lake into whitecaps. I'd heard more than a few limbs from the very oldest and largest trees around the cabin breaking off and crashing to the forest floor. Each day brought a new wave of dashed hopes until it felt like it might never rain again. Hidden Lake would slowly dry up, and my coveted waterfront property Up North would be situated not upon the shore of a paradise but at the edge of a one-hundred-fifty-eight-foot-two-inch-deep hole in the ground filled with rotting fish and vegetation.

We needed a storm. I only hoped it would wait until after the fireworks.

At eight o'clock I climbed into the boat and aimed for the birches. An unfamiliar boat was tied at your dock when I floated up. I was at once relieved and irritated. Having other people around might mean that whatever grudge Beth was holding against me would be kept stuffed behind her impeccable manners. It also meant that I might not have a chance to get updated on your situation. It wasn't something she'd broadcast to all the neighbors, after all.

Your bangles caught my eye as I tied the boat. They hadn't left my wrist since the day I found them, but now I wondered whether it might be better to leave them outside. Beth would surely recognize them and wonder why they were on my wrist rather than her daughter's.

The bracelet had slipped on fairly easily when I was in the cool water of Hidden Lake. Now I was hot and my hand was swollen. I pulled and tugged and lost a layer of skin cells to the keen metal rings, but the bangles would not release me. I glanced at the darkening mantle of clouds. Maybe Beth wouldn't notice in the gray light.

The sound of what seemed to be crying reached my ears when I was halfway up the stairs to the deck. A few steps more and I could tell that this was not crying at all. It was categorically different from crying. It was an almost animal sound of pure anguish. I stood transfixed at the back door. Should I knock? Should I turn around and go home? Did I dare disturb whatever tragedy might be unfolding inside?

Before I could decide on the right course of action, the door burst open. Tyler rushed past me and down the stairs. I ran to the edge of the deck and leaned over the railing.

"Tyler, what's going on?"

But he was already in your father's boat, yanking on the engine cord.

"Tyler!"

The motor roared to life. Tyler steered the boat into open water. I rushed into the house. Your father sat on the couch, his arms encircling your mother, who was letting out a series of staccato wheezes as her lungs gathered enough air for the next animal howl. A small, rumpled man twisting a fishing cap in his hands stood before them.

"What happened?" I blurted.

Only the old man looked my way. It was Ike Fenton. He glanced back at your parents and then stepped toward me. I heard him swallow and grind his few remaining teeth. He leaned in close.

"I found Cami."

Beth wailed. A blinding white light flashed in the windows. Thunder cracked and faded into a low grumble.

There would be no fireworks that night.

20

I was already back in my boat when your dad came running down the stairs.

"Stop! Kendra, the lightning!" He grabbed hold of the line. "Get out of the boat!"

"But—"

"Now!" He gripped my upper arm, and I climbed out. "You can't go out in a metal boat in a storm, didn't your grandpa ever teach you that?"

"Tyler's out there in a metal boat right now," I yelled. "Where is he going?"

"He's gone to Ike's. You shouldn't go there, Kendra. You shouldn't see it."

"You can't just leave Tyler out there." Even as I said it, a part of me thought, *Why not?*

A bolt of lightning struck just beyond the western tree line. Your dad's next words were obscured by an angry crack of thunder.

"What?" I shouted.

"I said take the wooden one."

My heart felt like it was imploding. I could not get in that boat.

He was already halfway up the stairs. I stood helpless for a moment before following. We wrestled the boat from its weedy purgatory behind the garage and back down to the water. When I couldn't make myself step into that wooden boat, Robert helped me in and shoved the oars in my direction.

"No motor?" I asked.

"Motors are metal."

The wind whipped my hair across my eyes. "What happened to Cami?"

His face said everything I needed to know. Well, almost everything.

"I should go," he said. "You want me to go?"

Of course I did. I didn't care about what happened to Tyler. Why was I even out here? And yet I heard myself saying, "No. Go up to Beth. I'll bring him back." They couldn't lose both of their children in one day.

He nodded.

I put my back into it and cut through the whitecaps, fighting to keep my course, not knowing why I was making any effort at all. Maybe it was simply the desire to do something, anything, rather than stand impotently in your parents' living room, trying to comfort a woman who could not be comforted.

As I rowed, Robert got smaller and smaller, finally retreating up the stairs and into the pale-yellow cottage. Little waves pressed against the wooden hull and splashed up over the sides. Lightning flashed—closer now—and the crack of thunder was so loud I jumped up in my seat and almost lost hold of the oars. I thought of Andreas's life jacket, which he'd never worn. I wished I had it now. Wished I had him now.

I beached the wooden boat on Ike's frontage a few feet from Tyler's metal one as the first fat drops of rain buried themselves in the sand like missiles. Tyler was just up the beach on his hands and knees. A blue tarp lay half crumpled at his side. My first instinct was to run to him, despite everything, but I was bolted to the ground.

"Tyler!" I thought I shouted it, but he didn't seem to hear. One foot found the will to lift, then the other. "Tyler?"

He sat back on his heels and screamed a string of obscenities at the angry sky, which answered back with a wave of ferocious rain and another crack of thunder.

I was almost beside him now, careful to keep his body in my line of vision to block whatever the tarp had concealed. When he looked at me, his face was unrecognizable. None of the cool, confident swagger. No sneer. No I-get-what-I-want smile.

I tried to say, "What is it?" even though at some level I knew. I inched closer and held my hand out. To help him up? I didn't know. What else was there to do? He gripped it, pulled me down on my knees, and buried his head in my neck, his body heaving and shivering.

Over the slick wet blackness of his hair, I saw everything.

The purple skin where skin was left. The raw, bloated flesh that had been picked at by fish and turtles. The sticks of driftwood that were your exposed bones. The empty holes marking where your twinkling eyes once dared me to smoke cigarettes and swim naked and live each fleeting day to the fullest.

I squeezed my eyes shut. I couldn't breathe. Couldn't think. The insides of my eyelids flashed red for an instant as lightning struck, closer. Thunder galloped through my head.

Tyler pulled away. "This is your fault! She was getting better! And you had to tell everyone in the world! You had no right to do that!"

He kicked a clod of wet sand into my face. I scrambled to my feet and took two steps back.

"Shut up!" I screamed. "She shut *me* out! Don't you get that?

Don't any of you get that? She never believed me. She never returned my calls. She dropped *me*! I endured you for years because I didn't want to lose my best friend. I didn't want to lose your family. And now I wish I'd told them earlier, because I lost them anyway. I wish you *had* drowned." I choked on the last word, then recovered. "This is your fault, Tyler. It's your fault. And you know it."

Tyler clenched his hands into tight fists and released a long, low growl that crescendoed into a yell as he ran into the roiling lake. He ran until he was up to his thighs, then up to his waist, pounding on the water, taking out all of his anger and sorrow on the thing that had ultimately stolen your life away. Then he disappeared under a wave. I watched the spot, watched for his black hair to resurface. But there was nothing but water.

I felt a darkness creeping into the edges of my vision, like a movie scene that would end in just a few seconds. One more shot of your body. One more shot of my face staring at the lake. One more shot of the churning waves. Then nothing. A moment of black and then everything would go on. It would be the next day or a week later. The sky would be clear. And Tyler Rainier would be no more. He'd never be able to hurt me again.

And he'd never have to answer for any of it.

I ran into the water that tried to throw me back to shore as it must have thrown your battered body after the storm lifted you from the cold, spongy silt at the bottom of the lake. I felt around with my hands, floundered, and went down. The swell of the water pushed its way past my lips and into my lungs. I rose up, gasping and choking. Then my leg hit something. I dove under, found Tyler's arm, and wrenched us both back up into the storm. Lightning flashed from cloud to cloud. Thunder cracked. With everything I had left, I dragged Tyler to the beach and threw him onto the sand, where he coughed up a lungful of water.

"Get in the boat," I demanded once I could breathe again. When he didn't move, I kicked my own clod of sand in his face. "Get in the boat!"

He got to his feet and looked at me with such undisguised contempt that I actually braced myself to run from him. Then he pushed past me and made for the boats.

Though I wanted to scrub my mind of what lay in the sand beyond the tarp, I could not leave you exposed. Trembling with fear and adrenaline, I pulled the tarp back into place over your tortured body and secured the corners with rocks. When I turned back to the lake, Tyler was in the aluminum boat.

I ran toward him, waving my hands and shouting. "Not that one!"

No sooner had I yanked him out onto the sand than a thick shaft of lightning connected with the water a few hundred feet away. We locked eyes. All I was sure of beyond the sound of the thunder in my ears was that my heart was still beating.

I snapped out of it first and pushed your shell-shocked brother toward the old wooden rowboat. Together we shoved it into the water and jumped inside. The bottom of the boat sloshed with rainwater.

"Keep your feet up," I commanded, then I took my place at the oars and started to row.

21

I f we were the characters from *Beaches*, who do you think
would be Hillary and who do you think would be CC?"

You posed this question during my sixteenth summer
on Hidden Lake. We were lying on the diving platform your
dad had anchored in deep water, shading our eyes against the
afternoon sun. We had watched your mom's old VHS tape
of the movie two nights earlier when a storm had driven us
inside.

You answered your own question. "I think you'd be Hillary
and I'd be CC."

"You'd be CC? I don't think so."

"Why not?"

"Because . . . you don't sing. And anyway, you have dark
hair like Hillary."

"You don't sing," you said.

"I can sing."

"Better than me? Go on. Sing." You knew I wouldn't.

"You sing," I said.

You immediately belted out the chorus of "Wind beneath My
Wings." Your voice had nothing of the power of Bette Midler's,

but it was fairly on key. I wasn't sure I could do any better, and I wasn't about to try. You sat up on your elbows, a smug smile on your lips. I rolled onto my stomach and dipped my fingers in the water.

"It's not just that, anyway," I said, trying to build my case. "It's like the song says. One gets the attention and the other one—she's beautiful, but people don't really know who she is. I won a writing contest and my name's been in the paper. I've got a whole scrapbook of it."

You scowled. "Yeah, and I bet only one page has anything on it. Anyway, my name was in the paper for the swim team. And you're pretty."

I shrugged, though I hoped you really thought so. I hoped it wasn't just something you said to me to flatter me into submission.

"So," you continued, "you're saying you've got some sort of star quality and everyone adores you?"

"Well, not necess—"

"Are you delusional? You're the most boring person I know. If it weren't for me, you'd never even leave the house." You looked out across the water. "Scott's coming. Let's ask him."

"Oh, like he's seen *Beaches*."

"Let's just ask him."

Scott pulled his boat up a few feet from the diving platform.

"You've seen *Beaches*, right?" you asked before he could even say hello.

He looked at you as though the line of questioning was a trap—which was what it was beginning to feel like to me. "Maybe."

"That's a yes," you said. "So which one of us is Hillary and which one is CC?"

"Huh?"

You motioned to yourself and then to me. "Who's Hillary and who's CC?"

"Oh, man. Don't bring me into this."

"Come on. This isn't hard. Which one of us is smart and quiet and which one is loud and exciting?"

"Easy. Kendra's the smart one and you're the loud one."

You turned your triumphant smile on me. "See?"

I laughed. "You realize he just insulted you, right?" I turned to Scott, sure I could formulate the question to get him to say the right answer. "Which one of us do you think could be famous someday?"

"For what?"

"Anything. Singing, dancing, acting, writing. Anything."

"I don't know," he said, washing his hands of the whole thing. "Cami, you want to go to town?"

You ignored the question and turned on me. "You think I couldn't be famous and you could? For what? Your writing? Look, I've read some of your stuff, and—don't take this the wrong way—it's mind-numbingly dull. There's no point. Nothing happens. People just sit around and say stuff that sounds smart but doesn't really mean anything. I mean, I don't blame you. It's probably hard to find something interesting to write about when nothing's ever happened to you."

"Stuff has happened to me," I mumbled. "Anyway, Robert likes it."

"He's just trying to be nice."

I don't know why you said that. Why you said any of it. If I'd told my school counselor what you said, she would have told me you were just jealous. But what could you possibly be jealous about? Everything about your life was better than mine. You lived in a gorgeous house most of the year—you were sure to show me pictures—and went on amazing trips with your rich family.

You had more friends than I ever would. Each summer you dropped their names more and more. They were tributaries that flowed into the Great River Cami, feeding you, always feeding you. I was a dry creek that, paradoxically, only ran in the summer. Was I even on the map? Did Ashlee or Stacey or Brielle or any of those other girls ever hear my name drip from your lips? Was even a single one of them jealous of what I had with you? Or was I forgotten the moment you left the lake in August?

"I will go to town, Scott," you said pertly. You got into his boat, kissed him deeply, and gave me an aw-poor-baby frown before striking an alluring pose for his benefit.

I fought back tears as you slowly disappeared from view. More and more of our conversations had been ending like that, with stupid little disagreements that, at the time, seemed deeply important. We were constantly poking at each other to see where the tender spots were.

I stayed on the platform another half hour, convincing myself of all the reasons I was CC and wondering if Robert really was just trying to be nice when we talked about my stories. He certainly gave me plenty of critical feedback for someone who was just humoring me. But you'd planted doubt in my mind. If I wasn't any good at it, how could I spend my life doing it? What if I never reached the success your dad had reached? Wouldn't I be wasting my life when I could do something that actually mattered? Or at least something that would get me a boyfriend rather than a mentor?

When I was sure you and Scott must really be gone, I swam back to your dock, wrapped myself in a towel, and let myself into the house. In the study, your dad was pounding away at the typewriter. Disregarding the fact that I was dripping wet, I sat down in the leather chair across from him and did not wait for him to look up.

"What's the point of writing?"

He finished typing the sentence he was in the middle of, hit the carriage return, and looked at me. "What do you mean?"

"You're not helping anyone. You're not doing anything useful or even talking to anyone."

"I'm talking to you right now."

"You know what I mean. How do you justify spending your life behind that desk?"

He tented his fingers and stuck out his bottom lip but said nothing. I let the silence hang there between us. I needed an answer. If I was going to put any more effort into writing, I wanted to know what the point was. I didn't want to waste my life. I didn't want to be Hillary. I didn't want to end up alone and bitter and full of regrets. I wanted to be CC. I wanted adoration. I wanted fame. I wanted fans. But I didn't want my life to end up empty.

"Writing is about making sense of the human condition," he finally said. "It's about communicating truth, which is useful and helpful to people on a far more elemental level than a lot of stuff we think of as necessary to life."

"But nothing you write is real," I said. "You tell stories about made-up people with made-up problems. You're a professional liar."

He smiled. "Oh, Kendra. You know better than that."

He looked back down at the page in the typewriter, and a moment later the sound of the keys clicking, sending the inked hammers to slam another letter into place, was all I could hear. I stalked out of the room and closed the door behind me.

"Where's Cami?" Beth said as I passed the kitchen. She was slicing celery into dozens of little green Cs.

"She went to town with Scott."

"I see." She put down the knife. "Kendra, would you please dry off better before you come into the house?"

"Sorry."

"Are you staying for dinner again?" It wasn't an invitation.

"No. I'm going home."

Beth went back to slicing celery. "Did something happen?"

I scratched a mosquito bite on my elbow, trying to come up with an explanation for our little fight that didn't sound totally petty. "Not really."

She put the knife down again and looked long and hard into my eyes. "Your mother and I used to be friends, you know. We let something get between us, and we never dealt with it. I've always regretted that. You understand what I'm saying?"

I nodded, though I didn't really understand. The words she was saying seemed designed to help you and me make up. But the tone was like she was blaming me for her fight with Jackie.

She slid the little celery pieces into a bowl and started in on the shell of a hard-boiled egg. When she didn't say anything else, I headed home.

Later that night as the fireflies began their dance, you knocked on the cabin door, and I opened it to find a person I hardly recognized. Your beautiful black hair that I had always been so jealous of had been shorn into a boy's cut—practically shaved on the sides, no more than an inch or two long on top—and heavily waxed so it stood up in a carefully messy arrangement. Were it not for the silver bangles on your wrist, I might not have known you.

You came to apologize for being "kind of a jerk earlier." I said it was okay, but nothing could soften the sting of your criticism. I did not ask you about your haircut because I was sure you wanted me to. And I did not forgive you.

190

We sat in the loft and you French-braided my hair and we agreed that we were both CC. But I still thought you were Hillary.

"Anyway," I said, "CC says she'd be nothing without Hillary. That her friend was everything she wished she was. And Hillary was the one that John wanted."

"Yeah, he never really wanted to marry CC." Your fingers paused in my hair. "Who do you think you'll marry?"

"I don't know."

"If you had to marry someone you know right now," you persisted, "who would it be?"

"No one."

"But you have to."

"Um, no I don't."

You pulled my hair too tight. "Don't marry Tyler."

"Ow! What? Why would I ever marry Tyler?"

"Just don't."

"Shut up. I would never marry Tyler. Why would you even say that?"

You tied off the braid with a rubber band but said nothing.

"I know who you would marry," I said. "Scott."

"Nope."

I twisted to look at you. "I thought you really liked Scott."

"He's fun, but I'd never marry him. I'm never marrying anyone."

"Why not?"

You tucked an errant hair behind my ear and looked at me earnestly. "Because when you get married, you give up all your power."

"Pfft. Where'd you hear that?"

"Think about it. As long as you don't give a guy what he wants, you're in control. The minute he thinks it's his right to have it, you don't control a thing. Then you're just there to do his bidding."

I swallowed down the sick feeling in my stomach, thinking of what Tyler expected from me now. "Wait, Scott never—"

"No."

"Then what—"

"I'm just saying. That's what happens. Girls have it, guys want it. And when they get it, there's no getting the worms back in that can. They're in control from there on out."

"You don't seriously believe that. Your parents aren't like that."

"Ew! What my parents do is none of my business. I just know that Scott's never getting any, and neither is anyone else." You stood up and started down the ladder. "I gotta get home. Beth's all up in arms that I went to town without telling her—thanks a lot for that—and she's really not happy about my hair. I don't want her mad about me staying out late too. Later, CC."

"Bye, CC."

Hillary.

22

When I deposited Tyler on the dock the night of the big storm, I briefly considered asking Robert to drive me back home. I knew he would have. But I couldn't ask him to do anything. Not that night. Instead, I bailed some water and maneuvered the old wooden rowboat back out into the storm.

Part of me wanted to go back to Ike's to confirm that what I had seen beneath the blue tarp was real. Maybe it wasn't you at all. Maybe it wasn't even human. Maybe my mind had filled in details that weren't actually there—the scraps of fabric that had once been clothes, the mouthful of metal fillings from a neglected childhood spent in a poor orphanage overseas, the short black hair you'd never grown out, the silver chain and teardrop opal pendant I'd given you the summer after we'd argued about who was Hillary and who was CC. But I couldn't go back. I couldn't face the horrific reality beneath the tarp.

In the middle of the lake, in the middle of the storm, I stopped rowing. I was breathing heavy, heavy, faster, faster, huge quantities of air that should have filled my lungs but only left me gasping for the next breath, like the time I fell out of the willow tree and got the wind knocked out of me. Every muscle shuddered. My guts were full of rocks. Already veiled in sheets of gray rain, the wooded shores of Hidden Lake seemed to recede until the monstrous water was all there was, sucking hungrily at the little wooden boat.

I don't remember getting to shore or going into the cabin or sitting down on the scratchy plaid couch in my waterlogged clothes. In fact, my only clear memory of the long black night is the exhausting dance between unrestrained crying and numb silence.

The next morning, I woke tangled in my sheets and settled into a new reality. One where I'd never have a chance to talk to you ever again, where we'd never be able to clear the air and start over. One where there was no longer a future, only a past. With nothing else to do, I started searching out that past, rummaging through scraps of notes and shells and seagull feathers until I found a short stack of photos in the bottom right-hand drawer of my desk.

People put too much stock in photographs. The camera *does* lie. Frequently. Because the people being photographed are lying. They lie with their smiles, with arms draped around each other, with sunglasses muzzling what their eyes would otherwise say. I didn't have a lot of photos of our time at Hidden Lake. We were too busy living life to record it. But I did have a few.

There was nothing special about any of the photos, beyond the fact that they were developed from actual film and had not been self-consciously posed or overlaid with a filter to make us all more attractive than we might otherwise be. A picture of you burying me in the sand. One of us both doing backbends on the beach. A few from the summer your dad got us that disposable underwater camera. A photo I took of Tyler the first year he was here, which I'd had on the wall near my bed until I couldn't stand to look at him anymore. One of Tyler and Scott trying to look big and muscular, standing up in the old wooden rowboat. One of you squinting into the sunny middle distance, unaware that I was taking your picture to finish up a roll of film.

I flipped through our lives together in less than two minutes, stopping on the last photo I remember being taken of us. We are on your dock. Your hair is still as short as a boy's so that your scalp could be seen on the sides. The necklace I gave you reflects a glint of sunlight at your throat. On your left wrist are the silver bangles you never took off, the ones I had now not taken off in weeks. Your fingers are laced in mine. The cottage glows yellow over our shoulders. Just in front of it and out of focus are two sets of male legs. One set belonged to Tyler, but the other did not belong to Scott. He was in the water taking the picture. It took me a moment to remember the other guy's name.

There were only two weeks left of vacation when Tyler finally appeared at the cottage that summer. Newly graduated from Stanford, he was even more smug and self-confident than usual and had brought his equally cocky roommate, Baz, along with him. Baz wasted no time in hitting on me—trying to get me to laugh at lame jokes, sitting by me every chance he got, leering at me in my swimsuit, taking every opportunity to brush my arm when there was plenty of room to get past without touching. It was like Tyler had brought a far less subtle clone along with him.

This behavior abruptly ended on day three when Baz became sulky and reserved and Tyler resumed his role as my malevolent shadow, making no secret of the fact that he considered me to be his rightful territory. The next day Baz turned his charm in your direction, much to Scott's displeasure and your total indifference.

After nearly a week of this, you and I were painting each other's nails in the loft in my cabin, the only place we could truly get away from the boys. On the floor beside my bed, you held my left hand and drew the polish-laden brush down the length of one fingernail.

"What do you think of Baz?" you said.

"Pretty hot. And pretty full of himself."

"Who's not?"

"Scott," I said. "He's good-looking, but he's not full of himself."

"Oh, yeah. Of course not," you said. "He's just a guy."

"What does that mean?"

Your bracelets jingled as you dipped the brush and moved to my pinky. "Well, what does he have to be full of himself about? I mean, he's not even in college. He's working some construction job and only getting a couple weeks off this summer. Baz has met Kevin Spacey."

"So?" I said. "You think too much about guys. I know that's the only reason you're going to California for school. You think there's more hot guys there than in Michigan."

You scoffed and motioned for my other hand. "At least I'm not a big lesbo like you."

I pulled my hand away. "Excuse me?"

"Tyler told me all about it. It's no big deal. I mean, whatever. Though you could have told me."

"I'm not a lesbian."

You shrugged. "Like I said, it wouldn't matter to me if you were. But as your best friend, don't you think I ought to know something like that? That's a big secret to keep."

"But I'm *not* a lesbian. And I can't believe Tyler would have the gall to make up that kind of story after . . ."

You stopped polishing. "After what?"

"Nothing."

"Yeah, right, nothing. After what?"

I shushed you. You were always so loud. "You know you can hear everything in this place."

"What happened with Tyler?" you whispered. "So you're not a lesbian, fine, I believe you. But only if you tell me what happened with Tyler."

I rolled my eyes and shook my unpolished hand at you to get you back on task, to make you look at my hand instead of my face.

"Fine." We were going away to college in mere days. I had nothing to lose now, right?

You started on my thumb. Finger by finger, I quietly spilled the secrets I'd been storing up for years. His furtive touches beneath the dinner table, his body pressing down on mine in the shallows, his hand up my shirt in the truck bed, his forced kiss in the tent, and finally his conquest in the wooden rowboat.

I didn't tell you how, in the summers after Tyler had finally gotten what he wanted in the boat, I'd let him have it again, time after time. How he'd whisper flatteries and veiled threats. How he'd wear me down, get me alone, and push until I gave in at least once every summer. I didn't tell you any of that. I would never tell you. I would never tell anyone.

When I ran out of things to say, your reaction surprised me. Mostly because you didn't seem surprised at all. You just kept blowing on my nails.

"He said you posed for him to draw because you were a lesbian and you weren't interested in him."

"*Shhh.*"

"Stop shushing me!"

"He put something in my lemonade, I know he did," I whispered severely, "and took my clothes off when I could barely move. He's a predator, plain and simple."

You stopped blowing for a moment and looked me straight in the eye. "If he was doing all those things, why didn't you say something? Why didn't you do something? Why didn't you call the cops?"

"Because he was your brother! You think we could have been friends after that?"

You were silent a moment, considering. "Look, I know you want to make your life seem more exciting, but you can't do it by throwing accusations around about people. If rumors got started about that kind of thing, it could seriously jack up someone's life."

I was trying to hold it together. "Oh, you mean like rumors about someone being a lesbian? I *cannot* believe you think I'm making this up. What kind of person just makes up stories like that?"

"I don't know, maybe a writer? Which is what you like to claim to be. But you're not. And you never will be. So you may as well stop trying and wasting all of my dad's time."

I tightened the top of the nail polish and threw it at your chest. "What is wrong with you? Get out. Go home. And don't bother saying goodbye when you leave the lake."

You quickly gathered your beauty supplies up in your bag and started down the ladder, turning just enough so I could see one last gesture from you. Grandpa came into the cabin just as you stomped out. I heard him say something to you, but I didn't hear your voice in return. A moment later he was shuffling around beneath the ladder.

"Kendra, you up there?"

I worked to hide the tears in my voice. "Yeah."

"Everything okay?"

"Yeah."

"Cami seemed upset."

I said nothing.

"Not my business, of course," he continued, "but you only have a week left. Think hard about how you want to leave things."

First Beth, now Grandpa. But neither of them understood. They didn't see the way you tore me down every chance you got. The way you'd changed. The way you'd chosen Scott over me. The way you'd chosen your rotten brother over me. He wasn't even your real brother. You'd known me longer than you'd known him.

In the days following, I waited for you to show up at my door, if not to apologize, then at least to pretend nothing had happened so we could go on as before. But you didn't. Finally, on the last day of summer vacation, I took the boat over to your cottage. Robert sat on the deck with a cigar in his mouth and a distant look in his eyes as Beth noisily packed up the house inside.

"Kendra," he said when he noticed me, "haven't seen you all week. You ready for school?"

"I guess so."

"Listen, you need any ins there, you let me know. I know a lot of people."

"Thanks, Mr. Rainier. Is Cami in the house?"

"Oh, yeah. Sorry. Go on. I won't keep you."

I opened your bedroom door without knocking, and you looked up, ready for a fight.

"Oh, it's you," you said. "Come to apologize?"

"I came to say goodbye."

"I thought you told me not to bother."

"I didn't think that was the best way to leave things."

You just stared.

"Look, I know you think I'm lying about Tyler. I don't care.

It doesn't matter. You can believe whatever you want about him or anyone else. But it seems dumb to lose your friendship over it. I don't want to get up to the lake next summer and have you mad at me."

Your expression softened slightly. "I don't either."

"Fine."

I turned to go, but you hopped off the bed. "Wait. You haven't told anyone else all that stuff, have you?"

"No."

"And you're not going to."

I frowned. "No."

"Good."

You smiled and pulled me into an intense hug, the kind of hug you used to give me when we were younger, every time we saw each other in the morning and every time we had to say good night. I squeezed you back, but there was no feeling in it. Had you just made me promise not to tell anyone because you didn't want me spreading lies about your brother? Or because you believed me but you didn't want him to get in trouble?

As you pulled away, your smile faded. You looked into my eyes for a long time. Too long. I glanced away.

You took a step back. "See you next summer."

But that was the last time I would see you—until I saw you on Ike's beach.

23

The day after our awkward goodbye, I packed my bags into Grandpa's old truck and settled in for the two-hour drive to the McDonald's near the Soaring Eagle Casino off M-20, where we would eat a late breakfast of Egg McMuffins while we waited for Jackie to pick me up. She usually shuffled in around the time they stopped serving breakfast, still groggy from the night before, which was always her last hurrah with her girlfriends at the casino before she had to act like a responsible adult again. I'd hug Grandpa and thank him "for putting up with me," as Jackie invariably instructed, then I'd hunker down in the car and watch them stand about four feet away from each other and exchange a few words before they parted ways. Grandpa would go back up to the lake until deer season, then move back downstate after the hunt. Jackie and I would drive another hour south to our tiny gray house in Lansing and order a pizza for dinner.

This time, Jackie was late. We ate our McMuffins. Grandpa sipped his coffee. I sucked down my orange juice. I threw away the greasy wrappers and napkins. Then I threw away our cups.

Grandpa thumbed through a newspaper that had been left on the table next to us. I read the comics, twice. Eleven o'clock rolled around. Eleven thirty. I tried to make myself care about the rest of the newspaper.

"Should we call the casino? Or the police?" I finally asked.

Grandpa looked at the clock. "Let's give her another twenty minutes or so."

I sighed and sank back into my seat. "Why is she like this?"

"Everyone's late sometimes."

"But why is she *like* this?" I persisted. "She's totally selfish. All the time. She's had all summer to screw around. She can't just be on time to pick me up?"

Grandpa said nothing.

"Is that the way you raised her?" I said, trying to get a rise out of my eternally even-keeled grandfather.

He looked at me not unkindly. Then he got up and went to the counter. He came back with some fries and a tiny paper cup of ketchup. I knew it was just to keep my mouth busy, but I was grateful nonetheless.

Jackie finally rolled into the parking lot at 12:08 p.m. I didn't wait for her to come in and order her standard large Diet Coke for the road. I met her in the middle of the parking lot, and suddenly I was the mom. "We've been waiting for hours."

She tried to walk past me, but I shifted in front of her.

"Don't you have any respect for other people's time? Grandpa's been stuck here reading the same newspaper since before ten o'clock."

"Then let him tell me about it," she said.

A car honked at us to get out of the way. I followed her into the restaurant. Grandpa smiled and waved as she walked in with me on her heels.

"Everything's fine," she said to him without being asked.

"Sorry to keep you waiting." She stood at the counter and ordered her drink.

Grandpa put his hand on my shoulder and said in a quiet voice, "Don't let it ruin your day. We had a good summer, didn't we?"

Did we? I know he did. Every summer was good for him. But had I? Tyler and Baz jostling for position. You accusing me of lying about Tyler and telling me I would never be a writer. Grandpa and Beth harping on me to make up with you without having the first clue what I was upset about, as though there were no legitimate reason to stay angry at someone. I could think of lots of reasons.

I thought of Beth's comment about how she and Jackie used to be best friends. What had happened between them? Whatever it was, it had to be Jackie's fault. Beth was perfect, no matter how coolly she treated me. And now that I thought about it, maybe that was Jackie's fault too.

I put my bags into the car, gave Grandpa a hug, and slumped in the passenger seat to watch the weirdly distant conversation I knew was coming. Only this time, after the first few words were spoken, Grandpa closed the distance between himself and his daughter. I couldn't roll down the window because the car wasn't running, so I opened the door so I could hear what they were saying. But they were too far away and too quiet.

A moment later they both turned their backs to me, but not before I saw Grandpa pull out his wallet. So that's what this was. Jackie had probably lost big at the casino, and now her daddy was going to have to bail her out. A grown woman. Pathetic. I couldn't even look at her when she got into the car.

Ten minutes down the road, I couldn't hold it in any longer. I hated confrontation, but right then I hated Jackie more.

"That must be humbling."

She didn't take her eyes off the road. "What?"

"Asking your dad for money when you're almost forty."

"Mind your own business, Kendra. Don't pretend to know what's going on in other people's lives. Because I can guarantee you have no idea."

She kept looking straight ahead, the only sound the whir of the tires on the road and the low murmuring of a talk radio station that was mostly static. I turned the radio off.

"So tell me, then. What don't I know?"

"Kendra," she warned.

"Sorry. That's too vague. How could you possibly know where to start? Here, I'll make it easier for you. What did you do to Beth Rainier?"

She finally glanced my way. "What is with you today?"

"Come on. I know you used to be best friends. I know something happened. I just want to know what. Tell me one thing— one thing!—about you. Tell me why you won't go to the lake anymore. Tell me why no one will let me be mad at Cami, why everyone insists we make up the second we have a disagreement. Tell me why Beth has never liked me. Tell me what happened with you and Beth that was so terrible you haven't spoken since you were eighteen."

"Kendra, my life is none of your business. You want permission to be mad at your friend? Do it. Be mad. Whatever she did to you, don't forgive her. I don't care. It doesn't matter. You'll never be good enough for them anyway."

"What does that mean?"

She lifted a hand from the wheel and flung it out to the side in a gesture of giving up. "Just believe me when I say I'm not the only person who can hold a grudge, okay? Beth does a pretty bang-up job herself."

I didn't know what to say to that. It occurred to me that I

had indeed taken Beth's side when I had zero knowledge of the situation. I'd taken Beth's side just like you had taken Tyler's side. But there was something my mother was not telling me. That was when I began to wonder if there was something you weren't telling me either.

24

"Can I come in?"

It was late in the afternoon on July 5th that your father stood on the other side of my screen door waiting for permission to enter. I was sitting on the couch, staring at nothing, coffee table strewn with the photos that could not tell me what had happened to you. I didn't have the energy to voice even such a simple word as *yes* or *no*. He came in anyway.

He walked slowly and sat down heavily on the still-damp cushion next to where I was hunched, feet tucked up underneath my body.

"Get any sleep last night?" he asked. When I didn't answer, he said, "Me neither."

I knew I should say something, but I couldn't form a clear, sensible sentence in my mind. I thought of the empty and unhelpful things people had said to me at Grandpa's funeral. It would have been better if they'd said nothing at all, if they had simply made eye contact and nodded, affirming that my unarticulated feelings of devastation were real and true and right. They should have known that words couldn't fix anything.

Robert was turning something over and over in his hands.

"What's that?" I finally managed.

He looked at the object as though to remind himself of what he carried. "This is for you. This is the first picture I ever took of you and Cami the year we brought her home. I thought you would want to have it." He motioned to the table littered with small, rectangular windows into the past. "I see we had the same idea today."

I took the photo from him gingerly, as though it might cut me, and stared into a lost summer of pleasant surprises and easy laughter. A summer with no fear, no sadness. There it was—perfect and innocent and incorruptible. Robert had taken the photo from a few yards out in the lake. You and I sat on the end of your dock, toes drawing shapes in the water, the cottage that same soft-focus yellow glow in the background. One more artifact to add to my collection, even if it could not add to my understanding.

God must have known even then that the girl on the right would end up decomposing in the very lake her toes tickled. He must know even now how old I would live to be, and whether I would ever recover from what I saw last night. If I would ever forget your empty eye sockets.

"Thank you," I said.

Robert ran the back of his hand under his nose. "They came and got her last night."

The photograph blurred and swam in my vision. "What happened?"

He sat back. "We don't know for sure yet. They're doing an autopsy. That might be able to tell them something about when she died. I don't know if they'll be able to tell us if it was an accident."

I caught his meaning. "She was a great swimmer."

Robert nodded. "Yeah. She was," he said thickly.

"Did Tyler tell you Ike saw her in March?"

He nodded again. "You got anything to drink around here?"

"No, sorry. Not like what you want. I can make some coffee."

"That's okay. I've got plenty at home. Out of gin, though." He stood up. "I'll leave your boat and take the wooden one back."

I stood with effort. "I have your book Andreas borrowed." I retrieved the German edition of *Blessed Fool* from the desk in Grandpa's bedroom.

"He's gone then?"

"He left last week."

"I'm sorry."

I gave an unconvincing shrug.

"Did he like the book?"

"He did. Said it helped him a bit with mine."

Robert took the book from me and eyed the cover. "It's hard to believe this was nearly twenty-five years ago. It was published just a couple years after you were born."

"I just reread it, you know."

A tentative smile broke out on his face, chasing away some of the sorrow that had been lodged there. "Did you? And what did you think this time?"

"I liked it."

He waited for more.

"I mean, it ticked me off. But I liked it."

"What ticked you off?"

"Misty mostly."

The smile broadened. "She ticked me off too."

I struggled for the next words. "Listen, I hate it when people ask me this, but . . . how much of it really happened?"

"You mean what's fiction and what's fact."

"I know it's ridiculous to ask."

"And you know what the answer is, don't you?"

"Probably the same answer I give."

"Probably."

He headed for the door.

"Robert?"

He turned back, eyebrows raised expectantly.

"Are you Arthur?"

Suddenly he looked sad and old and broken. His eyes took on a strange liquid quality, like when a glass has been filled just beyond the brim. He wavered a moment, lips fighting to form the words. "Are you Jess?"

He had read it. He had read my book.

We stared at each other for one heavy moment, neither of us expecting an answer because we already knew. He knew without a doubt that his adopted son had done something terrible to me. And I knew that the man standing in the doorway was my father.

25

The big storm had broken summer's relentless heat. As Robert and Beth awaited the outcome of your autopsy and cremated your remains and planned the memorial service downstate, the weather at Hidden Lake changed from one hour to the next. Cold, foggy dawns gave way to sunny mornings, which were chased away by afternoon thunderstorms and nights without sunsets.

The sun shone now in a near-cloudless sky as I stepped off the sidewalk into the parking lot of Redeemer Lutheran Church in Battle Creek. I had just watched your family file out of the sanctuary as the closing hymn pealed from the organ. Robert with his hand at Beth's back, Tyler close behind, a grandmother I had met a time or two at the cottage, a smattering of aunts, uncles, and cousins. Family that, I now realized, I might rightly claim as my own, that I'd always known about but never known.

A few carloads of Hidden Lake families had made the four-hour drive south to pay their respects, and now some were piling back into vans and trucks to reverse the trip before the next predicted storm hit. Others were headed to your house for a catered reception that would undoubtedly be fancier than the luncheon in the church basement they'd attended just four months ago when my grandfather died. Despite an offer to carpool with Scott Masters and his parents, I'd opted to come alone. I didn't want to be at the mercy of someone else's schedule and have to sit in a cramped back seat for hours on end as people speculated about your last days while spouting clichés and platitudes about death and life. I didn't want to talk to anyone.

I followed the train of cars down tree-lined streets and parked down the road from the sprawling brick Victorian house I'd seen in pictures but never in person. The wide front porch was sprinkled with finely dressed people, some sucking down cigarettes, their smoke wafting into the house through the open door. I walked in far enough to hit a patch of fresh air. Smells of hors d'oeuvres—chicken satay and sweet-and-sour meatballs and warm brie—mixed with coffee and beer and perfume. The smells of a party, but none of the sounds. People spoke in hushed tones if they spoke at all.

Every wall in the house was graced with one of Beth's detailed paintings of pores and fingerprints, bacteria and follicles. Scaly dry skin like desert rock formations. Sweat glands like rotting flesh. I fought against the memory of your face under the tarp and weaved my way through the crowd into the kitchen, where women moved at a brisk pace, plating fruit kabobs and crackers spread with goat cheese and chutney. The thought of food turned my stomach. I found a narrow staircase at the back of the house and went up, not caring where it led as long as it led away. I put my ear against the heavy oak door at the top and opened it when I heard nothing on the other side.

I found myself in a marble-tiled bathroom that housed a large claw-foot tub. Through another door was your parents' elaborate master bedroom, complete with its own sitting area and fireplace and more Beth Rainier originals on the tastefully cream-colored walls. I tiptoed out to the hall and peeked into what had to be Tyler's room. Compared to the master bedroom, it was sparse and peaceful. A dark gray comforter covered a platform bed with no headboard. The modern-style black desk sported a functional black lamp and a single potted succulent—fake. No skin diseases in here. And no Tyler Rainier originals either, despite all the art classes.

A peek into the closet revealed no clothes—of course, Tyler had long been on his own three time zones away—but there were a number of identical white boxes stacked on the highest shelf. My fingers itched to look through them, but my conscience prompted me to close the closet door. Looking in a room when the door was open was one thing. Looking in a closed box in a closet was another.

I left Tyler's room and walked a few paces down the hall. The next door was closed but for a crack that light poured through. I peeked through the opening to see Scott Masters sitting on what had to be your bed. He was flipping slowly through a large book.

"Hey, Scott," I said gently.

He looked up and offered me a sad smile. "Hey, Kendra."

In the eight years since I'd seen him, Scott had put on a few pounds around the middle and grown a beard. Seeing him in a suit today rather than swim trunks or cargo shorts was slightly surreal.

"I had to get out of there," he said. "All those people."

"Yeah." I looked around a room as tightly packed with stuff as Tyler's had been empty. Too much furniture, too many knick-knacks on the shelves, too many posters on the walls. "It looks like she still lives here."

"I think she ended up back home a lot," he said without looking up from the album in his lap. "Between schools."

I had forgotten that you didn't stay at Berkeley like you'd

always planned. That in fact, you had left five different schools after a semester or two, either flunking out or just drifting on to some new place with new people. Robert had emailed me once that he thought you might end up at Michigan State, just down the road from where I grew up. But I never saw you in town, and when I asked if you were there, he told me you'd changed your mind. I wondered at the time if I was the reason for that, if you just didn't want to risk running into me.

"She showed me a photo of this house once," I said. "I was always so jealous of this place. I was too embarrassed to send her a picture of mine."

"What's wrong with your house?"

"Mom and I just lived in a dinky little two-bedroom with a weedy yard in kind of a crappy part of town. It was all she could afford, being a single mom without a college degree. Sure couldn't compare to this place."

I sat down on the bed and leaned over the photo album as Scott turned the pages backward, slowly going back in time, photo by photo. Christmas morning, first day of school, birthday parties, candid family shots.

"Tyler isn't in any of these," I said.

"I think this is from before Tyler." He turned another page and pointed. "This must be the first picture of her in America. The ones before it are from Korea." He turned the page. "See, here she is with Beth and Robert at the airport. And here's the orphanage." He turned another page and pointed to a photo of perhaps a dozen young girls lined up in front of metal beds. "Can you tell which one is her?"

I scanned the faces in the photograph. The girls were rigid, standing at attention like little soldiers. All except one, who stood with one hip out of joint. "That's her. Has to be."

Scott smiled. "I bet you're right."

I considered the man next to me. Tall, handsome, friendly, successful. Single. You guys had been a summer fling for at least five years. For all I knew, when I stopped coming up to the lake, you and Scott just kept going. I always thought you'd marry Scott, no matter what you said. A girl could certainly do worse. And yet, here he was and you were in an urn.

I swallowed the knot that was forming in my throat. "I wish you and Cami had stayed together. None of this would have happened."

He let the album rest on his thighs. "It would never have worked."

"Why not? You were good together."

He looked at me as though I had just asked him what color the sky was.

"I mean, from where I stood it looked good."

"We were never really together," he said. "Not like you think. I wanted it to be more. But she wasn't really interested, you know?"

I thought of your long-ago comments about control and power and wondered how far Scott had pushed, how far you'd let him go. "Well, you could've fooled me," I said.

"Me too, and she did for a while. Eventually I realized I was just kind of a guard dog for her."

"A guard dog? You mean a lap dog?"

"No." Scott untied his shoes and shifted his feet around inside them. "Sorry. These things are killing me."

I took my own shoes off, and your bangles jingled on my wrist. "What about these? She never took them off from the moment you gave them to her."

"I thought those were hers," he said. "I'm glad you have them now. Anyway, it just wasn't meant to be. I think Tyler kind of messed her up. She never trusted guys after that."

The bottom dropped out of my stomach.

"But I guess I don't have to tell you that sort of thing, huh?" he continued. "Great book, by the way. Think they'll make it into a movie?"

I tried to catch my breath. "I don't know."

"They should. It's very cinematic. They could get that red-headed kid from the Harry Potter movies to play Blake. Break him out into a different kind of role, you know?"

I nodded. "Sure."

"I better get back downstairs," Scott said, sliding the open photo album onto my lap. "My dad's probably wondering where I am." He stood up, shoes still untied, and gave me a chaste peck on the cheek. "Maybe I'll see you on the lake. I've been so busy working I haven't had much time for it. But maybe soon. Once the busy season is over."

I nodded again, and he walked out to the hall, shutting the door behind him.

I stared down at the picture of all those little Korean girls, at the one at the end with her hip out of joint. And like the weight of all the stones I'd ever gathered pressing on my chest, I suddenly saw that I was not the only one keeping a secret all those years. Who wished she could tell someone. Someone who would understand. Someone who would still love her no matter what.

And then I realized, you had told someone. You had told Scott.

Not me.

I flipped the next page, back to the time before you. I flipped through vacations Robert and Beth had taken, photos of Robert's first box of *Blessed Fool* arriving in the mail, a photo of him signing that first book contract, photos of Beth and Robert's wedding, until I got to the first page of the massive album, which held a single photo centered on the page. A young Robert sitting on my grandfather's plaid couch, holding a baby.

I peeled back the plastic page cover, got a fingernail under the bottom corner of the photo, and gently lifted it from the sticky album page. Written on the back in blue pen in Robert Rainier's unmistakable hand were three words.

My best mistake

It was me. It had to be me. I was his mistake.

I shut the album and put it aside, then stared at the photo in my hand. Where was Jackie? Why wasn't my mother sitting beside my father, arm around him, smiling for the camera? Was she the one taking the picture? Or had my grandfather taken it? Did my grandfather know that Robert was my father? Why had no one told me? Why hadn't Robert? There had been ample opportunities over the years.

I stood up and floated slowly around your room, taking in every vacation snapshot, every necklace, every eye shadow, every souvenir you'd picked up along the way. I ran my fingers over the trendy clothes stuffed into your closet. I should have had all of this. Robert was my father. My real father. Yet two adopted children had laid claim to my childhood, my house, my identity, my inheritance. And what had I gotten? A mother who resented me for existing and a breathtaking financial burden in the form of student loans to get me through college, while you wasted every dollar Robert had invested in your unfinished education.

I thought of all the money flowing through every inch of this house, of my unpaid bills at home, of my unfinished book that was keeping me from paying them. It wasn't fair. It wasn't fair that you had all of this. It should have been mine. Your life should have been mine.

I tamped down the tears that were threatening to leak out and put the photo into my purse. I had to get out of this room, out of this house. I had to get back to the cabin. I reached for the doorknob, but someone was already turning it from the other side. I stepped back as the door swung open, revealing Tyler, collar unbuttoned under his loosened tie. He looked just as surprised to see me as I was to see him.

"What are you doing up here?" he said.

I tried to slide past him into the hall, but he blocked my escape. I let my hands drop to my sides and tried to focus my mind and my body on just standing still rather than running straight through him.

"What's wrong with you?" I practically shouted.

"What?"

"What's wrong with you? What happened to you?"

Tyler pushed his way into the room and shut the door. "Calm down."

"Something had to have happened to you," I continued at the same volume. "No one does what you did. No one acts the way you did. A normal teenage boy doesn't assault his sister or her friends. So what was it? And don't tell me you don't know why you did those things. What happened to you?"

With every sentence I uttered, Tyler's face hardened a little more until he looked like he was trying to decide whether to answer me or slap me across the face. Then he turned abruptly and left the room. Down the hall a door slammed, a lock clicked, a wall was punched.

Adrenaline raced through my body like an electric charge. I hurried down the main stairs and out the front door. I was shaking so violently I could hardly open my car door. I sat down inside, pounded the steering wheel, and screamed.

Everything was falling apart. Just when I should be happy—watching my dreams coming true, fulfilling my potential, starting my career—every strand of my life seemed to be unraveling.

Whatever chance I might have had to reconcile with you was gone. The kind and considerate man I had started falling for in spite of myself was gone. I would never finish my book on time, and even if I did, it would be half-baked and terrible and everyone would know that my first novel had been a fluke. I'd end up alone and bitter and forgotten. Like Jackie. And the worst of it was, I couldn't stop thinking about how all of this was affecting me. There was no room in my thoughts for your family's brokenness or yours. Only my own.

I pulled the photo out of my purse and stared at it through tears. Then I pulled myself together and opened up my phone's GPS app.

"Take me to Jackie's," I said.

"Okay," the soothing voice crooned. "Let's go."

26

The look on my mother's face as she opened her front door wasn't exactly surprised. More like disappointed. Cheeks slack, a single wrinkle splitting the space between her perfectly plucked eyebrows. She looked older than she did even four months ago at her father's funeral, which wasn't really old at all. Maybe she was just tired.

I spoke first to relieve her of having to lie about how nice it was to see me on her doorstep. "I need to talk to you about something."

She set her mouth in a line. "I wish you'd called first. I'm on my way to Pontiac in a few minutes to sign the final papers on Grandpa's house."

For a moment I lost the train of thought I'd been following since I'd gotten on the highway. "You sold his house?"

"Of course I did. No one was living in it, the market's been better. I can certainly use the money."

She lingered on that last word a little longer than the rest. I knew she thought that having a book published had made me rich. Everyone thought that. I didn't have the time or the energy to set her straight right then.

"I'm sure you can spare five minutes."

She took a step back from the doorway. "Why didn't you call?"

"I was already downstate. For Cami's funeral."

She sat on the couch. "Yes, I heard about that."

"I'm a little surprised you weren't there," I said as I perched on the very edge of a chair.

But I wasn't surprised at all. Jackie had never even met you. You only lived an hour away during the school year, and she'd never suggested us having a sleepover. When you told me to ask her and I said I did and she said no, I was lying. I never asked. I didn't need to. She'd always refused to talk about anything or anyone associated with Hidden Lake. Now I was finally putting the pieces together of why. She didn't want to have to face her past with Robert. Just like I hadn't wanted to face mine with Tyler until I just couldn't avoid it any longer. Maybe you had felt the same.

"I never knew Cami," Jackie said.

"She was your daughter's best friend. You'd think that might count for something. More than that, she was your daughter's sister, wasn't she?"

The wrinkle between her eyebrows deepened. "What are you talking about?"

I pulled the photo from my purse and held it out to her. "Why was I never told that Robert Rainier is my father?"

Jackie took the photo and pursed her lips. "Who told you such a thing?"

A flicker of doubt flashed in my mind. What if I was wrong? Robert had never actually said it. What if the baby in that picture was someone else?

Jackie regarded me with a calculating stare. Then all at once her face softened, the wrinkle disappeared, and I knew I'd guessed right.

"It seemed like things would be simpler that way," she said. "Anyway, Beth insisted."

That was it, then. The unforgivable sin that had driven her and Beth apart and the reason Beth had never liked me. Jackie had slept with her boyfriend.

"Did Grandpa know?"

"Yes."

"So I'm the only one no one thought to tell?"

She handed the photo to me and leaned back against the couch.

"How did it happen?"

The wrinkle was back. "Oh, Kendra, I don't have time to get into this right now."

"Get into what? All I want to know is what happened. You owe me that. I'm through minding my own business. And anyway, this is my business."

"What happened was that we were stupid kids who made a mistake and you were the consequence. He pushed things too far. I got pregnant. End of story."

I frowned. "That's not what happened in *Blessed Fool*."

"That's fiction. I would have thought you of all people would be able to tell the difference. It's not like the stuff in your book really happened."

"Yeah, it did."

Jackie's prickly demeanor changed in an instant to something that resembled maternal care. "What?"

"Not all of it," I said. "Not exactly as I wrote it, but it happened."

"Who?" She barely got the word out.

"Cami's brother, Tyler."

She covered her mouth.

I squeezed my eyes shut and let out a heavy sigh. "My brother."

"No," she said. It wasn't a leading sort of *no*, not a cinematic, gaspy type of *no* that meant the character was taken aback by the enormity of what was just said. It was simply *no*. A short, declarative sign of disagreement. *No, Kendra, you are incorrect about your experience.* Just like the letter.

I'd never considered that Disappointed Reader might be her.

But that wasn't the point at this moment. The point was that I was tired of other people telling me about my own life. Of other people determining the veracity of my words and the validity of my feelings.

"Look," I said slowly, forcefully, "all fiction is based in reality. That's why we read it. That's why we write it. To process reality. To deal with all the crap that happens to us."

She looked about to jump in, but I barreled on.

"I made a quiet Korean guy named Tyler into a loud redheaded guy named Blake, but it's the same guy. I've told myself—I've told other people—that it's not, that one was just a jumping-off point for the other, but that's a lie I have to stop telling. And I think Robert did the same thing with Misty and Arthur and all the rest. I think you were just a really terrible person for a while there when you were younger, and you don't want to own up to it and ask the people you hurt to forgive you."

She took a slow breath. "And I suppose you've worked it all out with Tyler? Best friends now?"

"No, obviously," I said. "It's complicated. But I do want to get past it—so it doesn't define the rest of my life, so he doesn't get the last word."

Jackie was quiet a moment. She looked at her watch.

I stood up. "I know you need to go. So do I. I just wanted to come here and tell you I know. And it's going to take some time to work through this."

Jackie stood and shouldered her purse. "That's rather dramatic. What is there to work through?"

"Seriously? My dad has been there all the time. All the time I needed one."

"And I bet he treated you just like a father, didn't he? I seem to remember you thanking him rather extensively in your book. I don't remember reading my name in there."

I had no answer for that. She was right.

"Don't worry about it," she said. "I didn't expect any accolades. But don't pretend things are worse than they really are."

"Don't tell me how to feel about this. It's more than that. Cami had the childhood I should have had."

"A lot of good it did her."

"Don't. She was dealing with other stuff. Lots of other stuff."

Jackie screwed up her face. "Three months out of the year you had the exact same childhood up on the lake. Was the time you were with me so terrible?"

I slipped the photo of me and Robert back into my purse. "That's a long conversation." I started toward the front door at a clip. Then I stopped. This summer was about getting answers, not getting the last word. "Maybe you could come up to the lake before the summer's over and we could talk about it."

She looked away. "Can you get texts up there?"

"No. Call the cabin. Or just show up. The door's always open, you know."

We walked to the front door and stood awkwardly at the threshold for a moment. I waited for my mother to hug me, to be a real mother. A good mother. A mother who would cancel her plans and make a pot of tea and invite me to stay with her for a while. But she only put a hand on my arm and said, "I'm sorry that happened to you. I wish I had known."

I nodded, then we walked down the steps and split off to our cars.

"You know that's why there's no door on Grandpa's bedroom,"

she said suddenly. "That's where Robert and I were—locked behind that door. The next day your grandmother took it off its hinges and threw it in the bonfire. She made the curtain while it burned."

A smile spread across my face. "I knew there had to be a story there."

We got into our cars and headed different directions: Jackie to sign away her childhood home, me to get back to work on my book. As the flat cornfields and wind farms of mid-Michigan rippled into the forest-draped hills of the north, I felt my remaining energy reserves draining away. It had been a long and emotional day, and all I wanted to do was crawl into bed and sleep for a week.

I was twice startled back to full wakefulness by the rumble strips on the edge of the highway. Twenty minutes from the cabin, the predicted rain hit like buckets of rocks being dumped on the roof of my car, and I could hardly see the road ahead. I pulled up as close to the cabin door as possible and made a dash through the pelting rain. Inside, I peeled off my soaked cardigan and kicked off my heels.

"There you are."

If the voice had been almost anyone else's, I might have jumped back and screamed. Instead, it was the most welcome sound I could imagine. I looked at the man standing by the stone fireplace, his wavy dark hair only a little less damp than mine, and feared that I was seeing things, that in a moment he would disappear.

"The door was unlocked," he said, "as you said it would be."

I gave my head a little shake. "Of course. That's fine. You're a pleasant surprise on a really bad day."

Concern was written large across Andreas's face. "I heard. Robert called me."

"Is that why you're here? Or was there something you missed . . . in the translation?"

"The translation is fine." He took a step toward me. Thunder rumbled lazily in the west. "I thought you might not want to be alone. But I don't want to put you out."

I stepped off the doormat into the room, closing the distance between us just a little more. "No. No, it's no trouble at all. I . . . I'm glad you're here."

Andreas gave a crooked smile. "How is the writing going?"

"It's good. It was good. Up until . . ."

He pressed his lips together and nodded. "I don't want to be another distraction."

I smiled. "I'm sure you will be."

27

changed out of my wet funeral clothes and into a faded old U of M T-shirt and a pair of shorts I fished out from under the bed. I curled up beneath an afghan at one end of the couch, sipping the hot tea Andreas had made while I was changing. The rain came down in relentless sheets outside, and Andreas regarded me with a curious expression.

"You're sure you don't mind? I know you have a lot of work to do."

"No, not at all. I can work with you here." Afraid I was sounding too eager for his company, I added, "But don't you have things to do in Chicago? Mutual funds to keep an eye on?"

"Actually, it is good for me to be up here again. I am going to begin working on another translation."

"A book?"

"Yes."

"Anything I've heard of?"

He raised one eyebrow. "Yes, I think so. It's one of Robert's. *The Soldier.*"

I rested my mug on my knee. "You're kidding me. They're publishing that in Germany?"

"I'm publishing it. With my friend."

"The same one that's doing my book?"

Andreas nodded. "I asked Robert about the possibility when I was up here. The contracts aren't signed yet, of course. But I can still get started."

"Will anyone want to read it?"

He shrugged. "I don't know. I hope so. That generation is nearly gone. History has a tendency to turn into myth when there are no eyewitnesses left alive to tell what it was really like. And myths are dangerous. It was myths about history and about the Jews that Hitler used to convince so many regular Germans of the justice of the Nazi regime. It is myths about the West that radical Islamic groups use to recruit jihadists, and it's myths about Muslims and Central and South Americans that the US uses to suppress immigration when people are fleeing from war and violence and poverty."

"Of course, but would Germans want to read about the war from an American perspective?"

"Haven't you ever read about Hiroshima from a Japanese perspective?"

I thought a moment. "Yes. When I was in school we read *Sadako and the Thousand Paper Cranes*."

"And have you ever read about your border wars from the perspective of an immigrant? Or about American slavery from the perspective of a slave?"

"Of course."

"Then of course there will be Germans who want to understand the war from the perspective of a former enemy."

I picked at the dirt under my fingernails. The rain was turning to tiny balls of hail outside. "I've been trying to do something similar with Tyler. To see things from his perspective, to understand why he did what he did."

"Mm. And how is that working?"

I let out a heavy sigh. The hail was getting louder, and I raised my voice to compensate. "I think I may have messed up."

Andreas waited for me to continue.

"I know something must have happened to him. I mean, a fifteen-year-old pursuing an eleven-year-old? That's not normal."

Andreas nodded in silent agreement, his expression nearly obscured as the clouds pressed in heavier and the room got even darker.

"And I found out today that he must have done something to Cami too, but I don't have any details."

"Wow."

"Yeah. Cami once said something about abuse in his past. I tried to get him to talk about it today after the funeral. But I was kind of belligerent and it was bad timing. Too much emotional stuff going on already. He left the room angry. And as awkward as things have been between us all summer, now they'll be ten times worse."

Andreas let out a little laugh. I countered with a quizzical look. He ran his fingers through his hair and lifted his hands in surrender. "I just—"

He was interrupted as a violent gust of wind threw open the casement window in Grandpa's bedroom. We both jumped up, but Andreas got there first. He shut the window firmly and latched it. I snatched a towel from the bathroom and mopped up the rainwater that was spattered across Grandpa's beautiful walnut desk. Then I dropped the towel on the floor and pushed it around the wet spots with my bare foot. When I looked up, Andreas was watching me with hurt in his eyes.

"What?" I asked.

"Why would you kiss him?"

"That's not exactly what happened." I picked up the towel and headed for the kitchen.

"I couldn't help but see it," he said, following behind. "You go out to talk to him, then you take off your clothes and swim away, and an hour later you're back on the beach in a bikini, kissing him. Why would you be so careless?"

I laid the wet towel on the washing machine and looked for something else that needed my attention, but there was nothing. The dishes, the floor, the countertop were all clean and in order. Even my rocks had been washed and dried and were now lining the edge of the fireplace mantel. I opened the fridge for no reason. I wasn't hungry. I felt sick.

Andreas was standing in the doorway, waiting for an answer.

I shut the fridge and pushed past him. "It's more complicated than that."

"Okay, then tell me. Because what I saw was—"

"You don't know what you saw. Just because you read *That Summer* doesn't mean you know anything about what really happened. Don't pretend to know what's happened between me and Tyler."

His face fell. I cringed at how much I sounded like my mother. I paced around the small living room like a captive animal. Why did it have to be raining so hard? All I wanted to do was walk. Out to the lake, down the shoreline trail that took me to my rock-picking spot, to the place where I could empty my mind entirely and just focus on colors and textures and the accumulating weight of stones in my pockets.

Andreas caught up with my frantic movements and laid a hand on my arm. "Kendra, stop. It's none of my business. I'm sorry."

He was so close.

"Andreas, I . . . it's a big mess and it's never going to make sense. There's always been some part of me that liked his attention, even though I knew the whole time it wasn't the right kind. Maybe there was just a part of me that needed to be noticed. It felt good to be someone's obsession. For a while, anyway."

Andreas tilted his head down to catch my gaze. Then he drew me into a soft embrace and spoke into my still-damp hair. "*Dein Leben war wirklich nicht einfach. Du hast etwas Besseres verdient. Ich wünschte nur, ich wäre derjenige, der es dir geben kann.*"

I stood there in that warm moment, my head against Andreas's shoulder, not caring that I didn't know the meaning of what he'd just said. I felt completely safe and whole for the first time in a very long time.

Andreas stepped back into a room that was more shadow than light. "I need to confess to you. I know a thing or two about obsession. I didn't want to translate your book only because it is a beautiful book. When I heard the interview on the radio, I thought, 'I have to meet this woman.' And when I saw your picture . . ."

I smiled. "I thought you said you weren't crazy."

"Not in a bad way," he said.

I let out a little laugh. "Well, um, did you get any dinner?"

"Not yet."

"We could order a pizza. But we'd have to pick it up. No one will deliver out here."

"I can do it if you don't mind me driving your car. I flew up this time and took an Uber from the airport in Traverse City."

I picked up the phone handset. "I can't imagine what that must have cost." I spun the rotary dial—this number I had no trouble with because I had only ever dialed it on this phone. After I made the order, I drew out a meticulous map, complete with street names, stop signs, and landmarks.

"If you can't find it with this," I said, "I can't help you."

"I'll find it."

"You're sure you don't want me to come with you?"

"No, you're exhausted. Stay here and have a glass of wine."

"I don't have any wine."

"This is a grocery store?" he said, pointing to one of the buildings on the map.

"*Ja.*"

Andreas smiled. "I will pick some up."

I handed over the keys. "Watch out for deer."

Once he was gone, I realized I hadn't peed since before the funeral, and though I hadn't consumed anything since breakfast and I had wept buckets, my bladder had reached emergency status anyway.

When I was washing my hands, I looked at myself in the mirror. The rain and humidity had turned my hair into a wild mane, and the crying I'd done earlier had liquefied my mascara, which had run and then dried under my reddened eyes in asymmetrical smudges. This was what I'd looked like during my entire conversation with Andreas? And still it seemed that perhaps he might feel about me the way I could no longer deny I felt about him? Maybe he really was crazy.

I washed my face, brushed the tangles out of my hair, and twisted it into a low, loose bun. The screen door creaked but did not slam. It was far too early for Andreas to be back.

"Kendra?"

I stepped out of the bathroom and flicked on the living room light. Tyler was still in his suit, though the tie was gone.

"You are here," he said. "I didn't see your car."

I stood silently at the light switch and waited, afraid to say the wrong thing. Afraid to say anything.

"I'm flying out tomorrow," he finally said. "But I have something to say to you before I leave."

28

"an we sit down?"

I took a seat on one of the plaid wingback gliders. Tyler took the spot Andreas had so recently occupied on the couch. He stared at his hands. The silence lengthened, I unwilling to start, he apparently unable. He stood up and walked a few paces and looked out the window. Suddenly the guy who was always already staring at me any time I glanced his way could not make eye contact.

"I had a lot of time to think on the drive up. You want to know what happened to me. So you can 'understand.'" He put the last word in air quotes.

"I think you owe me that much."

"Wrong. Maybe I owed you an apology, which I already gave you. I don't owe you this. I don't owe you an explanation. But I'm going to give you one."

I settled further into the chair and motioned for him to continue. He put his hands in his pockets and then pulled them out again.

"I was born to a very poor mother. She was not married. She was probably a prostitute. I wasn't the only kid of hers at the orphanage. There were three of us. The two girls were adopted fairly quickly. I was not. No one wanted an angry little boy. Eventually, a farmer adopted me so I could work on his farm. Then his wife got sick and died, and he brought me back to the orphanage, saying he didn't need me to work the farm anymore because he was going to shoot himself when he got home."

He turned toward me a little, the weak light from the window briefly edging his features and setting the little droplets of water on the shoulders of his suit to sparkling.

"Then when I was ten, another couple came to adopt me. They posed as husband and wife, and maybe they were, I don't know. But they didn't take me into a family home. They took me into their business."

He turned back to the window, his shoulders rising slightly with a breath and then falling again. Silence.

"Tyler?"

He let out a big sigh and spoke to the window. "My customers for the first few years were men. Some old and lonely, some young and wealthy. Sometimes the same man would come to see me many times, sometimes once a week. Some only wanted to look at me. Some wanted me to touch them. Most wanted more."

My throat swelled. "Tyler, I—"

"You wanted to know what happened. And you're going to listen to it. All of it. And then maybe you'll stop whining about what I supposedly put you through."

I swallowed, but the lump of emotion expanding in my throat would not be moved.

"When I was thirteen, I was sent out to recruit. To become friends with boys and girls who needed money. To gain their trust and offer them jobs. They didn't want to do that kind of work. So sometimes we offered them drugs. Sometimes we kidnapped them."

I became aware that my mouth was hanging open and shut it. Disappointed Reader's words scrolled across my mind.

`Did you ever consider that antagonists have stories of their own?`

"One day on the street I ran into a lady who had worked at the orphanage. I think she could tell by looking at me I was not well. Everyone who worked for this couple took drugs. It was the only way to get through the day. I was very thin. She knew I was in trouble. She told me, 'Chin-Hae, God doesn't want this for you. If you continue this way, you will die on the street. Do you want to die on the street?' I started to cry—even though I was nearly fourteen years old. I told her no, of course I don't want to die, but that was a lie. I did want to die. I could think of nothing better."

Tyler walked back to the couch and sat down. He stared at his hands.

"She took me back to the orphanage and called the police, and I testified against the couple. I stayed at the orphanage and worked there. And then one day they told me that a couple from America would take me. Not that they wanted me. That they would take me. I never asked how it all went down. I didn't care. I wanted to get out of that place. I wanted to start over. And that's how I came to live with the Rainiers."

He finally glanced my way.

"They had me see a therapist every week. Brought me to church on Sundays, art lessons on Tuesdays. Mom thought that art would be good therapy for me because it was for her. They really wanted me to have a better life. I worked hard in school, got a good job. Considering everything, I think I turned out as well as I could have."

Except for the sound of the rain outside, the room was silent.

"So," Tyler said. "You 'understand' now? You satisfied?"

I nodded, but then I quickly realized that I wasn't. What had happened to him was unequivocally terrible. Worse than what had happened to me. But it didn't make my experience—or yours, whatever it might have been—any better to know that his was worse. Just like when women at readings told me about their own assaults. It wasn't a contest of who was worse off. It was all bad. It was all wrong.

"I'm sorry that happened to you, Tyler."

He stood up and buttoned his suit coat.

"But it doesn't excuse you," I continued. "It doesn't make what you did to me somehow okay because it's more 'understandable.'"

I could feel him stiffen in the dark.

"You were doing the same sort of thing to me as those people were doing to you. Only you were the one in the position of power. And I was a safe target. Wasn't I? Who was I going to tell? Who would believe me?"

"Yeah, sure," he said. "Who were you going to tell except everyone in the world?"

I followed his gaze to the bookshelves. "Writing that book was *my* therapy," I said. "I had to tell someone. I tried to tell Cami, but she didn't believe me."

"Of course she did." Tyler sat back down on the couch. "When she was between Berkeley and Boston, we got into a big fight about it after she went through my closet and found all my drawings."

The large white boxes in Tyler's closet in Battle Creek flashed into my mind.

"I did get to be a pretty good artist," he said. "At first my therapist told me to draw all the things that made me angry or sad, so I drew all those men. And I drew myself. But that just made things worse, so she said I should draw something that made me hopeful." He looked me in the eye. "That's when I started drawing you."

He picked at a loose thread on his cuff.

"Cami found all of it. She started screaming at me and told me she knew everything I'd done to you—and she did. You didn't leave much out, and she didn't forget any of it. And it's not like she thought I wasn't capable of it."

He said no more, so I pushed him. "What happened between the two of you?"

"Nothing like what happened with you. The first time I tried anything, she beat the crap out of me. She never put up with the stuff you did."

Of course you didn't. You always were so much stronger than me.

"Maybe that's why she didn't want to believe you when you told her everything," he said.

"What do you mean?"

"You know. Like maybe she felt guilty. Like she should have told someone about what had happened to her so that it wouldn't happen to someone else. Or like if she had just given in, maybe I never would have bothered you."

"Would you have?"

The sound of tires on the gravel outside reminded me that the world was bigger than the confined space we were occupying.

I took a deep breath. "That's Andreas."

"Your German's back?"

Outside, the car door shut.

"Robert called him and told him about Cami."

Tyler's mouth quirked in a small but genuine grin. "I think he's good for you."

The screen door slammed. Tyler stood up. When Andreas

spotted him, the happy look on his face died. I thought of the story he'd told me about the bar fight in Chicago. While some women may like the idea of one guy fighting another guy to defend her honor, I was not one of those women. I put a calming hand on his arm, took the rain-spattered pizza box from his hands, and set it on the coffee table.

"Tyler's on his way out," I said.

Andreas sucked his cheeks in a moment, then said, "I was sorry to hear about your sister."

"Thank you," Tyler said. "Well, I'll get going so you can eat your dinner."

"When do you leave tomorrow?" I asked.

"My flight is at eleven, so I guess I'll get going by eight."

Part of me was happy to imagine him two thousand miles away. And yet there was another part of me that needed more. A part that didn't want to end on such an unfinished note. My eyes drifted to the curtain in the bedroom doorway, stirring slightly in the draft that made its way through the closed window.

"I'm going to have a bonfire tonight," I announced. "And I want you to come."

"It's raining."

"Looks like it's clearing up to me. Come back at ten. Come in the wooden boat. Robert told me I could have it."

He looked at Andreas, who shrugged and said, "Whatever she wants."

Tyler nodded and walked out into the dregs of the storm. As the sound of his car died away, I got busy in the kitchen pulling out plates and napkins and cups.

"There are no wine glasses here. We'll just have to use regular old tumblers."

I could feel Andreas's questioning eyes upon me as I brought everything out to the coffee table and sat on the couch. He must have thought I was crazy or stupid to invite Tyler back. Probably he was disappointed in me for allowing Tyler any more of my time or emotional energy after what he'd done. But he kept it to himself, and for that I was grateful—because I wasn't sure I'd be able to explain myself. And anyway, I had a lot on my mind.

As I filled my plate and got comfortable, I wondered how much of what Tyler had revealed to me he had ever told anyone beyond his parents and his therapist. How much had you known, and when had you known it?

"I didn't know whether you prefer red or white, dry or sweet, so I got a Cabernet and a Riesling," Andreas said.

"Bitter, sweet—they're both good in their own way. I'm not picky."

He opened the Cabernet. "Neither am I. Not about wine, anyway."

Grateful for a new line of thought, I said, "What are you picky about? Besides your footwear."

"What is this?"

I pointed to his shoes. "How much did you pay for those?"

"Crass Americans," he said with mock disgust. "I don't know. A few hundred dollars."

"Have you worn your flip-flops since you went back to Chicago?"

"Not in public." He grinned and took a bite of pizza.

Our eyes met briefly, and for a moment I forgot how everything in my life was falling apart and realigning itself in new and strange ways. Andreas was a bright yellow umbrella on a rainy day, the beam of a flashlight on a moonless night.

He took a sip of wine and finally dove in. "So why was Tyler here?"

I leaned back into the corner of the couch, resting my glass on my knee. "He came to give me some answers."

"And?"

"I can't tell you what he said. It was . . . horrible what happened to him before he came here. It doesn't excuse him. And I don't think he expects me to forgive him."

Andreas put his glass on the table and picked at a snag in his thumbnail. "Do you forgive him?"

I hesitated. Did I? I felt bad for him—more than bad. I couldn't imagine how someone could ever recover from what he'd been through. Certainly Tyler could not be expected to forgive his abusers, could he? And all the other children he'd recruited or coerced into that life? Could they ever forgive him? Weren't some things simply unforgivable?

Andreas was looking at me, waiting for an answer to an impossible question.

"I don't know."

29

By the time the wine was gone, the rain had stopped and a few stars were peeking out from behind the thinning clouds.

"I don't know how you think you'll get a fire going," Andreas said. "Everything must be soaked through. How will you get the wood to burn?"

You have to understand, of course, that he'd never met Grandpa. I led him to the far side of the shed beneath the overhang and pulled away a smartly tied tarp. The woodpile Grandpa had left behind was seven feet wide and came up to my shoulder and was dry as the leaves I'd pressed in the Oxford Unabridged Dictionary over a decade ago.

"We'd better not burn it all," I said. "I want some for the fall."

"Just how big of a fire are you making?"

"Big enough."

Andreas hauled the wood while I crumpled newspaper and arranged dry kindling in the wet sand. I made a teepee of logs over my tinder and held a lighter to it. Though it had been inside, the paper was damp from several days of high humidity. It caught, smoked, and fizzled to black.

"You see?" Andreas said.

"Be right back."

I retrieved the gas can from the shed, soaked the wood with gasoline, and flicked the lighter. The whole mess went up in a whoosh. The wood caught. I fed the fire slowly, methodically, widening its circumference log by log until it was nearly four feet across.

"Don't you think that's big enough?" Andreas cautioned.

"Getting there."

When Tyler came ashore a little after ten o'clock, flames were hungrily licking the cloudy black sky.

"Couldn't have done this a couple weeks ago," he said. "You'd have started a forest fire."

"Where's the boat?"

"At the dock."

"Bring it ashore and make sure it's empty."

Tyler beached the boat and came back to the fire.

"No, I mean bring it up here," I said. "Andreas, give him a hand, would you?"

The men left the orange glow of the fire, their faces registering confusion. With Andreas at the bow and Tyler at the stern, they shuffled up the beach and set the heavy boat on the sand. I looked it over and removed the oars.

"You can take these back to your dad," I said. "We only need the boat."

"What's this all about?" Tyler said.

"About half a bottle, I'd say," Andreas quipped.

I faced my two skeptics but directed my words at Tyler. "On my way home today, I stopped at my mom's house to confirm a suspicion I had." I paused a moment, looking for the right words, settling on one true sentence. The truest sentence I knew. "Robert is my father."

I waited for Tyler's reaction, braced myself for skepticism or accusations of lying or even laughter at such a pronouncement. He only raised his eyebrows and waited for me to continue. It was my turn to spill some secrets.

"I found a picture in the photo album in Cami's room where he's in my cabin and holding a baby—he's holding me. On the back of that picture he wrote, 'My best mistake,' the same thing he wrote on the dedication page for *Blessed Fool*. 'For my inspiration and my best mistake.' And that book is the story of how I came to be and how he ended up marrying Beth instead of Jackie, even though she was carrying his child."

And even though, I now realized, Beth and Robert had never been in love.

"That's all just the prelude to what I really want to say. Mom told me why there's only a curtain in the doorway of my grandfather's bedroom. It's because she and Robert were screwing around behind that locked door—making me—and my grandmother was so angry that she took the door off of its hinges and burned it in a bonfire on this very stretch of beach."

I pointed to the old green wooden rowboat. "For more than a decade, this boat has been a reminder of something I wanted to forget. And I bet you want to forget it too. I want you to know that I do honestly want to forgive you. For everything. I want to. I don't exactly know how, but I think if we could get rid of this boat, it would be a small step in that direction. A sign to me that I don't have to be defined by the past." I hesitated for just a moment, then pushed the words out past my teeth. "And you don't either."

Tyler gave a little nod but still said nothing, almost as if he knew I had more I needed to say. I was surprised to find that he was right. Tyler wasn't the only one who needed forgiveness in this situation. I had also done something for which I needed to atone. Nothing like what he had done. But I did not stand on this beach an innocent.

I fiddled with your bangles on my wrist, knowing that I had missed something I should have seen. I'd worn my pain like blinders, and in my tunnel vision I hadn't seen that I was not the only one hurting. If I had, I might have been a better friend, and you might have been standing next to me on that beach. You'd have gotten the gas can before I even had the chance to think of it. The whole fire would have been your idea.

"I hope you might someday forgive me for any harm my book has brought to your family." My voice broke on the last word. "Because I didn't mean for it to hurt anyone."

We were all quiet for a moment, looking into the hungry flames, looking into ourselves.

Finally, Tyler spoke. "Are we going to burn this thing or what?"

I let out a half laugh, relieved at the breaking of the tension. Tyler took hold of the stern. I grabbed the bow. Together we heaved the boat onto the fire, sending sparks dancing into the night sky like fireworks. The wet wood on the bottom of the boat hissed in protest. But the fire was hot and insatiable and began to chew its way through. We backed away from the hungry flames and watched a part of our shared shame being consumed. A chemical reaction, wood becoming ash, water, and carbon dioxide, like releasing a long-held breath.

I looked around. To my left was the man who had defined my past. To the right was a man I could imagine as part of my future. And at that moment I felt nothing but gratitude that I even had a future. Unlike you.

"Were they able to determine anything from the autopsy?" I asked.

Tyler shifted his weight. "No sign of a struggle. Alcohol but no drugs. She had a lot of rocks in her pockets, but nothing big—may have just been collecting them. They couldn't be sure if she actually died from drowning or if it was hypothermia."

"And they can't know if it was just an accident?"

"No."

I almost didn't ask my next question. "What do you think?"

He took a long, slow breath and let it out in a whoosh. "I don't know. One minute I think maybe she'd just had enough—she'd been caught in this destructive cycle for so long. The next I think maybe she just did something stupid and no one was there to get her out of the mess she was in."

No one was there. I wasn't there. You'd always been there for me—to make an excuse, take the blame, save me from punishment. But when you needed me, I was nowhere to be found. I was too busy with me. Too busy trying to become a famous writer so that I could rub it in your face. I wasn't CC. And I wasn't Hillary. I wasn't any kind of friend at all.

I picked a stone from between my toes and threw it into the fire. "I guess you better get back so you can get some sleep before your flight."

"You two drink up all that wine?" Tyler said.

"There's a bottle of Riesling," Andreas said.

"I'll get it," I said.

I trudged down the path and into the house, not bothering to wipe the sand from my feet. I opened the Riesling, poured three glasses, set the bottle down, and began to cry. Stupid. No reason to cry. Already cried enough today.

I tightened every muscle in my face, like squeezing the excess moisture from a sponge, and wiped the wetness from my cheeks. No one would know. My mascara had already been washed off. My face was probably already red from the wine and the fire. I took the three glasses outside and passed them out.

Tyler took a long, slow drink. "Gah, that's sweet! And a tumbler? Honestly, Kendra. I'm having a proper bar setup shipped to you for next summer. I'm sure Andreas will thank me."

I reddened yet more at the insinuation that Andreas would be up at the cabin with me the next summer.

Andreas caught my eye and gave me a half smile. An I-know-you-feel-what-I-feel smile.

And I did.

I held my tumbler up to his. "To new chapters."

"New chapters," he said.

30

Tyler flew back to LA. I spent the next several days struggling through my first draft, making some progress, doubling back, plodding on again. It was working and it wasn't. I was trying to write something that felt completely foreign to me—a love story. But I was still in an emotional quagmire, and there was so much I didn't understand about love. How could I make this story tell the truth when I didn't know it myself?

Andreas spent his time translating—flipping pages, scrawling notes in German, scowling at his laptop. When we needed a break from our work, we worked on getting to know one another better over meals and walks. I introduced him to the simple joys of rock collecting and identifying plants and insects and birds. He introduced me to the idea that men could be willing listeners and restrained lovers.

Despite the warm embrace and knowing glance we'd shared the night of your funeral, Andreas never touched me. Any time he was at the cabin, he seemed always to have a book or his laptop in his hands, as though to leave them empty might be dangerous. At night, he slept at your cottage as Robert's guest, though it was nearly a week before your parents reappeared on the lake and invited me to join them and Andreas for dinner. I was glad for the distraction, even if I was nervous about seeing Beth.

"It'll do her good to entertain," Robert said over the phone. "Get her out of her own head for a while. Bring your appetite. I've got plenty of brisket."

During dinner, Andreas and Robert conversed easily about *The Soldier* and the war in general, leaving me to struggle for appropriate words to say to the bereft and grieving woman I now knew to be Robert's second choice for a wife. There were plenty of things I wanted to ask her: Was she jealous of Jackie's ability to have an unwanted child when she had tried for years unsuccessfully to have a natural-born child of her own? Was she ever able to forgive her? Were some things unforgivable?

But instead of asking any of these questions, I poked at my food and made what I thought were benign comments about the weather. When your mother suddenly stood up and went into the house, I tried to rewind the tape to see what I'd said wrong.

"Don't worry about it," Robert said. "She's been like that all week."

"I don't blame her," I said.

"No," Robert agreed, "but I don't think we should tiptoe around her either. We've been worried about Cami for so long, I'm not sure she knows what to do with herself now that there's nothing to worry about. You and I, we have somewhere to put our grief—into our work. Beth doesn't have that kind of outlet."

"What about painting?"

Robert shook his head. "She's too clinical about it. She looks at a picture and paints almost exactly what she sees there. She doesn't filter and interpret and reshape reality, she reproduces reality. She doesn't process life like you and I do."

"Have you been writing then?" I asked.

He looked out at the sparkling lake. "A bit. You? How's that next book coming?"

"It's coming, not as easily as the last one did."

He nodded. "Do you think you'll ever write about this summer?"

"I'm sure I will." I purposely avoided looking at Andreas. "Pieces of it may already be filtering into what I'm working on now."

Robert drained the rest of his beer and leaned toward me. "I want to show you what I'm working on right now." He stood up.

"I have something for you to look at too," I said.

I sent Andreas down to the boat to retrieve it while I followed Robert past the empty kitchen and into his study. I envisioned Beth in her bedroom, lying facedown on her pillow in a pool of tears, and I wondered why Robert was out here with me instead of in there with her.

He situated himself behind the desk. I sat across from him on the same leather chair I'd sat in countless times before as I waited breathlessly for him to render his verdict on my youthful storywriting attempts. He put on his reading glasses and lifted the sheet that was in the typewriter a little. He looked like he was about to start reading, but then he stopped. He opened his mouth again. Closed it. Cleared his throat.

A light knock on the door. Andreas squeezed in and handed me a book. Then he melted back through the door, and it shut quietly behind him, leaving me and your dad—my dad—and the charged atmosphere hanging in the study like a cloud.

"Why don't I go first?" I offered.

Robert seemed relieved.

"Last month you asked me to sign a book for you, and I didn't know what to say. You've been so integral to my success.

You've written letters of introduction for me, talked me up to the right people, put your stamp of approval on my writing before it even got out into the world. You've taught me so much over the years about how to tell a good story. You encouraged me when no one else did. And I could have written all those things on the title page of this book, and they all would have been true. But they're not what I need to say to you."

I held out the book. Robert took it from my outstretched hand, turned it right side up, and opened the cover.

> ~~Robert,~~
> Dad,
> I cannot be the daughter you lost.
> But I can be the daughter you've always had.
> Love,
> Your Best Mistake

Robert took off his reading glasses and rubbed his eyes. He looked up at me briefly, then buried his face in his hands. Only his shoulders, with their intermittent shudders, let me know he was crying. I came around the desk and put a hand on his arm. The moment I touched him, he got to his feet and pulled me into a fierce hug. I pressed my face against his chest and felt like I had always wished to feel as a child. Covered, encased, a caterpillar in its protective cocoon, safe from the predators outside. I let the years of loneliness and jealousy dissolve to make room for what came next.

"I'm sorry," he whispered again and again. "I'm so sorry."

After what seemed like a long time and yet not long enough, the hug ended, and father and daughter stood there looking at each other for who we truly were, as we should have for the last twenty-six years.

"I don't think you can ever understand how many times I longed to do that, Kendra."

I didn't say I wished he had. He knew that. Saying it would only hurt. And I'd hurt enough people.

"Well, now you can, whenever you want," I said.

He smiled sadly. "I'm sorry we never told you. It was such a mess. Beth—well, we thought it would be easier on you not to have this weird, broken family."

I nodded. "It is what it is. And now it's all out in the open. But it will still be weird, you know."

"Yeah. I guess it will. I'm just so sorry. I can't stop thinking about what *wouldn't* have happened if we hadn't hidden the truth. What could have been avoided. I mean, we might never have adopted. And Tyler—"

I held up my hand. "Don't go down that road. It won't help anything." I pointed at the floor. "We have to start from here, you know? And Tyler needed you too."

He gave a resolute nod. We wiped our eyes and resumed our places on either side of the desk.

"Now then," he said. "My turn." He cleared his throat and put the reading glasses back on.

"If it's not something you can read out loud, I can read it for myself," I offered.

"No, no. I can read it. I want to read it."

He lifted the paper in the typewriter again and began in the deep, clear voice I only ever heard him use when reading his own material.

"Dearest Cami, we have long feared that you would lose your battle with your demons someday. That fear drove your mother to be your fierce protector, though I know it didn't always feel that way. She worked hard to build a wall of rules and discipline around you to try to guide you on the narrow path, and all the while she was building, you were searching for ropes and ladders and dynamite to get out."

I let a light laugh escape my lips, and Robert looked up with a knowing smile before continuing.

"She loved you more than any woman has loved a daughter, whether natural-born or chosen as we chose you. Though we often disagreed about how to bring you and your brother up, we did the best we knew how. I am sorry"—he choked back a swell of emotion—"profoundly sorry for all the ways we must have failed you, for all the times you felt that we did not understand, for any moment that you didn't feel unconditionally loved. Your mother and I will spend the rest of our lives second-guessing everything we did and said. I can only find comfort in the thought that you are happy and content now in the presence of the God who created you, who gave you your unquenchable spirit, and who pursued you, relentlessly, to the end. All my love, Dad."

Robert sat back and took off his glasses. The sigh that escaped his lips filled the room with a ponderous sorrow. Words seemed inadequate at such a moment, so I walked around behind his chair and placed my hands on his shoulders. He covered the hand that would not allow your bangles to come off with his own.

"I've written scenes of such violent death and destruction on this machine over the years," he said, "and nothing's been harder to write than this."

The typewriter keys were shiny, polished for decades with the oils from his fingers. I looked at the letter that had been so hard to write, eyes swimming. I rubbed the tears out of them. When my vision cleared, my breath caught like a burr in my throat. In this devastating, heartfelt letter to Robert Rainier's dead daughter, every single *a* drooped beneath the line.

I pointed to one. "What's going on here?"

"Oh, that started up a few years back. The guy I used to have up here who could fix stuff like that died back in 2007. You get used to it though."

I felt sick. "I have to go."

"Is everything okay?"

"Yes, fine. I just—I need to get to bed. I'm exhausted. And you should go see how Beth is doing." I started for the door.

"Kendra," Robert said, holding up the book. "This means a lot to me. But I think for the moment it would be best if we didn't talk about this in front of Beth. There's still a lot of hurt there. And now with Cami . . ."

"I understand."

I rushed out of the cottage and found Andreas sitting out on the deck, looking out at the stars that had taken up their appointed places in the night sky.

"I'm heading home," I said.

"Are you okay?"

"Fine. I'll see you tomorrow."

I headed down the steep staircase, hands gripping both railings, head swimming in a swill of confusion and grief and the revelation that my Very Disappointed Reader had written that screed against me on the very typewriter the renowned Robert Rainier had written his bestselling books on. It wasn't Tyler, it wasn't Jackie, and it wasn't Robert, I was sure. That left only you or Beth. But Tyler had said that you believed what I'd told you, that you had believed it long before *That Summer* came out. It made no sense for you to then write an anonymous letter defending Tyler. And if you were going to criticize me, what would possibly keep you from signing your own name to it?

That left only Beth.

31

did have a life before you. Before Cami. BC. But it's hard to remember. It's like trying to remember time in the womb, before light, before language. I know I filled my summer days somehow. I know I fished with Grandpa. I must have built sandcastles and splashed in the lake. I collected feathers and caught frogs and picked flowers. I watched sunsets and found shapes in the clouds. I did what kids do. But I did so much of it alone, without witness, that it can feel sometimes like it didn't actually happen. Like maybe I dreamed it.

I do remember the moment I woke up, the moment BC changed over to real time. Incredibly, it started with Beth.

"Grandpa! Mrs. Rainier invited me to dinner! Can I go?"

I was nine years old, shouting through the screen door to my grandfather, who was inside reading the newspaper. He didn't answer, as I knew he wouldn't. He never answered when I shouted. Just waited for me to come close enough to talk at a civilized volume.

I went into the house and ran up beside his chair. "Mrs. Rainier invited me to dinner."

"Really?" I know now why he sounded so surprised.

"Can I go?"

"When?"

"Tonight. Now. Can I go?"

He put down his newspaper and looked out the window toward the lake, where Beth was waiting in the old wooden rowboat, which wasn't quite so old back then.

"Please?"

"Did she say why?"

Why? Wasn't it obvious? "For dinner."

Grandpa stood. "Why don't you stay here. I'm going to talk with Mrs. Rainier a moment."

I sat on the couch, fidgeting and flummoxed. Why hadn't he just said yes? What could they possibly be talking about?

After an interminable amount of time, Grandpa came walking slowly back up the sandy path to the cabin. The second he was inside, I pounced.

"Can I go?"

"You may. But be on your best behavior."

I was already running out the door. "I will!"

I'd known Robert and Beth Rainier, as I'd known nearly everyone else on the lake, for as long as I could remember. Grandpa didn't spend much time with them—or anyone else of their generation, preferring the company of the older folks, all of whom are gone now, with the notable exception of Ike Fenton. But I saw the Rainiers now and then in town or at the restaurant or in their boat, drifting by my dock.

And like all children allowed to run wild, I tended to trespass. I disappeared for hours, running down overgrown trails through the woods or following deer tracks along the shore. I played with other people's dogs, sat on other people's docks, used other people's bathrooms. I was a child of the lake, and back then everyone knew everyone else and didn't think twice about offering Fred Brennan's granddaughter a cookie and a glass of milk.

Though the Rainier cottage was on almost the opposite side of the lake, it was less than a mile away by land if one was willing to go off-road and knew the best way to avoid the marshy area that was all muck and rot and goose poop. So every so often, I ended up at the yellow cottage up the hill. Sometimes I'd sit with Robert on the deck and he'd tell me a story. Sometimes Beth would give me lemonade and strawberries and stand at the kitchen counter with her arms crossed as I sat at the table, napkin on my lap. Treats notwithstanding, I preferred Robert's easy smile to Beth's formal manner. And I loved Robert's stories.

I was never with both of the Rainiers at the same time. Beth never joined us on the deck. Robert never joined us at the table. So when Beth had told me that she and Mr. Rainier wanted me to have dinner with them—both of them—it felt like something big was about to happen. I felt very important and grown-up to be asked. But I couldn't have anticipated the surprise that was awaiting me.

When I walked into the house and found you sitting on the couch, there was a moment—just a moment—of confused disappointment. They'd invited another little girl to dinner too, so maybe I wasn't as special as I thought. But when Robert kneeled down beside me and introduced you, everything changed.

"Kendra, this is Camilla. She's nine years old, just like you, and she's from Korea."

I held out my hand to be polite, but you didn't shake it.

"We adopted Cami last month. She doesn't know much English yet, but she likes a lot of the same things you do, and we thought that you might like to play together this summer. How would you like that?"

"Sure," I said.

It would be fun to have a playmate. Someone who could share in my adventures. I missed the kids at school, especially when it got to be August and the joys of summer were wearing thin. Now I wouldn't have to come up with ideas of what to do during the day all by myself. Now I'd have someone to play games with. We could build a fort and have a club with secret passwords.

All the new possibilities for fun that you opened up spread before me like a candy store, and I decided then and there that you were made for me, that we would be best friends, and that nothing could separate us from that moment forward. Yes, at the end of the summer, we would both go back to our own towns and schools, but those times would just be temporary, like dreaming. The summers on Hidden Lake would be our real world.

But now, sitting on the far side of our friendship, with summer barreling on toward August, the truth hit me hard. Hidden Lake was not the real world. It was the dream. And I was now permanently awake in a cold reality where you were gone and your mother blamed me for it.

The knowledge that Disappointed Reader was there, less than a mile away by land and closer yet by water, ate at me. I stopped writing. I stopped eating. I stopped sleeping. I was worse off than I'd been when I'd first come up in June, hoping to prove the letter writer wrong. I'd started a response that day that I never finished. And though I'd straightened out in my mind what had happened with Tyler, Beth still did not know that what I had written about was the truth. She thought I was dragging her damaged son through the mud. She didn't know how wrong she was.

I had to tell her. Time was slipping through my fingers like sand. I had to get myself writing again. And if I didn't straighten things out with your mom, what kind of relationship could I hope to have with your dad?

My dad.

Our dad.

It was the third week of July that the letter turned up again. It had been missing for weeks, biding its time in the pocket of a pair of shorts, and rediscovered when I had to stop putting off the laundry. Once stiff and crisp and able to draw blood, it was now worn and pliable. The corners had been rounded off a bit from handling. The once perfectly straight folds were askew. Reading it over now, with the knowledge I had about Tyler's past and from the viewpoint of it being written by his mother, I felt less indignation than shame.

```
Your book, while perhaps thought "brave" in
some circles, is anything but. It is the work
of a selfish opportunist who was all too ready
to monetize the suffering of others. Did you
ever consider that antagonists have stories
of their own? Or that in someone else's story
you're the antagonist?
```

I found Andreas out on your deck and held out the letter. "It's from Beth."

He shut his laptop. "How do you know?"

"The *a* drops below the line a little. When I was reading what Robert was writing the other night, I saw the same thing. This was written on the same typewriter. Look at the first paragraph."

He glanced over the stinging indictment. "Does she think *you're* the antagonist in Tyler's story?"

"No. In Cami's. It was after my book came out last May that she stopped communicating with them. I think Beth blames me for that and thinks I was unfair to Tyler in *That Summer*. And maybe I was. If I had known what he'd been through, maybe I wouldn't have written that book at all. Or at the very least, I would have written it differently."

He handed the paper back to me. "What will you do?"

"I have to talk to her. I was thinking maybe I'd invite them over tonight."

"Do you think she would even come?"

"Only one way to find out." I knocked at the back door and put my face up against the screen. "Robert?"

"She's really not up to it," Robert said, hanging in the doorway, blocking my way in. "She's hardly left Cami's room."

"Is she mad at me?" I asked.

He was silent for a beat.

"There was nothing in my book that Cami didn't already know," I said.

"Maybe not," he said. "And maybe it's all just coincidence after all—the timing, I mean. But there's a lot in there that Beth and I didn't know. All of it, in fact." He paused and swallowed. "I tried to tell her when I was done with it that it wasn't her type of book. But she wasn't going to not read your book."

I sighed. "I have to talk to her. This will not just fix itself in time. And I can't just avoid her like my mother did. I'm not going to stop coming up here, and I doubt Beth is either."

"Why don't you come back over after dinnertime. Then you two can talk in private while Andreas and I work."

So it was that later that night as the sun sank in the western sky—a little earlier than last night, which was just a little earlier than the night before—I found myself standing alone outside your bedroom door, letter in hand, heart in throat, ready to face my accuser.

I knocked lightly and opened the door though there was no answer. Your bedside lamp threw soft shadows against the wall. Beth sat on the edge of your bed, holding a large jar filled with stones.

"May I come in?"

Beth said nothing. I slipped in and shut the door behind me.

"What's this?" I asked, indicating the jar.

Beth looked at the object in her lap. "They're from her pockets. The coroner set them aside." She tipped the jar, and the rocks clinked against the glass. "I thought maybe I could figure out if it was just an accident."

I examined the jar for some indication of the method one might use to determine if someone had purposefully weighed themselves down with its contents.

"I thought if they looked intentional," she continued, "like she'd picked them because of their beauty or rarity, that it might mean it was an accident. That she was just collecting rocks and wasn't thinking about the temperature of the water."

I studied the rocks. Were these carefully chosen treasures? Or hastily chosen aids to suicide? Granite, mostly, and gneiss. Schist and sandstone. Some pretty specimens here and there, but not necessarily your typical haul back in our rock-collecting days. Still, there was no telling. My tastes had changed over the years. I'd tired of pinks and reds and focused more on grays and blacks. I'd abandoned stones that were round and smooth from decades of sand and wave action in favor of jagged rocks that highlighted the structures of their composite minerals. Perhaps you had simply been looking for something a little out of the ordinary.

"What do you have there?" Beth asked, indicating the paper I held in my hand.

I folded it up and shoved it in my pocket. I lowered myself onto your bed next to Beth. "Mrs. Rainier, I feel like I need to tell you what happened between me and Cami."

She continued to stare at the rocks in the jar, but she seemed to be listening.

"I stayed away from Hidden Lake for eight years after high school even though it was my favorite place on earth, the only place I felt wholly *me*. I stayed away because I had confided in Cami about something important and she said she didn't believe me. And then she followed that up by calling my writing boring and let me know that she didn't think it would amount to anything. I took that really personally. Too personally. I spent the next seven years trying to get good enough so that I could come back and prove to her that I had what it took to make a name for myself. I wanted to make Robert proud, but more than that I wanted to make Cami jealous. I wanted her to be as jealous of me as I'd always been of her. I wanted her to admit that I was CC and she was Hillary."

Beth finally looked at me with questioning eyes.

"From *Beaches*. It was this stupid argument we had. It doesn't matter. Anyway, I published my novel and it did well, and I thought about coming back up to the lake last year to get that apology. Only I was so busy those first few months with publicity and talks and stuff that I didn't have time. And then I realized that I really didn't care about that anymore. I didn't need Cami to acknowledge the book's success—it spoke for itself."

I paused and took a breath and tried to slow my racing heart. This was it. There would be no going back now.

"You know what it was that brought me up to Hidden Lake this year?" I said. "Criticism. In a letter. Someone had accused

me of using people in my writing. Of being a selfish opportunist. That letter made it so I couldn't write anything else. I
was obsessing over it. I came up, in part, to prove that person
wrong."

I searched Beth's face for a reaction to what I was saying, but
her expression was unreadable. She didn't look angry or guilty
or any of the other ways I might have expected her to look.

"But a funny thing happened," I continued. "I realized that
some of that letter was right. I had been careless with people.
I'd been honest about my own experience through my own
point of view, but I hadn't considered what that might mean
to others. And that was thoughtless and selfish of me."

Beth squeezed her eyes shut and shook her head. "Why are
you telling me all of this, Kendra?"

"I guess I just wanted to say I'm sorry. I'm sorry about ex-
posing your family the way I did. About hiding behind my writing instead of dealing with it face-to-face. I'm sorry I wasn't
there for Cami when she needed me. I should have made time
for her before everything in her life got so out of hand. By
the time I tried, it was too late. I'd ignored her for too long,
and I guess she didn't want to have anything to do with me.
I'm so sorry I let her down and let you down. I wish I could
apologize to her."

I looked Beth directly in the eyes.

"And I wish I could tell the person who wrote that letter that
she was right. Not about everything, but about some things."

There. I'd said what I needed to say. Now it was in Beth's
hands.

She put a hand on my arm, the first time I could remember
her ever touching me. "I wish Cami knew how much people
loved her. Robert and I knew that adopting older children would
be a challenge. I wanted so badly for us to be enough for them,

for things to work themselves out because they had their needs provided for and two parents who loved them no matter what. *No matter what.* And now I am trying to figure out what I did wrong, and not just in a general sense, like, oh, I was too strict or something, but every specific choice I made, every word I said."

She wiped a fat tear off her cheek.

"And I'm so angry." She looked at me. "Not at you, though. I was. I was angry when I read your book. I was angry at you for writing all that stuff. I was angry at Tyler, despite everything I knew he'd gone through. How could he have done those things to you? I'm so, so sorry."

I waved a hand at her. "It's not your fault."

"And I've been so angry at Robert. He always acted more like a father to you than he did to them. He invested so much of himself in you. And I didn't think you deserved it because I couldn't stop thinking about how Jackie didn't deserve it." Beth sighed and turned the jar in her lap, the stones tinkling against the glass so much like the sound of your bangles. "I just wish I knew. When someone jumps off a bridge or shoots themselves, at least you know. At least you know that."

"Even great swimmers can get hypothermia."

Beth nodded lightly.

"Maybe you should talk to Robert about it. Even if it seems like he's got it together, he really doesn't."

"I know." She smiled weakly. "What about you? How are you holding up? I know it's been a long time since you and Cami were together, but I also know that you never get over losing your best friend, no matter how you lost them."

I thought of *Blessed Fool*, of my mother, of what she had done to Beth when they were eighteen. Your criticism of my writing was nothing compared to Jackie's betrayal, and in light of it I felt as ridiculous claiming I'd been wronged as I'd felt claiming PTSD when there were soldiers out there watching their comrades shot down all around them. Men like Ike Fenton.

Ike had been the one to discover your body. Had it sent him back to those horrific days on the beach at Normandy? I looked at the stones in the jar. Could a man who had seen so much death and despair, who had been the last person to see you—could he help answer Beth's unanswerable question? Could he read intention in those stones?

"You're all alone over there now, aren't you?" Beth said.

"Not completely. Andreas spends a good deal of time with me. Though I don't know how long he'll stay at the lake."

"He's a very kind, conscientious man, isn't he? I thought Robert was out of his mind having a houseguest after everything that's happened, but Andreas is a good distraction."

I smiled. "That he is."

A tentative knock sounded at the door, and then Robert's face appeared in the crack.

I stood. "I'll get going now."

"Kendra?" Beth said. "You know I didn't write that letter, don't you? I might have thought some of the same things that person did, and I can understand why you might think I'd have a reason to criticize, but I didn't write it. No one who's been married to a writer as long as I have could have written that letter. I know you have to follow the story where it leads. And I know that in the writing of it, you found some relief. I would not deny you that comfort."

"I don't understand. It had to be—"

Robert opened the door the rest of the way. "What's this?"

"Um, nothing," I said. "Nothing you need to worry about. I'll let you two talk."

I slipped out of the room and shut the door. I found Andreas out on the deck, looking at the stars through a hole in the clouds. He smelled of cigar smoke and summer. Of simpler times.

"I still can't get over how quiet it is out here," he said. "Listen."

I leaned on the rail and listened to the night crickets and katydids, gray tree frogs and leopard frogs. Creatures I'd learned to identify by sound even when I couldn't see them. I easily picked each of their distinct voices out of the evening din.

But I hadn't recognized your voice. Now I knew—it had to be you.

You were my Very Disappointed Reader.

32

ome on, I'd really like to come with you." Andreas stood in my doorway, backlit by the morning light. When I'd told him of my intention to visit Ike Fenton, he'd invited himself along, which is why I had tried to get myself out of bed early enough to leave him behind. But a restless night had me running late, while his Germanness had him running right on time.

I self-consciously gathered my unbrushed hair in my hands. "I'm just not sure it's a good idea."

"You told me the man is in his nineties."

"That doesn't mean his trigger finger doesn't work."

"Bah. That doesn't scare me. Has he ever *told* you that he hates Germans?"

"No, but—"

"Have I ever told you that I'm a pretty fair marksman?"

"That doesn't do you a lot of good without a gun."

Andreas smiled. "I will just borrow one of his if I need it."

"Fine, you can come. But no talking. I don't want to derail him. As far as I know, he's the last person who talked to her before she died. I'm just hoping maybe something he says will help me put the pieces together."

"What do you think happened?"

"As far as I can see, there are only two possibilities. One, she made a poor calculation about the lake while she was under the influence and her death was an accident. Two, she knew exactly what she was doing and her death was on purpose. And I don't see how any of us who care about her can live with that ambiguity. Especially Beth."

Outside, a hot, bright morning had already burned away what mist might have been on the lake. Andreas jerked the line off the cleat. I looked at him intently.

"I feel like I need to prepare you for this. Ike Fenton is not a normal man, and he does not live in a normal house. As far as I can tell, it started as an ice fishing shack that he's just added junk to for decades. Like plywood and aluminum siding and cinder-block walls, but also an old pop-up camper and part of a chicken coop and a 1957 Chevy truck. Whatever castoffs he found on the side of the road. I'm not kidding. And I've never been inside, but I've heard stories, and I think it's basically going to be like the set of a horror film."

Andreas laughed. "Okay. I'm prepared."

"And remember, let me do the talking."

I started up the motor, steered us into deep water, and shivered despite the heat. How many times had I passed unknowingly over your watery grave that summer? How close had I come to finding you when I found your bracelet?

We tied the boat at Ike's rickety dock, and I sat for a moment. I had prepared Andreas to see a crazy house, but I'd neglected to prepare myself to see the spot where you had lain under the tarp just a couple weeks ago. The spot where I'd pulled Tyler out of the water during the storm. I took two long, slow breaths.

"Are you okay?" Andreas asked. "Kendra?"

"Yes. I'm fine."

I took his hand and he pulled me up onto the dock. I was so grateful that he did not let go. We walked hand in hand down the narrow wooden planks.

"*Ach, du lieber Himmel.*" Andreas's facial expression was a clear enough translation of his words for me.

"I told you."

The ramshackle porch was lined with rusty coffee cans filled with plants that looked like they may once have been tomatoes. Now they were yellowed, spindly waifs cowering under the hot sun. An old boot caked with dried mud lay on its side in the dead grass, as did a defunct toilet. The yard was liberally sprinkled with windmills, mobiles, and bird feeders Ike had constructed from empty beer cans and milk jugs. I stepped gingerly onto the rotting porch and gave the door three firm knocks, fully expecting the whole structure to fold like a house of cards. A moment later it creaked open a bit, revealing a shock of thin white hair and bushy eyebrows knit together above pale blue eyes.

"Hi, Ike. It's Kendra Brennan. Fred's granddaughter."

"I know who you are. Who is this?" He looked at Andreas.

"This is my friend Andy," I said.

"What can I do for you?"

I didn't know how to start, so I started with something I knew would get us through the door. "We were wondering if you could tell us about the sturgeon you caught."

Ike's eyebrows shot up, and a broad, nearly toothless smile broke out across his skinny, wrinkled face. "Yes, yes, of course. Come right in. Let me get you two some coffee."

He disappeared down a crooked hall. We searched for a place to sit in the cramped sitting room. Stacks of ratty *National Geographic* magazines served as end tables to a drooping couch and one stiff wooden chair. Here and there on the walls hung the dusty heads of a few unfortunate deer, along with an assortment of antlers and disembodied hooves screwed into wooden boards. The windowsills were littered with an array of turtle shells, bones, and bits of birch bark. On a makeshift shelf of cinder blocks and unfinished two-by-sixes was a small army of stuffed rodents.

"*Meine Güte, die Hütte ist komplett verrückt.*"

"Shhh."

I spotted a pair of menacing green eyes underneath the sun-faded drapes and realized that, in this house, I could not assume the creature to which they belonged was a domestic cat. It might be a possum or a raccoon or a bobcat.

Ike lurched back into the room with an old metal TV tray holding three mugs of coffee. "Take a load off."

I considered the stains on the couch—what they were, how long they might have been there, whether they might transfer themselves to my shorts—and sat on as little of it as possible. We each took a mug of coffee. No cream or sugar was offered. Instead, Ike put the tray down on a teetering stack of magazines and pulled the wooden chair directly in front of us, sitting so close that his knobby knees nearly brushed ours.

"So you want to hear about the big fish?" he said enthusiastically.

I took a casual swig of the coffee and nearly choked on it.

"Hope you like it strong," Ike said with a grin.

I smiled and muscled down another mouthful to be polite. Andreas was trying not to laugh.

"It was July 6th, 1982," he said slowly, deliberately, obviously relishing every practiced word. "I was out on the lake early— about three o'clock in the morning. There was a full moon. I like fishing with a full moon. Easier to see what the heck you're doing. But you never can tell with a full moon. Weird stuff happens sometimes. There was a lunar eclipse that night."

He gave us a knowing look, but I wasn't sure just what it was I was supposed to know.

"It started getting darker and darker. I just sat there for a while with my line in the water and watched that moon get eaten up. And at the *very moment* the moon was totally eclipsed and turned bloodred, that's when I felt a tug on my line. And then it wasn't a tug. It was a yank!"

Ike jumped in his seat, so I jumped. Hot coffee sloshed over the side of my cup.

"Don't worry about that, sweetie," Ike said. "I don't even remember what color the carpet started out as."

I tried to smile. Ike was already forging on ahead.

"I fought that beast all night if I fought her an hour. I fought her as the moon reappeared in the sky. She pulled me all over the lake, trying to shake me loose. But I kept fighting back." He squeezed his eyes shut, then opened them. "Finally, around 6:30 in the morning, she realized that no fish can escape from Ike Fenton. I reeled her in slowly and pulled her up to the side of the boat, but I couldn't hoist her in without capsizing, she was so huge. Lucky for me, your grandfather had just gotten out on the lake. I flagged him down, and he helped me tow her in and get her up on the dock."

Grandpa. I could have asked him to confirm this story if I'd only known about it when he was alive. How many other stories had I missed out on?

"Fred said he'd help me load her into my truck to take her to be processed, but I didn't have the heart. So we slipped her back into the water and she swam away. Haven't seen her since. But she's still down there somewhere. They can live a hundred years, you know."

"You didn't take a picture?" I asked. "Seems like you'd want to show off a prize fish like that."

He frowned. "Picture would have been nice all these years to shove in people's faces when they didn't believe me—say it's impossible! No rivers or creeks going in or out or something. Something about glaciers and kettles. I don't know how she got in this lake, but I know how she got out—at the end of my line! Don't need to prove it to anybody else. I know I caught the dang thing."

"Yes, it seems like you're quite the hunter," I said, indicating the collection around us.

"Couple of the deer I shot, though the real big one there is my father's kill back in '48. The one over by the front door I hit with my truck about ten years back. The squirrels and shrews and such I collect. I find them in antique shops and flea markets. And then once people know you collect something, you know how it is. Suddenly you get a squirrel for every birthday and two for Christmas. Sometimes they just show up on the doorstep, so I bring them inside and give them a home. I've got raccoons and possums and a badger and—well, you should see what I got in the cellar."

From the look on his face, Andreas seemed to be thoroughly enjoying himself. I had to admit it was amusing. I didn't want to forget why we were there, but it was obvious that Ike didn't get many visitors and apparently had a lot to say once he did.

We followed him down a dark hall, where he raised a trapdoor to reveal a metal spiral staircase. When he disappeared beneath the floor, Andreas and I each motioned to the other to go first. I caved and carefully picked my way down the steps.

The claustrophobic space was lit by one bare light bulb that swung gently after Ike pulled the chain. A narrow, winding pathway led through the most macabre assortment of animal relics I'd ever seen. Mammals, birds, and reptiles looked out with their dead plastic eyes. Everywhere I turned there was a wing, a talon, a mouthful of teeth, a grimacing face with black lips pulled back.

"Now, strictly speaking, not all of this is legal," Ike said conspiratorially. He held up his right hand. "But I didn't kill no owl or eagle, believe me. I just acquired them over the years. Now I got them, I don't really know what to do with them. I figure once I die it don't matter. So I'll just keep them all under wraps down here until they bury me. Then they'll be someone else's problem. Don't know whose. I try to give 'em away every chance I get, but they're not everyone's cup of tea."

"Hey, you didn't give my grandpa that screech owl, did you?"

"Certainly not! That was for Leila. She loved that little guy from the moment she saw him. Gave it to her back in 1972 for her birthday. I always liked her. Real shocked when she died young as she did. But I guess it wasn't so easy having Jackie Brennan for a daughter—no offense. Probably wore her heart right out."

I filed that comment away as we filed upstairs. I would have to come back another time and find out what Ike knew about my mother and my grandparents that I did not. For now, I was only interested in one thing.

We settled back down in the living room.

"More coffee?" Ike offered.

Andreas shook his head.

"I'm good, thanks," I said.

He gave Andreas a sidelong glance. "You don't say much, do you?"

"I came over," I interrupted, "because I wanted to talk to you about Cami."

Ike turned serious.

"You said you talked to her back in March," I said, "and that she was at the cottage working on something."

"That's what she told me."

"Did she say anything about what she was working on?" Of course, I already knew what you must have been working on—the letter—but you didn't need to come all the way up to Hidden Lake to write a letter.

Ike looked thoughtful for a moment. "No, I don't think so."

"She didn't give any hints about where she was going after that?"

"I don't know any more than what I told you before." He took a loud sip of his coffee. "Well, now, wait a minute. That's not actually true. She did say one thing, but it didn't make no sense to me. She said it more than once."

"What was it?"

"Something like, 'People should pay less attention to the ones who're wrong and more to the ones who're right'? Or something. It was something like that."

```
Your problem is that you paid more attention
to the people who had done you wrong than the
ones who'd done you right.
```

"Then she asked me to mail a letter for her when I was down-state for the funeral," Ike said. "I asked her why she didn't just mail it herself, but she said she needed it to get mailed further south. Something about it getting where it needed to be faster because I'd be near one of those big postal hubs or something."

"Who was it for?"

"Don't know. I didn't look. None of my business. Figured

it was a bill or something if it needed to get somewhere fast. The whole thing made no sense at all to me, but I didn't see no point in arguing with Cami Rainier. Always been difficult, that one."

I rolled my eyes and gave a little chuckle of understanding. If anyone knew the futility of arguing with you, it was me. But then, without warning and without my permission, a well of emotion boiled up behind my eyes and I found I couldn't speak. In that moment I'd give anything to argue with you again.

Ike put a bony hand on my forearm. "Listen, Kendra. I seen a lot of death over the years. Some kinder than hers and some much worse. You never forget what death looks like. I'm not gonna tell you time will make it better or you'll get used to it and all you'll remember are the good times, yadda yadda yadda. I've lost a lot of friends. I'm the only one left of the old-timers up here anymore. It's a lonesome way to be no matter how long ago you lost someone."

A hot tear dripped down my cheek, and I felt Andreas's hand on my back.

"Sweetheart, I'm sorry," Ike continued. "I'm truly sorry that you saw what you did. That's why I covered her up. No one should have to see that. But don't fixate on it. Don't keep bringing it to mind. That don't help a dang thing. You know what I did in the war whenever I felt those kinds of scenes crawling back into my brain? I turned to the man at my side who was alive and kicking and started telling him a story. True, fake, didn't matter. Just something to send the mind down a better road. Ol' Robert tells me you're a writer."

I nodded and wiped my cheek with the meat of my hand.

"So I guess you're just as good a storyteller as an old fisherman like me."

I smiled. "I don't know about that."

"Eh? And what about your mute friend over here? Maybe he could take your mind off it. You got any stories? What'd you say your name was? Andy?"

"Andreas Voelker," he said without even trying to sound American. "And *ja*, I know many good stories."

Ike seized on this new knowledge about his quiet houseguest. "I'll be. You didn't tell me your friend was German. Well, I got some stories for you, Herr Voelker."

"I would love to hear them," Andreas said. "Could I come to visit you tomorrow?"

"Don't know how my old heart will handle visitors two days in a row, but sure. You fish?"

"No, but I can sit in a boat." He winked at me. "Just learned how this summer."

Ike slapped his knee and laughed. "Then you're welcome in mine. You at Fred's?"

"I am staying with Robert Rainier at the moment, not at Kendra's."

"Right, right. That's your place now, eh?" he said to me. "Look, I'm sorry about the washing machine. Fred said I could have it when he went into the nursing home. I'd offer to give it back, but it's part of my septic system now."

"That's quite all right," I said. "I have a new one."

"You can have the shotgun back. I got plenty of guns of my own." He reached under the couch, pulled out Grandpa's shotgun, and thrust it into my surprised hands. "Andreas, I'll pick you up tomorrow morning at five."

"Andreas works nights," I said. "He'll be sleeping at five."

"Not if he wants to sit in my boat, he won't be."

"Five o'clock is fine," Andreas said. "I have been thinking of adjusting my hours anyway."

"Great. I'll bring the coffee."

"*Wunderbar*," Andreas said, raising his mug and then downing the entire thing in one long draught.

"Ha! I like this guy." Ike stood up and led us to the door. "I bet she told you not to talk because I hate Germans, didn't she? Well, that's one story about me that ain't true. Killed a lot of 'em, but I ain't got nothing against 'em."

We started down the porch steps when a glint of sunlight off a bottle in the garden caught my eye. Shortcross Gin. Robert's brand. I handed the shotgun to Andreas and picked up the bottle. "Where did you get this?"

Ike squinted. "Oh, that. Washed up back in early April. Good bottle. Woulda been better if there'd been some gin left in it." He laughed at his own joke.

"Mind if I keep it?"

"Well, now, I been collecting bottles to line the garden beds . . . but I do like the colored ones better, so I guess so."

"Thanks," I said. "And thanks for your time today, Ike."

"Anytime." He pointed at Andreas. "Five o'clock. If you're not on Robert's dock, I go without you."

"I'll be there."

We got back into the boat, and Ike shut himself back inside his house.

"What's with the bottle?" Andreas asked.

"It's from Robert's icebox, I'm sure of it. How would it end up washing up on Ike's beach except that Cami had it?"

"So she was intoxicated. You said the autopsy showed that. But it still doesn't tell you if it was an accident."

"No."

Andreas started the engine and guided us back to my dock.

"You're not really going fishing with Ike," I said as he tied the boat.

"Of course. He's lonely, and I think talking with him, hearing his stories, can help me with my translation of *The Soldier*. The opportunity to talk to someone who was there is one we won't have much longer."

I started down the dock to the shore, shotgun in one hand, empty gin bottle in the other. "You're really changing your sleep schedule? It seems you're getting quite cozy up here at Hidden Lake. How long are you planning on staying?"

"That depends," he said. "How long will you have me?"

33

The summer you chopped off all your hair, I asked your dad what the point of being a novelist was. He said it was to tell the truth, which is the best answer he could have given. I was simply too young to understand what he meant.

To a kid, the truth is obvious. Easy. Black and white. It's what happened. What you can see. And it is only through your own eyes that you can see it. But novels are about looking through someone else's eyes, seeing what someone else sees when they look at the world, and realizing, perhaps for the first time, that other people are just as real and alive and hurt as you are.

I was beginning to see that the truth of my situation was much bigger and much harder than I thought it was. I had seen only my abuser, not the victim of sex trafficking. I had seen only my neglectful mother, not the woman who was so ashamed of what she'd done that she couldn't risk seeing those she had wronged. I had seen only an unsupportive friend, not the friend who needed me to focus less on myself so that I could see that she too was going through something difficult. I had seen myself only as a brilliant novelist, not as the woman who exploited other people for my own gain.

Robert once said that I would be a good writer because I was a keen observer. I believed that about myself for a long time, but I was, as you might say, delusional.

And now I was trying to write a love story when I'd never really seen one work.

It was August, and all forward progress on my second novel had ground to a halt. The fact that I'd been right about what happened with Tyler didn't matter. The fact that I knew who had written the letter didn't matter. The fact that I was Robert's daughter didn't matter. And I was pretty sure that even if I knew without a doubt whether or not your death was just an accident, that wouldn't matter either.

I had thought my ability to write was dependent on knowing I was right, when it was really dependent on actually having something to say. Something that needed to be said. Something that burned inside of me. When I wrote *That Summer*, I'd known exactly what I wanted to say. I'd needed to say it for years, and it took me years to say it. But the deadline for book two hadn't given me enough space to discover the next thing worth saying.

Maybe *That Summer* was all I had. Maybe there was one book in me and no more. There was certainly no way I would make my deadline. I would have to get Lois to cancel my contract and find a way to pay back a portion of my advance to my publisher—an advance that was already spent. I'd have to get a real job to pay the bills, but that wouldn't be enough to get me out of my contract. Robert or Andreas, even Tyler, would probably loan me the money. But I could not, would not ask any of them for help.

Anyway, I did have one major asset. The cabin.

Though by no means rare in a state that is forty percent water, waterfront property in Michigan is so desirable it can fetch double the price of regular property. The thought of selling made me physically ill. But maybe I could at least get a loan based on the value of the property.

And pay it back . . . with what? If I wasn't a writer, what was I? I wasn't qualified for any job that might make enough to pay off that kind of loan, plus I still had a portion of my student loans to cover.

I had been turning this problem over for days when Andreas suggested a trip into town to pick up a package waiting for him at the post office. I jumped at the chance. After all, it had been during a trip to town with him that the first rumblings of my story had bubbled up in my brain. Maybe I could recapture a bit of that magic.

Andreas drove my car without directions, and I lost myself in the passing landscape. Black-eyed Susans and coneflowers were giving way to goldenrods and asters. The meadows were browning, and the corn was higher than the car. Here and there, the top of a maple tree had already turned orange. In just three weeks it would be Labor Day, and northern Michigan would empty out like a tub with a pulled drain. The tourists would all be back to work and school. The people with summer homes would be emptying pipes and latching shutters and locking doors. The first snow would likely come before all the leaves managed to give up and release their grip on life.

And where would I be? I couldn't stay in the uninsulated cabin. I'd be downstate looking for a job. And Andreas would be back in Chicago.

This excursion into town already wasn't working. I wasn't recapturing the enchanted feeling of that first week with my accidental houseguest, the feeling that had inspired me to start writing a love story between two people from different worlds— not terribly unique, I know, but it had been fun to write up to the point everything had stalled out. Instead, I was just getting more depressed as I looked upon everything I stood to lose if I couldn't figure this out.

When we got into town, Andreas dropped me off at Biggby to catch up on my email while he swung by the post office. I quickly dispensed with the spam and then began the distasteful task of figuring out my future.

I emailed Lois to ask her how to go about canceling my contract and repaying the advance. I emailed a realtor to ask about assessing the value of my property. I emailed my bank to see what kinds of loans might be available to someone in my situation. And I emailed my editor to give her an honest report about my non-progress. I was just hitting send on the last message when Andreas walked in empty-handed. I shut my laptop.

"You ready?" he asked.

"You don't need to check email?"

"I did it on my phone when I was in line at the post office."

On the way back to the cabin, I did not feel the lightness of spirit I was hoping to feel after sending out those emails, a lightness that would have told me I had done the right thing. It had been a very long time since I'd felt so directionless. I'd had such concrete goals and such well-laid plans for reaching them when I was in college. Now I felt like I was back in Robert's office trying to decide if I wanted to be an entomologist or a geologist or a painter. He was the one who'd steered me toward writing in the first place. Had I done it all for him? What would he think of me if I gave up now?

"How did you know you wanted to go into finance?" I asked Andreas.

"I didn't. I wanted to travel, and that takes money. I found a job that made me a lot of money and sent me on international trips."

"So you didn't feel called to it? Like you were meant for it?"

"Not especially. I was good at math, so it just made sense. How did you know you wanted to be a writer?"

"I wanted to be like Robert, I guess." We passed by the empty spot where the burned-out house used to stand. "I wanted to be noticed."

The phone was ringing when we walked into the cabin. Andreas carried his rather large package into Grandpa's bedroom as I picked up the receiver.

"Hello?"

"Kendra! Oh, thank goodness I got you. What are you doing to me, girl? Paula called me and she's freaking out. What kind of an email is that to send? What is happening over there? Is the isolation making you crazy? Are you about to go on a *Shining*-style murder spree? Talk to me!"

I pulled the phone cord as long as it would go and tucked myself into the closet, on top of the washing machine. "Calm down, Lois," I said in a low tone. "I've given this a lot of thought."

"I don't think you have, Kendra. If they cancel the contract because of non-delivery, it's going to be that much harder for me to sell to another publisher. News gets around."

"I'm not asking you to sell to another publisher, Lois. I'm . . . thinking of quitting."

"No you're not. This is just a slump. You're just scared. Everyone goes through that, especially on second books. Let me ask for an extension for you. Nobody wants you to quit. The world needs your voice. Kendra, give me forty-eight hours. If I can get you an extension, will you please just consider it?"

I sighed. "I'm not sure it would matter. I can't just pound out another book. Believe me, I've tried. I actually got pretty far in the past few weeks, despite all of the crazy stuff that's happened up here this summer. It's just all wrong. I could probably finish it, but it wouldn't be any good. It wouldn't be this voice the world supposedly needs—which I'm beginning to doubt anyway. It would just be a story, and not a terribly unique one. I think it would only let people down. Isn't a bad second book just as bad—no, worse—than no second book at all? I'd rather be remembered by a few people for one good novel than the alternative."

"Forty-eight hours. Please."

"Okay. Forty-eight hours."

Lois let out an exaggerated *whew* sound. "You gave me three gray hairs today, Kendra. And I hold it against you."

I laughed lightly. "I'm sorry."

"Talk soon."

I slid open the closet door to see Andreas leaning in the kitchen doorway. I hung up the phone and pretended that there was nothing strange about me sitting in a closet.

"So what did you get in the mail?" I asked, brushing by him.

"It's on the desk."

I stopped in the doorway to Grandpa's room. There on the desk was the opalescent dove-gray typewriter sitting primly in a shaft of sunlight, a translucent piece of white typing paper already rolled into place.

"Does it work?" I asked.

"Try it out," he said. "I took the liberty of starting a little something for you."

I sat at the desk and looked more closely at the paper. At the top, Andreas had typed out,

`Dear Cami,`

For a moment I couldn't speak.

"I thought perhaps you might want to talk to her about the letter," he said gently. When I just kept staring at it, he said, "I'm off to Ike's. I'll leave you to it."

The screen door whapped as he headed down to the dock. I sat at the desk, hands in my lap, and stared at those two black words. *Dear Cami.* Eight letters for eight years. How could I account for eight years of silence?

I always blamed you for our extended estrangement. Your reaction when I told you the things Tyler had done and your criticism of my writing and my potential infuriated me. They were convenient excuses not to come back up to the lake when I was already busy with school and work and writing. Grandpa sent occasional letters with an invitation to at least spend a weekend on Hidden Lake, but I always politely declined, citing my heavy class load and my (actually quite flexible) work schedule.

When news of your slow spiral into an aimless life of drugs and alcohol and partying filtered into my world, I felt no pity for you. After all, every misstep you made could only make me look better in comparison. While you were dropping out of college, I was getting into an award-winning writing program. While you were sucking on an oversized pacifier at a rave, I was publishing in an esteemed university's literary journal. While you were keeping your parents up at night, I was busy making your father—my father—proud.

During those eight silent years, I was building up a body of work that would prove you wrong on the one point in order to show you that you were also wrong on the other. If I really could become a writer, that would somehow show that I'd been telling the truth about Tyler.

But you knew that, didn't you? You knew that I'd spoken the truth that day. But, like me, you didn't know what to do with it. That information could change your whole family's life forever. So you kept it locked tight and asked me to do the same. Because you were ashamed and scared. Like I was.

What I didn't understand—didn't think I would ever understand—is why you couldn't trust me with your story when I trusted you with mine. Maybe you thought that if I talked, you'd have to talk. Maybe you were more understanding about Tyler's past because you knew more or suspected more. Maybe you were just disappointed in me, because you'd put a stop to it while I had let it keep happening. Maybe all this time that I thought you were the weak one and I was the strong one . . . it was really the other way around.

These are all things I could write to you in the letter Andreas had started for me. But what difference could it make to put them down on paper? You'd never read it.

Anyway, if I had the chance, if you were standing before me right now and I could ask you just one question, it wouldn't be about why you didn't trust me with your secret. I would want to know why you went so crazy when *That Summer* was published if you had already come to terms with what Tyler had done. Because if you were angry with me on behalf of your family, you would have banded together with them against me rather than pushing them away.

Instead, you fell in with people who were not your people. People who didn't love you. People who promised you release through drugs and hookups, which only imprisoned you in a cycle of highs and lows you could not escape.

Once there was a girl who could breathe under water. She spent so much time under water that she discovered it became harder and harder to breathe air and walk across the hot sand. Eventually she could not come out of the water at all. And the people she left on land began to forget her.

And then my book came out.

I poised my fingers over the newly refurbished typewriter.

```
Dear Cami,

I know you wrote that letter. I know you are
my Very Disappointed Reader. I know you are
angry. I realize now that there were things
I didn't know about Tyler's past that, had I
known them, I might have written a different
book, or no book at all. I should have been
more careful to change the details of what
happened and where it happened. I know now
that I didn't do enough to protect your
family. I was irresponsible with Tyler, but I
thought I had been very careful with you. You
weren't even in it.
```

I stopped typing.

You weren't even in it.

I had left you out of the story entirely. I could lie to myself all day and say that it was to protect your identity, to keep your name from being sullied by what your brother had done. But it wasn't and I knew it. It was because I hadn't thought you mattered to the story. Because, blinded by my own giant ego, I had ceased to see you. Like the burned-out house on the county highway that I didn't notice anymore.

Until it was gone.

34

My agent called the following day with news that my deadline had been extended until November, giving me two more months to deliver an acceptable manuscript. I buckled down, forcing myself to write one sentence, then the next, then the next. From early morning to the point at which the days got so hot that it was impossible to think, I dutifully typed away in the loft with a fan blowing the heavy air into my face.

Afternoons were spent in the lake. Properly protected from the sun with waterproof SPF 70 sunscreen and wearing the new longer swim trunks he'd bought at an end-of-season sale at Walmart, Andreas worked on his swimming skills and was even getting a bit tan. The times I reached in to correct a technique or he offered his hand when we got out onto the dock were the only times we touched.

Page by page, my international love story was slowly progressing in what felt like natural ways. In real life it stalled, and I began to wonder if I had misread him. I had thought that he'd been flirting with me when he was speaking Ger-

ERIN BARTELS

man the first time we went into town. But I really had no idea what he was saying. He could have been making fun of me to my face and I wouldn't know it. I had thought his dislike of Tyler and his desire to protect me from him was because he had feelings for me. But his attitude toward Tyler was one anyone might take after reading *That Summer*. Asking me how I could have kissed him could have been just an indictment of my weak character rather than the jealousy I had made it out to be.

Robert's assertion that Andreas couldn't take his eyes off me had reinforced these initial impressions, had caused me to hope. But one looked at another person for any number of reasons. Maybe he wondered why I wasn't eating or talking much. Maybe I had something stuck in my teeth. Maybe he wasn't even looking at me. He could have been looking at the lake or a bird or nothing at all.

Maybe I'd made something out of a lot of nothing. It was convenient for Andreas to stay at the lake while he did his translation work, a nice escape from city life and the chance to smoke a cigar with Robert Rainier any time he wanted. I began to think that it was entirely possible that it was Robert, not me, he was interested in spending time with.

By mid-August I decided to change the approach I'd been taking to the novel. Rather than write a standard love story with a happy ending, I'd write what I was more familiar with—a story without resolution. It wasn't what I thought my editor wanted. It wasn't what I thought readers wanted. But it was what I could write.

The moment I made that decision, everything changed. Instead of forcing my fingers to push buttons to fill up white space on the screen, my hands could hardly keep up with my head. My daily output went from hundreds of words to thousands.

I stopped breaking in the afternoons to swim in order to keep my momentum going, sometimes writing for ten hours of the day.

When I got to the end, I started immediately back at the beginning, rewriting and revising what I'd written earlier in the summer, fitting it into my new framework. I saw Andreas less and less. I hardly ate at all. Eating meant I had to stop writing. And I couldn't. I couldn't stop typing because I couldn't stop my brain. It was all I could do to get to sleep each night, and some nights I didn't sleep at all. I suppose in that much, Robert was right. I had shown up, day in and day out, and the story had come.

It was the first day of September that I finally felt I was finished. I had a good, solid draft that held together and told a definite story, a story I felt fit to tell. A story that was true in its own way. A story I would not be ashamed to send to my editor.

But first, someone else needed to read it. I would send it to Lois, of course, but I needed a man to read it as well, to be sure I had written the male character with authenticity. It was too raw to show Robert. I wouldn't want him to think it was the best I could do. The only other man to ask was Andreas, but that was even more uncomfortable. It would be like if I had asked Tyler to read over an early draft of *That Summer*. Andreas was the inspiration for the story, and there was no way he wouldn't see himself in it—and see how I really felt about him.

It would have to be Robert. And Robert only read on paper. I'd have to get it printed at the copy shop in town.

"I'll come with you," Andreas said when I told him I couldn't hang out because I was going into town.

"I'm just emailing my manuscript to Lois and getting it printed out for Robert," I said as we got into the car. "It won't be much fun."

"*Das macht nichts. Ich verbringe gerne Zeit mit dir. Außerdem fehlst du mir.*"

"Zeit? Like Zeitgeist? Does that have something to do with time?"

"Ah, you caught that? You are learning. Soon I will have to be careful about what I say to you in German."

I pulled out onto the road. "I don't think you have to worry about that. Lucky guess. At this rate it will be decades before I can hold a simple conversation."

Out on the highway I was startled to see that the corn was dry and some fields had already been harvested. The teasel and mullein were already brown, and the forests were dotted with yellow and orange. My time at Hidden Lake was running short.

"I'll have to close up the cabin next month," I said. "It's not insulated. Grandpa used to stretch his time there until November with the fireplace and extra layers, but it won't be long before the nights are just too cold to stay comfortable."

"Did you ever think of insulating the cabin so you could stay up there year-round?"

"Ike is there year-round," I said, "and I can't believe that that claptrap of his is insulated all that well. He probably just has shredded newspaper stuffed in the walls. Are you still enjoying your early mornings with him?"

Andreas smiled. "Yes, though it hasn't worked out quite like I thought."

"How so?"

"I thought I'd be listening to his crazy stories while we fished, but he doesn't like anyone talking out on the lake. Scares the fish away. So I have to wait until he's made a few catches and heads back to shore. Then he makes breakfast and we chat. I'm getting a lot of good material though."

"Material for what?"

"I'd like to write about him someday."

I looked at him to see if he was kidding. "You mean like a novel?"

"No, more of a biography."

I laughed. "Does he know this?"

"I've mentioned it. He didn't think anyone would care to read it."

"I'm not sure I disagree with him. Do you think you would be able to substantiate any of his stories?"

Andreas snickered. "It will be a challenge, I'm sure. But that's half the fun of writing, isn't it?"

"I guess," I said. I pulled onto the exit ramp and got into the right turn lane. "I can drop you at Biggby and join you once I get my manuscript printed."

"Sure."

Forty-five minutes later, I met up with Andreas at the coffee shop. I dug through my email inbox, sent my manuscript to Lois for a read-through, and sent an encouraging "almost there" email to my longsuffering editor. The last email in my box came from Andreas. It contained nothing but a few links.

"What's all this?" I asked.

"Contractors in the area who do insulation."

I smiled. "I don't have the money for this."

"Your friend's company is in there. Scott. The one who redid that restaurant we went to. Maybe he'd give you a deal."

"Maybe."

Back in the car, Andreas picked up the box containing my manuscript and lifted the lid. "*Untitled*. Very catchy."

"Shut up. I haven't had time to think about the title yet."

He turned to the first chapter. Though almost all of what I'd written when I started drafting earlier that summer had been rewritten and revised and edited until it hardly resembled what I'd started with, I had only changed one word in the first couple sentences.

Leila Marie was never late, never early, never on time. She was never any of these things because she was never invited, not even to her own wedding.

During our drive back to the cabin, Andreas read the entire first chapter, which ended with the introduction of the love interest, whom I'd made an Iraqi doctor rather than a German investment banker. When I stopped the car on the gravel drive, he carefully put the pages back into the box and closed the lid. I held out my hand for it.

"Could I read the rest?" he said. "You've already got me hooked."

"That's a good sign, I guess." I shut the car door. "Though I'm not sure it would be your cup of tea. Women are more the target market."

"They were with *That Summer* too, and I loved that."

Inside, I put the box on the coffee table.

"Anyway," he continued, "it's a love story, isn't it? Everyone likes falling in love."

He was looking at me like he wanted to say more. But I guarded my heart against the feeling welling up inside. I'd make no more assumptions.

"Yes," I said. It was nearly a whisper.

I stared at the box on the coffee table and felt vaguely un-settled. I'd been so confident when I sent it off to Lois. Why did I suddenly feel like it was all wrong?

"So what do you think?" Andreas said. "Could I read it?"

"Sure," I said. Though I was anything but.

Andreas picked the box up. "I'll read it straight through, and Robert can have it tomorrow night."

I had no reasonable reason to refuse. He went into Grandpa's bedroom and closed the curtain. I retreated up to the loft and paced around for a few nervous minutes until I found something to distract me from the fact that Andreas was reading my manuscript. I'd let the laundry pile up again while I was drafting so feverishly. I gathered it from the floor and beneath the bed and brought it down to the kitchen. I dumped in the soap, started the water, and ran my fingers through every pocket to make sure no rocks made their way into the washing machine.

Once more, the letter turned up. I almost missed it because by this time it felt more like fabric than paper. I closed the lid went back up to the loft, and unfolded the thing that had driven me up to Hidden Lake three months earlier. The sentences in the creases were beginning to fade. I'd read it many times before in other people's voices, but I'd never actually read it in yours. And that's what I did now.

Kendra,

Your book, while perhaps thought "brave" in some circles, is anything but. It is the work of a selfish opportunist who was all too ready to monetize the suffering of others. Did you ever consider that antagonists have stories of their own? Or that in someone else's story you're the antagonist?

Your problem is that you paid more attention to the people who had done you wrong than the ones who'd done you right. That, and you are obviously obsessed with yourself.

```
I hope you're happy with the success you've
found with this book, because the admiration
of strangers is all you're likely to get from
here on out. It certainly won't win you any
new friends. And I'm willing to bet the old
ones will steer pretty clear of you from here
on out. In fact, some of them you'll never
see again.

Sincerely,
A Very Disappointed Reader
```

Each time I had read that letter since it arrived at my apartment in March, I believed that every line was about Tyler, which was why I found it so unbelievable that you could have been the one who wrote it. But it wasn't all about him, was it? Reading it now, I finally saw that it was also about you.

You were the one who longed to be noticed and appreciated. You had done me right so many times, for so long before our friendship started to fall apart. And I never fully saw it. Because it truly was all about me. I was CC. Only now, I really didn't want to be.

I looked at the date typed in the upper right-hand corner of the page. March 25. The day before Grandpa's memorial service. Ike had said that when he came back up from Pontiac, you were gone.

```
In fact, some of them you'll never see again.
```

It was then that I realized that perhaps I had not been carrying around a scathing review from A Very Disappointed Reader for five months.

Perhaps I'd been carrying your suicide note.

35

Labor Day weekend was fast approaching. Your parents would be closing up the cottage and heading back to Battle Creek for the cold months. I could not let them leave the lake. Not yet. Beth needed to know if you had chosen death or if death had chosen you.

I found your parents at the kitchen table, Robert reading the newspaper and Beth making checklists of what still needed to be done before they left. I placed the letter and the empty bottle of Shortcross Gin I'd found at Ike's on the table between them.

"Cami was my disappointed reader," I said.

At their confused looks, I went on.

"The date matches up with when Ike said he saw her up here. And the *a*'s drop below the line. This was written on your typewriter when Ike saw Cami up here, and when he came back from Grandpa's service she was gone. She asked him to mail a letter for her when he was in Pontiac."

Beth had picked up the letter, and her eyes were now swiftly running across the lines. She got to the bottom and handed it to Robert.

"And it's about more than just the book. It's more than just her being angry about me telling a story I shouldn't have. It's about what I missed. In the book and in real life."

"I'm not sure I understand," Beth said.

"I left her out of the story. Like she was completely inconsequential to me. Like she didn't matter at all." I tapped the empty bottle. "Ike found this in early April. This is your brand, isn't it?"

"What are you trying to say?" Beth said.

"This is my fault."

She put a hand on my arm. "Kendra, of course it isn't."

I pulled away. "Look at the last sentence. Is that not clearly a cry for help? Or a threat?"

The looks on their faces told me they understood what I was trying to say. Robert pulled a chair out for me, but I did not sit down.

"Kendra, I think maybe you're blowing this out of proportion. Maybe she wrote this letter, but to have such a strong reaction because she wasn't in the book? Don't you think that's a little unreasonable, even for Cami? It's certainly nothing anyone would commit . . ." He trailed off rather than say the word, the terrible word.

"Let's slow down," Beth said. "How can you be sure it was Cami who wrote this at all?"

"No, I think she's right on that," Robert said. "It was written on my typewriter."

"And the date," I said again. "And it was sent to my apartment, not to my publisher. It was from someone I knew, typed on your typewriter, and it wasn't either of you or Tyler."

"How do you know it wasn't Tyler?" Beth said.

"We already talked about it. It wasn't him."

"But it would only make sense to be him," she insisted. "It

doesn't say anything about being upset about not being in the book. I think you're drawing conclusions there."

"It wasn't him. Believe me. I paid him plenty of attention. When he was around, almost all of my attention was focused on him. This went on for years."

There was a moment of heavy silence before Beth said, "What are you talking about?"

I sighed. "It was somehow just easier than putting him off."

I could tell from her face that Beth did not understand this weak line of reasoning. Just as readers wouldn't have. And I could tell from Robert's face that somehow he did.

"Anyway, I just needed to tell you the truth. She wrote it, and I don't think it was an accident." I turned to leave but then changed my mind. It would be nine months before I'd be in this house again. "Before I go, would you mind if I had a moment alone in Cami's room?"

"Of course," Robert said.

I walked down the hall to your room and shut the door. I could hear Robert's muffled voice, low and calm. Then Beth's, louder. I tuned them out and lay down on the bed, thinking of all of the conversations we'd had in this very spot. All the secrets we'd shared. All the shenanigans you'd gotten me into and out of. I thought of the cigarettes and the rainstorm. Then I remembered the box.

I rolled over on my stomach and hung the top half of my body off the bed so I could see underneath it. There, tucked far below, was the shoebox full of treasures I had never quite gotten a good look at. I reached through the dust bunnies and dragged it out. It was too dirty for the pristine bed, so I dropped onto the floor beside it. Then, with just a moment's hesitation but no real shame, I invaded your privacy.

Inside, there were dozens of notes from me you had saved

over the years. The pink bandana that had declared our sovereignty over Mermaid Island. A picture of us, taken before you cut your hair, both in bikinis, laughing. Your arm is around my waist. Mine is around your shoulders. The sun is shining brightly, and we are happy in the way only two young, invincible girls can be. Only those who've felt so fiercely about one another could have hurt each other the way we did. Only those with so much to lose could have felt so deeply the loss.

Now our friendship was just a forgotten box of memories left to gather dust under a bed that was never slept in.

A knock sounded on the door. I quickly put the lid on the shoebox and slid it under the bed, but the photo I tucked under a pillow. I sat on the edge of your bed, facing the door, and said, "Come in."

It was Robert. "Beth's gone to bed."

"I'm sorry."

"For what?"

"For everything. For all the ways I messed up your lives. If I'd never been born, none of this would have happened."

He looked about to argue, then seemed to consider that. "Well," he said finally, "if you want to play that game, you have to go further back. Back to me and Jackie. Then back to our parents and their parents. All the way back to the first man and the first woman. There's no point in what-ifs except in writing. Which, by the way, how's that going?"

"Great, actually. I printed the manuscript out today and I was going to ask you to read it, but I wasn't sure you'd have time or the mental space with all that's going on. Then Andreas kind of usurped your position. He's reading it at my place right now. Only I'm not sure it's right anymore. It was great this morning, though." I laughed.

"That's how it goes." He sat beside me. "What's it about?"

"When I started, it was going to be a love story. But then I realized I didn't really know anything about love, so I couldn't get to the happily-ever-after part. Then I rewrote it to be a tragic romance."

He nodded thoughtfully. "I certainly know a thing or two about that."

I pulled the photo out from under your pillow. "This was in Cami's box beneath the bed. Would you mind if I kept it?"

"Looks like you were going to anyway."

I let out a little laugh. "Yeah. I guess I'm making stealing people's photos a habit." At his cocked eyebrow, I admitted, "I took one from an album in Cami's room after the funeral."

Robert smiled. "Take the whole box."

I looked at the bangles on my wrist. "That's okay. I think I've got everything I need for now."

He patted me on the back. "Okay."

I stood up. "When are you leaving the lake?"

He stood as well. "The Wednesday after Labor Day. Give the highways time to clear out a bit."

"Is that when Andreas is leaving too?"

Robert smiled again. "I think he'll stay on."

"Here?"

"No, at Ike's."

I nearly choked. "Seriously?"

"I was surprised too. Not that he wants to stick around while you're still up here, but that he didn't just ask you if he could stay with you again."

"That is weird. He'd rather live with Ike Fenton? I feel somewhat rejected."

Robert laughed. "It's not like that, I don't think."

"What is it, then?"

"I don't want to talk out of turn."

I narrowed my eyes. "You two have been talking about me behind my back?"

"Maybe a little. All good stuff, though. I think he just wants to respect your space. And perhaps flee from temptation a bit."

My face flushed hot. "Oh."

"Anyway, I want to have you both here on Labor Day. Say, four o'clock?"

"Sure."

He showed me out and waved as I headed back across the lake.

When I got back into the cabin, I found Andreas still reading my manuscript on Grandpa's bed.

I snatched the page out of his hand. "Stop reading that."

36

ndreas looked up, startled. "What's wrong?"

"All of it." I started boxing the manuscript back up. "It's all wrong."

"Whoa, whoa, whoa," he said. "Slow down. You're just having second thoughts. Give it time to settle a bit. Let your agent read it."

Lois. I needed to call her immediately and tell her to stop reading. I took the box with me into the kitchen and dialed her number. She answered on the third ring.

"Lois, did you start reading that manuscript I sent you today?"

"I'm sorry, I haven't had time just yet, but I'll get to it when—"

"Don't read it. Delete it. It's not done. I'll send you a new file as soon as I can, but forget about that one. Please. Don't even let it linger in your recycle bin. Erase it from existence."

"Kendra," she drew out in a warning tone, "you're not starting over again, are you?"

"No, I just need to make some adjustments. I promise I'm not starting from scratch."

When I got off the phone, Andreas was standing in the living room, his hands outstretched in a "what gives?" gesture. "I was on the tenth chapter. I was loving it."

"I'm sorry, but it's just not there yet. I have to get rid of Kahil."

"How can you get rid of him? He's the love interest. This is a love story."

"Not exactly. A love story ends with them getting together."

He frowned. "And this doesn't?"

I shook my head. "Sorry to spoil it for you. But I'm changing it anyway."

He sat on the couch and gave me a calculating look. He opened his mouth. Closed it. "They don't get together?"

I shrugged. "No."

"So it's not a love story."

"It's a love story, it's just not a happy one. It's more like *Romeo and Juliet* or *Casablanca*."

He stuck his bottom lip out. "So who will you replace your foreign lover with? Someone more Leila's type? An American? Maybe someone she met in college?"

"Her best friend."

"You're making her best friend a man? That will mean a lot of changes."

"No, it will still be Annie. But that's what the story will really be about. A friendship. One that falls apart little by little—so slowly, in fact, that they don't even know it's happening until it's too late."

"But what about the love story?"

"It doesn't make any sense. Right now there's really no good reason for Leila and Kahil not to get together. If they really love each other, they would make it work."

"Then why not just keep your foreigner and make it work?"

I slumped onto the couch. "I don't know how. Apart from

movies, I've never seen two people who were really, truly in love, so I'm not sure what I'm writing is true to life."

He sat back, draped his arm across the top of the couch behind me, and looked at me intently. "You've never been in love?"

I held his gaze. "Not with anyone who loved me back."

The corner of his mouth quirked up just slightly. "That can't be true. Maybe you just misread the signs."

I scoffed. "Maybe. I seem to be good at that."

His smile grew. "I suppose sometimes the signs are too small, so they're hard to read. Sometimes a man is overly cautious because he doesn't want to move too fast, doesn't want to presume."

"I guess. But I think most women like a guy who takes the lead in things like that, as long as he's respectful."

"What would your advice be to a man who was falling for you, then? What kind of sign would you be able to read?"

I had to smile. "I don't know. A touch when there doesn't have to be one."

Andreas ran the back of one finger down the length of my arm. "Like this?"

I felt my cheeks getting hot.

"What else?" he said.

"He wouldn't always keep two feet of space between us."

Andreas moved closer until his leg was touching mine and brought his arm down from the top of the couch to encircle my shoulders. "What else?"

"He would tell me."

"What would he tell you?"

"He would tell me . . . that he came back to the lake to see me for more than just the fact that I had been through a tough time. That he had missed me when he was gone. That he didn't want the summer to end because he didn't want us both to have to go back to our real homes and our real lives." I looked into his eyes. "He would tell me that it had taken all of his power not to lay Tyler out when he first met him, and that when he saw Tyler kiss me, he wasn't just upset that I had put myself at risk—he was jealous that another man had kissed me at all."

"All das und noch viel mehr."

"And he would say it in English so I could understand him."

Andreas smiled and held my gaze. "All that and more."

Then he leaned in and kissed me. He finally kissed me. Soft, tender, and full of love. Like I'd been given a second chance at my first kiss.

37

The Saturday before Labor Day, a large delivery truck lumbered down the winding gravel drive, dropped off four boxes, did a thirty-seven-point turn, and lurched back up the hill. Tyler had made good on his promise to send a proper bar setup, despite the fact that I didn't know what any of it was for and it would surely end up collecting as much dust as my rocks did. The next day, Scott Masters was at the door, tape measure in hand. Andreas had invited him to come over and give me an estimate for insulating and drywalling the cabin. The amount was breathtakingly out of my price range, even with the friends and family discount, but Andreas seemed to think that didn't matter.

I sent Scott away with a stern order not to accept any money from Andreas and to put the Brennan cabin out of his mind until at least a year or two down the road. The two of them talked for too long after Scott got into his truck, though, and I was sure they were cooking up some way to ignore my directive.

Labor Day dawned cool and clear. I was looking forward to seeing Robert, and I hoped that Beth had been able to process the new information I'd given her. I was doing okay on some points. I could accept that you had written the letter. What I had trouble with—what I was sure I would always have trouble with—was the fact that I had contributed in some way to your death.

Certainly I had never been able to fathom the wild child I knew settling down and growing to a ripe old age, but I could never have guessed just how young and tragically you would die. Since I had seen you lying on Ike's beach, there had been many nights I'd awakened sweating and gasping. The nightmares were beginning to fade, and now in my dreams I knew that your body was somewhere close, but I did not always see it. Robert and Beth had been spared that, at least, though I often wondered if Tyler had similar nightmares and whether I might meet him in them some dark night.

At noon I sat in Robert's boat with a large bowl of salad on my lap as Andreas, who'd swung by to pick me up, manned the motor like he'd been born on the lake. As I walked up the stairs to your deck, I heard a voice that was out of context. It was not a Hidden Lake voice. Surely Robert and Beth had not invited a stranger over. Not when this had promised to be such an intimate meal.

It took a moment after I got up onto the deck to get my bearings. Of course I knew that voice. It belonged to my mother. But to see her there, lounging in an Adirondack chair and accepting a drink from Robert's outstretched hand as Beth looked on with a trace of a pained smile across her face, was just this side of believable, like watching a street magician levitate.

"Kendra! Andreas! There you are," Robert boomed. "Look who's here."

"I see," I said through a strange, plastic smile. I tried to look properly enthused, but I knew I must be failing.

Jackie got up and held her hand out to Andreas.

"Andreas, this is my mom, Jackie. Mom, this is Andreas. He's been up most of the summer translating my book, and now one of Robert's, into German."

"It's so nice to meet you," she said. "Rob's told me so much about you."

"When did you get here?" I said.

"About an hour ago," Beth offered. "We've just been catching each other up on the last quarter century."

I tried to read Beth's expression. Was she happy about this visit?

"Andreas, I know what you're having," Robert said. "What about you, Kendra?"

"Oh, wow," I said, "I'd take just about anything right now. Surprise me."

Robert went inside, and Jackie patted the chair next to her. "Sit down, Andreas. Tell me all about yourself."

Why was she being so friendly?

I sat next to Beth and leaned in close. "Did you know she was coming?"

"No," Beth whispered. "She called on the drive up."

"Are you okay with her here?"

She looked at me. "Are you?"

"I'm afraid I kind of suggested it. Though I told her she should come up to visit me, not you." I leaned closer yet. "I never thought she'd take me up on the invitation."

Jackie laughed at something Andreas said.

"I think it's good for her," Beth said. "Anyway, it was a long time ago. We all made mistakes. We can't change that." She patted my arm.

"What are you two whispering about over there?" Jackie said.

"I was just telling Kendra about Martin," Beth lied. "That

Polish exchange student who was up here with Paul's family that one year, you remember him?"

Beth and Jackie started talking about all of the escapades with Martin, some of which involved hopping trains, just as you and I had once schemed about doing. Robert came out with our drinks.

"What is it?" I said when he handed me a glass of deep amber liquid.

"Scotch. You'll need it if Jackie's staying with you."

"I heard that, Robert. I won't impose, Kendra. I'll stay at a hotel."

"On Labor Day weekend?" Beth said. "Did you make a reservation?"

"She can stay with us," Robert said.

Beth, Jackie, and I all shot Robert the same incredulous look.

"No, you already have Andreas. She'll stay in Grandpa's room," I said in a parental tone that brooked no argument.

There was no more talk of sleeping arrangements, but I could feel the strain the conversation had put on Beth and Robert. He'd just been trying to be polite by offering a bed to Jackie. But I didn't blame Beth for not wanting my mother loose in her house.

Drinks and cigars were followed with drinks and steaks, then more drinks and cigars, until it was getting on the late side and Robert and Jackie were both a little giddy. Despite the prospect of spending one-on-one time with my mother, I didn't touch the Scotch after the first unpleasant sip, and I noticed that Beth drank only water. Funny that it should take me this long to realize how much she and I had in common, both feeling the burden to stay alert and sober minded when others were descending into alcohol-induced idiocy.

As the night was wearing thin, Beth gave me a knowing glance and then retired to the kitchen to tackle the dishes, leaving me to watch Jackie, who had latched herself to Robert like a lamprey. I tried a few times to subtly indicate it was time to go, but clearly I would have to be the parent in this situation.

"Come on, Mom," I finally said. "You can't make up for twenty-five years in one night. Let's go. They'll be here tomorrow."

After saying our goodbyes, I drove Jackie's car around the lake to my cabin, though I would far rather have had Andreas take me home in the boat under the stars.

At the cabin I got her tucked into bed, but she was too wired to go to sleep.

"He's very nice," she said.

I sat on the edge of the bed. "Yes, he is."

"He lives in Chicago?"

"Yes."

"So, what now? Has he asked you to move to Chicago?"

"No."

She fluffed the pillow and put it back under her head. "Not everyone is worth changing your life for."

"Yes, I'm very aware of your position on that."

"Don't get catty, Kendra. I'm not saying he's not worth it. Maybe he is. But you only have one life. You don't want to screw it up."

"Like you did?"

She rolled over. "I can't have this conversation right now. I'm tired."

I picked at a peeling fingernail and tried to recall if I'd packed any polish back in June. "When you realized you were pregnant, why didn't you just get married?"

She expelled a little puff of air. "I'm sorry you had to have me as a mother, but it wouldn't have been any better with Robert

Rainier as a father. When Beth married him, she had a lot of work to do to get him to the point where anyone would even consider allowing him to raise a child. And if the two of us had been together—it would have been worse. We were just terrible people, and we made each other more terrible when we were together."

"Did you love each other?"

"I don't know. Maybe." She turned back toward me. "We did the best thing we thought we could do for you, Kendra. And you turned out all right."

I stood to leave but lingered in the doorway a moment. "Why don't we stay here tomorrow, just you and me. I'm not sure Beth's up for more company right now."

I slid the curtain closed before she could answer. I brushed my teeth and slipped under my covers. The cabin was chilly. It wouldn't be long before I'd have to drain the pipes and latch the shutters. Where did I go from here? Where would Andreas go? And would we go there together?

38

The first thing I did the next morning was build a fire. I made coffee, opened my laptop, and started my rewrite. Unexpected houseguest or no, I was going to get some work done.

It was nearly eleven o'clock by the time Jackie rolled out of bed. I made eggs and toast, not knowing that my own mother was now gluten free. She ate the eggs and I ate the toast.

Then we picked up where we'd left off, Jackie finally filling in some of the vast gaps in my knowledge about her. We talked about her wild past, which sounded a bit like your wild past, only she'd started from a younger age. It was my arrival in the world that had gotten her to clean up her act. So at least I managed to perhaps save one life, though I hadn't been aware of it. Did that balance out what I might have done to yours?

She told me of her close friendship with Beth, of its disintegration when she came between Beth and Paul, the man Beth was really meant to end up with. Of how Beth and Robert had ended up together instead, just like their characters had in *Blessed Fool*. She told me how she'd made life all about her. She told me about my longsuffering grandmother, who had died in her late forties the same year I was born. I wish I could tell you about it.

Through it all, I kept thinking about your letter.

```
Did you ever consider that antagonists have
stories of their own? Or that in someone
else's story you're the antagonist?
```

My mother seemed to have been an antagonist in a number of people's stories. But that wasn't the whole picture. She'd also been a victim. Of drug dealers, as you had been. Of some guys who only wanted one thing, as I had been. She wasn't all bad, just like I wasn't all good.

Robert too. He'd been the good guy in Tyler's story and in yours. He'd been the bad guy in my grandparents' story, the guy who'd corrupted their daughter, even if she did plenty of corrupting herself. He'd been the bad guy and the good guy to me—both the absent father and the devoted mentor.

The one person in my life I could not imagine as an antagonist was Andreas. He came to the cabin around three o'clock as my mother was preparing to leave. He brought her bag out to the car, lingering outside afterward to give us a moment to say a private goodbye.

Jackie and I shared a stiff hug. "Stay in touch and let me know where you end up," she said.

When she'd gone, Andreas fed the fire and then handed me something from his pocket. "Robert gave it to me to give to you."

I unfolded the letter I had left at their house and wondered what I should do with it. Was it something I should put in a shoebox and store under my bed? Something I should put in a file in some cabinet? For what purpose? To pull out later and remind me of how I had failed you as a friend? To remind me of this grim summer? Of the body under the tarp? Those were things I wanted to forget. And yet every time this letter turned up, it would all come rushing back, just as other bad memories had when I saw the old wooden rowboat.

I took two deliberate steps and tossed the letter into the fireplace. The flames licked the edges, then burst through the center. In a moment it was gone.

The next day, Beth and Robert closed up their cottage and headed downstate. Other houses around the lake had emptied out as well, and by the end of the week, the only houses with lights still on and docks still in the water were Ike's and mine. Andreas spent much of his time with Ike, getting down as many stories as possible because there was no telling which summer might be Ike's last.

In the quiet, empty cabin, I sat by the perpetual fire and revised my second novel. And as I did, as I added you to every page, it came alive.

At the end of each day, I collapsed in bed, utterly spent. Until finally, on the last day of September, it was finished. I went to town, which was now devoid of tourist traffic, and sent it off to Lois. Then I handed off my laptop to Andreas and went out to pick the last rocks of the season.

Two days later, early in the morning when it was still dark, Andreas woke me up. "Come on, we're going fishing."

I rolled over. "It's too cold. And you don't know how to fish."

"Ike taught me."

"Then go fish with Ike."

He tugged on my hand. "Come on. It might be your last chance this year. You told me you used to go fishing every morning with your grandfather."

"He had coffee."

"I have coffee. And I finished your novel."

I sat up. "Let me get dressed."

Ten minutes later, I was shivering in the boat on the mist-heavy lake. The trees were at peak color, a tapestry of gold and bronze and rust woven together with the deep gray-green of conifers and softened by silver steam rising from the still water. Andreas had taken us to one of Ike's favorite fishing spots. Though it felt early to me, Ike had already been out on the lake and was back in his house, probably frying up the catch for breakfast.

Andreas and I were utterly alone. And I was not anxious. I did not fear what he might say about my novel, and I did not fear him. This was a man I could trust.

He expertly prepared our rods and held one out for me.

"That's Grandpa's," I said.

He handed me the other one. My old fishing rod, Jackie's before that, Leila's before that. It had seen many mornings out on Hidden Lake, caught many fish. The handle still fit perfectly in my hand. We cast off opposite sides of the boat, turned slightly apart from one another, looking at the lake cradled within the tree-covered hills rather than at each other. The perfect position to discuss a book.

"So, what did you think?" I said.

"It's wonderful."

"Not *wunderbar*? I wish it was *wunderbar*."

Andreas laughed. "*Ja, es ist wunderbar.* But I was specifically told I needed to express myself in English so I could be understood."

I smiled and slowly turned the reel handle to draw my line back in. "Do you think it's as good as *That Summer*?"

"Better."

"Please."

"It is. It's a beautiful story."

I cast my line again and felt a lump of emotion creep up my throat. "I wish Cami could read it."

Andreas reached over and put a hand on my knee. We were quiet for several minutes until he finally said, "I guess Ike caught the last fish this morning."

I laughed. "That's okay. It was never about the fish for me. Or for Grandpa, I don't think."

"For all his fish stories, I don't think it is for Ike either."

We reeled in our empty lines and sat face-to-face, drinking black coffee from an old thermos.

"I have to close up the cabin," I said. "It's too cold. And I'm going to have to have reliable internet when the edits and marketing plans start coming in."

Andreas nodded. "I still think you should get the place insulated. And I checked, they can run DSL up here. Fiber optics can't be that far behind."

His mouth was quirked in that confounding half smile I had grown to love.

"Maybe next year," I said. "If I have the money."

"I have the money right now."

"I told you, you're not paying to update my cabin. I'm not going to abuse you just because you have means."

"What if it were our cabin?"

You know how when you've stayed under water too long, you become ultra aware of the involuntary action of your lungs? How they start to strain against your will to hold your breath because they know they need air? That's how I felt when I heard those words.

When I didn't—couldn't—answer, Andreas kept talking. "I know we haven't known each other very long, but I think I know what I need to know to know that I don't want to go back to Chicago without you."

I found the surface. "Andreas, I can't just move to Chicago."

It killed me to say it, but if I did this wrong, if I just went along to get along as I had always done in the past, how would I ever be able to call my life my own? I wanted everything that I did, from this moment on, to be something *I* did. Not something done to me.

"I can't just move in with you," I said. "That's not the kind of future I want for myself. I grew up in a broken home. If I'm going to be with anyone, it has to be a real commitment, not just living together."

A smile crept back over his face. "Maybe I'm hard to understand even when I am speaking English. I don't want you to just move in with me. I was thinking of something more permanent. When you're ready." He reached across and took my hand. "I love you, Kendra."

Tears pushed at the backs of my eyes. "How do you say it in German?"

"Ich liebe dich."

I leaned forward over the space between us and kissed him. *I* kissed *him*. I chose him. A man who gave me all the right kind of attention. Who desired all of me: my mind, my body, and my spirit—my past, my present, and my future.

"So, is that a yes?" he said. "I don't want to get the wrong translation."

"Of course it is."

Andreas took both of my hands in his. "There, you see? You can write a love story. One with a happy ending."

Epilogue

In ideal conditions, a work of fiction tells the truth. Probably our dad knew when he'd hit on it, the same way he'd know if he got stung by a bee. For me it was more like the mosquito I didn't know I should have slapped until I was scratching at an angry red welt behind my knee.

Sometimes the truth hurts. Sometimes it's ugly. Always it shows us just a little bit more of who we are. And when we don't like what we see, we have the chance to make a change. To be less of the person we wish we weren't and more of the person we wish we were.

If you could read this, I would want you to know that I am happier now than I have been since the summer I first met you, that perfect, enchanted summer of smiles and easy laughter. When I was a child, you were everything I could have imagined desiring in a best friend, everything I wished I could be. Gorgeous and gregarious. Daring and dangerous. Haughty and hilarious. Everything you did, you did to the fullest.

There are so many things I wish I'd done differently in my life. It used to be that most of those things were centered on Tyler. I spent over a decade wishing I'd been stronger, firmer, harsher, thinking that if only I had come across with enough force and authority, he would not have taken advantage of me. Or that if I had just had the guts to tell someone, he would have been punished as he deserved.

Now I don't care about any of that. Now all of those things I wish I'd done differently? They're about you. I wish I'd been more observant and less self-absorbed. I wish I'd asked you why you cut your hair, why you threw rocks so hard at your brother, why you hated that he stared at me, why you never seemed to be quite as happy with your life as I thought you should be. I wish I could have seen that I wasn't the only one hurting. I wish it hadn't all been about me.

And I wish I'd come back to Hidden Lake sooner.

Maybe it wouldn't have changed anything. But maybe it would have been enough to show you that you were and are loved unconditionally. By your best friend. Your sister.

You might be interested to know that my second novel ended up with the same title as my very first short story, the one you hated, the one I destroyed. You might also be interested to know that the day it released was the day your bangles finally came off my wrist.

For weeks I had been anxious about the book's reception and busy getting ready for the media blitz my publicist had cooked up. That, combined with the recent stress of traveling to Germany to meet Andreas's family, made it so that I could hardly eat for weeks. Early in the morning on release day, I was all soaped up in the shower and the bangles slipped right off and clattered to the tile floor. I almost put them back on, but for some reason I set them aside. They didn't quite match the ring Andreas and I had picked out, and I wasn't sure they'd be right for the wedding. And what if once I put them on, they wouldn't come off again?

I finished getting ready for a full day of visiting indie book-shops in Chicago to support the release of *The Girl Who Could Breathe Under Water*. I was almost out the door when I doubled back to the bathroom.

"Kendra, the car is here," Andreas said from the hall.

"Be right out!"

I slipped the bangles over my hand.

And I haven't taken them off since.

Author's Note

When I was nine years old, a friend's older brother molested me in their van during a game of hide-and-seek. This occurred after a string of other lesser, though not less uncomfortable incidents of being grabbed and pulled under water in a pool, trapped in a room, held down by the weight of his body, and otherwise intimidated and harassed.

By God's grace, nothing worse than that ever happened to me, though of course worse does happen to many girls and women, usually at the hands of someone they should be able to trust. Many of us spend years, decades, or perhaps our whole lives keeping these things secret for many reasons—to preserve a friendship or a career, to avoid shaming our family, because we don't think others will believe us, because we've seen that many victims who come forward are accused of lying or of causing their own abuse. There are many compelling reasons to keep quiet, to not rock the boat.

Even I hesitate to tell you much more about my own story. It's been more than thirty years since it happened. I know where he is. I've spoken to him a number of times since. I would not be surprised if at some point in my life, I see him again. And I have my own suspicions about what might have happened to him to have influenced his behavior.

If you've experienced sexual harassment, abuse, or intimidation, I'm not here to tell you what you should do about it. I'm not here to shame you for not going public or getting law enforcement involved. I'm not going to tell you it's your Christian duty to forgive your abuser. Your story is your business, and the way you handle it is your decision. The way I ultimately handled mine was by writing this book.

I will say this: if you are currently in a dangerous situation or an abusive relationship, whether at home, at work, at church, or anywhere else, please tell *someone* you can trust, and please start making an exit plan. You were not meant for this. You do not deserve this. You are worth far more than this. Please, please get out.

Healing is a long road. Forgiveness is a longer one. Or maybe it's part of the same lifelong journey. But you don't have to walk that road alone. Turn to your friends. Turn to God. Ask for help and understanding. And don't stop asking until you get them.

The first person I told my story to was a teacher in sixth grade—who, as it happens, went to prison a few years later as a sex offender. I think I was in college before I risked telling anyone else. That confidant is now my husband. After I started writing this book in 2015, I told a few others. A couple close childhood friends. My sister. My mother. In 2016, I wrote about my story on my blog. And now anyone who cares to read this book will know a bit about it. With each telling, it's gotten easier and I've felt a little weight lifted, like removing another stone from my pocket.

You don't have to let your past trauma define your future.

It will always be part of how you became the person you are today, but you get to decide whether you're going to let that hold you back or you're going to harness it and use it to propel you forward. As in the story of Joseph in the book of Genesis, what man means for evil, God can and does use for good. And as Paul reminds the believers in Rome, "We know that God causes all things to work together for good to those who love God, to those who are called according to His purpose" (Rom. 8:28). God exchanges His beauty for our ashes, His hope for our despair, His glory for our shame. He is in the business of redemption. And He can redeem your story.

I am thankful to Him for His patience with me as I have walked the road of forgiveness, for His grace when I stumble, for His forbearance when I am tempted to blame my own missteps on others. And I am grateful He's afforded me the opportunity to write this book.

I am also thankful to those who read early drafts—Valerie Marvin, Heather Brewer, and Nancy Johnson—and offered thoughtful critique and advice, as well as to Ulrike Köebele for her work translating Andreas's German lines and giving me insight into the types of challenges inherent in translation work. Thank you to Steve Anderson for making sure all of the boat and fishing activity was up to snuff (and to his wife, Pat, for volunteering him for the task).

Thank you to the Women's Fiction Writers Association (WFWA) for the 2015 writers retreat in Albuquerque, New Mexico. I wrote the first scenes of this story on the patio at the beautiful Hotel Albuquerque in Old Town, a place that feels like a second home to me now, surrounded by fellow writers who feel like family. I've been so honored to be able to serve as an organizer of this marvelous retreat for the past few years.

I am especially thankful to Zachary Bartels, not just for

reading what is a difficult book for a husband to read but for *believing* me when I first told him what had happened to me. Nothing means more to someone telling her story than that the one she tells it to believes it is true.

I am grateful to the pub board at Revell Books for being willing to take a chance on this novel, and especially to my agent, Nephele Tempest, and my editor, Kelsey Bowen, for championing it. Thanks also to Andrea Doering, Michele Misiak, Mark Rice, Laura Klynstra, Karen Steele, Jessica English, and everyone else at Revell and Baker Publishing Group for your support, your considerable talent, and your good work in every aspect of the publishing journey.

Mostly, reader, thank *you*. Because without you, I'd just be talking to myself.

Turn the Page

for a Special Sneak Peek
of Another Captivating Story from

ERIN BARTELS

COMING SPRING 2023

Liner Notes

I never wanted to live at my Uncle Mike's. Partly because I swore I'd never have anything to do with my dad since he clearly wanted nothing to do with me. Being my dad's twin brother, Uncle Mike is about as close to my actual dad as anyone could be. And partly because he's the type of guy whose entire life screams *failure*, and the more your path crosses with his, the more likely you are to become a failure yourself. And truthfully, I do a good enough job of that on my own.

But then, if Uncle Mike hadn't taken me in when Slow and Rodney kicked me out, I wouldn't be covered in mud and sitting in this pit with Natalie Wheeler.

Yeah, that Natalie Wheeler. Daughter of reclusive-guitarist-turned-producer Dusty Wheeler and onetime-flower-child-singer-songwriter Deb Wheeler, who also happen to be Uncle Mike's across-the-street neighbors and longsuffering landlords.

Uncle Mike's house was never meant to be a house. It was just the break trailer for the construction crew that built the Wheeler estate twenty years ago back in 1970. Uncle Mike was on the crew, and the Wheelers rented him the property cheap after their sprawling contemporary glass and stone house was finished. I guess because they either liked him or pitied him.

I'm not one hundred percent sure which impulse first inspired Natalie Wheeler to give me the time of day, but right at this moment, I don't really care. Right at this moment, I'm seeing more clearly than I ever have in my short and disappointing life that maybe I'm meant for something . . . better. It doesn't really matter to me how we got here.

That said, it probably matters to you—or if it doesn't yet, it will shortly—so maybe I should start earlier. Maybe the night I first made it through the door of the Wheeler house. The night I first saw Natalie. Even if she didn't see me.

SIDE A

Track One

I wasn't invited.

I should probably make that clear right off the bat. Because I don't want you to get the wrong idea about me. I'm nobody special. I don't know anybody important, and nobody important knows me. I just happened to know somebody who knew somebody. Or rather, I happened to have the same name as somebody who knew somebody.

The invitation I pulled out of the dented, rusty mailbox at the end of the short gravel drive did say Michael Sullivan, but it wasn't for me and I knew it. It was for my uncle, who I happen to be named after. Not because my dad wanted to honor his brother, but because my mom preferred his brother to him and she wanted to get back at him for missing my birth twenty-two years ago because he was out on a bender somewhere. Only I go by Michael, not Mike. The invitation said Michael. Probably because Mrs. Wheeler is a classy lady

The invitation arrived on Wednesday, December 27, 1989. I knew Mike wasn't going to be around for New Year's. I hadn't been living with him long, but it was long enough to notice a few patterns.

One: he smoked a pack of Camels every day.

Two: he never slept at home on weekends.

Three: he was bad with money.

Four: he listened almost exclusively to Lynyrd Skynyrd.

Five: he was wildly superstitious.

And when it came to ringing in the New Year in style at the Wheeler house, four out of five of those facts worked in my favor.

As I came back inside with the mail and knocked the snow off my boots, I heard Mike on the phone talking to his friend Carl. I knew it was Carl because of the voice Mike was using. He used one voice for work, another voice for girls, another voice for friends, and another voice for Carl, who was a friend but also someone who often loaned Mike money and rarely got any of it back. I slipped the thick envelope (which had been sent through the post office even though I could see the iron gate at the end of the long Wheeler drive from the kitchen window—like I said, classy) into my pocket and listened as Mike convinced Carl to pay for gas for a road trip out to California, where Lynyrd Skynyrd was playing the Cow Palace on Sunday the 31st. Then they'd swing by Vegas on the way back to Michigan, where Mike was certain he'd win enough money to cover what he owed Carl as long as Skynyrd opened with "You Got That Right" and closed with "Sweet Home Alabama" (see also: superstitious). When he hung up the phone and started throwing some underwear and jeans into a duffle bag, I knew what I was going to be doing on New Year's Eve.

Mike left the next morning without so much as a "Stay out of my room"—which the lock rendered unnecessary anyway. You might think he could have invited me to go along with him. I like Lynyrd Skynyrd okay. The guys and I occasionally threw in a cover of "Simple Man" when we played gigs, which wasn't as often as Rodney had wanted but proved to be more often than I managed to show up (see also: being kicked out).

A good uncle might have made an effort to bring his aspiring rock star nephew out to California to live it up a little at a big concert. And I was over twenty-one, so I wouldn't have been a drag on them in Vegas. But I knew he wouldn't ask me to come. I was bad luck.

The day I was born and my mom named me after him, Mike lost a thousand dollars and his motorcycle in a poker game. (It's unclear if my dad was with him that day—reliable sources are scarce.) For the next couple decades, whenever something went wrong in Mike's life, which seemed like it was more often than in most other people's, there was some way in which I was to blame. He routinely cheated on his girlfriends, but they dumped him because it was my eighth birthday or I had talked to him earlier in the day or I was watching the same TV show at the same time. When he got injured on a construction job, it was because my Little League team got mercied, not because he had been up drinking the night before. The day I got my first guitar—a right-hander even though I'm left-handed—he was sentenced to one hundred hours of community service after his third drunk and disorderly offense. The night I first kissed a girl, he was stranded in Detroit with a dead car battery.

The only reason he let me come live at his place when I found myself homeless back in August was because I promised to pay him rent and he needed the money. Most of the time he tried to stay out of the house—which was just fine with me—and when we were there at the same time, he was always looking at me sidelong, like I was contagious or something.

So when he left without me on Thursday morning, I was nothing but relieved. I had three boring days of work at Rogers Hardware in downtown West Arbor Hills to get through, days when I'd be marking down Christmas lights and stocking gardening supplies that people would look at for the next three freezing, snowy, slushy months but no one would actually buy until after Easter. Then it would be New Year's Eve, and I would finally see what was on the other side of that iron gate across the street.

The temperature had been rising a little each day since Christmas. The trees had all dropped their snow, and I could hear little streams of meltwater running down the drive into the street when I went out to get the paper off the damp concrete stoop. When Sunday rolled around, it was windy and warm, nearing forty degrees in the afternoon. I'd spent the morning sleeping late and eating three bowls of half-stale Cocoa Puffs because the milk was going to expire, then digging around in my drawers for something to wear to the party.

The invitation had been printed in gold on heavy paper, but it said "Come As You Are" at the bottom of it. "As I Was" usu-ally meant ripped jeans, a concert T-shirt, and a denim jacket, though I'd been trying to save up for a leather one I'd seen at the mall. But that didn't seem right for a party announced in gold lettering. I had khaki slacks for work, but that wasn't really "As You Are" for me. That was just something I had to do to keep a roof over my head and gas up the car and pay for pedals and strings and maybepleaseGod a better amp someday.

However, Uncle Mike had a closet over on the other side of the thin wall, and for all his faults, he always looked cool. Actually, maybe that was the problem with him. What you saw was not exactly what you got. It fooled people into trusting him when he was only slightly more dependable than his brother— which was not at all.

He'd locked his bedroom door, as always, but the trailer was made of cheap, second-rate materials and it wasn't hard to pick the lock. I had plenty of experience doing just that to get into various houses or apartments when I either forgot my keys or was locked out by the people I was staying with, sometimes accidentally, sometimes on purpose.

Mike was a middle-aged contractor, and I was a skinny wannabe rock star built more like Steven Tyler than Henry Rollins, so most of his clothes would be too big on me. Definitely I'd have to wear my own pants. But Mike was also secretly sentimental, so he never got rid of certain things, even if he couldn't button them over his growing gut. He had faded T-shirts from concerts I wish I'd been old enough to go to, a motorcycle jacket from his glory days of roving across the country following bands and girls and pipe dreams, his old army junk from Vietnam.

I settled on a pair of my least ripped jeans, Mike's Goose Lake Music Festival tee—nothing said I'm a legit Detroit musician like a nod to the legendary 1970 concert—and the black leather motorcycle jacket, which I knew would land me in either the hospital or, more preferably, the morgue if he ever found out I'd touched it and gotten my bad luck all over it. I tied my hair at the back of my neck and wondered if I should have taken a shower. I pulled out a few strands around my face so it didn't look too polished or purposeful—cool wasn't cool if it wasn't effortless—and laced up my black motorcycle boots. No, I didn't own a motorcycle, though when I was little I apparently rode on the back of my dad's once—there was a picture of it somewhere. Then I was ready to go.

It was 4:59. The party didn't even start until 9:00.

I caught the tail end of a football game I didn't care about, half watched the news talking about Panama and Israel and some bomb threat on some airline, then turned up the volume when *Life Goes On* came on, but it was a rerun. I killed the TV and turned on the radio instead, but it was mostly year-end junk. Top songs of 1989, but not actually playing any of them in full, and most of them were pop shlock—Paula Abdul and Debbie Gibson and Milli Vanilli.

I secretly did like some of that crap—it was just so catchy—but synthesizers and drum machines wouldn't get rid of the churning I'd started to feel in my stomach when I thought of walking through the door at a party I wasn't really invited to and where I wouldn't know anyone.

I turned the radio off and popped *Slippery When Wet* into the tape deck, following it up with *Hysteria* and then *Appetite for Destruction*, which I turned off after "Sweet Child o' Mine." Axl's pinched, perfect whine still ringing in my ears as I crossed the dark street and approached the open gate of the Wheeler house. I thought of how Axl would walk into a party, shoved my hands into my jeans pockets, and put a friendly sneer on my face, the kind of expression I used to get through gigs without a panic attack.

The winding driveway was already lined with cars at 9:15. Nice cars. Some new, some classic, all perfectly shiny except for the spatter of salt water just behind the tires. Who washed a car in the winter? Rich people. What did "Come As You Are" mean to rich people? Ties and sport jackets? I didn't own a tie, and I'm not sure Uncle Mike did either. Well, maybe. For court dates.

I could feel my heart rate tick up and sweat gathering on my scalp and palms. I almost turned around and called this what it was—a bad idea. But then the last thing Rodney said to me when he and Slow gave me the boot from our crappy apartment in Plymouth (which he always told people was in Detroit) replaced Axl's aching E-flat in my brain. *"The minute you're not a drain on this band, the minute you actually have something to offer, that's when you can come back. Not one second sooner."*

Knowing Dusty Wheeler . . . that would be something to offer. That might make up for me missing the odd gig or five. That might make up for the fact that my equipment kind of sucked. That might make up for Slow's girlfriend hitting on me right in front of him, which, hey, wasn't my fault to begin with but also didn't bother me all that much because she's pretty cute and is one of the few people who makes me feel kind of good about myself in kind of a bad way.

If I could get a demo to Dusty, I'd be worth something to those guys. Maybe they'd even give a few of the songs I wrote the time of day. Maybe I could actually sing lead once in a while instead of Rodney, who was always a little flat and on the unintelligible side.

I picked up my pace and pushed through the panic. I wasn't going back to that trailer. That trailer was the past, evidence of a forgettable life in a disappointing family. My future was waiting for me at the end of this driveway. I might as well go get it.

The house my uncle built was nothing like I'd been imagining every time I saw those iron gates. It was a plain, one-story stone rectangle broken up by other rectangles—front door, garage door, windows. If Robin Leach had taught me anything, rich people—to say nothing of the rich *and* famous—were supposed to live in over-the-top miniature palaces with columns and fountains and hedge mazes. I mean, wasn't the extravagant lifestyle half the reason for getting into the entertainment business?

Maybe I was dressed just fine.

I'd never have known a party was going on from the silence when I got to the door. I stood there a minute, listening hard, listening for voices, music, laughter—anything to indicate I hadn't gotten the date wrong or imagined the cars lining the driveway. Nothing. Should I ring the doorbell? Or just walk in? I didn't have time to make a choice. The door opened and the raucous party sounds spilled out, along with three black guys in black suits and a white guy in khakis carrying a basketball.

"Oh, sorry," the white guy said when he realized he'd practically shoved me off the wide stone porch.

"See if he wants to join us, Bill," one of the others said, holding his hands up for the ball. Bill tossed it his way.

"He can't join us," said another. "He's not part of the bet. Dennis, give me that ball."

Dennis palmed the ball and held it at least nine feet in the air. "Come and get it."

The shorter guy laughed, then started in on some fancy footwork, faking one way then another, then leaping up and knocking the ball from the taller man's hand.

Bill spoke up. "The bet doesn't matter. There's no way you two can win anyway, even if we have three." He leaned way down to me. "You wanna play?"

I looked at the other three guys once more. They looked sort of familiar. The way your math teacher looks when you see him at a bar after you've graduated. Like you know you know him, but you aren't sure who he is out of his proper context.

"Come on, kid," the third black guy said. "We'll sign the ball for you after and you can keep it."

Only then did it dawn on me who I was talking to. "Thanks," I said, waving a hand. I meant to say "I'm good" next. Like, I'm all set. But it came out, "I'm no good." Which was true. But still.

A couple of the guys looked surprised to be turned down.

"Ah, forget it," Dennis said. "Joe, you're with me. Isiah, you're with Bill." They all turned away and focused on the basketball hoop above the closed garage.

I swallowed down my embarrassment, opened the front door,

and hoped that our paths wouldn't cross later in the night. It wasn't a strong start, I'll give you that.

The door shut behind me. I was in a large foyer carpeted with shoes save for a path to a closet and four large blank spots left by the size seventeens now out on the driveway. Beneath the shoes, the floor was made of the same stone as the porch was. The floor-to-ceiling windows—through which the four most famous Detroit Pistons could no doubt see me staring dumbly at the floor, but in which I could only see my reflection—must make it feel like you were still kind of outside during the day.

I hated taking my shoes off in public. But worse than walking around in dingy socks at a fancy-stationary party was being the only guy whose big black boots were mashing down the carpet. I sat on a bench positioned against the far wall and started untying the laces.

To my left there was an open stairwell leading down to the lower level, and a burst of deep male laughter bounced up it and onto the main floor. But I could also hear the party somewhere behind me, on the other side of the wall at my back. Kitchen noises and voices and someone playing a piano—rather well, in fact.

I placed my boots in one of the empty spots on the floor and headed for the kitchen. Best to get a drink first. It was easier to walk into a roomful of people if you had something to do with your hands. Plus the kitchen was where moms hung out, and most moms could be counted on to offer you food and give you helpful information, like pointing out where the bathroom is or guiding you to the area where the people your age were hanging out. I mean, not my mom. But most moms.

The kitchen was large, but with as many people as there were in there, it could hardly be called spacious. I squeezed by a lady in a pink top wearing a silky scarf that nearly touched the floor and scanned the room. One of these women had to be Deb Wheeler. Should I introduce myself? Assume they had seen me once or twice over the past several months—though I had never managed to get a glimpse of them—and would know who I was? Or should I stay under the radar since I hadn't actually been invited?

A lady with short, bright red hair and too much makeup—meant, no doubt, to hide her advancing years—pushed an open bottle of Perrier into each of my hands.

"Take these out to Pinky and Stevie, would you?" At my look of confusion, she added, "At the piano."

I followed the sound of the piano through the dining room overflowing with food and into a sunken living room with wall-to-wall white carpeting. Beautiful people lolled on white leather couches in front of the large fireplace on the opposite wall or congregated in little pockets and corners of the vast room. Above the fireplace on the stone wall hung a large rug with American Indian designs woven into it in white, black, yellow, and a rusty red. Overhead, an enormous chandelier made of deer antlers lit the vaulted ceiling and threw twisted shadows across the room. To my immediate left, by yet more windows, was a shiny black baby grand piano at which a black man with long braids and a slight white woman with short brown hair swayed and played and sang a duet. Stevie and Pinky, presumably.

His voice was familiar. Hers was not. It was lower and bigger than you might expect for someone her size. Kind of soulful. Kind of sexy.

I edged around so I could see their faces. The man was wearing dark sunglasses. Of course. I don't know why I should have been surprised that Dusty Wheeler hung out with Stevie Wonder. But I was. I thought of the men playing two-on-two outside.

Who else had been across the street in the past few months while I sat stupidly clicking through network television on my uncle's saggy couch? Who else might be here even now? Was this girl someone important? Some famous jazz singer I didn't know about? I couldn't think of anyone named Pinky.

The song ended and the crowd clapped—and I would have if I hadn't had the two bottles of Perrier in my hands—and Stevie turned my way. "You play?" he asked.

How, in this packed and noisy room, did he even know I was standing there?

"Mike doesn't play piano," Pinky said without looking at me. "He can't even keep a beat."

Well, that was uncalled for. And not even true—the beat part, at least. How would she know anything anyway? How did she even know my name?

"I brought you water," I said.

Stevie held his hand out, and I placed the bottle against his open palm.

Pinky frowned and said, "You're not Mike."

"No," I said, holding the other water out. She made no move to take it.

"Why are you wearing his clothes?"

"Excuse me?"

"I can smell the Camels on them."

"Lots of people smoke Camels."

She looked at me skeptically, not quite meeting my eyes.

"He let me borrow his jacket," I lied. I didn't know how this girl knew Mike, but I sure couldn't have her ratting on me when he got home.

She slid off the bench, and Stevie slid to the middle and resumed playing. A thin strip of pale skin showed between her boxy black cropped sweater and the waistband of her silver stretch pants. Large silver hoop earrings glinted on either side of a face devoid of makeup but also not needing it.

I took a step toward her. "Do you want this water or not?"

"Are you his nephew?"

"Yeah."

"Ah."

What had Mike told her about me? Was she one of the girls he talked to on the phone sometimes? She seemed way too young for him.

She put her hip out of joint and held out her hand. "Are you ever going to give me that water?"

I waved the bottle in the air, but she didn't make a move for it. I set it down harder than I should have on top of the piano, and a little shot of water jumped out the open mouth of the bottle.

"Relax, man," she said, snatching the bottle and putting it to her lips. "Not a great first impression you're making. An impression, no doubt. But not a great one."

"Yeah? Same to you."

I headed back through the dining room, through the kitchen, and into the foyer, then down the steps I'd seen a few minutes earlier. The lower level was as packed with people as the living room. Blues played at high volume on the hi-fi, and on the television—smaller and older than I expected—hordes of reunited Germans smiled and popped champagne at the Brandenburg Gate in Berlin. Then the screams and whistles and fireworks half a world away were replaced by shots of revelers in Times Square. Add in the chatter and laughter and the room was uncomfortably loud. And that's saying something, coming from someone in a band.

If I could still consider myself in the band.

I could smell cigars, but no one was smoking. There must be another room. I went past a wall of overflowing bookshelves through a door and into a long hallway painted in high-gloss black and red. It had the feel of some kind of back entrance to a club you needed a secret password to get into. A man came through a nearby door and let a haze of smoke out with him, along with the clack of billiard balls. He nodded at me as we squeezed past each other in the narrow hall. I took a breath and stared at the green door that had closed behind him.

That's where Dusty Wheeler would be. Smoking cigars and playing pool. Stuff rich guys did with their rich buddies. A place the little pixie with the sultry voice and the attitude probably wouldn't venture and therefore the best place to be. I opened the door with more confidence than I felt and more racket than I should have. Someone scratched at the billiard table and shot an accusing glance up at me in the doorway.

I stifled the urge to back out the door and headed into the room like I belonged there. There was a bar to my left, reminding me that I still hadn't gotten a drink, only delivered a couple. Behind it stood a short, rather portly, monumentally scruffy man with an unkempt salt-and-pepper beard and a mane of hair that looked like it hadn't been combed since the Carter administration. His rumpled white shirt was open at the neck to allow the little tufts of his gray chest hair to breathe. Hard to do in the smoky air. A cold draft swirled into the room from a cracked sliding glass door, but it wasn't enough ventilation with half a dozen guys smoking in there.

"What'll it be, son?" the man said without a smile.

"Uh . . ." I stalled. What were other people drinking? I scanned the room.

"We don't have that," the bartender quipped, still unsmiling.

"A beer?"

"We got that."

He turned to a small fridge that looked like a reject from the set of *The Honeymooners*. I dug in my pocket for some cash. A bottle of Miller Lite appeared in front of me.

"Gotta keep that lithe figure," the bartender said.

I couldn't tell if he was making fun of me, so I assumed he was. I lifted a crumpled five.

"Keep your money, buddy. This is a party." He picked up a fat cigar from below the counter and sucked it back to life.

I turned my back to him and leaned on the brass bar rail. There was no trace of Times Square or Berlin or the chatter of the last room, despite it being just next door. Here the only sounds were an occasional low voice, the clacking of the balls on the pool table, and the low sounds of an upright bass, a high hat, and a muted trumpet squeezing out a laid-back tune from the reel-to-reel in the corner. The walls must be soundproof. I'd have to ask Uncle Mike about that.

"You just gonna stand here all night?" the bartender said.

I shrugged. "Maybe."

He came around to the other side of the bar and nodded at the pool table. "You play?"

"Sometimes."

"Meet me back here at two and we'll play."

"Two o'clock? In the morning? People will still be here then?"

"No, that's why I'm telling you to meet me at two. Geez, you kids today are idiots sometimes." He wiped his hands on his wrinkled pants and looked to me for an answer.

"Sure," I said, knowing full well I would not be staying up to shoot pool with this crazy old man at 2:00 a.m.

He gave me a nod and left the room.

I tugged on the beer and watched the guys play pool. They took their shots without rushing, without posturing, without even putting much muscle behind any of them. They floated around the table, one way then another, like they were following some kind of choreography, like the shots were all there and didn't need to be looked for or planned, just made. Like life was all laid out for them.

Ten minutes later I stood up straight and felt swimmy. Buzzed on one beer. I hadn't eaten anything since the three bowls of Cocoa Puffs nearly twelve hours ago. I'd have to risk running into either the Pistons or Pinky to go get some food.

I left the room as quietly as possible. Across the hall a bright red sign above another green door flashed RECORDING. Was Dusty in there?

Back through the loud room with the blues and the Berliners and up the stairs to the main floor and the foyer full of shoes. Through another wall of floor-to-ceiling windows in the front hall, I could see across a dark courtyard to the sunken living room with the piano and the white couches. Which meant anyone in the living room could see me. I examined the faces in the crowd. Dusty Wheeler would be, what? Mid- to late fifties by now? Maybe sixty? I'd only ever seen one picture of him, backing up Jimi Hendrix at Woodstock. He was way in the background, grainy, out of focus, a collection of black dots on white newsprint. Really it could have been anyone, but the caption listing the people in the picture had included his name.

I saw Pinky walking past the window, the fingers of her right hand just grazing the glass, the crowd parting ahead of her. I poked my head around a corner in time to see her open and close a door at the end of a long hallway. Coast clear, I headed for the dining room and piled a small plate with shrimp, cheese, olives, and any number of fancy little items I didn't have names for, then sat in a chair in the corner and commenced inhaling.

People drifted in and out. Some glanced my way, some offered me a smile, some bothered to say "Happy New Year" and raise their glass. But no one actually introduced themselves.

No one asked my name. No one wanted to know my story. No one knew me coming into this night, and no one would know me going out of it.

Eventually I wandered into the now-empty kitchen and checked the clock on the wall. 11:47. It would be midnight soon. A new year. A new decade. A bright new future, if newspapers and magazines were to be trusted. *Time* and *Newsweek*, which traded on fear and disaster all year long, were suddenly awash with optimism about the coming decade. The toppling of autocratic regimes. The waving of flags. The tearing down of walls. The dawn of a new era of democracy and peace. "Come Together" and "Kum Ba Yah" and "We Are the World" all piling up like an accident on I-94. It was big. Big enough that you kind of felt the energy of it as a buzzing electrical field all around you.

Why was everyone so hopeful?

I turned to leave, to head back down the long dark driveway lined with beautiful cars, and realized I was not alone. A woman was standing in the kitchen doorway, looking at me. Salt-and-pepper hair fell in waves down her back. A long white and gold floral dress hung on her gaunt shoulders like it was still on the hanger. Her large hazel eyes sparkled with a light that was flickering but not quite out.

"You must be Mike's nephew," she said, extending a thin hand.

I shook it gently. "Yes, I'm Michael."

She smiled at me, and I felt a little prick of golden joy in my chest.

So this was Deb Wheeler. Or what was left of her. While there was only one picture of Dusty Wheeler, I'd seen several of his gorgeous wife in her younger years. Doe-eyed with long wavy brown hair and a set of pipes that every girl I knew tried to pretend she had but never did. Deb had put out three records in the late 1960s. Then she never recorded another song.

I tried to reconcile the woman before me with the one from the album cover I saw on the top of my mom's stack any time my dad reappeared for a few days and then disappeared again. She listened to lots of different kinds of music, but *Homeward* had been her go-to soundtrack when it came to that sacred mixture of righteous anger and heart-searing loneliness a forsaken woman felt. But that Deb was vibrant and attractive and a little bit dangerous. That Deb looked like trouble—the good kind. This Deb was shrunken and fragile.

She kept smiling, but her eyes looked suddenly sad. "I'm so sorry. I haven't been a very good hostess tonight. I was just resting in the bedroom."

She opened the fridge, and the light from inside it traveled through the fibers of her dress, the way sunlight used to shine through the girls' dresses at church the few times we went. But there was nothing alluring about this. Deb Wheeler looked like she'd just stopped by on her way to the grave.

She shut the fridge without getting anything out of it.

"Do you want me to get you something?" I asked. "The dining room's still full of food."

"Oh, no, I'm not hungry. I just opened the fridge out of habit."

She padded across the room, fuzzy red house slippers poking out from under the long skirt of her dress. She pulled out a stool at the counter, sat down, and motioned at me to do the same. I obliged, grateful to finally have someone to talk to.

"Mike said you're in a band?"

"Yeah." I wanted to ask her when she interacted with Mike, but she kept talking.

"And what is it called?"

"The Pleasure Centers. I didn't pick the name."

"Mm, and what do you play?"

"Guitar."

"Genre?"

"Oh, you know, just rock music. Like sort of metal but not real hard-core stuff usually. Good melodies. Some harmony. We have a couple ballads the girls like. Kind of like Guns N' Roses meets Bon Jovi meets Scorpions."

"Arena rock."

My heart rate ticked up a notch at the thought of having to play in front of tens of thousands of people. It was what I wanted, but it also kind of made me feel like throwing up. "Well, we haven't played any of those yet."

"Hair band?"

I cringed at the term I'd always hated and looked at my hands. "Not exactly."

"Spandex or leather?" she said, a mischievous twist to her mouth.

I laughed. "I just wear jeans mostly. Rodney did try the spandex thing once. His sister's aerobics pants. Ripped the seam in the back and she beat the sh—" I caught myself. "Oh, sorry."

"Michael, my entire life has been lived with musicians, artists, and writers. There's absolutely nothing you could say that would shock me."

I glanced at the clock. "Almost time. Don't you want to join the party?"

She put a bony hand on mine. "You're good enough company for me. Anyway, if we stay here I know I'll have a handsome young man to kiss at midnight."

"What about your husband?" Where was Dusty Wheeler anyway? This night was kind of a waste if I didn't meet him.

"Oh, he's in the recording studio tonight. They're laying down a few tracks for some project while they've got everyone in town. They've been at it off and on most of the day. 'The New Year Sessions' or something is what they're calling it." She pointed at the clock. "One minute."

Who was *they*? Who else was in that room? "He wouldn't take a break to ring in the new year with you?"

"I wouldn't want him to. That's why we've stayed together so long when practically every other musician's marriage has fallen apart. I've always been one hundred percent behind his work, and he's always been one hundred percent behind mine. Every opportunity is met with an enthusiastic yes. No jealousy, no nagging, no resentment, no compromise." She looked at the clock again. "Thirty seconds. Too bad you'll be stuck kissing this old lady."

I smiled. "You're not so old."

"No, I'm not." She smiled back. "And I do believe you're old at heart."

I wasn't sure what she meant by that. But somehow coming from her, I assumed it was good.

The countdown started in the living room.

Ten.

"Here we go," she said.

Nine.

She watched the clock.

Eight.

I examined the side of her face.

Seven.

She looked in my eyes.

Six.

"Mom?" came a voice from the dining room.

Five.

"In here, Natalie."

Four.

I turned on the stool for my first glimpse of Natalie Wheeler.

Three.

I was looking at the piano player.

Two.

Pinky.

One.

Screams and shouts from the living room. Two thin hands grasped my face, two lips pressed against mine, and then that killer smile again as Deb turned to the young woman in the doorway. "Natalie, this is Mike's nephew, Michael. Michael, this is my daughter, Natalie."

"We've met."

Erin Bartels is the award-winning author of *We Hope for Better Things*, *The Words between Us*, and *All That We Carried*. A publishing professional for twenty years, she lives in Lansing, Michigan, with her husband, Zachary, and their son. Find her online at www.erinbartels.com.

THE PAST IS NEVER AS PAST AS *We'd Like to Think*

In this richly textured debut novel, a disgraced journalist moves into her great-aunt's secret-laden farmhouse and discovers that the women in her family were testaments to true love and courage in the face of war, persecution, and racism.

CONNECT WITH ERIN

Check out her newsletter, blog, podcast, and more at

ErinBartels.com

[f] @ErinBartelsAuthor   [🐦] @ErinLBartels   [📷] @ErinBartelsWrites

Author photo: © Matthew Mitchell Photography